Why readers are addicted to Friend Request . . .

'Addictive, thought-provoking and **truly hits home**'

'**Engaging characters**, good plot – intriguing from first page to last!'

'**Absolutely brilliant**, I could not put it down'

'**One of the best** books I have read in a long time'

'**Kept me on the edge** all the way through'

'Wow. **What a story**. Couldn't put it down'

'If you like a story that makes you think and **keeps you guessing** this is the book for you'

'**Hooked** me in from the start'

'Brilliant book and with an **unexpected twist at the end**'

Praise for
Friend Request

'I read it in one go . . . supremely grippy with an excellent twist!'
Marian Keyes

'A read-it-in-one-sitting thriller . . . Twisty and gripping but always relatable, *Friend Request* is the ultimate it-could-happen-to-you read'
Erin Kelly

'Brilliant'
Jenny Colgan

'Tightly plotted and brilliantly tense, this is a devour-in-one-sitting must'
Heat

'Laura Marshall ramps up the tension page by page until it's impossible to know who to trust . . . I loved it!'
Rachel Abbott

'Imagine getting a Facebook message from a school friend whose death you blame yourself for . . . That's the eerie premise for Laura Marshall's unnerving novel'
Good Housekeeping

'An astonishingly good debut'
Sun

'Sharp, relevant and tightly plotted, and with a fabulous twist, psychological thriller fans should definitely say yes to this impressive debut'
Sunday Mirror

'An incredible debut novel that's not to be missed . . . a fast-paced, exciting thriller with some unexpected twists and turns'
Hollie Overton

'A slick psychological thriller with a killer hook'
Red Online

'Utterly gripping and so astute on the dangerous dynamics of teenage girl friendships'
Tammy Cohen

'This thriller grips you right from the tag line . . . An accomplished debut novel with insights into social media, its dangers and how much we leave ourselves open online'
i News

'I couldn't put it down!'
Jenny Blackhurst

'Pulp fiction at its finest, *Friend Request* is a mystery with a genius premise'
Stylist

'Twisty and gripping with huge depth and heart . . . You must read this!'
Emma Kavanagh

'Intriguing and compulsive, this deftly plotted debut asks uncomfortable questions about the nature of friendship – both on Facebook and in real life. I raced to the end'
Louise Candlish

'A cleverly plotted, enticing mix of suspense, regret and redemption . . . I will never look at social media the same way again'
Heather Gudenkauf

'A gripping read'
Closer

'An accomplished debut novel which not only boasts an engrossing storyline, but also perfectly captures teenage angst and the need to be accepted'
Irish News

'Just try to keep the chills away when Louise gets a Facebook request from a "friend" who's been dead for 25 years'
Cosmopolitan US

Laura Marshall grew up in Wiltshire and studied English at the University of Sussex.

After almost twenty years working in conference production, in 2015 Laura decided it was time to fulfil a lifetime's ambition to write a book, and enrolled on the Curtis Brown Creative three month novel writing course. *Friend Request* is her first novel and was shortlisted for both the Bath Novel Award and the Lucy Cavendish Fiction Prize 2016.

Laura lives in Kent with her husband and two children.

For more information visit Laura's website
www.lauramarshall.co.uk or find her on
@laurajm8 and lauramarshallauthor

Friend Request

LAURA MARSHALL

sphere

SPHERE

First published in Great Britain in 2017 by Sphere
This paperback edition published in 2018 by Sphere

7 9 10 8

A CIP catalogue record for this book
is available from the British Library.

ISBN 978-0-7515-6835-6

Printed and bound in Great Britain by
Clays Ltd, St Ives plc

Papers used by Sphere are from well-managed forests
and other responsible sources.

Sphere
An imprint of
Little, Brown Book Group
Carmelite House
50 Victoria Embankment
London EC4Y 0DZ

An Hachette UK Company
www.hachette.co.uk

www.littlebrown.co.uk

To M, C, and A, *with love*

Chapter 1

2016

The email arrives in my inbox like an unexploded bomb: *Maria Weston wants to be friends on Facebook.*

For a second I miss the Facebook reference, and just see 'Maria Weston wants to be friends'. Instinctively I slam the laptop shut. It feels as though a sponge has been lodged in my throat, soaking up water, swelling and clogging, leaving me struggling for breath. I attempt to breathe deeply, trying to get myself back under control. Perhaps I was mistaken. I must have been mistaken because this cannot possibly be happening. Slowly I raise the lid of my laptop. Hands shaking, I go back into the email and this time there is no denying the bald fact of it. Maria Weston wants to be friends with me.

It's been a fairly unremarkable day up until now. Henry is at Sam's tonight, so I've put in a long day working on some initial plans for a client who wants everything from walls to carpets and sofas in varying shades of beige and taupe, but at the same time doesn't want the house to look boring.

When I saw I had an email, I was glad of the distraction, hopeful of a personal message rather than yet another company trying to sell me something.

Now though, I'd be grateful for marketing spam, and I long to go back to the mild tedium of a few minutes ago. This must be someone's idea of a sick joke, surely. But whose? Who could think this funny? Who even knows the effect it would have on me?

There's an easy way out of this, of course. All I have to do is delete the email, go to Facebook and decline the request without looking at the page. A part of me is screaming out to do this, to end it here; but another part of me – a quiet and buried part – wants to see, to know. To understand.

So I do it. I click 'Confirm Request' and I'm taken straight to her page: Maria Weston's Facebook page. The profile photo is an old one from a pre-digital age which has obviously been scanned in. Maria, in her green school-uniform blazer, long brown hair blowing in the wind, a small smile playing across her face. I scan the screen, searching for clues, but there is very little information on the page. She doesn't have any friends listed or photos uploaded other than the profile one.

She stares at me dispassionately from behind my computer screen. I've not felt her cool gaze for over twenty-five years, not been the recipient of that look, which tells you she's sizing you up, not in an unpleasant way, but appraising you, understanding more of you than you want the world to know. I wonder if she ever realised what I had done to her.

The red brick of the school buildings lurks in the background, familiar in a way but strange too, as if it belongs to someone else's memories, not mine. Odd, how you spend five years going to the same place every day, and then it's over, you never go there again. Almost as if it never existed at all.

I find I can't look at her for long, and my eyes roam around the kitchen, wanting something mundane to fix on, a break from this bewildering new reality. I get up and make a coffee, gaining comfort from the ritual of putting the smooth shining pod into the machine, pressing the tip of my finger onto the button in the precise way I always do and warming the milk in the frother.

I sit there amidst the trappings of my very comfortable, very middle-class, nearly middle-aged life. The kitchen gadgets and the photo on the fancy fridge of me and Henry on our first holiday alone last summer, a selfie taken by the pool: our skin salty and sun-kissed, a shadow around Henry's mouth where the dust has stuck to the remnants of his daily ice cream.

Outside the French windows, my tiny courtyard garden is wearing its bleak late-autumn clothes, paving stones slick with the earlier freezing rain. Chipped plant pots trail the dead brown remains of my doomed summer attempt at growing my own herbs, and the darkening afternoon sky is a dull sheet of slate grey. I can just see one of the tower blocks that loom here and there like malevolent giants over the rows of Victorian terraces all turned into flats like mine that make up this part of south-east London. This room, this home, this life that I have built up so carefully. This little family, with only two members. If one of us falls, then what is left is not a family at all. What would it take to tear it all down, to bring it tumbling and crashing to the ground?

Perhaps not as much as I thought. Maybe just a nudge in the back; a tiny push, so slight that I would hardly feel it.

The kitchen with its muted dove-grey walls and bleached wood worktops is warm, uncomfortably so. As the coffee machine hums its everyday tune, I half-listen to the news on the radio, which chatters all day every day in my kitchen: a sporting victory, a cabinet re-shuffle, a fifteen-year-old girl who has killed herself after her boyfriend posted naked pictures of her online. I flinch at the thought of it, sympathy for her mixed with a shameful gratitude that there were no camera phones around when I was that age. I move over and open one of the French windows, feeling the need for fresh air, but an icy blast slams it shut again.

My coffee is ready, and I have no alternative but to sit back down at the laptop, where Maria has been waiting for me: steadily, impenetrably. I force myself to meet her eyes, searching futilely for any hint of what was to happen to her. I try to see the photo as a casual observer might: an ordinary schoolgirl, an old photo that's been sitting on some mother's sideboard for years, dusted and replaced weekly. It doesn't work; I can't see her like that knowing her fate as I do.

Maria Weston wants to be friends with me. Maybe that was the problem all along; Maria Weston wanted to be friends with me, but I let her down. She's been hovering at the edge of my consciousness for all of my adult life, although I've been good at keeping her out, just a blurred shadow in the corner of my eye, almost but not quite out of sight.

Maria Weston wants to be friends.

But Maria Weston has been dead for more than twenty-five years.

Chapter 2

1989

I've been awake all night in an attempt to maintain some kind of hold on what has happened, on what I have done. My eyes are red and prickling with tiredness, but I daren't go to sleep. If I sleep, when I wake up I'll have one blissful, terrible second when I'm unaware – and then it will all come crashing in on me, its power multiplied indefinitely by that one un-knowing second.

I think of the last time I saw the dawn in, lying in Sophie's bed. This time it's a more tempestuous and bleaker affair. A ceaseless summer rain has been falling all night, and the branch of a nearby tree is thwacking intermittently against my windowpane. It's not just the chemicals keeping me awake, although I can still feel them coursing, unwanted, around my veins. I've been sitting here on the floor for four hours, as my bedroom turns gradually from darkness to a dull grey half-light. I'm surrounded by the debris of my elaborate preparations for the evening that, twelve hours ago, stretched out invitingly, bright with the promise of acceptance and approval. There are three dresses strewn on the bed, with the accompanying pair of shoes for each lying discarded in front of the full-length mirror. My eyes rest dully on the stain on the carpet where Sophie dropped my new bronzing powder and I made a clumsy attempt to wipe it up with a bit of tissue dipped in a glass of stale water.

The dress I wore lies in a crumpled heap next to me – I've pulled on an old sweatshirt and leggings. There are dark smudges under my eyes and my lips are dry, the remains of my lipstick clinging to the cracks and bleeding into the skin around my mouth.

I've been sitting here on the floor for so long only because I can't move. I would have expected my heart to be racing, but in fact an iron fist grips it so tightly that I am surprised it is beating at all. Everything has slowed to a funereal pace. If I move my hand to brush my hair behind my ears or pick something up off the floor, however quickly I do it, it's as though I am moving in slow motion. My brain struggles to make sense of it all, my thoughts moving sluggishly through the past couple of months, trying to figure out how it has come to this.

I suppose it all began a couple of months ago, the day the new girl started. I'd spent break listening to Sophie talking to Claire Barnes and Joanne Kirby, not saying much myself. We were all sitting on that bench at the far edge of the play-ground, the three of them with their skirts rolled over at the waist so many times there was hardly any point in wearing them. Matt Lewis was watching Sophie from the other side of the playground and I could tell what he was thinking. It was that day, the first one of the year where you could smell spring in the air. I sat on the end of the bench, enjoying the feeling of the sun on my face, hoping they wouldn't expect me to contribute anything. The sky was the most amazing blue, and Sophie and the other two were sort of shining, their impossibly glossy hair reflecting the sunlight, their smooth golden skin glistening. Of course they knew the effect they were having, they weren't that stupid.

Sophie was redoing her mascara and talking about a boy she'd got off with the weekend before at Claire Barnes's sixteenth birthday party. Obviously I wasn't invited. Claire and Joanne only tolerate me tagging along because I'm friends with Sophie, and sometimes I feel like I'm hanging on to even that friendship by the tips of my fingers.

'Basically, we were kissing and all that, and then – well, you know the most embarrassing thing that can happen to a boy? That happened.'

Claire and Joanne shrieked.

'Oh my God!' Claire said. 'That is so embarrassing! You know I got off with Mark that time, at Johnny's party? We went down the fields and I was down there, you know, giving him head, and nothing much was happening and I looked up and guess what? He was asleep!'

Sophie and Joanne fell about laughing and I smiled, to show that I understood the joke. At least I know what giving head is, even if I am hazy on the details. I've tried to imagine doing it to someone, even someone I really like, but I can't. I have no idea how it works, for a start; what you would do with your mouth, your tongue. I shuddered.

Claire leaned in to the other two as if about to impart some great piece of wisdom.

'It's all right for you two, it's still all quite new to you, but I'm actually getting a bit bored with sex, you know. It's all

Dan wants to do. You know sometimes I'd like to go into town or go to the cinema or something?'

Sophie and Joanne fell over themselves to agree. It's funny, Sophie's always so cool, so together, but sometimes when she's with Claire I can see her soft underbelly, the cracks in her facade. They'd recently started letting me go into town with them after school. We would all walk down in a group, but when you get to the path by the river it's too narrow to walk anything but two-by-two, and I could always feel Sophie and Joanne silently jostling to be the one that got to walk with Claire rather than with me.

Until tonight, I'd never even kissed a boy, and I remember praying that day that the others wouldn't find out. Sophie knows, but I don't think she'd tell. At least they never try to involve me in those conversations. I'm always so frightened of saying something stupid, something that will betray my lack of experience. Most of what I know about sex I've learned from the pages of *Just Seventeen* magazine, although God knows it could be more helpful. The problem-page woman seems to assume you have a basic knowledge, so there are always phrases and words I'm not sure about. You'd think maybe sex education at school would have covered this, but no, so far it's been an ancient 1970s video of a woman giving birth, and some embarrassed talk about penises going into vaginas. Well, even I knew that. The only lesson that had promised to be interesting was the one where Mrs Cook was going to teach us how to put a condom on a banana but guess what: Mrs Cook was ill that day so we had to make do with hearing from one of the other classes in our year who'd done it the week before.

The new girl's name was Maria Weston. She looked OK,

sort of normal uniform, not trendy but not square either. Miss Allan made Sophie look after her, but Sophie basically showed her where the toilets were, and the lunch hall, and then ignored her for the rest of the day. Esther Harcourt tried to make friends with Maria, but even a new girl could see that Esther, in her hand-me-downs and thick-rimmed glasses was not the route to social success at our school. Funny to think that I used to hang out with Esther all the time at primary school. I loved going to her house because her mum let us go off into the woods for hours, although they were vegetarian hippies so we got some odd stuff for tea. I sort of miss her in some ways; we did used to have a laugh. Couldn't be friends with her any more though – nightmare.

Anyway, at lunch Sophie hadn't even sat with the new girl, and Esther was already staying away by then because Maria had been so cold to her at morning break. As I got closer to the tills, I started on the daily task of scanning the cafeteria trying to work out where I was going to sit. Maria was sitting on her own at one end of a table with a group of real swots at the other end, including Natasha Griffiths (or, as Sophie calls her, 'Face and Neck' due to her orange foundation and white neck). Face and Neck was holding forth on the subject of her English homework and how brilliant Mr Jenkins said it was, and how he'd asked her to stay back specially after class at the end (I bet he did; everyone reckons he's a right old perv). I was about to pass Maria, wondering whether it was going to be OK to sit with Sophie (she was with Claire and Joanne on the far left corner table which for some reason is the cool table – basically unless you are only having a yoghurt for lunch it's fairly embarrassing to sit there), when I caught Maria's eye. She was eating her jacket potato and listening to Natasha banging on about her Shakespeare essay, smiling like she could already tell how full of crap Natasha is, and something made me slow my pace.

'Is anyone sitting here?'

'No, no one!' she said, moving her tray to make room for me. 'Sit down.'

I unloaded the shameful fat-filled lasagne from my tray and sat down, pressing the sharp end of my apple juice straw into the little silver disc until it popped, a bead of amber liquid oozing from the hole.

'So, how's your first day going so far?'

'Oh, you know, good; of course it's difficult ... you know ...'

She trailed off.

'So, crap basically?' I grinned.

'Yeah.' She smiled in relief. 'Total crap.'

'Where did you go to school before? Did your mum and dad move?'

Maria concentrated very hard on cutting the skin of her potato. 'Yes, we lived in London.'

'Oh right,' I said. April seemed like a funny time of year to move, so near the end of GCSE year.

She hesitated. 'I was having a bit of trouble with some of the other girls.'

I sensed she didn't want me to press her, so I didn't.

'Well, everyone's really nice here,' I lied. 'You won't have any problems like that. In fact there's a group of us that goes into town most days after school, you should come.'

'I can't today, my brother's picking me up outside school to walk home. But I'd love to another day.'

First lesson after lunch was maths, and Sophie swung into the seat next to me, freshly made up after a bitching session in the toilets and reeking of Christian Dior's Poison. I told her that I'd been talking to Maria and that I'd invited her to come into town with us. She turned to me.

'You've invited her out with us?' There was a dangerous edge to her voice.

'Yes ... is that OK?' I tried to check the tremor in my voice.

'Does Claire know?'

'No ... I didn't think anyone would mind.'

'You could have checked with me first, Louise.'

'Sorry, I thought ... she's new, and ...' I rearranged the books on my desk needlessly, panic building. What had I done?

'I know that. But I've heard some things about her already, stuff that happened at her old school.'

'Oh, it's OK, she told me about that.' Maybe this would be OK. 'None of that was true.'

'She would say that though, wouldn't she? Did she tell you what it was about?'

'No,' I admitted, my cheeks beginning to burn.

'Right. Well, maybe you should get your facts straight before you go inviting people out with other people.'

We carried on doing our algebra in silence for a few minutes, although I noticed Sophie was still looking over my shoulder to copy my answers.

'She can't come tonight as it happens,' I ventured eventually. 'She's got to meet her brother.'

'I heard he was a bit of a weirdo as well. Anyway, I can't go into town tonight. I'm doing something with Claire.'

I clearly wasn't invited to this mystery outing, so I said nothing. I was surprised Sophie couldn't feel the heat radiating from me, shock and worry oozing through my pores.

When the bell went she scooped up her stuff and went straight off to the next lesson. At the end of the day she didn't even say goodbye to me, she just went giggling off, clutching Claire Barnes by the arm, without looking back. I was so frightened that I'd ruined everything with her. Shit shit shit. What was I going to do?

Chapter 3

2016

I'm still sitting shell-shocked at the kitchen table, Maria's Facebook page open in front of me. Questions crowd my mind. Who is doing this, and why now? I try to wrap my mind around the horrifying possibility that somehow, somewhere, Maria is still alive. When a new Facebook notification pops up, I click on it with trepidation.

> Sharne Bay High Reunion Committee invited you to the event Sharne Bay High School Reunion Class of 1989.

Reunion? I click feverishly on the link, and there it is: Sharne Bay High School Class of 1989 Reunion, taking place two weeks on Saturday in the old school hall. On top of the request from Maria, it's a sucker punch right in the solar plexus. Can it be coincidence, getting this the same day? I click on the Facebook page of the group organising it, and although there's no way of telling who has set it up, it seems bona fide. There's a post pinned to the top of the newsfeed from our old English teacher Mr Jenkins, who apparently still works at the school. There were all sorts of rumours that used to go round about him – keeping girls back after lessons, looking in through the changing-room windows, stuff like that – but I don't suppose there was any truth to them. We all thought the PE teacher was a lesbian because she had a glass eye, so we weren't the most reliable of witnesses. The rest of the newsfeed is full of excited chat from people going to the reunion, dating back a couple of months. Why has it taken until now for me to be invited? My neck is flushed and there are treacherous, foolish tears prickling at the back of my eyes. How easily, how stupidly, I am transported back through the years; how quickly that familiar rush of shame washes over me: shame at being left out, being left behind. Still not really one of the gang. An afterthought.

I click on the list of attendees, furiously scanning for his name. Yes, there it is. There he is, eyes crinkling away at me from his profile photo, his right arm around someone out of shot. Sam Parker is attending this event. Why hasn't he said anything to me? Obviously we hardly spend hours chatting, but he could have mentioned it when I was dropping Henry off. Maybe he's hoping I don't find out about it.

Other names I recognise jump out at me: Matt Lewis, Claire Barnes, Joanne Kirby. For a heart-stopping second I see Weston and think wildly that it's Maria, but no, it's Tim Weston. My God, her brother. He wasn't at school with us – he was a year older and went to the local sixth-form college – but he used to hang out with Sam and some of the other boys in our year so I suppose it's not so surprising that he's going. There are loads of other names – some I know, others that I don't remember. So many names, but not mine.

I keep scanning the list of attendees until I find Sophie. I knew she'd be there. I click on her profile. I've looked at it before, but always resisted the temptation to befriend her. This time I go straight to her 'friends' section, but Maria's not there. Of course that doesn't mean that Sophie hasn't received the same request I have, only that she hasn't accepted it. She's got five hundred and sixty-four friends. I've got sixty-two and some of those are work-related. I've thought about deleting my account before, to prevent myself from getting sucked into that terrible time-wasting vortex where you find yourself poring through the wedding photos of someone you've never met instead of meeting a work deadline; but actually it's important to me, particularly in the last couple of years. Since Sam left, I have had to shrink my world, in order for the important things not to fall apart: Henry; my business. I don't have the time or energy for anything else, but Facebook means I haven't completely lost touch with my friends and old colleagues. I still know what's going on in their lives – what their children look like, where they've been on holiday – and then on the odd occasions that we do meet, the thread that binds us is stronger than it would otherwise have been. So I keep posting, liking, commenting; it stops me from falling out of my world completely.

The wind is rising outside and a strand of the wisteria that trails around the outside of my French windows taps on the glass, making me jump. Even though I know it was the wisteria, I get up and peer out, but it's nearly dark and I can't see much beyond my reflection. A sudden sprinkle of rain rattles against the windowpane, as if someone has thrown a handful of gravel and I jump back, heart thumping.

Back at the kitchen table, I click on Sophie's profile photo. It's one of those faux-casual ones where she looks impossibly gorgeous but manages to give the impression it's any old snap she's thrown up there. Look closely and you'll see the 'natural' make-up, the semi-professional lighting, the filters applied in the edit. Lean in closer and you might see the lines, but I have to admit she's worn well. Her hair is still a tumbling waterfall of molten caramel, her figure enviably but predictably unchanged since her teenage years.

I wonder if she's ever looked for me on here, and I click back to my own profile picture, trying to see it through her eyes. I've used one that Polly took, me sitting behind a table in the pub, glass of wine in hand. Under my newly critical gaze it looks like the photo of a person self-consciously trying to look 'fun'. I am leaning forward on the table in a short-sleeved top and you can see the unattractive bulge of my upper arms, in grim contrast to the gym-toned, honey-coloured limbs on display in Sophie's photo. My mousy brown hair looks lank and my make-up is smudged.

My cover photo is one of Henry taken last month on his first day at school. He's standing in the kitchen, his uniform box-fresh but marginally too big, looking heart-wrenchingly proud. Only I had known his private worries, confided to me last thing at night from deep beneath his duvet: 'What if no one wants to play with me, Mummy?'; 'What if I miss you too much?'; 'What will I do if I need a cuddle?' I had reassured him as best I could, but I didn't know the answers to those questions either. He had seemed too small to be going off on his own into the world, out there where I couldn't protect him. I wonder briefly if Sophie knows that Sam and I have a child, or even that we were married. I push down the thought of Henry, trying not to think about what he might be doing at Sam's tonight, trying not to worry about him; it's like trying not to breathe.

I think about what it will mean if I become Facebook friends with Sophie, and scroll through my timeline, trying to see it through her eyes. Lots of photos of Henry; posts about childcare stresses and working-mother guilt, especially when Henry was starting school and only went mornings for the first two weeks. I wonder if Sophie has children. If she doesn't, she's going to find my timeline extremely tedious. If she scrolls back far enough at least she'll see the photos from our summer holiday, Henry and I tanned and relaxed, all tension eased away by warmth and distance from home.

What she won't be able to see is that I was married to Sam, that's if she doesn't know already. I removed all the evidence of him from my timeline two years ago when I realised that he'd deleted his own Facebook account, the one with the story of us on it. He had simply started again. All the holidays, the days out, our wedding photos carefully scanned in several years after the event: gone, replaced by his shiny new narrative. He wiped me clean away like a dirty smear on the window.

I check to see if Sophie is Facebook friends with Sam, and she is. He must have his privacy settings very high, because all I can see are his profile photos, which are either of him alone or landscapes, and the date two years ago when he 'joined Facebook'. I struggle to tear my eyes away from his photo. I know that I'm better off without him. Yet there is still a part of me that yearns to be with him, the two of us luminescent in a dull world that wants everyone to be the same.

I start clicking through the photos on my laptop, trying to find a better one for my profile picture, wondering whether to take a new one, although selfies are always horrendously unflattering, so maybe not. What about one of those 'amusing' ones where you put a picture of the back of your head, or a blurred photo? Mind you, maybe she's looked for me before and seen the current one, so if I change it today and then send her a friend request, she'll know that I've done it on purpose to impress her.

That brings me up short: impress her? My God, is that what I'm trying to do, even after all these years? I look back through the prism of time and it's perfectly clear that Sophie was using me to shore up her own ego; that she needed someone less attractive, less cool than her to stand beside her and make her shine even brighter. I couldn't see it then, but she was jostling for position as much as I was, just a few rungs up the ladder. But receiving this message from Maria has plunged me back to the playground and the lunch hall, where fitting in is everything and friendship feels like life and death. My professional achievements, my friends, my son, the life I've constructed – it all feels like it's been built on shifting sands. My feet keep sliding out from under me, and I can sense how little it will take to make me fall.

In the end I leave the photo as it is and merely send a friend request, after some deliberation not including a message. After all, what on earth would I say? *Hi Sophie, how've you been these past twenty-seven years?* That's a bit weird. *Hi Sophie, I've had a Facebook friend request from our long-dead schoolmate, have you?* Even weirder, especially if she hasn't.

I sit at the kitchen table, abstractedly chewing the inside of my mouth, eyes on the 'notifications' icon. After two minutes, a '1' pops up and I rush to click on it. Sophie Hannigan has accepted your friend request. Naturally she's the sort of person that's always on Facebook. She's not sent me a message, which makes me feel a bit sick and panicky, but I trawl through her profile anyway. While it might not give me much of an insight into what her life is really like, it certainly tells me a lot about how she wants the world to see her. She changes her profile picture once or twice every week, an endless succession of flattering images accompanied by the inevitable compliments from friends of both sexes. One of her male friends, Jim Pett (who appears to be married to someone else) comments on every one: I would, one of them says; I just have, another. Oh Jim, you always have to lower the tone, she replies, mock-disgusted, loving it.

I know that Facebook offers an idealised version of life, edited and primped to show the world what we want it to see. And yet I can't stifle the pangs of envy at her undimmed beauty, the photos, exotic locations, the comments, the uproarious social whirl, the wide circle of successful friends. There's no mention of a partner though, nor any sign of children and I catch myself judging her a little bit for this. It seems that even after what I've been through I still see it as a marker of success for women: finding a partner, creating life.

When it comes to sending her a message, I am paralysed by indecision. How can I explain what has happened? But who else is there that I can talk to about this? Once I might have spoken to Sam, but that's out of the question now. I decide to keep it simple and try to be breezy:

Hi Sophie, it's been a long time! I type, cringing at the desperation that she will surely sense oozing from every word. Looks like we are both in London! Would love to see you some time! Too many exclamation marks but I don't know how else to communicate breeziness. Clearly I shouldn't have worried about that because a message pings back immediately.

> Hey! Great to hear from you!! Love to see you!! Are you coming to the reunion?

Hope so! I type, my fingers slipping on the keys. Waiting to hear about a possible diary clash but would be great to see everyone!

I'm conscious of the mismatch between the brightness of my tone and the confusion and distress I feel as I type. A voice inside my head (probably Polly's) is telling me to stop, to ignore the reunion altogether, but I can't do it.

I know! Gonna be great!! she replies.

My God, these exclamation marks are killing me. I can't do this on email; I need to see her. I gather myself and begin to type.

> Be great to catch up properly before the big day – fancy meeting for a drink?

I press send before I have a chance to change my mind. Up until now the messages have been flying back and forth like nobody's business, but there's a slightly longer hiatus after I send this one. I hold my breath.

> Sure, why not? Why don't you come over to mine for a drink – how about this Friday?

I exhale, shaking. I feel a bit strange about going to her house – I would have preferred somewhere neutral – but I can't keep this up much longer so I agree. She gives me her address, a flat in Kensington, and we say goodbye with a flurry of kisses and smiley faces from her and a couple of self-conscious kisses from me.. Another notification pops up straight away. I've been tagged in a post by Sophie Hannigan: Looking forward to catching up with my old mate Louise Williams on Friday night! I click the like button with trembling hands. I am thankful that this first encounter with Sophie took place online, giving me time to compose myself privately afterwards. *I'm an adult now*, I think. *I don't need her approval*, but I'm not even convincing myself.

Outside, night is falling. I close the laptop and sit unmoving at my kitchen table for a long time. First the Facebook request, then the reunion, now this meeting with Sophie … I feel as though I'm on a ride, or a journey, that nobody asked me if I wanted to go on. Although I am profoundly shocked by the turn events have taken, at some level I've always been expecting this to happen, or something like it. I don't know who is driving or where we are going, but wheels have been set in motion and I don't know how to stop them.

Chapter 4

2016

I notice the photo is missing just before the doorbell rings.

It usually sits on top of the freestanding shelving unit next to the fridge: a selfie of me and Henry on the beach, framed by an unfeasibly blue sky, our eyes screwed up against the brightness of the sun. The unit also acts as a holding area for unpaid bills, letters from the school, shopping lists and scribbled reminders to myself about things I need to do. I knew that adjusting to life as a single, working mother would be hard emotionally, but the practicalities took me by surprise. Sometimes I feel that I am hanging on to life by my fingernails, always just seconds from falling.

I leave Henry sitting at the table, painstakingly forking individual pieces of pasta into his mouth, and open the door.

'You're early.'

'Yes, well, even though I have babysat for you a million times, I know there's going to be a list of instructions as long as my arm: current favourite book, the precise angle he likes the door to be left open, the configuration and pecking order of the cuddly toys. These things take time. Can I come in then?'

'Sorry.' I step back and Polly whirls past me, divesting herself of an enormous striped scarf, which is practically the length of her entire body, and a Puffa coat, and unzipping knee-length leather boots to reveal greying leggings which don't quite meet her mismatched socks, a stripe of unshaven leg visible in the gap between.

'How's things with you?' I ask, hanging up her coat and scarf.

'Oh, the usual. Work's a nightmare; you were so right to get out of there, set up on your own.'

She's said this pretty much every time I've seen her since I left Blue Door Interior Design three years ago, but we both know she'd go crazy after just one day of sitting alone at home like I do, with only the odd meeting to break things up a bit. She thrives on the chat, the office gossip, the vibe that thrums between colleagues in a busy, demanding workplace. Whereas I don't miss it one bit. I go out for occasional drinks with some of my old colleagues, but apart from Polly I wouldn't describe any of them as friends.

'I know, although sometimes I wish there was someone else to share the load,' I say pointedly over my shoulder as we walk to the kitchen.

Polly grins. I'm always trying to persuade her to leave Blue Door and come into business with me. We'd be able to take on some of the work I have to turn down.

It was hard at first, going it alone, but it felt like the right time. Henry was almost one, and I was due back at Blue Door after taking the maximum maternity leave. The thought of going back to work full-time, being out of the house the whole time Henry was awake, alarmed me. Sam had been worried about how we would all cope when I was back at work – in fact, he was keen for me to give up work altogether but financially it wasn't doable; and actually I was ready to get back to work again, just not to rejoin the rat race. I think we all thought it would make for an easier pace of life if I was working from home, building up the business slowly. It didn't really work out like that though.

I got in touch with someone I'd worked with years before, Rosemary Wright-Collins, and it turned out she was looking for someone to do the interiors for all her properties. Rosemary is a property developer with impeccable taste and a huge wallet, and it was a real coup to get her as my first client. The fact that I did, and that she is still using me for every new project she takes on, is a huge source of pride for me. She's even written a glowing testimonial for my website. But it did mean that I had to hit the ground running, sort childcare for Henry, get straight back into professional mode.

'Caro's driving me insane,' Polly goes on. 'She's got a new man again and she keeps phoning me what feels like every ten minutes to ask me what various text messages mean, what she should wear, whether she should shave her whatsit. I do not know what I did to deserve such a sister. I mean, for God's sake, how am I to know if women these days are shaving their whatsits? Aaron would be so delighted if I ever wanted to have sex that I don't think he'd care if I was covered in a fine down from head to toe ... Henry! How's my favourite boy?'

She swoops down and kisses his head.

He smiles through the tomato sauce.

'Hello, Polly.'

'He's been looking forward to you coming all day,' I say. 'Apparently you read more stories than me.'

'Well, Thomas the Tank's all new to me, the girls were never interested. You got any new ones, H?'

His face lights up.

'Yes! Daddy got me three new Thomas books: Charlie, Arthur and Diesel. Will you read them to me?'

'Of course! That's what I'm here for!'

'Mummy? Can I go and get them?'

'Yes, if you've had enough pasta. Just let me have a chat with Polly though, and then when I've gone she'll read them all to you.'

'Tell you what, H, why don't you go and make a start on a massive train track while I talk to Mummy, and then I'll come and play with it when she's gone out. Deal?'

'Deal!' says Henry, visibly bursting with joy at the prospect and scurrying out of the kitchen, already mentally constructing the track.

Polly sits down at the table and pops a piece of cold pasta from Henry's plate into her mouth. I kneel on the floor by the shelving unit, and pull it away from the wall slightly, its contents wobbling precariously on their shelves. I run my hand along on the floor behind it just to be sure, but there's nothing there.

'What *are* you doing?'

'I keep a photo on here usually – you know, that lovely one of me and Henry on the beach.'

'Oh yes, I know. And . . . ?' She gestures to me on the floor.

'It's gone.'

'What do you mean, gone?'

'Well, I haven't moved it, and it's not there. It's always there.'

'Maybe you were dusting it, and you got distracted and put it somewhere else? You know what you're like.'

'But where? It's not exactly huge in here.' There are units down either side of the galley, and then the room opens out slightly at the end, with just enough space for a small dining table by the patio doors. The photo is nowhere to be seen.

'Or Henry's moved it?'

'Yes, maybe. Henry!' He comes in, a wooden bridge in one hand and a plastic elephant about twice the size of the bridge in the other.

'Have you seen the photo of me and you? The one that's normally on the shelf there?'

He shrugs. 'No. Can I go back to my track?'

'Yes, OK.' I turn to Polly. 'Well, where is it, then?' Maria's friend request hums in the background of my thoughts all the time, colouring my view of the world. A few days ago, I wouldn't have given the missing photo a second thought, and even now the rational part of me says I'm being ridiculous; but in a small, scared corner of my mind, I can't help but wonder: has someone been in my flat?

'Oh, don't worry, it'll turn up. It's got to be somewhere. So, who's this old school friend you're going to see tonight?' asks Polly.

I fill the kettle with water, playing for time, anxiety about the missing photo still playing at the edges of my mind. I'm unsure how much I want to share with Polly. I've never spoken to her (or anyone, in fact) about what happened with Maria. It's too big, too unwieldy. I don't know how to configure my tongue into the right shapes to explain it. That was one of the reasons it was such a relief to be with Sam. I never had to explain it to him because he was there. Sometimes I wonder if I would have put up with so much for so long if it hadn't been for the fact that he was one of the only people who knew what I had done. He had seen the very worst of me and yet he still loved me, in his own way.

'Oh, just a girl who I lost touch with years ago. She contacted me on Facebook, thought it would be nice to meet for a catch-up,' I say, trying to keep my voice light. Tonight's not the time to go into it; if I start explaining what happened to Maria, even the heavily edited version that I would have to tell Polly, we'll be here all night, and I haven't even figured out what I'm going to wear yet. I can't ask Polly for help with that, much as I'd like to, because then I'd have to explain why it matters so much to me to look good tonight.

'That's great,' says Polly. She's always on at me to go out more, see my other friends. She thinks, and she's probably right, that I've neglected them in my eagerness to focus on Henry in the wake of the split from Sam. The only one who hasn't dropped away is her, because she refuses to.

'So she would have known Sam too, this girl you're going to see?' Polly goes on, frowning.

'Yes, of course.'

'Does she know that he's left you for that ... that ... *floozy*?' Polly's fury at Sam's treatment of me, and her contempt for Catherine, his new, younger wife, knows no bounds.

I feel a fierce pang of love for her. She and Aaron and Sam and I never really progressed as a foursome, beyond the occasional dinner together. I used to wish that we were more of a gang, like some of the other couples that I knew who holidayed together, but I'm glad now that Polly stayed so very much mine, and that Aaron and Sam never gelled.

'I don't even know if she knows that Sam and I were married,' I say. 'Although I wouldn't be surprised if she knows the whole story; she always knew all the gossip at school.' Well, not the whole story. No one knows that. Not even Polly.

'Hmm, OK. Now,' Polly says, and I can tell that whatever's coming next, it's something she's planned to say to me before she arrived, 'have you thought any more about what I said? About internet dating?'

'I don't know, Polly. I'm not sure I'm ready to meet anyone.' I spend longer than necessary looking for teabags in the cupboard. 'You know I need to concentrate on Henry, and work. I don't have a lot of time for anything else.' It's not time that's the problem. It's me. I think I might be broken. After all those years with Sam, I wouldn't have a clue how to go about conducting a new relationship.

'That's exactly why you should do it! You need something else, something that's just for you. I totally understand why you've had to devote all your energy to Henry, especially with him starting school this year, but it's been two years since Sam left. That's a long time, Lou.'

It feels like yesterday. The pain has dulled a little, but it's still there, like a gap where a tooth has been extracted. Some days I can leave it alone, but others I can't help probing it with my tongue to see how much it still hurts. No matter how things were at the end, I can't forget how we felt like one person rather than two separate beings, how we were swallowed up into each other, the times I saw myself reflected in his eyes looking better than I had ever looked. How we used to be everything to each other, not needing anyone else. I drag my thoughts away from him, back to Polly.

'I know,' I say reluctantly. 'You're probably right. I'm OK on my own though. Better, even.'

'Well you're certainly better off on your own than being with him. But you could be more than OK, you could be happy. You deserve some fun, and to be with someone who will treat you well, put you first. Look after you.'

'Sam did all that,' I say defensively. Sometimes I think Polly forgets how happy Sam and I were until a few years ago when things started to go wrong. How much he loved me, needed me even. At sixteen he hadn't seemed to need anybody. He was so sure of himself, verging on arrogant, although I never would have said so at the time. I kept my devotion to him a secret back then because I feared he would scorn such puppyish emotion. But when we met again ten years later, he was different: a little softer, a little more vulnerable. Something in him responded to and was grateful for the uncritical, teenage adoration I still felt for him.

'Oh my God!' says Polly. 'Why are you still defending him? What he did to you was so wrong.'

'Yes, I know. But it wasn't all his fault.'

'Yes it was! It was totally all his fault!' Polly pulls her unruly hair into a ponytail and twists it around in frustration. This is a conversation we've had many times before and both of us know it's never going to end in agreement, so I pull her back.

'So … this online dating thing, what would I even say about myself?'

'Aha! That's where you don't need to worry.' Polly smiles with the air of a poker player pulling out a trump card. One of the many things I love about her is her inability to hold a grudge. She can be really cross with you about something one minute, but make her laugh and it's all forgotten. 'There's this site where your friend puts up your profile – they write it, say what kind of man you're looking for, everything. You just sit back and wait for the offers to come rolling in.'

'And this friend would be … ?' I smile, squishing the tea-bags against the inside of the mugs and adding milk.

'Ta-dah!' Polly does jazz hands around her face. 'Seriously though, what have you got to lose?'

It's not so much what I've got to lose as what I could potentially gain. Do I really want to open myself up to the possibility of hurt again? I've worked so hard to get to where I am today – independent, self-sufficient, just me and Henry, happy in our little bubble. Making sure that Henry is OK has been my only concern apart from my work, and although there are days when I wish I could turn the clock back, actually I'm OK: healthier, happier. In fact I can't imagine ever being with anyone else. I'm scared that I'm spoiled. A phrase I heard my mother use when I was a child echoes in my head: *damaged goods*.

'OK, don't be cross,' Polly goes on, 'but I've set you up a profile on the site. Why don't you have a look and see what you think?' She pulls my laptop towards her from the other side of the table.

'Wait!' I jump forward and snatch it from her. Maria's Facebook page is open on there.

Polly draws her hand back in confusion. 'The profile's not live yet, I set it up so you can check it before I upload it.'

'Oh, no, sorry, it's not that,' I say, opening up the lid, hoping she doesn't notice the barely perceptible tremor in my hands. 'It's just that my laptop's password protected. I'll do it.'

I hit a few random keys as if typing in a password, then close down Facebook and hand the laptop over to Polly. She opens a new window and taps away for a few seconds.

'OK, here you are: Independent, funny female seeks similar male, 35–50, for country walks, delicious food, and nights in and out.'

'I hate country walks.'

'I know, but they all seem to love them so I thought you might give yourself more of a chance if you said you did.'

'Right, OK . . . and delicious food? Won't they think that's a way of warning them that I'm really fat?'

'They'll be able to see your photo, so they'll know you're not. Look.' She clicks on the photo. She's used one I've never seen before, taken at a barbecue at her and Aaron's last summer. I'm wearing a bright print cotton dress and sunglasses, holding a glass of wine and laughing. I look happy and carefree. I don't look like me.

'So?' says Polly hopefully. 'Can I upload it?'

'Oh God, go on then.' She's never going to let this go, and I suppose there's no harm in putting myself on the site. I don't have to go on any dates, after all.

'Yay!' says Polly, clicking away happily. 'Right, you get changed. I'll do this then I'll go and play with Henry. I've set you up a new email address for all the replies, OK? So you can keep it separate. I'll send the details to your normal email address.'

I try on about five of my 'best' outfits, but I look over-dressed and try-hard in all of them, so in the end I aim for casual but funky in a denim skirt, leggings and roll-neck jumper. Henry and Polly are absorbed in a train-crash drama when I pop my head into the sitting room to say goodbye, but Henry tears himself away to give our parting the gravity he feels is its due. Farewells are a serious matter for him, not to be taken lightly.

As I walk towards Crystal Palace station, my phone vibrates in my pocket. I pull it out, and see with trepidation that I have a Facebook notification. When I click on it, though, it's only a status update from Polly. Having fun matchmaking and living vicariously through Louise Williams on matchmymate.com, she's written, tagging me so that it will appear on my page too. Thanks for letting everyone know I reply, adding a smiley face so she knows I'm not pissed off. Everyone and their dog seems to do internet dating these days, so I don't mind my friends knowing. I think with a smile of the reaction some of them will have to Polly's post, already looking forward to the comments, and I realise with a jolt that I've been looking for a way back into my life. Maybe this is it.

Chapter 5

2016

I'm rummaging in my handbag for my Oyster card when I first get the feeling someone is watching me.

There's nothing specific that I can put my finger on, just an awareness, a prickling on the back of my neck. I glance around, but the station is busy with a mix of commuters on their way home and locals on their way into central London for a night out. I try and force myself to breathe evenly: I'm overreacting, letting my imagination run away with me. But my fingers stab uselessly inside my bag, the tension from them running all the way up to my shoulders, which are hunched as if in readiness for an attack.

I look around, my eyes sliding unseeing over the men to search out women of my age. Could that be her, that woman in the expensive-looking camel wool coat standing by the entrance? She pulls a compact from her bag and turns towards me slightly as she checks her make-up under the harsh fluorescent light. No, it's definitely not her, but it strikes me what a futile exercise this is. My mental image of

Maria is decades out of date anyway, and who knows what blows life has dealt her if she has somehow survived? My chances of recognising her are slim to none, yet still my eyes sweep the ticket hall: not her . . . not her . . . not her.

I move swiftly through the barriers and half-run down the stairs, trying to look as if I'm hurrying to catch a train, not running from something, or someone. I arrive breathless on the platform, more so than the run warrants, and push my way through the waiting passengers to the far end. My ragged breath is visible in the dark air before me, but a line of sweat trickles down my back. There's still five minutes to wait for the train, so I stand close to the back wall, my bag gathered to me, eyes scanning the busy platform. When the train arrives, I get on and walk quickly down the first carriage, slipping into the second and pausing in the vestibule next to the toilet. I stand there a moment, trying to slow my breathing, but then the electronic door to the toilet slides open to reveal a young man vomiting into the toilet. I wince and walk down into the second carriage, taking a seat by the window. I rest my head against the glass, closing my eyes for a second against the houses that flash past with their glimpses of cosy family life through the lighted windows. I jerk round when I feel someone slip into the seat beside me, but it's a young girl, talking very fast and angrily on her phone. She doesn't take the slightest bit of notice of me.

At Victoria I cross the concourse, trying to keep my eyes ahead, telling myself I'm being absurd. Even if someone were following me, I'm in a crowded station. I am safe. I join the crowds surging down into the Underground and stand on the platform. We are packed in so tightly that I can only see those people closest to me, everyone else just a sea of hot bodies, cheeks still red and cold from the freezing air outside, sweating in their winter coats. There's no way anyone could still be watching me now; it's too busy.

By the time the tube pulls into South Kensington, I've convinced myself that I was being paranoid. I've allowed the fear I felt when I first got Maria's friend request to overlay my life like an Instagram filter, turning everything a shade darker. No one is following me. I walk evenly up the steps from the platform, the knot in my stomach easing a little. The easiest route to Sophie's flat, and the one I planned when I looked up her address earlier, is through the tunnel which runs under the roads to the museums. During the day it's thronged with people – families going to see the dinosaurs in the Natural History Museum, tourists on their way to the V&A, but now although it's not deserted, it's quiet. I consider carrying straight on with the majority of people as they stream out of the main entrance, but then I give myself a mental shake. I've allowed myself to become cowed, afraid. I'm being ridiculous. I turn down the tunnel.

I'm about halfway along when I hear the footsteps. I can see a man about fifty yards ahead of me, but otherwise I am alone, apart from whoever is behind me. I speed up just a fraction, I hope not enough for anyone to notice, but I'm sure the footsteps speed up too. They echo around the tunnel; proper shoes, not trainers. I speed up a bit more; so do the shoes. I risk a glance behind me and I can see a figure in a black coat, hood up. I daren't look for long and I can't tell at this distance whether it's a man or a woman. I'm not far from the end of the tunnel now and I am filled with a need to be outside where there are cars and people. I start to run, and so does the figure behind me. My handbag is flying up and down and the carrier bag in my hand containing a bottle of wine that I spent forty minutes choosing in the supermarket last night bangs against my leg with every stride. Blood roars in my head and my chest starts to burn, and then finally I see the exit, and a group of women in suits coming towards me, chatting and laughing. I slow my pace, breathing heavily. One of the women looks at me with concern.

'Are you OK?'

I force a smile. 'Yes, I'm fine. Just . . . in a hurry.'

She smiles and goes back to her conversation. Once they have passed me and I am nearly at the exit, I look back. There is no sign of the figure in the black coat; no one there at all but the group of women, their laughter echoing around the tunnel.

Out on the street, I lean against a wall for a moment until my breath, which has been coming in panicky gasps, slows to something approaching normal. Out here in the street-lit world, full of people and cars and life, my fear seems suddenly out of proportion. What did I think was going to happen?

I force myself to check the map on my phone and start walking, legs still wobbly, in the direction of Sophie's flat. Soon I find myself walking down a row of elegant, cream Georgian terraces fronted by black wrought iron railings and sporting carefully tended window boxes. Normally I would be peering enviously through the large sash windows at antique furniture and painstakingly restored fireplaces, my own flat seeming cramped and plain in comparison. Some of them are still one house, with the basement converted into a homely but expensive-looking kitchen with room for a squashy sofa as well as the obligatory kitchen island. Today, however, I can't focus on anything except Maria.

Workers rush past me in their daytime uniforms, wrapped up against the freezing wind, hurrying home to hot baths, warm rooms, dinners cooked by loved ones. I pass a group of teenage girls dressed in onesies and sheepskin boots with their hair in enormous curlers. They are dancing along together, oblivious to the cold, arms linked, hysterical with laughter. I feel a twinge of envy laced with shame, and am filled with a sudden longing to be curled up on the sofa reading Henry a Thomas the Tank Engine story.

When I reach Sophie's door, I glance up at the lighted windows behind the plantation shutters, firmly closed to keep out the darkness. I take a moment to compose myself, and then press the top buzzer. Seconds later there's a pattering of feet, and a figure gradually takes shape, refracted through the stained-glass panels in the front door. And then the door is opening, and there she is. We look at each other for a couple of seconds, both of us seemingly unsure about how to play this. Then she breaks into a smile that lights up every corner of her lovely face.

'Louise!' She goes to kiss me on the cheek and then thinks better of it and pulls me into her, enveloping me in her arms, her perfume, her personality. I'm overwhelmed by memory, by sheer sensation. The intervening years, during which I have worked so hard at forgetting, melt away and for a moment I'm sixteen again – awkward, conflicted, intensely alive.

Close up she is not quite the glossy creature of her Facebook photos but she's not far off. With a flagrant disregard for the inclement weather, she's dressed in skinny jeans with bare feet and a silvery gossamer-light vest top accessorised with a chunky statement necklace. Her honey-streaked hair falls around her tanned shoulders and she is lightly but expertly made up. I was reasonably confident when I studied myself in the mirror before I left the house, but now I just feel frumpy.

'Hi, hi!' she exclaims. 'It's so good to see you!'

She even talks in exclamation marks.

'You too,' I manage. 'You look great. How are you?'

'Oh, I'm great, really well, really, really well,' she gabbles, pulling me into the spacious tiled hallway, studying me with her head on one side. 'Aw, you look exactly the same.'

Upstairs in her top-floor flat it is almost stiflingly warm, and I can feel sweat begin to soak into the fabric that presses into my armpits and pool between my breasts. I'd like to take my jumper off but I can't risk Sophie seeing the dark circles under my arms.

Her flat is immaculate with airy, high-ceilinged rooms and solid wood floors, but it somehow manages to be cosy at the same time. An extravagant crystal chandelier hangs in the centre of the living room.

'What a gorgeous flat,' I say as I hand her the wine I brought.

'Oh yeah, thanks. Come through to the kitchen.'

I follow her into a small but tasteful and expensively fitted-out kitchen, where she shoves my wine into the fridge and pours us both a glass from a different bottle.

'Is it . . . just you here?'

There's a pause.

'Um . . . yeah.' Her eyes flick to the fridge, which has photos and appointment cards stuck to it with magnets. She seems uneasy and I guess she's unwilling to admit to being single. Even though I'm in the same position, there's a tiny, secret, mean part of me that is glad she too is alone in her forties.

We take our wine back to the living room and she gestures to me to sit at one end of the purple velvet sofa, curling herself in the opposite corner like a cat. The sofa is so deep that if I want to keep my feet on the floor, I can't rest against the back, so I balance on the edge, legs primly together, shifting my wine glass from hand to hand.

Despite her studied insouciance, I can tell she is nervous too, rattling off questions – what do I do for a living, do I enjoy my job, where do I live – leaving me little opportunity to ask any of my own.

'And your parents, how are they?' she asks when we've exhausted the other avenues.

'They're really well. Still living up in Manchester.' There's not much more to say. We haven't fallen out exactly – I think you'd have to be closer than we are for that to be possible. It's just that there's a wedge between us, as there is between me and everyone who doesn't know the real me, doesn't know what I have done.

'Do you get up there a lot?' she goes on.

'Not that much. It's difficult, you know, with work and everything.' It's not that difficult really. Manchester's not much more than a couple of hours on the train from London. The truth is that it's an effort, spending any time with them. Our relationship is superficial, the conversation skating over the surface of life, never plumbing its depths. It's a struggle to keep up the facade for longer than a few hours every now and then.

'And your parents?' I ask.

'Oh, they both passed away. Dad when I was twenty-one, and then Mum a couple of years ago.' Her tone doesn't change from the bright cheeriness of a moment ago but I sense a brittleness behind her words.

'I'm really sorry to hear that.'

'Yeah, thanks.' She dispatches my condolences neatly. 'Sooo, tell me more about your work. Do you find it hard, working for yourself?'

I go on too long about the perils of setting up my own interior design business and the awards I've won, and after a while her eyes begin to glaze over. She does perk up a bit when I mention being featured in the local paper back in Sharne Bay when I won a design award, but only because she too has a story about being featured in the same paper when she ran a charity race.

'And you?' I ask eventually. 'What do you do for work?'

'I work in fashion.'

'Oh, great. Doing what?'

'Oh, bits and bobs, you know. Sales, marketing. This and that.'

I sense that for some reason she's being deliberately obscure, so I don't ask any more. I notice that she doesn't ask me about a partner, or children. Is that because she knows about me and Sam, or because she doesn't want to talk about her own relationship situation? She seems edgy, as if her incessant questioning is a way of keeping the conversation on the track she wants it on. When she finally runs out of questions, silence falls, and I rack my brains for a new topic. Sophie looks down, fiddling with her glass, uncharacteristically uncertain.

'It's so good to see you, Louise,' she says. 'You know, you were really important to me. You were the one I could … talk to, I suppose. You seemed to properly care about me, not like some of the others.'

I am verging on speechless. Surely I was the one who had gained from our friendship at school, not her? She was my pass to the other world, the one who kept me from being Esther Harcourt. Looking back, I suppose I provided the uncritical, adoring acolyte she so desperately needed, but at the time I was so desperate to keep her that I never thought to wonder what was in it for her.

I start to reply, but she cuts in, as if already regretting what she's just said. 'Soooo … excited about the reunion?' She smiles, giving the distinct impression that she is well aware that I only found out about it recently. How very Sophie. The conversation has swung so swiftly back onto the regular track that I wonder if I imagined that lowering of her guard.

'Yes, yes. Should be great,' I reply. 'Can't wait.'

'You do know Sam's going? I heard about you two, such a shame.' So she does know. Does she genuinely think it's a shame? I was never entirely sure whether anything had happened between her and Sam when we were at school, and a ridiculous teenage part of me pulses with jealousy. She regards me soulfully from under her eyelashes, concern oozing from every pore. 'Will it be a bit awkward, d'you think?'

'No, it'll be fine. It was very amicable,' I say, as if reading from a script. I could call it My Life As I Want It To Be. Hearing his name from her lips, with the past draped heavy around me, makes the weight on my shoulders press down just that little bit harder. 'How did you hear?'

'Oh, you know how these things get around,' she says. 'I still see a few of the old gang – Matt, Claire. People talk. I think it was Matt who told me actually – he came to your wedding, didn't he?'

He came alone, standing awkwardly around in his work suit, not knowing anyone. I remember Polly talking to him, saying afterwards that he was nice. I think she fancied him a bit. Before she was married, obviously.

What did he say to Sophie about Sam and me, I wonder? There's nobody who knows the intimate details of our relationship. Nobody who knows how we used to spend whole weekends in bed, totally absorbed in each other, turning down invitations to see friends, being everything to each other.

'You had a baby too, didn't you?'

'Yes,' I say through gritted teeth. 'We had a baby. Although he's not a baby any more; he's four now.' I suddenly wish desperately that I was at home, peering in through the gap of Henry's door to check if he's asleep, going in to kiss him, to breathe in the sleeping scent of him.

'Oh, sweet.' She couldn't be less interested, and anyway Henry is the last thing I want to be talking about with her.

'What about Tim? Tim Weston?' I ask, as if the name has just occurred to me. 'Do you ever see him?'

Sophie looks at me sharply. 'No, I've not seen him for years. Why do you ask?'

'Oh, I noticed that he was listed on Facebook as going to the reunion and I know he was friends with Matt's brother, so I thought . . .' I tail off. As an introduction to the thing I want to talk to her about, it's been a spectacular failure.

Sophie starts listing all the others that are going, filling me in on the lives of various people of whom I've heard nothing since I left school in 1989. There was no sixth form at Sharne Bay High, although even if there had been there was no way I would have stayed on for it, not after what happened. I went to sixth-form college in a neighbouring town to do my A levels, and after I left home for university, I never looked back. My parents moved to Manchester to be nearer my grandparents during my first year away, so I never spent any holidays in Norfolk and didn't keep in touch with anyone, throwing myself determinedly if unenthusiastically into university life. By the time Sam and I got together, which was well after our university days, I had completely lost touch with everyone from school, and although I knew Sam saw Matt Lewis from time to time it was very rare and I never joined him.

Maria's friend request sits in my stomach like a lump of undercooked pasta, preventing me from engaging fully in the conversation – not that it matters as I can barely get a word in. I have that shaky, breathless feeling you get when you know that there's a huge conversational bomb upcoming, but the other person has no idea. I've got my finger in the pin of the grenade, but she can't even see it.

Eventually there is a lull, so I seize the moment and launch in.

'Sophie, there's actually a reason I got in touch ... something I need to talk to you about.'

'Yes?' she says cautiously, taking a sip of wine.

'I got a rather ... strange friend request on Facebook.' I take a beat, wanting to give myself a few more seconds of normality. Once I say it, once I let someone else in to this . . . whatever it is, that's it, game over. Things will never be the same. 'It was from Maria Weston.'

I don't think it's my imagination that Sophie pales and her eyes widen for a millisecond, before she slips her mask smoothly back into place.

'Oh, did you get that too?' She laughs. 'From the girl who drowned?'

So it's not just me. There's a certain comfort in that. But surely even Sophie can't be so heartless as to be laughing about this. The only possible explanation is that she is faking it, pretending a nonchalance that you might feel about a girl with whom you had had nothing to do, a girl whose life never touched your own.

'Yes, of course the girl who drowned.' This comes out rather more forcefully than I intended, and Sophie looks taken aback, perhaps even a little frightened, although she hides it quickly.

'Is that why you're here?' she says, laughing again. 'It's obviously a sick joke, probably from someone who's going to the reunion. I bet everyone's had the same request.'

'I suppose so,' I say. This is in fact the supposition I have been clinging to for four days like a shipwreck victim to a broken piece of the hull. 'But who would do something like that? And why me? I didn't even know about the reunion when I got the request. Mind you, I suppose it's obvious.'

'Why obvious?' Sophie asks, getting up from the sofa and pouring herself another glass of wine from the bottle on the coffee table without offering me one. She sits down in the armchair on the opposite side of the table and sips her drink, her face unreadable in the shadows.

'You know. The way I treated her . . . and what we did . . .'

I blunder on. 'Although hardly anybody knew about that. Did they?'

'I don't know what you're talking about, Louise. I barely knew her.' She places her wine glass firmly on the coffee table.

I can hardly believe what I am hearing. I have lived the last twenty-seven years in the shadow of what we did, of what I did. Of course my life has carried on – I have studied and worked, shopped and cooked; I've been a friend, a daughter, a wife, a mother. Yet all the time, in the back of my mind, this one unforgivable act has loomed – squashed, squeezed, parcelled, but always there. The awkwardness I have been feeling all evening subsides and is replaced by anger. I thought I would be able to talk to Sophie about this.

'Yes you did! You know what we did: we made her life a misery. And what about that night, at the leavers' party?'

'I honestly don't know what you mean,' she says with finality, standing up and picking up her glass. She bends over and takes mine although there's still an inch of wine left in it, and moves towards the door to the kitchen, a glass in each hand. 'Listen, it's been really great seeing you but I'm afraid I'll have to love you and leave you. Oh—' she breaks off as the doorbell rings. 'That'll be Pete.'

'Who?' I say in confusion. I had wanted to tell her about the missing photo, and how I thought someone had been following me on the way to her flat.

'Pete – my date?' she says in response to my blank face. 'Sorry, I did say just a quick drink, didn't I? I'm sure I told you I wouldn't be able to give you a whole evening.'

She puts the glasses down, checks her face in the ornate gilt mirror hanging over the sofa, shakes her hair out over her shoulders and trips lightly down the stairs. I sit on the sofa, my face burning. How is it possible that she can still make me feel like this? I should be furious at her rudeness, but instead I feel embarrassed and foolish. I hear a man's voice and Sophie laughing, then two pairs of footsteps coming up the stairs.

'This is my friend Louise.'

'Oh! Sorry to interrupt,' says the man, looking embarrassed. He's early forties, mid-height with closely cropped greying hair. He's not good-looking exactly, but he looks at ease both in his own skin and in his clothes, dressed casually in black jeans and a faded blue denim shirt under a dark woollen overcoat.

'Oh no, it's no problem – she's just leaving, aren't you, Louise?'

I scramble up from the sofa, red-faced, gathering up my bag in what feels like an unnecessarily scatty manner.

'Yes, don't worry,' I say to him. 'We were just having a quick drink. I've got somewhere else to be anyway. Nice to meet you.' I offer a hand, which he shakes for a few seconds too long.

'I'll see you out,' Sophie says, shepherding me briskly out of the room and down the stairs. In the hallway she hands me my coat and opens the door.

'It's been really fun seeing you,' she says brightly. 'See you at the reunion, I guess!'

Her tone is determinedly upbeat, but I can't help noticing that she is reluctant to meet my eye for any length of time. We say a brief goodbye and I find myself alone on the street, even more confused than I was before I went in. I am struggling to come to terms with Sophie's rewriting of the past, although I suppose I shouldn't be, seeing as I've been doing exactly that myself for years.

I take a few paces down the road then turn to look back. Through the coloured glass in the front door I can see that Sophie doesn't immediately go back upstairs, but is standing with her back to the door, leaning against it as if she needs the support. She stays that way, perfectly still, for thirty seconds, then, with a defiant flick of the hair, she is gone.

Chapter 6

1989

Sophie didn't mention Maria for the next few weeks, so I took my lead from her and said nothing either. I saw Maria around school, and sometimes we chatted, but I had Sophie's words ringing in my head, *I've heard some things about her already*, so I didn't let it go too far. I saw Maria sitting with Esther Harcourt at lunch a couple of times, both of them laughing their heads off, Esther looking happier than I'd seen her since primary school.

Three weeks after that first encounter with Maria in the cafeteria, I was walking down the corridor when I saw her standing alone at the end of the lunch queue. I was going to have to join her, unless I turned back and didn't go to lunch at all. Sophie had left with Claire at the end of double French without speaking to me so I assumed it was one of those days where she wasn't going to sit with me. Maria was facing straight ahead, so I touched her arm. She jumped, and whipped round to face me.

'Oh! Hello,' she said, her eyes brightening.

'Hi. How are you?'

'Good, thanks. Yeah, I'm OK.'

I could see Sophie and Claire Barnes ahead of us at the front of the queue, Sophie throwing her head back to laugh, her shining hair flying over her shoulders. I felt a sudden spurt of anger. Why should I have to sit alone on the days when she doesn't deign to sit with me? I turned back to Maria and smiled.

When we got to the puddings, Maria helped herself to a doughnut, so I did too. I never do that when I'm with Sophie. It was so nice to be able to have whatever I wanted. She looked a bit embarrassed when we got to the till because she had one of those tokens for free school dinners, but I pretended I hadn't noticed.

Before I had a chance to suggest we sat elsewhere, Maria had placed her tray down on the table behind Sophie and Claire, who were sitting with Sam Parker and Matt Lewis. I could hear them all talking about the drugs they'd taken the previous weekend. They'd gone to one of those raves they go to over on some farm near where Claire Barnes lives, where apparently everyone takes Ecstasy or speed. I've never been invited, not that I'd be allowed to go anyway. I remember thinking that day that I'd be too scared to take drugs, although part of me was a bit intrigued. Maria rolled her eyes.

'God, people who take drugs are so BORING,' she said, taking no trouble to lower her voice. 'They can't talk about anything else.'

It might have been my imagination, but I thought I saw Sophie's back stiffen slightly.

'Have you ever done anything?' she asked.

'I've tried dope,' I said in a low voice, barely more than

a whisper. 'It didn't really do anything for me, apart from making me feel sick.'

'Same,' she said, grinning. 'Like I said, *boring*.'

A wave of laughter built inside me, and soon we couldn't stop giggling, neither of us really knowing why. I saw Sophie half-looking round a couple of times, but even that couldn't stop me. When we'd finally calmed down, Maria said, 'I could go into town, if you like. After school? My brother's not collecting me today.'

She said it casually, but I could hear the hope in her voice.

'Sam!' I heard Sophie say behind us, mock-horrified. I looked over as she laughed artificially loudly and gave Sam a push on the arm. He took her hand and snaked it around behind her back, smiling lazily and looking straight into her eyes as she struggled uselessly to free it.

'Get a room, you two,' said Matt Lewis casually, but I could see the whites of his knuckles around his fork and his eyes that never left Sophie's face.

'I'd love to,' I said to Maria.

I'd forgotten that it was the first day of the fair, and after school the market square, instead of being full of stalls selling polyester skirts and mixed nuts, was a riot of colour and lights. We wandered around looking at all the rides, competing fairground tunes jangling discordantly in our ears. Maria bought a stick of candyfloss the size of her head and I had a toffee apple, the tangy sweetness as my teeth cracked through the shiny layer of toffee giving way to disappointingly woolly blandness within. Because it was only four o'clock it was mostly little kids on the rides, but we went on the waltzers anyway, the kidney-shaped carriage spinning on its axis as the carousel turned. We staggered off afterwards, heads fuzzy and stomachs heaving, clutching each other, breathless with laughter.

'Do you want to go and get a hot chocolate or something?' Maria asked, zipping up her coat against an unseasonably chilly wind. We got the good table in the window at the Oven Door and sat in cosy, companionable silence, watching the street outside.

'There's your mate.' Maria gestured towards the window, and there was Sophie sashaying down the pavement, mucking about and holding hands with Matt Lewis and Sam Parker. I felt a brief pang of hurt, but then Maria laughed.

'My God, she's such a slapper! What does she think she looks like?'

'I know.' I smiled, astonished at this heresy, and at my ability to find it funny. I'm not used to people laughing at Sophie.

'Shall we go to Topshop?' I asked, draining the last of my hot chocolate.

'Yeah, OK,' Maria said casually, failing to hide her pleasure at being asked.

We took loads of stuff into the changing rooms. Maria tried to persuade me to get this bright red miniskirt but it looked awful on me. She tried on this cool trilby but she said it made her look like she was trying to be Michael Jackson. When we came out, still laughing about the hat, there was Sophie again, sitting on a bench flanked by the two boys. This time she saw us.

'Hello, you two!' She sniggered. 'Having fun?'

I was about to mutter something when Maria said brightly and with a certain edge, 'Yes, thanks! You?'

Sophie looked taken aback, then smirked.

'Yeah, I'm fine,' she said, flinging a casual arm each around Matt and Sam. 'Having loads of fun.' Sam put his head on her shoulder and grinned up at us through half-closed eyes, but Matt held himself more stiffly, his hands placed awkwardly either side of him on the bench.

Maria raised her eyebrows and said, 'Mmm, looks like it. Well, if that's your idea of fun, I know what that makes you . . . Come on, Louise, let's go.'

She seized my arm and pulled me off in the direction of her house, which we'd discovered earlier was on my way home. As soon as we were out of earshot, I turned to her, half admiring and half terrified.

'What did you say that for?'

'Oh, come off it, Louise, she's such a cow. I can see that and I've only been here a few weeks. She deserves everything she gets. She's just using you to make herself feel better. She needs someone who'll hang on her every word, someone to hang out with on the days when Claire decides to ignore her. I've seen the way she treats you. All over you one day and then completely ignoring you the next? Deliberately flirting with the boy she knows you like?'

'What do you mean?' I asked, the flush rising up my neck belying my apparent lack of understanding. I'd obviously done a worse job than I thought of hiding my feelings about Sam. Also, no one had ever pulled me up on my friendship with Sophie before. I suppose somewhere inside I'd always known it was a bit unequal, but I thought that was the price you paid for being friends with someone popular.

'Oh, come on, I'm not that stupid. You like Sam Parker,

don't you? And if I can see that already, then she definitely knows.'

'Are you stalking me or something? All right, maybe I do like him,' I admitted. 'But only in that way where you know nothing's ever going to happen. I think Sophie fancies him anyway; she's not doing it to get at me. She's right for him. They match. He would never in a million years want to go out with me.'

'He might.'

'No, seriously. Boys like him don't go out with girls like me, that's just the way it is. At the most, I might get to be friends with him. But I don't even have that, he barely knows I exist.'

'Then maybe you need to change that,' she said. 'You never know if you don't try.'

I changed the subject then. Surely even a new girl could see that Sam was totally out of my league, even if I did have the courage to do more than smile at him.

We had such a laugh on the walk back to her house, Maria giving me her slyly observed take on various students in our year at school. For someone who'd only been in the school a few weeks she was astonishingly spot-on, identifying the frailties, insecurities and absurdities of people who to my uncritical eye had seemed achingly cool. She also did a pitch perfect impression of Mr Jenkins asking her lasciviously to stay behind after class to 'discuss her essay'. She hesitated outside her front gate, appearing to be involved in some kind of internal debate.

'Do you . . . do you want to come in for a bit?'

Inside, the hall carpet needed a hoover and was frayed at the edges, and there was a vague smell of bacon fat. The wallpaper was peeling and I could see that the handrail for the stairs had been removed, leaving a jagged groove in the wall. It was very quiet, but when Maria called out, her mum emerged from the kitchen, drying her hands on a tea towel that had seen better days. The resemblance between the two was striking: their long, wispy brown hair that fell somewhere between straight and curly, their eyes hazel pools, flecked with gold and green.

'Hi! I'm Bridget,' she said. I always feel a bit weird about calling my friends' parents by their first names, and generally try to avoid calling them anything at all. 'It's so nice to meet one of Maria's friends. Welcome!' She flung out both arms in an exaggerated gesture, tea towel flicking against the wall. 'So who are you?'

'Louise. Hi.'

'Oh, Louise! Yes, I've heard all about you!' I wondered what Maria had told her.

'Stay for a cup of tea! In fact, stay for dinner!' I was beginning to feel slightly suffocated and was about to make my excuses when Maria interrupted.

'Mum! Stop being so embarrassing. Come on, Louise, let's go to my room.'

'Shall I bring you up some tea and biscuits?' Bridget called after us as Maria hustled me up the stairs.

'No, Mum. We don't want anything.'

Maria closed the door behind us and sank down on the bed. The paint on the walls was chipped and the carpet didn't seem to quite fit the room, but Maria had obviously done her best, putting an Indian throw on the bed, covering the worst bits of wall with Salvador Dalí prints and filling the white Formica shelving unit with books.

'Sorry about that.'

'It's OK,' I said, lowering myself onto the bed beside her. 'Is – is she always like that with your friends?'

'She didn't used to be. Before ... well, before everything that happened at my old school she was fine. I mean, she still is fine really. It's just ... oh, never mind.' Maria's fingers went to her necklace, a gold heart on a chain that I'd noticed she always wore.

'What is it? You can say, I won't tell anyone if you don't want me to.'

'I don't want to go into it all. I had a bad time of it. Like I told you at lunch that first day, it was so bad that we moved schools, and home. It was awful for me, of course. But Mum took it even harder. She told me once that there's a saying, you're only as happy as your unhappiest child. If that's true then she must have been pretty fucking unhappy.'

There was silence for a while. It was clear that Maria wasn't going to say any more about it, so I changed the subject.

'I like your necklace. Where's it from?'

'I don't know. My dad gave it to me.' Her hand stole to it again, twisting the chain around her fingers. 'It was the first thing he'd ever bought me himself. Mum always bought the presents. I should have known he wasn't going to be around much longer. Are your mum and dad still together?'

'Yes.' I couldn't begin to imagine my parents splitting up. I didn't think of them as two separate people, more as an entity, mum-and-dad.

'Well, mine aren't. They separated before we left London. I think it was the stress of ... everything that happened.' What could have been so bad that it caused her parents to split up? I couldn't tell if she really didn't want to talk about it, or if she wanted me to force her to open up.

'So . . . what happened?' I asked.

She looked for a moment as if she was going to tell me, but then her face closed up.

'Let's talk about something else.'

I decided to take a different tack, telling her about the different teachers and their quirks and giving her the school gossip about who was going out with who. This was much more successful, and we were in her room for over an hour, punctuated by Bridget bringing up the unwanted tea and chocolate digestives. She lingered too long at the door, watching Maria and me laughing together, urging me again to stay for dinner, which I refused to do as I knew my parents would be expecting me back.

Maria and I said goodbye on the doorstep. I had that warm achy feeling that you get when you've been laughing too hard for too long. I had the uncomfortable realisation that I hadn't worried about what to say all afternoon. I hadn't turned every potential utterance over in my mind, examining it for possible embarrassment before letting it come out of my mouth as I have to with Sophie. Instead of feeling like a performance, my afternoon with Maria had been completely relaxed. I had simply let go.

As I walked down the front path, I almost bumped into a dark, thickset boy with the same hazel eyes as Maria and her mother. He didn't introduce himself, but looked at me suspiciously. I smiled, feeling flustered without knowing why, and let myself out of the gate. I didn't turn round, but I could feel his gaze, white-hot on my back all the way down the street until I reached the corner.

Later that evening I was in my room pretending to do my homework when the phone rang. I picked up the one on the landing outside my room.

'Hello?'

'Lou? It's Sophie.'

Her voice sounded gentle and hesitant, a world away from the strident confidence she had displayed earlier in town. For a moment I thought she was going to apologise. I slid down the wall until I was sitting on the landing floor, knees up to my chin, twisting the phone cord around my fingers.

'I'm worried about you. You hardly hang out with me and the girls any more.'

The girls? Sophie's the only one out of all of them that ever shows an interest in me. The rest of them barely know I exist, unless they want to copy my homework. There was a part of me that automatically wanted to apologise, to put everything back how it was before. But I still had Maria's voice in my head, still had the illusion of confidence that spending the afternoon with her had given me.

'What do you mean? You haven't even been speaking to me at school.'

'That's so unfair,' she said in injured tones. 'You're the one that's been ignoring me. I didn't have anyone to go into town with after school today. Claire was a right cow to me this afternoon. I was looking for you everywhere.'

'But you were with Matt and Sam! You looked pretty happy to me!'

'Oh, those two. I only went with them because I didn't have anyone else to hang out with. *You* certainly seemed like you were having a nice time.'

'Yes . . . I was.' My resolve was fading. Could she really be upset? Had I read everything wrong? 'But obviously … if I'd known you wanted to come with us, you could have done.'

'I don't know about *us*,' she said carefully. 'I wanted to go with you.'

'What's wrong with Maria? She's really nice.'

'I'm sure she's all right, although sorry but she was quite rude to me this afternoon. Also, what do you actually know about her? Where has she suddenly appeared from? The things I've heard about her … well, I shouldn't gossip. If you want to be friends with her, then of course that's up to you. But don't dump your old friends, Louise, otherwise you're running the risk of losing them. If you're not careful you'll end up like Esther Harcourt.' Sophie gave a little laugh – but a worried one, indicating that although she was joking there was a grain of truth in what she said. 'Obviously it's up to you who you hang out with but if I were you I'd think very carefully about where your loyalties lie.'

After we hung up, I sat on the landing for several minutes, my hand still on the phone. I thought about defying Sophie, and what that might mean for me socially; about the parties and sleepovers that I felt I was on the verge of being invited to, and of how much I wanted that. I wondered whether I was ready to throw all that away for someone I liked very much but hardly knew, who could potentially end up being my only friend.

The next day at school I didn't have any lessons with Maria in the morning. At break I went straight from Biology to the library and sat there for twenty minutes pretending to read a book about Anglo-Saxon England. I was going to skip lunch, but Sophie stopped me on my way back to the library and hauled me off to the canteen with her. My jacket potato was dry and starting to crack inside, and, as I added a small pot of congealed baked beans (no butter), I could see Maria out of the corner of my eye, a few places behind me in the queue. I paid and Sophie shepherded me firmly with her over to the far left corner table, settling down next to me with a protective hand on my arm. I could feel rather than see Maria coming up behind me. She put her hand on the chair next to me, but Sophie was ready for her.

'Sorry, that seat's taken,' she said, smiling brightly.

'It doesn't look taken,' said Maria. 'It looks totally empty to me. Unless one of your really skinny friends is sitting there and has managed to slim down so much that nobody can see her.' She looked at me, hoping for a smile or at least an acknowledgement but I stared studiously at my tray, running my fingers over the brown moulded plastic bumps as though they were braille, and I blind.

'I'm saving it,' said Sophie. 'For a friend.' The emphasis on friend couldn't have been more pointed.

Maria risked one more glance at me, but my eyes were glued to the tray.

'Right. OK. I get the picture,' she said, and took her tray over to the furthest possible table.

As I left the canteen I looked over at her. I think of her now as she was then: sitting on her own, her lunch barely touched in front of her, hunched over, pale-faced and staring unseeingly at her maths textbook. I saw Esther Harcourt watching her too from another table where she also sat alone, unread book in hand.

Chapter 7

She stands on the bridge, staring down at the water, brown and uninviting on this sunless winter day. Her knuckles stand out, harsh white against the dark wood of the railings. A solitary drink can bobs under the bridge and out of view, the only bright spot in the murky ribbon that snakes its way through the city. She could dash across the road in a kamikaze version of the childhood game of Poohsticks, to see if it makes it to the other side; to see if she does.

It's an impulse she's familiar with, having lived with it all these years. She first felt it that night, all those years ago, and it has returned at intervals ever since. What would life have been like if she'd made a different choice then, not just for her, but for everyone around her? It's been hardest for her family. Things have never been the same for them. They've done their best to support her, to be there, but they didn't really understand. How could they?

She looks down at the water again as it flows beneath her, away from her, her thoughts returning as they always do to that other time and place; that other choice, its implications still reverberating through her life.

What she wishes more than anything is that she could make things right; rebalance the scales. The world was knocked out of kilter that night. If only she could find a way to set it back on its proper axis. Maybe then she would be able to get on with the rest of her life. To live it fully, engage with the world, instead of existing in this shadowy half-life, where no one knows who she really is.

She releases her grip on the railings and slowly walks away, leaving the swirling water behind her. Not this time, she thinks. Not this time.

Chapter 8

2016

It happens again on Monday morning, three days after my visit to Sophie's flat and exactly one week since the original friend request. Outside it's one of those sunny autumn days where you feel summer might not be over after all. Light streams through the French windows, warming the surface of the kitchen table where I am struggling to concentrate on work. I'm already late in delivering two proposals for potential new clients, and I'm falling behind on a project for Rosemary as well. I check Facebook constantly, dreading the moment. I've been praying that it was a one-off, an ill-judged joke by someone going to the reunion. With every day that passes, the tiny seed of hope that I'll never hear from her again has been sprouting.

When I get the notification that there is a Facebook message from Maria Weston, I can hardly get my hands to work fast enough, my fingers scrabbling desperately over the keys in my haste to get to the message.

Run as fast as you like, Louise. You'll never escape from me. Every wound leaves a scar. Just ask Esther Harcourt.

I sit for a moment or two, heart racing, reading the message over and over as if that will yield some further clue as to who is doing this, and why. *Run as fast as you like.* There *was* someone following me that night. I knew it.

Ask Esther Harcourt. I saw Esther once in town, after it happened. She averted her eyes as if my guilt might somehow rub off on her, as if she could catch my shame like it was a contagious airborne disease. She didn't even know the whole truth – if she had, she would have done more than look away.

She was the only person that Maria talked to in those last months before the leavers' party. There are spaces, huge gaps, in what I know about Maria. Esther might be able to fill them in. I've spent the weekend poring over every detail of my meeting with Sophie, and the thought of speaking to someone who genuinely cared about Maria is strangely comforting.

I type her name into the search box, but she's not on Facebook. I quash the terrible teenage part of my brain that immediately concludes that she doesn't have any friends. Many people are not on Facebook for a variety of excellent reasons. Once I have exhausted that avenue, I try simply googling her, which throws up a number of results. LinkedIn is the top one, and it's her. She is a solicitor, and still living in Norfolk. Her profile picture reveals that she has aged well; in fact, she looks about a million times better than she ever did at school. The bottle tops have been replaced by a sleek pair of angular designer frames and what on the teenage Esther was an unruly mass of bushy mousy hair is now a thick, glossy, chestnut mane.

She is a partner in the wills and probate department at her firm, one of the big ones in Norwich. It seems she is a proper high-flier, speaks at conferences, writes papers, the kind that probably gets invited back to school to give inspirational talks. I thought when I won that interior design award recently, and was featured in the *Sharne Bay Journal*, that they might invite me back to speak, but I never heard anything.

Now I know where Esther works I could call or email her, but I cannot shake the memory of our eyes meeting all those years ago, and how she turned her face away. A mad idea occurs to me and I pick up the phone. Two minutes later Serena Cooke has an appointment with Ms Harcourt to make a will. They'd taken my details and tried to fob me off with someone else but I insisted. Normally I would have had to wait, but she has had a last-minute cancellation for tomorrow morning. She'll probably recognise me straight away but at least she won't have had any time to prepare, and can't refuse to see me.

The next morning we're up early. Henry always goes to the school's breakfast club on a Tuesday anyway so I can work, but today I'm taking him a bit earlier than usual. He sits at the kitchen table in his pyjamas, spooning cereal into his mouth, bleary-eyed and red-cheeked, still carrying the warmth of his bed with him. I lean down to kiss him as I pass, mentally listing the things I need to remember like a mantra: book bag, lunch box, water bottle, reading book, school-trip letter, fabric samples, email Rosemary.

'Mummy?' Henry says, between spoonfuls.

'Yes,' I say, distracted and still swooping around gathering everything we both need for the day.

'At school yesterday, Jasper and Dylan wouldn't play with me.'

I sit down next to him, mental lists abandoned.

'What do you mean?' I say with a sinking heart.

'I wanted to play trains in choosing time, but they wouldn't play. I kept telling them, but they wanted to play outside.'

'You can't make your friends do what you want them to do, Henry. It sounds more like they wanted to play a different game, not that they wouldn't play with you as such.'

'No, Mummy. They didn't want to play with me. I asked and asked. Dylan said all I want to do is play with the trains. He said I'm boring.' He puts down his spoon and jumps onto my lap, wrapping his arms and legs around me, his hot face buried in my neck. My heart aches with love for him, and I try not to examine my feelings about Jasper and Dylan too closely. They are only four, after all.

'Can't I stay with you today?' The words are muffled but there's no mistaking the hope in them.

Guilt clamps around me like a vice. I'm not going to get much work done today. The fabric swatches and paint colours I was meant to be putting together for a client were going to have to wait anyway. I'm already late with them, what's one more day? I could easily cancel the appointment with Esther, call Henry in sick, spend the day snuggled on the sofa watching Disney films. I'm not going to, because my need to find out what's going on with the Facebook request is overriding everything else.

I unpeel Henry and manage to persuade him to get dressed by promising that I will play trains with him for a long time when we get home this afternoon.

'A really long time?' he asks beadily.

'Ages and ages,' I promise.

I drop him at breakfast club and drive east under a leaden sky. Once I leave the motorway behind, the A11 unwinds reluctantly before me. The landscape is dully familiar, despite the many years since I've been this way: vast skies, rippled with threatening cloud; flattened expanses of field after rolling field; the war memorial standing stark and alone as the traffic roars past, just before the mysterious-sounding Elveden Forest, conjuring images of Tolkien-esque creatures engaged in thrilling adventures but delivering only bike hire, rock climbing and other wholesome family activities. The wind is buffeting my car and a few miles past Elveden I pull over in a layby and sit for a moment, gripping the wheel, trying to calm my breathing. I check my phone, as I do every time I have a spare moment, but there is only an email from Rosemary asking for something I am meant to have done but haven't.

When I arrive, I am buzzed in and asked to wait in an elegant room complete with polished wooden floors and immaculately upholstered antique furniture. It's like an American movie's idea of an English law firm. I perch on the edge of an embroidered chaise longue, shifting this way and that, crossing and un-crossing my legs.

I was hoping for a few moments to get my bearings, feel my way, but as soon as I am shown in by the elegantly groomed secretary, it's obvious that the game is up. Esther raises her head with a welcoming smile in place but within a second it has faded and behind the tortoiseshell frames her eyes register shock. She waits until the secretary has gone before speaking, and when she does her tone is blunt and unfriendly.

'You're not Serena Cooke.'

'No, obviously ... I ... I wasn't sure if you'd see me.'

'I assume you're not here to make a will then?'

'No.'

'So why are you here?'

I'm still hovering by the door, having not been invited to sit. I tuck my hair excessively and needlessly behind my ears, a habit I've had since childhood. Something in the gesture must trigger a memory in Esther of our days running wild and mud-spattered in the woods near her house, because her face softens a tiny bit and she gestures to the padded leather chair in front of her desk. I sink gratefully into it.

'I didn't know where else to come.'

Esther raises an enquiring eyebrow.

'Something's happened.'

A second eyebrow joins the first. I steel myself.

'I got a Facebook friend request. It was from Maria Weston.'

The sympathy that in spite of herself is Esther's natural response to my obvious discomfort is replaced instantly by bewilderment, and something else I can't identify. Is it fear?

'From Maria? But that's not possible.' She's not used to having her composure rattled, I can tell.

'No, I know it's not. But, well, it happened. I wondered ... if you knew anything about it, or if you could throw any light?'

'Why on earth should I know anything about it?' she says, flushing. 'I'm not in the habit of setting up Facebook pages for long-dead school friends. I'm not even on Facebook myself.'

'No, of course not, I didn't think you set it up. I'm just . . . well, I'm frightened. I think someone might have been in my flat, and I'm sure someone was following me the other day.'

'What?' Her forehead creases in concern. 'Have you told the police?'

'What can they do? I've got no proof. The other thing is . . . I got another message yesterday. From the same person. Can I show you?'

She shrugs as if to say I'm leaving her no choice, so I hand my phone over. She presses her lips together as she reads it, as if to keep the words she wants to say from flying out. She taps the screen and her expression softens. She breathes out, a long, slow breath and I know she's looking at Maria's photo.

'What do you think it means, about asking you?'

'It's obvious, isn't it? Maria and I both suffered at the hands of bullies. Whoever wrote this knows that.'

I start to protest, but she interrupts. 'I know, I know, you never bullied me. You just dumped me the minute we arrived at secondary school and never spoke to me again. But I don't think there's any other word for what you and Sophie did to Maria, is there?'

I am hot with shame. I can't bear to look her in the eye.

'I shouldn't have come,' I say, looking at the floor. 'I suppose I needed to talk to someone about it, and Sophie was no good, so I thought maybe you might be able to – help me, I guess.'

'You talked to Sophie Hannigan about this? Are you still in touch with her?' Esther manages to give the impression that if I answer in the affirmative I will sink even lower in her estimation.

'God no, not at all, not since school. I tracked her down as well.'

'On Facebook?'

'Yes.'

'Of course. I bet she's on there all the time, isn't she? "Look how gorgeous I am, look at my amazing life." I can't stand it. That's why I'm not on there; it's all so bloody fake, as if it's actually designed to make you feel crap about your own life.'

I wonder how I am going to get past the barriers that Esther has been erecting since I walked into the room.

'Look, I know I treated Maria badly.'

Esther snorts.

'OK, worse than badly. When I think about it now I am so ashamed, it's like I was a different person. I can't believe that the me that I am now could ever have behaved as I did. Barely a day goes by that I don't think of Maria. But I can't change what I've done.' My God, I wish I could. The worst of it is that Esther doesn't even know what I have done, not really. 'I can only control who I am now. What I don't understand is why this is happening now. Is it something to do with the reunion maybe? Stirring things up in people's minds?'

'There's a reunion?'

Esther's mask slips and she has spoken before she's had a chance to arrange her face into the expression she wants me to see. For a second I see on her face the emotions I experienced when I heard about the reunion myself: disappointment, shame, self-loathing. Unlike me she has a live audience, so has to recover quickly.

'I wouldn't go to that if you paid me. You're not going, are you?'

'I thought I might,' I mumble. Why does it make me feel so ashamed? Why am I still so engaged with my teenage self, with my place in that long-ago universe?

'Still tagging along, Louise? God, have you not moved on at all?'

'Look, forget it,' I say, eager to be away from her. 'You obviously can't help me. Or you don't want to.'

Her face softens. 'It's not a question of not wanting to; I simply don't know anything about this. I haven't seen anyone from school since the day I walked out the door. Not deliberately anyway. Look, give me your number – if anything occurs to me, I'll let you know.'

'Thank you,' I say quietly, scribbling it down on a Post-it note.

She looks down at her hands, which are balled into fists, and I get the impression that she is digging her nails into her palms.

'It must have given you a terrible jolt, getting that request. Seeing her photo.'

'Yes. Must have been taken not long before – you know.'

There doesn't seem to be any more to say, so I leave with the firm intention of heading straight back home. However, without thinking, I find myself turning right at a crossroads and negotiating a hairpin bend, and before I know it the outskirts of Sharne Bay begin to roll out around me. Things haven't changed much, although there's a row of houses that

I don't remember, and the corner shop where we used to go for sweets has become a Tesco Metro. We're closer to the sea on this side of town, and I roll my window down to let in a waft of salty air.

As I drive through a mixture of the painfully recognisable and the disorientatingly new, my mind replays the encounter with Esther. Something is nagging at me and as I automatically bear right to loop round and join the road where my old school is, I realise what it is: that brief second where fear crossed her face. Why should Esther be afraid? If someone is playing a sick joke on me as some kind of retribution, then Esther surely has nothing to worry about. She was the one person who was never anything but kind to Maria. And she can't have anything to fear from Maria herself. Maria drowned more than twenty-five years ago.

Didn't she?

Chapter 9

1989

The next time I spoke to Maria wasn't at school. In fact she must have been avoiding me there because I had hardly seen her at all for over a week except in the lessons we shared, where she carefully sat where she wouldn't have to meet my eye.

I'd never been invited to one of Matt Lewis's parties before, but Sophie said Matt definitely said I could go. He barely knew who I was, but I think he would have agreed to anything Sophie asked. His mum and dad were away for the weekend. I saw his mum at parents' evening once. She'd started chatting to my mum while we were waiting to see Mr Jenkins and the contrast was hilarious: Matt's mum with her expensive highlights and flawless make-up, sporting a vivid electric-blue trouser suit, radiating sophistication and charm; Mum in her A-line skirt and beige car coat, funny little handbag on her lap, desperately trying to keep up her end of the conversation.

I got ready for the party at Sophie's, *Blind Date* blaring

from the telly in her room (Mum never lets me watch it at home) while she crimped my hair. I took practically my entire wardrobe over to hers and tried everything on in front of the full-length mirror in Sophie's walk-in wardrobe. Sophie was rifling through the rack, handing me things to try on.

'What about this?' she said, thrusting a black, fitted, velvet mini-dress at me.

'I'll never get into that,' I protested.

'Yes, of course you will,' she said, holding it out for me to step into and pulling it up over my hips. She took me by the shoulders and turned me round.

'Ah. I don't think it's going to do up,' she said. 'I'd try, but I don't want to rip it . . .'

I struggled out of the dress, my face hot.

'Ooh, this maybe?' she suggested, holding a red tube skirt. 'It's nice and stretchy. Maybe with that long navy T-shirt, although that might be a bit tight as well.'

'Don't worry, I'd rather wear something of mine.'

'Awww, really? OK.' She slithered into the tube skirt, smoothing it over her hips, turning sideways to look critically at her perfectly flat stomach in the mirror.

'What do you think? Bit tight?'

I ended up going with all black because it's meant to make you look thinner, and also I didn't want to stand out too much or get it wrong. Sophie had a bottle hidden in the wardrobe that we swigged from as we got ready. It consisted of a variety of different drinks all mixed together that she had nicked from her mum's drinks cabinet – gin, rum, vodka, some weird yellow stuff her mum got on holiday plus some coke to make it taste better.

Matt's house was on that estate where all the hulking great brand-new detached houses had been made to look like oversized cottages from a bygone age. As we got closer we could hear the thudding bass of the music, and there were loads of other people obviously going there too. Lights were blazing from all the front windows as we walked down the path. Groups of boys and girls spilled out of the house into the front garden, which was already filled with cigarette ends and empty glasses and bottles. The front door was ajar and we slipped through into a large hallway with a black-and-white tiled floor. A wide staircase led upstairs to our right, and to the left of it was a corridor that obviously led to the kitchen. Boys I'd never seen before greeted Sophie as we made our way through the throng into the kitchen, which was large and very hot. Matt was sitting at the huge oak table rolling a joint, with Sam to his right.

'Soph!' called Matt. 'You made it!'

'Of course,' she said, leaning down to hug them both. 'Hello boys.'

I don't know if it was my imagination but I'm sure her hand lingered longer on Sam's shoulder than it did on Matt's.

Matt peered uncertainly at me. 'All right? Good to see you, um . . .'

'Hi,' I muttered, flushing. He didn't even know my name, but it didn't matter, I knew I was protected by Sophie, a shining titanium wall made entirely of popularity and beauty.

'Have a drink,' said Matt, waving towards the marble worktop, which was sticky with spilled drinks, littered with cigarette butts and covered in half-empty bottles of spirits, huge bottles of cider, lipstick-stained plastic cups and several bottles of something very bright blue. I'd never been to a party like this before and I veered between wild excitement at simply being there and the acceptance that this implied, and a nagging fear that I would somehow say the wrong thing or make a mistake and that everyone would see me for what I was.

'Ooh, great,' said Sophie, pulling me over to see. 'Where did you get all this?'

'People brought stuff, and my brother got a load of it for me,' said Matt. 'Have whatever you like, Soph. And—' he gestured in my direction '—you too.'

'It's *Louise*, you idiot.' Sophie laughed. 'God, Lou, he doesn't even know your name! Honestly, you see her every day at school!'

'Sorry,' muttered Matt to me.

'Oh, it's fine,' Sophie said, smiling. 'What shall we have, *Louise*, vodka and coke?'

My head was already swimming from the effects of the drinks-cabinet concoction, but Sophie slugged vodka into two plastic glasses and topped them up with coke.

'Come on,' she said. 'Let's go and see who else is here.'

We left Matt in the kitchen staring longingly after Sophie, and made our way back through the hallway and turned right into the living room. This was the source of the music – someone had set up decks and a boy from school was DJing. There were a few girls I recognised dancing in the centre of the room, bodies moving effortlessly to the beat, completely absorbed in the rhythm, which thrummed like a heartbeat, insistent and demanding. I watched in fascination as Claire Barnes and a boy from the year above kissed on an armchair in the corner. Claire was sitting astride him and he had one hand on her bum and one caressing her breast through her top. They seemed totally in a world of their own, but I could see a couple of boys watching intently from the sofa on the other side of the room as Claire writhed and the movement of the boy's hands grew ever more urgent.

'We'll leave her to it, shall we?' shouted Sophie, but as she turned to leave the room, Matt came sidling up to us. The volume dropped temporarily.

'Want a pill, Soph?' he asked.

'Sure, have you got something?'

'Not at the moment but Max will be here later. He should be able to sort us out.'

He turned to me.

'How about you?' he asked politely. 'Do you want anything?'

'Oh, um, no. I'm all right, thanks.'

I cringed inwardly. All right, thanks? That's what you say when someone asks if you want a cup of tea. As the music rose again, a wild, irresistible beat, Matt took Sophie by the hand and pulled her into the middle of the room to dance. Sophie beckoned me to join them but I can't dance to that kind of music (or any kind) so I shook my head and took another gulp of my drink. I stood there for a while watching them, wondering how people learn to dance that way, and how they are able to do it so freely and unselfconsciously. Matt didn't take his eyes off Sophie as she moved to the beat, taking in every perfect inch of her as her top rode up to show an inviting strip of taut, tanned skin. I drained my drink, and decided to go and get another one, more for something to do than anything else.

Back in the kitchen, Sam was still sitting at the table. I

poured myself another vodka and coke from the bottles on the side, unsure what the ratio was supposed to be.

'Blimey, like your vodka, do you?'

It was Sam's voice. I'd obviously erred too far on the side of vodka.

'That's how I like it,' I said pompously, taking a sip and trying not to wince.

'Take a pew, Lou,' he said, laughing softly at his own joke.

I sat down opposite him, my heart beating very fast. I could feel the swell of my stomach under the flattering black clothes I had chosen so carefully, and my clumsy hands, large and in the wrong place wherever I put them. He was wearing a white T-shirt with a small V-neck and I had a strange urge to reach out a finger and stroke the soft triangle of lightly tanned skin that was on show. Already this counted as the longest conversation I had ever had with him.

'Soooo, Louuuu.'

He laughed again; he must have been stoned. 'Saw you in town the other day with that new girl.'

'Maria? Yes, she's . . . she's OK,' I trailed off lamely, thinking of my recent phone conversation with Sophie.

'I heard some . . . interesting stories about her. Matt Lewis's cousin knows someone who goes to her old school in London.'

'I heard there were some rumours. Do you know what they're about?'

The effects of the vodka and my interest in Maria were making me relax to the point where this was verging on feeling like a normal conversation.

'She's a wild one. She likes boys, she likes girls, she likes it all ways, if you know what I mean.'

I didn't, not really, but I got the general idea. I forced some more vodka down.

'Apparently she went so far that there was some boy who got totally obsessed with her, wouldn't leave her alone, stalking her and that. That's why she had to leave her old school.'

I tend to divide the people I meet, or certainly those of my own age, into two broad categories: those who are like me, and those who aren't. I was fascinated if a little disgusted by this new information about someone who (on my admittedly limited acquaintance with her) had seemed firmly in my category.

'Are you sure? She doesn't seem like that type.'

'Ah, it's the quiet ones you have to watch, Louise. Don't you know that by now?' He grinned. 'You're pretty quiet, aren't you?'

I flushed, my mind scrabbling around for a response, but thankfully we were interrupted by the arrival of Matt and Sophie. Sophie flung herself down next to Sam, leaning her head dramatically on his shoulder and declaring herself dying for a drink. Matt looked unhappily at them whilst he poured her another vodka and coke and then sat down next to me opposite them, his eyes on Sophie's hand, which kept nudging Sam's arm playfully. None of them seemed inclined to address any remarks to me, entering into an involved conversation about the exact nature of the drugs they had taken at a rave they'd been to recently, from which I was grateful to be excluded.

The kitchen was heady with smoke and I was starting

to feel a bit spaced out, unable to follow the conversation even if I'd had anything to add. I muttered something about needing the toilet, and none of the three even looked up as I rose and left the room.

I wandered upstairs, stepping over snogging couples and pairs of girls deep in intense conversation. I had a choice at the top of the stairs. To my left was what I guessed to be the master bedroom. The door was ajar and I could hear a furtive rustling and panting from within. To my right there were several doors to choose from. The first turned out to be the airing cupboard, but the second one I tried was locked, suggesting it was the toilet. I sank down and sat cross-legged on the floor to wait.

As the beat of the music downstairs faded for a second before rising again, I became aware of a noise coming from the toilet. At first I thought it was someone vomiting, but I gradually realised it was crying I could hear. A girl. She was obviously trying to keep the tears in, but it was no good. They were being wrenched out of her like a butcher tearing the innards from a dead animal. Gradually the gasps subsided and I heard the toilet flush. Despite my drunkenness, which was fairly advanced by now, I tried to arrange my face into a suitably nonchalant expression to indicate that I hadn't heard a thing. However, when the door opened my face dropped, because the girl in the toilet was Maria.

She looked at me with a mixture of shame and defiance.

'What's the problem?' she asked, daring me to mention what I'd heard.

'Nothing.' I hesitated. 'Are you OK though?'

'Oh, I'm fine, great.' Her speech was slurred and I realised she was even drunker than I was. 'Just fucking great. And even better now I've seen you.'

I reddened.

'I'm sorry about that day in the lunch hall. You don't understand what Sophie's like. If I get on the wrong side of her, I'm finished. At school, I mean.'

'Really? Seems like there's plenty of people at school who get along fine without following her around like a puppy dog.'

'But Sophie's my friend,' I say. 'One of my oldest friends.'

'I thought Esther was your oldest friend. Or non-friend now, I should say.'

'What do you mean? What's Esther told you?'

'Never you mind,' she said, attempting to tap her nose. The effect was somewhat spoiled by the fact that she was so drunk she missed her nose and ended up poking herself in the eye. For a moment she looked as though she was going to start crying again, but the balance tipped the other way and she collapsed in hysterical laughter, sinking down beside me on the floor. As she clutched my arm, laughter started to bubble up inside me and soon I had tears streaming down my face too. Every time the laughter started to die away, she would mime poking herself in the eye and it would start us off again.

Eventually we calmed down, and from inside her jacket she produced a bottle of something similar to the concoction Sophie and I had been drinking earlier, except this one had a purplish tinge. She passed it over and I took a swig, barely even flinching this time.

'So, what is it really?' I asked her. 'I heard you in there.'

'I saw my dad today,' she said, fiddling with the gold heart on her necklace. 'You remember I told you he gave me this . . . before he left?'

I remembered. The first present he had ever given her.

'He said he's not going to be able to see as much of us any more. He's moving out of London. Got a job up north somewhere.' She pulled the necklace forward harder. When she relaxed her hold I could see a faint pink line across the back of her neck. She looked as if she was about to say more but then seemed to change her mind. 'I don't want to talk about it.'

'Fair enough. What shall we talk about then?'

'Why you're such a bitch?' she suggested, elbowing me to indicate that although she was half-joking, I wasn't entirely forgiven.

'I really am sorry. It's just that Sophie's been so good to me.'

She looked at me sceptically.

'She has! Inviting me to stuff, you know. Like here.'

I glanced around nervously. The music pounded relentlessly away, reverberating through the house, and I could hear someone laughing raucously. Was it Sophie? Hopefully she wouldn't have any reason to come up here and see me talking to Maria.

'How come you're here anyway?' I asked her.

'Charming!'

'You know what I mean. I'd never have been invited if it wasn't for Sophie. Who got you in?'

'My brother, Tim,' she admitted. 'He's at college with Matt's older brother. He's in that room, with some slag.' She gestured to the master bedroom. The panter.

'Do you get on with him? Your brother?'

'Yeah, he's all right. He looks out for me, you know. Protective.'

I didn't know, not having any brothers or sisters.

'Sounds nice,' I said wistfully.

'Can be. Bit much sometimes.'

She looked as if she was going to say more, but then the bedroom door creaked and the dark-haired boy that I'd seen on the path outside Maria's house appeared, pulling on a T-shirt. The top button of his jeans was undone and I couldn't help looking at the line of dark hair that led downwards. He walked over to us.

'Are you all right?' he asked Maria, ignoring me.

'I'm fine,' she said, keeping her eyes on the floor. She kept her hair pulled down over her face, using it as a shield to stop Tim from seeing that she'd been crying. 'Leave me alone. Go back to your lady friend.'

'Are you sure you're OK?' he asked, eyeballing me with suspicion. 'Isn't this that girl who—'

'I'm fine, Tim,' Maria repeated, jumping to her feet. I scrambled up, not wanting to be left alone with him. 'We're going outside to get some air. See you later.'

'Don't leave without telling me, OK?' he called after us. Maria threw up her hand in a gesture that fell somewhere between waving and giving him the finger.

We made our way back down the stairs, through the kitchen where there was no sign of Sophie, thank God, and out of the back door. I hadn't seen anyone in the back garden earlier, so hopefully we could stay under the radar.

There were a couple of slatted wooden sun loungers on the patio, and we lay down on our backs under the clear, star-studded night sky. I could still hear the noise of the party – the heavy thud of the music, a buzz of chatter, the occasional whoop of laughter – but it had receded, as if it was happening far away, to people who had nothing to do with me. The air smelled cool and clean and I breathed easily for the first time all evening.

We were silent for a while, until Maria flipped onto her side and looked at me.

'So go on, what have you heard then?'

I continued to stare at the night sky with a studied calmness I was far from feeling.

'About what?'

'Me, of course. My mum thought we could leave it behind, but I'm not stupid, I know the rumours will have followed me here.'

'I haven't heard anything about you, honestly,' I lied.

I could tell that part of her wanted to talk, to share whatever it was that had followed her from London, which had already excited the attention or attracted the opprobrium of her new classmates. Whatever it was, it was making me feel on edge. I didn't know if I wanted to be drawn into her world, so I stayed silent, giving her no encouragement.

She remained on her side looking at me for a couple of minutes, until, seeming to come to a decision, she rolled back to face the sky. We lapsed into peaceful silence. My hand flopped over the side of my lounger and brushed against Maria's, and she linked her little finger to mine, our hands swinging gently together as we watched our breath curl into the night air.

'Hello, lovebirds!' Sophie's voice was strangely triumphant.

My heart leapt. I snatched my hand away from Maria's, swung my legs hastily round and sat up far too quickly, head spinning. The back door had swung open and a shaft of light illuminated the dark space between our sunbeds. Sophie was silhouetted in the doorway, Matt and Sam lurking behind her. What had they seen? I must have swayed, because Matt's expression changed from prurient interest to mild concern.

'Hey, are you OK? Are you going to be sick?'

'I'm fine.' I gripped the edge of the sun lounger.

'Come and get some water.' Suddenly, Sophie was all motherly concern. She pulled me up, put an arm around my shoulder and started to usher me inside. I allowed her to, only risking a look back when I was halfway through the open door. I expected to see anger, contempt or even pity. I wasn't prepared for the naked despair on Maria's face as Sophie led me away from her and back to the party.

Chapter 10

2016

As I approach the school, still thinking uneasily of my conversation with Esther, the landmarks start to mount up: the bus stop with its carpet of cigarette butts; the high fence that still runs the length of the playground; the noticeboard by the front gate with its tatty bits of paper advertising God knows what. The buildings are largely unchanged, the old part of the school still handsome with its Victorian red-brick facade, the 'new' buildings grey and blocky, the product of sixties architecture that once thought itself so terribly modern.

I was planning to drive straight past, take a quick look at the place, but amongst the faded notes on the noticeboard that look like they've been there since my time at school, a garish poster demands my attention. I slow to try and read it, and can just make out the rainbow-coloured bubble writing: School Reunion – Class of 1989.

I brake sharply and swing over to the side of the road, parking haphazardly half-on and half-off the pavement. I dart across the road, ignoring the hoots and furious gestures of a driver who has to swerve to avoid me, and read the poster from top to bottom: it promises a disco, pay bar and cold buffet; eighties tunes and old friends. I look behind me, feeling weirdly guilty, as if someone might catch me out. I hear Esther's voice in my head: *Still tagging along, Louise?*

I cross back to my car and sit at the steering wheel for a few minutes, staring over at the school, trying to get to grips with the emotions tumbling inside me. I'm a completely different person now to the girl who came here every day for five years, and yet I wonder whether that can be true. There must be some core part of me that is the same. The girl who did the things I did is me. That was what made being with Sam so safe. He knew the real me, and I knew he'd never tell anyone about what I had done. He would tell me so sometimes, when we lay together, absorbed in each other, the rest of the world shut out. Promise me that despite the terrible thing I had done, he would never leave me. But of course he did, in the end.

I start the engine and pull off. When I get to the end of the road I have a choice of turning left to head out of town, or right, towards the main residential part of Sharne Bay. I turn right, realising as I do that the contours of the road have been saved somewhere in my brain, a muscle memory that still works over twenty-five years on. Without thinking, I take another right towards my old house. The street is still lined with identikit 1970s houses, the front gardens neat and well cared for. There's at least two cars on every drive now – some people have even managed to squeeze three on.

Rather than turning the car around in this narrow street, I decide to carry on and rejoin the main road at a different point, but when I get to the junction where I need to turn right, I find the road has been made one-way, so I have to carry on. I turn left and right at random, trusting that I'll end up back on the main road at some point – Sharne Bay's a small town, I'm hardly likely to get lost. But as familiar landmarks begin to catch my eye – the post box built into a brick wall, that high box hedge on the corner – I gradually begin to realise that I am far from lost. I am on the road where Maria lived, a street of small Victorian terraces cramped together behind narrow pavements. These houses don't have driveways so the street is busy with parked cars, but there's a space opposite number 33, and I pull over, remembering the last time I was there, lying on Maria's bed, laughing until my stomach ached. I try to recall the last time I laughed like that, but I can't. Maybe it doesn't happen in adult life. It's stuffy in the car where I've had the heating on, so I decide to have a walk, get some air and then head back to London – leaving this nostalgia-fest, or whatever it is, behind me.

As I get out of the car, a bald man of about my age comes along the pavement with a baby in a buggy. As he passes me, our eyes meet and there's a second of non-recognition before I gasp and he does a double take.

Oh my God. A shard of ice slithers down my back. He looks older, of course, older than his years in fact, but I'd know him anywhere. It's Maria's brother, Tim Weston.

'Louise?' he says, standing stock-still in the middle of the pavement. 'Louise Williams?'

'Tim. Oh my goodness, I didn't know you still . . .' I tuck my hair behind my ears, then thrust my hands into my pockets to keep them still. 'What are you doing here? Does your mum . . . ?' I indicate number 33.

'What? Oh no – I live there now. Bought it from Mum. What are you doing here, Louise?'

'I've been seeing a client in the area,' I improvise hastily. 'I lost my way, and I pulled over to look at the map on my phone.'

'Oh, right.' He's looking at me dubiously. 'Where does the client live?'

My mind goes blank, and I can only think of my own old street.

'Turner Street, would you believe?' I smile, trying to deflect the suspicion that this piece of information is likely to garner.

'So has your mum moved away, or . . . ?'

'She moved to a bungalow a few years ago, so we bought it from her, me and my wife. Couldn't have afforded to buy otherwise.'

'Oh, wonderful!' I'm going wildly over the top, my heart fluttering in my chest. 'And this is your daughter?'

His face thaws slightly. 'Yes. Have to take her out in the buggy, it's the only way she'll sleep. Gives my wife a break too. She needs it sometimes, especially now she's back working again. She's got her own business, doing really well, but it's hard, she's . . .' He trails off as if he's thought better of letting me into his life to that degree.

I look down at the baby, fast asleep in her pink snowsuit, all rosy cheeks and long eyelashes.

'She's beautiful.' It took Sam and me so much time and effort and pain to have Henry, that I thought when he arrived we would relish every minute, every cry, every sleepless night. I thought that when people talked about sleepless nights, it was just a figure of speech. I didn't realise that it actually meant nights without any sleep at all. It soon became clear that Sam couldn't or didn't want to cope with the ferocious demands of babyhood, and that I was willing to take on all the caring duties because I was terrified that if I didn't, he would leave. I did other things too, to keep him happy, to keep him with me. I didn't know then that you can't stop someone leaving you.

Tim looks down at his daughter, smiling. 'Thanks.' There's an awkward pause and I cast around for something to say. What do you say to someone you haven't seen for more than twenty-five years who you know hates your guts, and with good reason?

'So, what do you do?' I fall back on that most conventional of dinner party questions.

'I'm in IT. I commute to London three days a week, then work from home the rest of the time – hence this.' He gestures to the buggy. 'How about you? You're an interior designer, aren't you?'

'Yes, that's right.' The unease which has been stirring inside me since I first heard his voice steps up a notch. Has he been keeping track of me? 'How did you know?'

'I'm not sure ... maybe someone told me ...' His forehead creases as he tries to recall who that might have been. 'Oh no, I know, I saw something in the local paper – you won an award, didn't you?'

'Yes, I did.' I was proud at the time, but now I feel curiously violated at the thought of people from my past having seen that article, knowing things about me whilst remaining anonymous themselves. I start to mutter something about having to get home, but he interrupts me.

'Have you heard about the reunion?'

'Yes, I saw something about it on Facebook,' I say.

'Are you going?'

'I'm not sure. Are . . . are you?' I know he is, I've seen his name on the Facebook guest list. Why am I so embarrassed about going to the reunion? Sophie doesn't have any shame about it, neither do all the others that have signed up for it.

'I thought I might,' he says, looking down. 'I know I'm not strictly class of eighty-nine, but obviously I hung out with a lot of you – and, you know, Maria was. I thought I might go, sort of on her behalf.'

The mention of her name takes my breath a little. Although she has occupied a private space in my mind for so long, until the past week I hadn't heard or spoken her name since I was a teenager. I had thought that Tim and I were going to get through this whole, utterly strange conversation without talking about her. Suddenly I realise I can't let the moment pass without at least trying to tell him how sorry I am.

'I think that's a really nice idea,' I say. 'Look, Tim, about Maria.' I screw up all my courage. 'I know I treated her badly, and I'm so sorry. I wish . . . well, I wish I could go back and change it.' I know he didn't think very much of me back then, and he was probably right. I don't think very much of myself either when I look back.

Tim looks away into the distance.

'I don't blame you, Louise,' he says stiffly.

'Really? I think Esther Harcourt does,' I say without thinking.

'Esther Harcourt? Do you still see her? She's a lawyer now, isn't she?'

'Yes. Do you remember Esther then?'

Part of me is surprised that someone like Tim, who was part of the cool crowd and didn't even go to school with us, should recall Esther.

'Yeah, she spoke at the memorial service, didn't she? And Maria saw a lot of her in the time before . . . you know. Mum talks about her a bit too. She's kept an eye on her career over the years. Esther was a good friend to Maria.'

The unspoken hangs in the air like a bad smell: *unlike some people.*

'How is your mum?' I think of Bridget the last time I saw her, the night Maria disappeared: the rising panic, her fear-drenched eyes locking onto mine for those few heart-stopping seconds.

'Not great, to be honest. She's not been at all well recently, and she's lonely. She never met anyone else after Dad left. Having a grandchild helps a bit, but she's never got over what happened to Maria.'

Of course she hasn't. How could you?

'Look, Louise, none of us know what happened that night.'

I try to keep my face neutral.

'Mum believes Maria killed herself, but I don't know . . . she's tougher than . . . she was tougher than she seemed, Maria. I know she was drinking that night. If she wandered off, if she was upset, she could easily have missed her footing up there.'

The baby stirs in her buggy, and Tim jiggles her gently back and forth. She sighs and relaxes back into blissful sleep.

'I know I was hard on you back then, but I felt so protective of Maria, especially after what had happened to her in London. And I was so angry; at our dad for leaving, and at Maria sometimes, for getting involved with that boy, although of course it wasn't her fault. Really, of course, I was angry at myself. I thought I should have protected her, I should have seen what was happening with that boy earlier. I thought it was my fault, that if I'd behaved better, not made such a fuss about leaving London, then Dad wouldn't have left.'

He assumes I know the story about the boy in London, thinks that Maria told me. Of course she didn't, but I don't feel I can ask him now.

'It wasn't your fault,' I say.

'Well,' he says with obvious effort, 'it wasn't yours either. I know you didn't behave well, but you weren't to know what was going to happen. No one did. I should have kept more of an eye on her at the leavers' party. We were close, Maria and I.'

How close, I wonder? Everyone used to comment on how protective he was of her, she even said so herself. Close enough to want to reopen old wounds, to punish the girls he sees as responsible for his sister's unhappiness?

'I knew she was . . . having trouble, you know . . .' he goes on.

Having trouble. It's kind of him to frame it like that, but I know the truth. We had made her life a misery.

'No one else can take the responsibility for what happened to her. Either she bears that herself, or it was an accident, a misstep, a one-in-a-million chance.' He's watching me closely, and I shift from foot to foot, wishing the encounter over.

It's a comforting fallacy, and I wish with everything in me

that his version of events was the true one. Or if that can't be (and of course it can't), I wish that I could tell someone the truth without being judged, or worse. I wish that I could loosen this secret knot within me, a knot that is tied so tightly I don't think anyone will ever be able to get their fingers into its intricacies to tug it apart, however hard they try.

Tim doesn't know it, but we are talking at cross-purposes here. He thinks we're talking about the fact that I abandoned Maria for Sophie and the promise of popularity, and how I was partly responsible for ostracising her at school. He thinks we are talking about a bit of schoolgirl bullying, not sticks and stones but words that were meant to hurt, and did. And it's true; I did do all that. I ignored her, I deserted her, I let her down. What Tim doesn't know is that I also did something else. Something much, much worse.

We say our goodbyes, and I drive slowly back through the streets of my childhood. As I put my foot down on the A11, something about my conversation with Tim tugs at the corners of my mind. It takes me a while to figure out what it is, but then I get it. *She's tougher than she seems*, he started to say, but then corrected himself. A slip of the tongue maybe, or perhaps seeing me threw everything up in the air, flung him back in his mind to 1989. But whatever the reason, there's no getting away from it: Tim referred to Maria in the present tense.

Chapter 11

Some days she feels like a prisoner in her own home. There's no reason why she can't go out, of course. Nobody could tell from simply looking at her. But on days like today, it feels as though someone has peeled back a layer of skin, leaving her face red raw, offering no protection from the elements. From anything. On these days she hides away, waiting until she feels able to face the world again; ready to put her mask back on, to keep smiling.

She wonders sometimes how long she will be able to keep it up. For ever? In some ways, she's so used to keeping this secret that it comes naturally. And on the days when it doesn't, when she yearns to open her heart, her mouth, to let it come spilling out, he is there to remind her, as he has been over all these years. Keep quiet. Don't tell. The consequences will be worse for you than for anyone else. He's just trying to protect her, she knows that, and is grateful for it.

So she carries on, shaking off those thoughts of the past that haunt her. It's not only the past that scares her; she fears the present too, some days, and not even staying at home helps. Sometimes she feels even more suffocated there than she does out in the world.

She keeps her circle small because she finds it hard to trust people. Even those who she does let in don't know the whole story, or even half of it. He is the only one who understands. Only he has helped her, reminded her that other people are not to be trusted with their story.

She doesn't need reminding that not everyone is what they seem. She of all people knows that only too well.

Chapter 12

2016

Waking the morning after my Norfolk trip, I feel relieved to be at home in something resembling normality, although I can't imagine how things will ever be normal again. I know Polly thinks I should do more for myself, reach out to the friends I've neglected over the past couple of years, but I can't cope with adding anything new to my life. I am only just managing as it is.

Henry always goes to Sam overnight on a Wednesday, so in the morning I begin gathering his things – underwear, spare uniform, Manky – and chucking them into his little rucksack. He's had Manky since he was a baby. At some point, when it began to get very ragged around the edges, Sam and I started calling it Manky Blanky and the name stuck. Things go back and forth from Sam's house to mine so I'm never quite sure what he's got there that he might need, but there is only one Manky and he is irreplaceable. As I shove a spare school jumper in, I feel something hard and sharp in the front pocket of the bag. I unzip it and peer in. When I see what it is, I sink down on Henry's bed, staring at the photo of me and him on the beach, both of us grinning and squinting against the sun.

'Henry, can you come here a minute?' I call.

He comes running in from the kitchen, licking jam from his fingers, but stops dead when he sees what I'm holding.

'Why have you got this in your bag, H?'

'I like to look at it,' he says under his breath.

'When?'

He seems to grow smaller. 'When I'm at Daddy's. Sometimes I miss you.'

Tears ache in my throat and sting the backs of my eyes. 'Come here.'

He rushes to me and leaps onto my lap, wrapping himself around me, his solid little body melting into mine.

'I miss you too,' I say, straining to speak lightly. 'But you have fun with Daddy, don't you?'

'Yes,' he says into my neck, 'but sometimes I want to look at you.'

'That's fine, H.' My voice cracks slightly and I swallow. 'You didn't need to take the photo, you could have just told me. Tell you what, why don't we make up a big frame with lots of pictures of you and me, and you can put it up in your bedroom at Daddy's?'

He gives me a final hug and goes back to his toast. I sit for a moment on his bed, looking at the photo of the two of us, arms around each other, bathed in sunlight. It feels like a million years ago. As I put the photo back in its place on the shelf, I can't help feeling relieved. I was being paranoid after all; no one has been in my flat.

I've got to stop neglecting my clients or I'm going to start losing them, so with Henry at Sam's I am able to finally get somewhere with Rosemary Wright-Collins's latest project. Having Rosemary as a client is so important: without her, my business would be floundering. Sam suggested once that I was misguided to work so much for her, that having most of my eggs in one basket was a mistake. He wanted me to turn down work from her, thought I was spreading myself too thinly trying to fulfil all her requirements and keep other clients happy. He was glad my business was doing well, I am sure he was. But it's not lost on me that he left me for someone much younger, much further down the career ladder. I know Polly thinks so.

On Friday, I pick Henry up from after-school club, and when we get home instead of plonking him in front of the telly, I play with him. We make a huge and complex track with his wooden train set and then he instigates a convoluted story where the trains have to save one of the cows from his farm set who is stuck on the line. Every time I attempt to bring the story to a close with some kind of resolution, he creates a new and apparently insurmountable obstacle that extends the game further. I watch as he pushes the little engines around the track, his face deadly serious, totally absorbed in the world we have created. It's cosy in the sitting room, but a chill creeps over me. This is why no one must ever know what really happened to Maria. I cannot allow anything to jeopardise Henry's innocent faith in the world as a benign place, where no one would allow a cow to be run over by a train, or take a mother from her child.

Once Henry is in bed, I sit at my kitchen table with a glass of red wine, the lamp in the corner casting a calming glow. The smell of the ready meal warming in the oven is beginning to waft through the room: onions, garlic, herbs. I scroll through my emails – the problem with working from home is that in a sense I'm always at work, unable to ever fully switch off. I open another window and go to Facebook. I've been checking it constantly both on my laptop and my phone, and each time there's no message the faint hope that it's over grows stronger. That it was someone playing a sick joke, a stupid prank – upsetting and disturbing, but no more than that. One of the school mums is spewing the details of her latest break-up on her page, but she has some of her ex's mates as Facebook friends and they are weighing in, disputing her version of events, calling her names. I am drawn in, as I used to be years ago when I watched the soaps on TV, but with the added fascination that this is real life, or at least something like it. I'm amazed by the extent to which some people live out their lives on here. This woman doesn't even say hello to me on the rare occasions I see her at the school gate, yet I know all the gory intimacies of her love life.

I go to Maria's page where I can see that Sophie has now accepted her friend request, but just as I'm about to close the window, I notice that Maria has another new friend listed: Nathan Drinkwater. I turn the name over in my mind, but it means nothing to me. I'm sure there was no one of that name at school with us. I click onto his page, but there's nothing there – no posts, no profile photo, nothing. Maria is his only friend.

There's a group Facebook message that I've been included on about a night out with some old colleagues. My instinct is to do what I would normally do – ignore it and let them assume that I'm not interested, too busy with the business and Henry. But I let the mouse hover over the reply button, trying to imagine myself in a bar with a glass of wine: chatting, catching up, swapping news. I am pouring myself a second glass of wine, and trying to persuade myself to accept the invitation, when the doorbell rings. I jump, and the bottle jogs in my hand, red wine slopping down the side of the glass, pooling like blood around the base and seeping into the oak table. I put the bottle down and walk cautiously along the corridor. Even though I've found the photo, I haven't totally shaken the feeling that I'm not safe, that there's someone watching me. I haven't forgotten the panic that surged through me as I ran through the tunnel at South Kensington. *Run as fast as you like, Louise.* I can see the outline of someone through the frosted glass of the front door, but I can't make out who it is. I stand in the dark hallway, framed by the light from the kitchen behind me, my body pulsing with every beat of my heart. I take a step back. I won't open it, creep back to the kitchen, let whoever it is assume I'm not in. But then the letterbox opens and a voice calls through:

'Louise? Are you there?'

I hurry to the door and yank it open.

'Polly!'

I enfold her in a hug, so thankful to see her that I hold her too long, too tightly.

'Hey, are you OK?'

I smile, biting back tears.

'I'm fine. Just glad to see you. What are you doing here?'

'Um, you invited me for dinner? When I was here babysitting last Friday?'

'Oh God, so I did. I'm so sorry, I completely forgot, what with everything . . .'

'How do you mean everything, what's going on?'

I'd forgotten for a minute that she knows nothing. Where to start? Should I even tell her anything at all?

'Oh, nothing much, just busy with work and stuff. How are you anyway?'

'Oh you know, same old, same old.'

We go through to the kitchen and she plonks herself down at the table.

'Something smells nice.'

'It's an M&S cottage pie for one,' I admit. 'Sorry. I've got some salad and bread and stuff, we can probably make it go far enough for both of us.'

'That's fine, I have wine and crisps,' she says, plonking them on the table. 'Who needs dinner?'

She glances at the shelving unit with the photo of me and Henry back on top of it. 'You found it then? See, I told you! I bet you just put it down somewhere and forgot, didn't you?'

'No, actually. Henry had it. He was taking it to Sam's. He said he misses me when he's there.'

'Oh, poor H.' Polly puts a hand to her chest in anguished sympathy.

'I know. Let's not talk about it, I can't bear it.'

By the time the pie is ready, we've worked our way through all the crisps and made a start on a second bottle. She's been regaling me with tales of her sister's love life, as well as filling me in on bits of news about my old colleagues at Blue Door. She is going to the drinks thing that I was havering about when she arrived and she's adamant that I have to come. She hasn't mentioned her girls yet, nor asked about Henry. Although she adores Henry, and I love Maya and Phoebe too, we don't talk about them that much. I do have friends that I made through Henry with whom the conversation nearly always revolves around fussy eaters, managing behaviour or the pros and cons of swimming lessons, but I love that that's not the case with me and Polly. She's a proper friend.

As I spoon the meagre pie out of its tin-foil dish onto two plates, adding several slices of French bread and a handful of salad, I ask how the girls are.

'They're OK. Well, Maya is.'

Maya is a robust and lively eight-year-old with an astonishing and enviable disregard for the opinions of others, whereas her sister at twelve grows quieter and more withdrawn every time I see her. I'd assumed this was the usual march of adolescence, the inevitable desire for independence, otherness, and the subsequent drawing away from one's parents and any adults associated with them.

'And Phoebe?'

'She's been having some trouble at school. With the other girls.'

An icy finger curls around my stomach, taking away my appetite.

'You mean – she's being bullied?'

'I'm not sure you'd call it bullying. It's so . . . subtle. Girls this age – they can be so *vile*.'

Don't I know it.

'What have they been doing?'

In some ways I don't want to know. I find this a difficult topic at the best of times, but right now I don't know if I will be able to keep my composure.

'It's hard to quantify. Leaving her out of stuff, not telling her about things until it's too late for her to go, undermining her confidence in the way she looks. I don't think she even tells me all of it. This new girl started halfway through term and she's thrown everything out of whack. She's turned Phoebe's best friend against her. She's a real alpha female.' She pauses. 'Actually, what she is is a fucking little bitch.'

The venom in Polly's voice shocks me. I've hardly ever even heard her swear, let alone speak so viciously about a child.

'Phoebe's always been so funny, so sparky, and now it's like she's shrinking. She's fading away, that person she used to be. And of course I knew she would change as she got older, grow away from me, but I thought that the essence of her, what makes her who she is, would still be there. But it's going; she's losing it. This girl, she's taking it away, she's taking Phoebe away.'

Polly is trying very hard not to cry. I am desperately sorry for her, but it's incredibly hard for me to respond in a normal way. This is such an emotive subject for me that I don't know what the normal response is. The only experience I have of it as a mother is Henry telling me that Jasper and Dylan wouldn't play trains with him in choosing time, which although it hurt my heart beyond measure, is hardly the same.

'Have you been into the school?' I manage.

'Oh yes, several times. They're doing their best, but like I said, it's subtle. There's only so much they can do. *Friendship issues*, they call it. Funny kind of friendship.'

She looks down at her barely touched plate. I want so badly for her to know that I understand, to offer some comfort.

'I had ... something similar when I was at school,' I say haltingly.

'Really?' Polly looks up. 'What happened?'

'Oh, I won't go into it all now, but ... I do understand. I remember what it's like to be a teenage girl.'

'Oh Lou, would you speak to her? She looks up to you.'

I must look sceptical because she goes on, 'No, she really does. She thinks you're so cool with your own creative business, and bringing Henry up on your own.'

'I don't know, Polly. I'm not sure I'd be able to say anything useful ...'

Oh God, what have I got myself into?

'Of course you would. You just said you had something similar happen to you. Even hearing that would help her. Please.'

Of course that's not exactly what I said, but I can't tell her that in fact I experienced it from the other side.

'OK, I'll give her a ring tomorrow.' What else can I say?

'Thank you. I really appreciate it.' She touches my arm lightly. 'Anyway, enough about that. I'm sick to death of thinking about it, to be honest. Let's talk about you – you haven't said much. Is anything up?'

It's my turn to look down, flattening the mashed potato with my fork. There's a part of me that longs to confide in her, to unburden myself to someone who genuinely cares about me and has nothing to do with the past. I am just so tired. Tired of keeping it all inside me, of never being able to fully let go.

'No ... not really.'

'I knew it! What is it? Have you met someone? Oh my God, is it someone from the website?'

She looks so hopeful that I am tempted to make something up, but I don't.

'No, nothing like that. I haven't even checked the email address you set up, to be honest. I don't know if my heart's in it, Poll.'

'OK, we'll do that in a minute. Tell me what's up first.'

I decide to go for a heavily watered-down version of the truth.

'I was contacted on Facebook by someone I was at school with.'

'Yes, that girl you went to see last Friday. Sophie, isn't it?'

'No, this was someone else. I've never told you about this, but at the end of my last year at school, a girl died at a party in the school hall.'

'What, she died right there in the hall?'

'No. She – they think . . . well, they think she must have been drunk or something. Our school was close to the cliffs at Sharne Bay. The last time anyone saw Maria she was wandering off in that direction. She was never seen again.'

I'm painfully aware of the huge holes in my story, the dark spaces that gape like missing teeth between my words. Polly, however, is agog.

'So they didn't find her body?'

'No, but that's not unusual, there've been several cases over the years where people jumped and their bodies were never found. It became a bit like Beachy Head, sort of a famous suicide spot. It depends on all sorts of things – the tides, the weather – whether bodies get washed up or not.'

'So who was the message from?'

'That's the thing. It was from her. From Maria.'

'From the dead girl?' Polly's fork stops halfway between

the plate and her mouth. 'But how horrible, that's sick. Who on earth would do that?'

'I don't know.'

'And why to you? Was she a particular friend of yours?'

I don't know how to answer this question. Apart from my parents (with whom my relationship is muddied by duty, guilt and prevarication) and Henry (who is biologically compelled) Polly is the only person in the world who loves me. I'd never been really close to my parents like some children are, but after Maria disappeared, our lack of communication became even more marked. It happened at that critical time in the mid-teens when children separate from their parents anyway. I was already drawing away from them towards my friends, my 'real' life. I suppose in the normal course of things I would have become closer to them again as I grew into adulthood, but Maria's death caused a schism between us so great that it was impossible to cross. I could never tell them what I had done, why I withdrew from them so completely. And they in their turn were baffled as to why the disappearance of a girl who, as far as they were concerned, I barely knew, had such a catastrophic effect on me.

Polly saw me at my lowest ebb when Sam left. I may not have told her the whole story, but she knows more than anyone else does. She picked me up and set me back on my feet when I thought I was never going to be able to get up again. In all my life I've never had anyone who was in my corner like she is, and I can't bear to risk losing that. I can't risk showing her who I really am, particularly in light of what's happened to Phoebe.

'Sort of,' I say. 'But not so much by the time she died.

It wasn't just me anyway, another girl I was at school with got the same request. The one I saw last week when you babysat. And there's something else.' I take a breath. 'That night when I went to Sophie's, I think someone was following me.'

'What? Why on earth would anyone be following you?'

'I don't know exactly . . . but this request, then the photo going missing . . .'

'But Henry had the photo, you just told me.'

'I know, I know. But I swear there was someone behind me in the tunnel at South Ken, and when I started running, so did they.' The footsteps clipping, keeping pace with mine, the burning in my chest, the bottle banging against my legs. 'And then I got another message from Maria's account. It said, "Run as fast as you like, Louise. You'll never escape from me." She was following me, she must have been.'

'That could just be a figure of speech though, couldn't it? It doesn't mean that anyone was actually following you that night.'

She doesn't believe me, and I don't blame her. Without the context of what I did to Maria, my story loses its power, but of course that's the bit I can't tell Polly. But someone has set up a Facebook page for Maria Weston, and someone followed me all the way from Crystal Palace station to South Kensington. I know it.

'This Facebook page though,' Polly says, echoing my thoughts, 'that is weird. Do you not have any idea who could have done it?'

'There's a school reunion next weekend, I thought I might go, see if – I don't know, if anyone else has had anything similar, I suppose?'

She regards me sternly. 'A school reunion? Seriously? Will Sam be there?'

'I don't know,' I say, eyes glued to the bottom of my wine glass and thinking of the event page on Facebook that told me exactly who was going to be there.

'Hadn't you better try and find out before you go? I don't think it's a good idea for you to see him socially, do you?'

Sometimes I wish I hadn't confided in Polly at all when Sam left me. She's not the sort of friend who forgets things, or allows you to do so. I love how fiercely protective she is of me, how angry she is at Sam on my behalf, but I can't allow her to stop me from doing this.

'Look,' I say, 'I'll try and find out who's going – there's probably someone I can ask, or maybe there's a Facebook page or something. I won't go if it looks like he's going to be there.'

I hate lying to Polly but I don't want to argue with her, I need her to be OK with me. She's right, of course. It's not a good idea for me to be in a relaxed, social environment with him, one full of drinking and reminiscing and heightened emotions, and Polly knows exactly why. I made the mistake of telling her that there was one time, not long after he left me, where he came round in the evening after Henry was asleep. I'd been drinking alone, so I poured a glass for him and he sat down with me, and for an hour or so it was as if he'd never left. There was a moment where he leaned over me to open the drawer where I still keep the corkscrew and time stood still, just for a second. He was so close that his features softened hazily, leaving only the feeling of his breath on my cheek, and a hot, melting sensation low in my stomach. I stood up quickly, my legs shaking and crossed the room, pretended to remember an early start, asked him to leave. Despite everything he had done to me, I still felt a pull to him. Part of me still does.

'Hmm … OK,' she says, seemingly mollified. 'Right, let's have a look at this email account, see if you've got any interest.'

I pass her the laptop and she logs in to the email account she set up for me.

'Oooh, there's quite a few!'

I scooch my chair round so I can see the screen, and she starts opening the emails.

'Oh,' she says. The first one makes lewd reference to the fact that Polly said I was interested in 'nights in and out'. '"I will go in and out all night if you want me to." OK, delete and on to the next.'

The next one goes into even more detail about exactly what it is he would like to go in and out of, and how he would feel about that.

'Oh dear. I think I should have phrased that differently,' says Polly, crestfallen. 'It was my first foray into the world of online dating. We should have got a teenager to do it for you. They're much more savvy.'

Most of the messages are variations on this theme, with a few genuine responses mixed in, all of whom seem to have taken my love of country walks and run with it. They are rock climbers, triathletes, iron men.

'I can't date any of these men,' I say. 'I get palpitations going outside the M25.'

'Hang on,' says Polly. 'We have a live one. "Hi there," it says. Well, that's friendly isn't it, a good start? "I must confess I'm not a huge fan of country walks, but I love to eat out and wondered if I could take you out for dinner?" There you go! He doesn't like country walks either!'

'That's not exactly the strongest basis for going out with someone, is it?'

'No, I know, but you never know. Let's have a look at his profile.'

Greg is 42 years old, and handsome in a non-threatening way. He's laughing in the photo, and looking at something over the photographer's shoulder.

'Lovely shirt,' says Polly.

'Again, Poll, not necessarily the criteria on which a lifetime's happiness is built.'

'Oh, stop creating obstacles. Let's reply.'

I sigh, but to be fair he is handsome and seems normal, as far as you can tell with these things, which is not very far at all; so I allow her to craft a reply, which she sends via the messaging function on the site. He must be online because a reply pings back straight away, and before I even have time to protest or think about it, Polly has arranged a date for me with Greg at 7pm tomorrow in a bar in central London. On her instigation, we are just going for a drink. She says that way if I need to get out of it I can do so after one drink without awkwardness, and if it's going well, then we can always go for dinner anyway. I can't imagine for a minute that it will go well if Greg is as nice and normal as he looks. It's years since I've been on a date, I'm bound to stuff it up.

When Polly has gone, I pour the dregs of the second bottle of wine into my glass and flip open my laptop. Facebook is still open from where I was checking it earlier and I see that I have a new message. My evening with Polly has dulled my fears a little and I assume it's the latest in the lengthy exchange of messages from my old colleagues about this night out, so I click on it with no trepidation.

What I see makes the blood drain from my face. The message is from Maria Weston, and it says:

> Did you enjoy your trip to Norfolk? I haven't forgotten what you did, Louise. I'm always watching you. I will never let you go.

Chapter 13

1989

Maria didn't stay much longer at the party. Sophie sat me down in the kitchen, gave me a glass of water and sat beside me stroking my hair. After about ten minutes, Tim came in and rummaged in a huge pile of coats on the kitchen floor. As he left the room with Maria's denim jacket, he looked back briefly over his shoulder and his eyes bored into mine, full of hatred and accusation. The intensity of his gaze frightened me and I looked away. From my position near the corner of the table I could see into the hallway. Maria stood by the newel post with her head down, her face shielded by a curtain of hair. She allowed Tim to help her into her jacket as you would a small child, and when he had done so he stroked her hair back from her face, saying something to her in a low voice that I couldn't hear. Then he steered her out of the front door, his arm wrapped protectively around her.

The party was brilliant after they left, one of the best nights of my life. I started to feel better so I had some more vodka and I actually danced, and for the first time ever it was OK. Sophie tried to get me to do an E but I was too scared and she was so sweet about it, said she understood, that she had felt the same before she tried it, that there was no pressure. Later, part of me wished I had just done it.

We went for a walk together at about four in the morning, all round Matt's estate. The streetlights were on, and in the half-light the houses looked like mini-castles. I'd never known such silence, broken only by the sound of our footsteps and Sophie's soft voice, telling me things I never knew about her, letting me in.

'A couple of years ago, not long before you and I became properly friends, me and Claire and Joanne were this tight group of three.'

I remembered. From the outside it seemed like they had won the prize, the three of them huddled together every day in a corner of the playground, screaming with laughter, an unattainable ideal of shared lip gloss and secrets. Everyone wanted to get close to them that year, but they were so tight that it was impossible.

'I don't know if you've ever been in a group of three friends, but it's a terrible number. When things were good it was amazing, but we were always falling out and it often seemed to be me that was frozen out. Do you remember that Dieppe trip?'

Summer 1987. Esther Harcourt had been in my dormitory, and on the first night there, we'd spoken for the first time in years. I'd been homesick and she'd comforted me, made me laugh, and I'd wondered whether I'd made a mistake cutting her out so comprehensively. The next day though when she'd put on her too-short jeans and bright blue cagoule, I'd known I'd made the right decision. I'd spent the day with Lorna Sixsmith, and that night I'd stayed up chatting to the others in our room while Esther had lain reading on her bed.

'We fell out badly during that trip,' Sophie went on, linking her arm through mine. We were passing the little shop that served the estate; it looked ghostly and abandoned under the streetlights. 'Well, I say we fell out; it was more like Claire and Joanne went off without me; I never really knew why. I hung out with Sue, so I wasn't on my own, but all the time I could see the two of them, whispering in corners, giggling at private jokes. On the coach on the way home, I was sitting in the seat in front of them and they were talking in a private language. Not a whole language obviously, but they had all these code words for things and people.'

Poor, poor Sophie. I could see her, sitting alone in a double seat, face pressed to the window, her forehead stinging against the cool glass.

'Obviously we're friends again now but Claire can be . . . difficult, you know? She's always trying to get one up on me; whatever I've done she always has to go one better. Everything's always on her terms. It was after that Dieppe trip that you and I started to get close, do you remember?'

Of course I remembered. The first time she sat with me at lunch, I was so excited I could barely sleep that night.

'That's why I got so upset about you and Maria. I know it's silly, of course you can be friends with whoever you like. It just felt like it was all happening again, you know? Like I was losing you to her.'

'You won't lose me, Sophie. You're—' Could I risk this? I took a deep breath. 'You're my best friend.'

She pulled me closer to her. 'Thanks. I know I can always depend on you.'

We walked on, arm in arm, having a real heart to heart; the only thing we didn't talk about was boys, whether there was anyone we fancied. Maybe Sophie felt it wasn't the time, that we were going deeper than that; I didn't ask her because I didn't want to know the answer. We did talk about our parents though.

'I know mine love me,' I said, 'but they have no idea about what's really going on in my life. All the time I'm at home, it's like I'm just marking time, waiting to leave the house and start living again. I don't feel like they know me at all.'

'My mum likes to think she's my best friend,' Sophie said. Her mum is like an adult version of her, always groomed and glamorous, poised and full of charm. Sophie once told me that she has a weekly appointment at the beauty parlour. I thought with a sudden pang of my mum's bare face and sensible shoes. She's probably never been to a beauty parlour in her life. 'Whatever happens to me,' Sophie went on, 'she's always got a story about how something similar happened to her, and some brilliant advice based on her own experiences. As if I'd take her advice. Look where she's ended up.'

'What d'you mean?'

'Her and my dad are always fighting. They wait till they think I'm asleep usually, but I hear them.'

'Do you think they'll get divorced?'

'I wish they would.' She laughed. 'Then I'd get two of

everything. Mind you, it doesn't always work like that. Do you know about Sam Parker's mum?'

'No,' I said, trying not to betray any emotion. 'What about her?'

'She just upped and left him and his dad a few years ago. Ran off with some other bloke. Sam hasn't seen her since.'

'God, how awful. Poor Sam.'

'I know. He never mentions her, but you can tell he's fucked up about it.'

We walked in silence for a few minutes, drinking in the stillness. Every house was in darkness and the cool air smelled crisp and clean, untainted by car fumes or cooking smells. With my arm tucked in hers, it felt like we were the only two people in the world.

As we turned back into Matt's road, Sophie's attention was caught by something on the front doorstep of the huge house on the corner.

'Fancy a cup of tea?' she said, grinning.

'What?' I looked at her in confusion. She grabbed my hand and pulled me towards the step. We were nearly at the door when the security light clicked on, bathing us in a harsh yellow light. Sophie snatched the bottle of milk from beside the step and we turned and raced madly towards Matt's house, breathless and giggling. I don't think I've ever felt so happy in my whole life.

Then the following Monday at school, Sophie invited me to go for a fag with her at morning break. We managed to dodge the teachers and half-ran down the path to the woods. It was totally out of bounds, and I felt really nervous but I didn't want to look stupid in front of Sophie so I tried not to look behind me. We came right through the little wood behind school and out the other side to the cliffs, which is even more out of bounds. Sophie went right to the edge and sat down on the chalky grass next to a sign saying 'Keep Back', dangling her feet over the precipice. I hung back, but she turned and beckoned me over, laughing.

'Don't be such a scaredy cat.'

I sat down next to her, the grass scratching the back of my legs, my feet hanging into thin air. I didn't smoke normally but I took the proffered cigarette she had lit for me. There was a faint print from her lipstick on the filter, and as I drew the smoke down I relished the bitter tang across my tongue and down my throat.

'We've had this idea,' Sophie said, her eyes on the horizon. 'Sort of a prank. To play on Maria.'

'A prank?' I pulled a tuft of grass loose and scattered the blades over the edge of the cliff. 'What do you mean?'

'She's a bit up herself, don't you think?'

I didn't say anything.

'Well, Claire thinks so, and then there's all these rumours going around about what a slag she was at her old school, and what she got up to. Have you heard about it?'

'No.' I remembered what Sam had told me at Matt's kitchen table, but that was just gossip surely, blown out of all proportion.

'It's some properly gross weird stuff, Louise. Apparently she was sleeping with this boy and she sent him a used tampon in the post. One that had actually been inside her – which was the idea supposedly, like it was meant to turn him on. So Claire had this idea that we could put a used tampon in her bag, for a joke. Not with real blood obviously – we're going to go up to the art room at lunch and soak one in red paint. I thought you could do it – put it in her bag I mean,' Sophie went on. 'You sit behind her in form, don't you, so it would be easier for you than for anyone else.'

'Oh, I don't know.' I shifted back a little from the edge, drawing my knees up, suddenly feeling the precariousness of my position. 'You sit next to me, can't you do it?'

'I'd have to lean right over though. She's directly in front of you, it'll be less noticeable.'

'I guess so, but – I mean, we don't know for sure that she did do that, with the tampon, do we?' I stubbed out my half-smoked cigarette, grinding it into the chalk beside me.

'Matt Lewis's cousin knows someone who goes to her old school. I swear to God she did it.'

'But even if she did, it just seems like . . .' What I wanted to say was that it seemed like a pretty horrible thing to do regardless. Maria hadn't spoken to me since the night of the party, nor I to her, but I had been hoping we could let our nascent friendship simply slide away, unnoticed. Now Sophie was asking me to raze it to the ground.

She took a deep drag of her cigarette and breathed out a plume of smoke into the salty air.

'Well, if you don't want to then of course it's your choice. I'm just worried about you – if you don't join in with it you might end up feeling a bit left out. People might wonder if you really are one of the group, you know? I'm not saying I would, but that's what the others might think.'

We sat there in silence for a couple of minutes. Sophie lit another cigarette from the stub of her first without offering me one.

'Right, we'd better get back to school then,' she said eventually, standing up and tugging her skirt down where it had ridden up slightly. She was slipping away from me, I knew it, and I couldn't help imagining the conversation where she told Claire and maybe even Sam that I had chickened out. I followed her along the path, and as we passed from the open cliff into the shadow of the woodland, I made my decision.

'OK, I'll do it.'

She grasped my hand.

'Yay! I knew you would. It's going to be so funny, honestly.'

I was overcome by breathless, shaky laughter and we walked back to school arm in arm, giggling all the way.

As soon as the bell went for lunch we went up to the art room. I kept guard while Sophie went into the room, coming out a few minutes later, smirking.

'That was quick. Where is it?'

'In my bag, of course. In a plastic bag as well. I'm not going to walk around dripping blood in the school corridors, am I?'

'What d'you mean, blood? I thought it was paint.' A horrible thought flitted across my mind.

'Yes, that's what I mean – paint.'

'Why haven't you got paint on your fingers?'

'I'm not totally stupid, Louise. If Maria tells, the first thing they'll look for is someone covered in red paint. I took some gloves from Mum's work the other day.' Sophie's mum is a dental nurse.

'The other day? When did you decide to play this joke then?' The blood in my veins dropped a few degrees. It all felt too premeditated, less of a prank than an attack.

'Oh, for God's sake, Louise, does it matter?' She pulled

me into a nearby toilet block. Inside a cubicle, she handed over a small see-through plastic bag, the kind you'd put your sandwiches in. I didn't look too closely.

'Right, so when we go back to class after lunch, that'll probably be your best chance, before we go to maths. Just tip it out into her bag. It's open at the top, isn't it, no zip or anything? Or get up and pretend to get something if that's easier, and slip it in as you walk past. Once you've done that, put the plastic bag into the bin in our classroom on your way out. Then there's no way to link it back to us if she tells.'

Back in the classroom, I sat at my desk, trembling from head to toe. Claire and Joanne chatted artificially to each other in their seats across the aisle from me, jittery and skittish with anticipation. Maria walked into the room with Esther, both of them laughing as they passed down the aisle. Maria was studiously avoiding my eye but there was a telltale flush on her chest as she hung her bag on the back of her chair and sat down in front of me. Her hair was neatly tied in a ponytail.

I put my hand into my bag and felt the sandwich bag, smooth and slippery, the tampon a squelchy lump between my finger and thumb. Was I really going to do this? I could feel Sophie brimming with supressed laughter to my right, and I anticipated the warmth I would feel as I basked in her approval later. I would be the one whose arm she sought as we walked into town after school, not Claire. Maybe she'd ask me to sleep over so we could relive what we had done, giggling together under the covers, partners in crime. I closed my hand a little tighter on the bag and its gruesome contents.

I tried not to look at Maria as I began to pull the bag

out; tried to force myself to visualise what would happen if I didn't do it, how scornful Sophie would be. I pictured myself walking home alone, studiously avoiding the sight of Sophie clinging ostentatiously to Claire as they swanned off into town together. I closed my eyes for a second, and when I opened them, the first thing I saw was the nape of Maria's neck, white and vulnerable, the clasp of her gold heart necklace just slightly off-centre.

Instantly I felt as though I'd sunk into a warm bath. Relief suffused me as I realised that I wasn't going through with it. I pushed the plastic bag back into my school bag with a shaking hand. Despite what I had already done to Maria, the way I had callously thrown aside our friendship, I couldn't do this to her. It felt so calculated, so gross, so spiteful. And although part of the relief I felt was for Maria, and how thankful I was that this wasn't going to happen to her, it was also for me. I was relieved that I wasn't the sort of person who would do something like this. I had thought for a horrible moment that I was.

There were only a couple of minutes left before the bell would go for maths. Sophie's leg pressed against mine under the table, and Claire and Joanne were openly staring, willing me to action. I knew Sophie was looking at me too, but I kept my eyes fixed on our form teacher, her words like a foreign language, floating meaninglessly over the pounding of the blood in my head.

The pressure against my leg lessened, and that was when I realised that Sophie was taking matters into her own hands. She reached into my bag and took something out, something that she held in her closed fist. If Maria hadn't hung her bag on the side of the chair nearest to Sophie,

I don't think Sophie could have done it without drawing undue attention to herself, but she simply reached across me, shook the bag and withdrew her hand all in one smooth motion. For a final touch, she slipped the sandwich bag back into my school bag with a pointed glare at me.

I don't know exactly what Sophie was expecting in terms of a reaction from Maria. I heard Maria say to Esther that she needed to check if she had her maths textbook. Before I knew it, my hand shot out and tapped her on the shoulder.

'Maria. There's something I need to—'

She cut me off as soon as I began to speak.

'Leave me alone,' she said in a low, cold voice without looking up from her bag.

'No, I know, but please—'

'I said, leave me alone.' This time she did look at me, hardening her face, determined not to betray the slightest hint of emotion.

I sat back, defeated, as she opened her bag and started to reach in. It felt as though the whole world was holding its breath. Her hand stopped. I could feel rather than see Sophie's anticipation next to me, but if she was hoping for screams and histrionics she was disappointed.

Maria stared into her bag for a few seconds, the blood that had rushed to her face whilst she was speaking to me seeping out of it, leaving her skin pale and thinly stretched over her bones. She withdrew her hand, inch by inch, and stood up slowly.

'I'm just going to the toilet. I'll see you in maths,' she said to Esther. Her voice was low but impressively steady.

As she left the room, she turned to look at me, her face impassive. If she was close to tears she didn't show it. The impression she gave was one of sheer fury, the kind that can fling objects across the room with its power. Without speaking, she told me she had the measure of me now, that she would make sure I would live to regret this day. I sat motionless at my desk, and felt a cold chill of fear trickle down my spine.

Chapter 14

2016

Usually I wake as soon as Henry pushes open the door, but the morning after my dinner with Polly, the first thing I am aware of is his warm body slipping under the duvet in the semi-darkness, his hair tickling my face as he snuggles into me. I glance at the clock; it's nine o'clock already, he's slept much later than he normally would. I pull him closer, burying my nose in the nape of his neck, wondering as I always do when he will lose this delicious smell. He won't smell like this when he's fifteen, but what about in five years' time? Will I still be able to breathe him into me like this? Sometimes I wonder what the effect of all this love will be on him later in life. All the experts seem to agree that you can't give a child too much love, but what if you can? What if you smother him with it, or ruin him for ever by raising his expectations of how other people will feel about him? Nobody will ever love him this much again.

He sighs happily. 'What day is it?'

No matter how many times we practise the days of the

week he is still none the wiser, each new day a delicious surprise.

'Saturday.'

'Is it a Daddy Saturday?'

'Yes.'

'Oh good.'

One of the only things I am grateful to Sam for is his timing. Henry was just two when he left and has no memory at all of Sam and I living together. He was recently invited to play at a new school friend's house, the first time he has had an invitation that didn't include me. At bedtime that night as I arranged the cuddly toys in their correct rows, he told me in great wonderment that Josh's mum and dad were both there, that they all lived together. I sold Henry the fantasy that he was lucky, he had two homes, and extra people to love him, but it was hollow on my tongue.

The wine I had with Polly has left me dry-mouthed and headachey. I leave Henry in my bed watching TV and stumble into the kitchen to make his jam toast. My laptop is still open on the table, a physical reminder of how the past won't let me go. I want so much to call Polly and tell her everything. The desire to unburden myself is like a hard stone in the pit of my stomach. But I have to keep reminding myself that I can't, I can't risk alienating Polly. She'd never understand, especially given what's going on with Phoebe.

What I wish more than anything is that my life could go back to the way it was before I got the Facebook request, to the time when everything was put away in its proper place inside my head. It has taken me so long to get everything into those compartments. I've only recently got back on track, got the things back in their boxes, made some new slots. And this time it's Maria who is in there, rummaging around, taking things out and holding them up in the cold clear light of day.

As the milk froths energetically away and the machine flashes, heralding the imminent arrival of my coffee, my phone starts ringing in my bag which is hanging from the back of one of the kitchen chairs. I rummage through old tissues, train tickets and broken pens, reaching it just in time before the voicemail kicks in. It's a mobile number, one I don't have in my phone.

'Hello?'

'Louise? It's Esther. Esther Harcourt.'

I stand very still, feeling my heart beating close to my skin. The toast pops up but I ignore it. Is it a coincidence that she has phoned the day after I receive another message from Maria? I've been thinking about Esther, and the fear that I saw on her face when I told her about the Facebook message. She seemed genuinely shocked, but that could have been merely because she wasn't expecting me to turn up on her doorstep. Hearing her voice, I realise how much I've wanted to see her again, but I'm so used to deceiving myself that I can't tell why. Is it because I think she might be the one sending the messages? Or do I need to be with someone who understands, even if she doesn't know the whole story?

'I've been thinking,' she says. 'There is something I haven't told you, but I don't know if it's relevant to what's happened.'

'What? What is it?'

'I'm meeting a friend in London today. We're spending

the afternoon together and then having an early dinner, but we should be finished by eight at the latest. Do you … could we possibly meet afterwards? We could talk about it properly.'

I am glad to have a real excuse to get away early from my date tonight, so we arrange to meet at 8.30pm in a pub near Seven Dials. I always feel more at ease in a proper pub as opposed to a fancy wine bar, and I sense that Esther feels the same, despite her expensive suits and general high-powered-ness.

I stick some more bread in the toaster for Henry and scrape butter onto the cold toast, the knife unwieldy in my hand. I stand at the counter eating it, staring mindlessly out of the French windows. A pigeon struts around the garden, pecking at unseen crumbs on the patio and I wonder vaguely what he could be eating.

I call Henry into the kitchen for his toast, and he comes ambling out holding Manky. One piece of his hair is sticking straight up from his head like a horn and his pyjamas are inside out and back to front. My heart swells with love for him.

'Thank you very much for my toast, Mummy,' he says gravely as he sits down, placing Manky carefully on the chair beside him. They've been talking about manners at school and, as in everything he does, he has taken it very seriously.

'You're welcome, Henry,' I reply, equally seriously. I wonder briefly, as I sometimes do, how different this scene would be if I had a brood of unruly children, pulling cereal boxes from the cupboard and knocking their drinks over, fighting with each other and answering me back. We had wanted to give Henry a sibling (as a pair of only children, neither of us wanted the same fate for him), but it had taken us so much time and money and heartache to conceive Henry, the thought of starting that journey again had been daunting, like finishing a marathon and then being told you've got to run another one straight away. My inability to grow a baby in my womb had made me feel like a failure. The one thing women are supposed to be able to do effortlessly, and I couldn't do it. When you first learn about sex, and pregnancy, all they tell you is how easy it is to fall pregnant. Nobody ever talks about when it's hard. Sam tried not to blame me, but I knew he secretly did. How could he not, when month after month there was no line, no big fat blue cross?

Now though, I love our tight little unit, the two of us against the world. Wherever we go, Henry holds tightly to my hand, as if to stop me from slipping away. If we're at the park, or soft play, he'll go and play with his friends but every now and then he'll come back to tell me he loves me.

I wasn't sure, before he was born, what sort of a mother I was going to make. Although things changed once it became apparent that we were going to struggle to conceive, prior to that I had never particularly wanted children, never felt that overwhelming biological urge that I've read about. But when he was born I surprised myself with my patience and my instinct, the way that, in spite of my inexperience, I knew what he needed and how to soothe him. The love that I feared wouldn't come consumed me entirely.

Perhaps I went too far in fact, subsuming my needs and Sam's in favour of Henry's. Sam certainly thought so. He wanted more of me than ever after Henry was born, but I didn't have much left for him. I don't know why he couldn't see that we were adults, we could look after ourselves; it didn't matter whether we were happy or not. All that mattered was that Henry was OK. That's still all that matters to me.

'Do you want to go and get dressed then?' I ask, smoothing down the sticking-up bit of hair. 'Then we've got a bit of time to play trains before I take you to Daddy's.'

His face lights up. 'Have we got time to make a really big track?'

'A huge one,' I say, smiling. He hugs me, and I don't mind that his sticky fingers are entwined in my hair. I just hold him very tight, the thought of leaving him at Sam's later sitting heavily on me, weighing me down like rocks in my pockets.

Whilst he's getting dressed, I pick up my phone with a heavy heart and scroll through the contacts until I find Phoebe's mobile number.

'Hi, Louise.' She sounds pleased and surprised to hear from me. I don't think I've ever called her before, although sometimes we chat on text.

'Hi, Phoebs. How are you?'

'I'm OK,' she says cautiously.

'Did Mum tell you I might call?'

'No, I haven't seen her this morning. I'm still in bed.'

'Oh, right, well.' I steel myself to lie to Phoebe, who I held in my arms as a baby. 'She told me you've been having some trouble with a girl at school.'

'Oh my God! Why did she tell you that?' Phoebe's clearly taken the 'teen' part of pre-teen to heart.

'She's worried about you,' I say. 'And we were talking, and

I mentioned that I'd had something … similar happen to me, and she asked me to talk to you.' It was similar, but not in the way I am allowing her to believe.

'Right,' says Phoebe, unconvinced. 'I can't believe she was talking about me behind my back.'

'She just wants to help you. And so do I.' I do want to help, desperately. Is there part of me that thinks I can somehow atone for what I did to Maria in some great cosmic trade-off?

'So what happened to you then?' asks Phoebe, curiosity getting the better of her.

'Oh, I won't go into all that,' I say, trying to sound light-hearted. 'But what you have to remember is that most bullying comes from insecurity. Even though this girl … what's her name?'

'Amelia.'

'This Amelia, she probably seems untouchable, full of confidence, she's actually probably massively insecure, that's why she feels the need to play you and the others off against each other.' If only I'd been able to see this myself when I was at school. If I could have seen that Sophie's unkindness sprang from insecurity, I might have been better able to keep myself from being sucked into it. If I had had more confidence myself, perhaps I wouldn't have been so easily persuaded to cruelty, so frighteningly keen to distance myself from anything and anyone even slightly tainted with the possibility of unpopularity.

'She's not insecure.' Phoebe is definite about this. 'Seriously, Louise, she's not.'

'Well, OK. The thing is the other girls probably feel like you do – scared of getting on the wrong side of her, scared of being left out. But if you can somehow band together with some of the others, you'll have more power, as a group. If she can't isolate you, she won't have such a hold over you. Is there anyone else, any of your other friends, who you can try and make more of an effort with, do things on your own with? Anyone who you think is maybe less in awe of Amelia than the others?' I wonder about Claire and Joanne, lip-glossed and bouncily confident in my memory. Were they struggling too? Was anything as it seemed to me then?

'Well,' she says slowly, 'there is Esme. And maybe Charlotte.'

'Great! There you go. Why don't you invite them over, or arrange to meet up with them without her. Once Amelia sees that you're not all going to roll over and do exactly as she says – well, maybe then you can all be friends.' I wonder whether Maria ever confided in anyone about what was happening to her, how different things might have been if she had had a concerned adult in her life to offer advice and comfort.

'I don't know about that,' she says. 'I don't think she's a normal human being. She's just a cow.' She giggles and I hear a glimpse of the old Phoebe, the one I used to push high on the swings as she whooped and squealed with delight. 'But I might try what you said about Esme and Charlotte.' She pauses, and then says almost shyly, 'Thank you.'

'You're welcome,' I say. 'The other thing to remember is that school, and your friends there, are just a small part of your life. I know it doesn't feel like it now, it feels like everything. But you're going to go on and do amazing things, and this Amelia, well, she may not.' I think of Esther with her high-flying career and her impeccably groomed hair; and of the look that flashed across her face when I told her about the reunion that no one had thought to invite her to. Will we hold them for ever, these hurts we bear from our teenage years?

I say goodbye to Phoebe and lay my phone carefully down on the table. What I have said to her is good advice, I remind myself. So why do I feel so guilty? I know why. It's because I've let her think I was the victim, not the perpetrator. Allowed her to imagine that I am like Esther, still bearing the scars of the humiliations I suffered at the hands of others, when in fact the opposite is true.

We leave late, what with the phone call to Phoebe and Henry being unwilling to leave our train game, and the traffic is awful so it's after 11.30am by the time we get to Sam's. I get out of the car to open Henry's door and unstrap him, loading his Thomas the Tank Engine rucksack onto his little back.

I lift him up so he can ring the bell, and as always it's Sam who comes to the door. His hair is messy and he's wearing jeans and an old T-shirt he's had for years, made of a faded soft cotton I've laid my head on a thousand times. You'd think I'd be used to it after two years, but it still takes me aback to see his face, so familiar, so much a part of me, in this unfamiliar context. I'm still poleaxed by what has happened to us, by the fact that I'm handing over our child to him, exchanging pleasantries at a front door that is Sam's but not mine.

'Can I go straight in?' Henry says to me.

'Yes, OK.' I kneel down to cuddle him, but he's already

gone, slipping from my outstretched arms like an eel. I still hate leaving him here, my stomach knotted with anxiety the whole time he is away, the clock inching its way to handover time agonisingly slowly.

I honestly think Henry is OK with parents who are not together, but I don't think I will ever get used to watching him walk away from me to a world I know nothing about. I always knew that when he was a teenager he would have an unknown life away from me that I couldn't control, but it feels so terribly wrong that he should have that now, aged four. There are people intimately involved in his life about whom I know practically nothing. A stepmother who doesn't come to the door. A little sister I've never seen. When he's not with me, how can I know if he is safe?

'You're a bit late,' says Sam.

'I know, sorry, we were playing trains, and then the traffic was bad . . .'

'It's OK, Louise, I don't mind.' He looks at me closely. 'But . . . is something wrong? Anything I should know?' He leans against the doorjamb, hands in his pockets.

'What do you mean?' Has he had the Facebook request too?

He is silent for a moment, as if weighing something up.

'Nothing. It's just you've seemed a bit . . . distracted lately. And you've been late with Henry a couple of times. I just wondered . . . Is everything OK?'

'Yes, everything's fine.' I fight the urge to run into the house and gather Henry up, take him away somewhere it can just be the two of us, for ever. Somewhere where I never have to watch him walk away from me into the unknown again.

'Are you sure, Louise? You seem . . .' he trails off.

'I'm fine. It's none of your business anyway, is it? How I seem?' I know I'm overreacting, but I can't stop myself.

He holds his hands up. 'OK, OK. I was only asking. I do still care about you, you know. I know things haven't worked out the way we planned.' I raise my eyebrows at this, the understatement of the year, but he ignores me and carries on: 'But I'll always care about you, whether you want me to or not.' I hear Polly's voice in my head, snorting: *care about you? He had a funny way of showing it.* How long would I have gone on pretending everything was OK, if I hadn't found the text message from Catherine on his phone that forced his hand?

I turn to go, but Sam stops me.

'Wait, Louise.'

I turn, confused. 'What?'

'Have you heard about this school reunion?'

'Oh. Yes.' Why is he suddenly asking me about it now?

'Are you going?' he asks, and I think I can detect a dangerous note of hope in his voice.

'I don't know. Are you?' I think of his name on the Facebook page. I know he is going.

'Yeah, why not? Should be a laugh.' He's aiming for levity, but I'm not fooled. I think of the sixteen-year-old Sam, so cool, so popular. Is he hoping to have a night where he gets to be that boy again, with the world at his feet?

'Maybe,' I say as I walk away from him down the path. 'I'll see you tomorrow at five.'

'OK, see you then.' He closes the door softly and I get back into the car, struggling to breathe normally. How is it that he can still do this to me? When am I going to get to the stage where he can't hurt me, where his words slip over me without even touching? As I drive away, I wonder whether I will ever be able to leave Henry with him without this terrible, gnawing sense of dread.

Chapter 15

2016

The rest of the day drags by. This is another part I haven't got used to: the empty weekends. When Sam and I were together, I relished the rare occasions when I got to spend time alone. Sometimes, despite my all-encompassing love for Henry, it felt as though they were the only times that I was truly myself, when I got rid of this interloper who had entered my life at the same time as Henry had, this mother. But when Henry is at Sam's now, I am lost. I know there are galleries and cinemas and museums I could be visiting, but I also know that if I do I'll see some nuclear family going to see a Disney movie, or following the signs for the interactive family museum workshop, and I'll feel a physical pain at the absence of the small hand that should be in mine.

I could see friends, I suppose, but Polly is often busy at the weekends ferrying the girls to their various activities, and even if she isn't I don't want to intrude on their family time – the spectre at the feast, reminding her and Aaron what life could look like if they're not careful with each other. I do have other friends, but it's frightening how easy it is to let them drift away. Turn down enough invitations and eventually even the most determined will stop asking. It would take a Herculean effort now to weave myself back into their lives and I don't have the energy for it. Instead I watch from the sidelines on Facebook, liking photos of barbecues, birthday parties, days out, knowing that I only have myself to blame for not being there in the pictures.

What I often do is take the opportunity to catch up on some work. Rosemary has sent me several emails about different problems with one of her projects, and I know she'll be surprised that I haven't responded yet, but I just can't settle to anything today. As soon as the clock crawls round to an hour whereby I can reasonably leave without being absurdly early, I'm out of the flat. I ought to have spent hours choosing what to wear, applying flattering make-up, styling my hair. The fact that I half-heartedly blow-dried my hair, bunged on a bit of mascara and lipstick and threw on jeans and one of my only 'going out' tops, doesn't exactly bode well for the date.

I get off the bus on Piccadilly and walk up through Soho. For a girl like me who grew up in the sticks, there's still something about living in London that gives me a thrill; not just the bright lights but the murkier depths too. When I first moved here, I was brimful of excitement at having an actual job in a real design agency, even if I was mostly making the tea. If I didn't have plans to go out or see anyone in the evening I'd go into Soho and walk around, absorbing the heady scent of garlic and wine, chips and cigarette smoke, rubbish and drains. I felt alive, anonymous but part of something that counted, a heady mix of out-of-towners going to see *Les Mis*, hen parties and work nights out plus a hint of the old Soho – bon viveurs, sex workers and criminals.

Soho has changed, even in the last twenty years. There are more chain restaurants, more tourists, less obvious grime. It makes me wonder if I've changed too. Probably less than Soho. I'm not so open to change; I have to be on my guard all the time. I've created this persona of stability, contentment, a real average Josephine. Sam was the only one who knew the real me.

I arrive a few minutes early and there's no sign of Greg in the bar. I've been studying his photo to make sure I'll recognise him. I get a glass of wine and sit on a stool in the window, where I've got a good view of everyone coming in. Despite my lack of enthusiasm for dating in general, I begin to feel butterflies at the prospect of this, my first date in seventeen years. Every time a dark-haired man approaches, my stomach gives a little flip, settling back down when it turns out not to be him. By 7.15pm, the flips have been replaced by a churning ache. I didn't give Greg my phone number as I didn't feel comfortable before I'd even met him, but he could email me if he was running late. I check on my phone but there's nothing. At 7.25pm I decide I've had enough. There's a group of younger women at a nearby table and I am sure they've clocked that I've been stood up and are laughing at me. I suppose this is what I should have expected, what I deserve. I've been foolish to allow myself to indulge in this fantasy where I could have a normal relationship. I should have known the past wouldn't let me go that easily.

I drain the last of my wine, flushed with humiliation, and

stand up to leave. As I come out of the bar my phone beeps, and I take it out, expecting a notification from the email address that Polly set up for me, which I've added to my phone. But it's a Facebook notification. Another message from Maria: Leaving so soon, Louise?

I stop, stock-still on the pavement, my legs almost giving way beneath me. It's noisy but all I can hear is my panicked breathing and the beating of my own heart. Someone is watching me. I look around, but the street is busy, filled with ordinary people meeting friends, lovers. There's a restaurant opposite with outside tables, the diners warmed by patio heaters. I try to scan their faces, but there are too many of them, tables behind tables, and anyway I don't know who I'm looking for. My phone beeps again:

> You don't deserve to be happy. Not after what you've done.

I pull the hood of my coat up and hurry away down the street, head down, almost running. She's right. I don't deserve to be happy. Of course there was no Greg. A nice, normal man would never be interested in me. And even if he was, I wouldn't know the right way to respond, how to be with him.

But how did she do it? It feels as though Maria has crawled inside my head, her fingers reaching out and scraping around inside my thoughts, taking the worst things I think about myself and serving them back to me. Then I remember Polly's lighthearted Facebook update: *matchmaking with Louise Williams on matchmymate.com*. Of course. Anyone can download a picture of a good-looking man.

Anyone can write an email. Maria was just lucky that all the other responses were so unsuitable.

I keep walking, staying on busy roads only, constantly looking around for possible danger. I am convinced for several minutes that someone on the opposite pavement is keeping pace with me, until they turn down a side street without a second glance. I double back on myself, switching from side to side of the street. Once I step into the road without looking and a taxi screams to a halt inches from me, the driver gesturing furiously at me. *Stupid cow.* I avoid the quieter side streets with their dark corners and shadowy, urine-soaked doorways, but even the well-lit, people-thronged areas seem menacing because I don't know where the danger lies. I don't know who I am frightened of, who I am running from.

At 8pm I get a text from Polly: How's it going? Do you need a pretend emergency phone call?

I text her back: Didn't show, on way home. I can't explain about meeting Esther without going into the rest of it, and I'm not ready to do that. Oh shit, she texts back. Call me when you get home? I can't, because I'm not going home. Going to pull duvet over head and hide. Will call in morning.

There's a pause, so she's either typing some mammoth reply, or wondering whether she should offer to come over and provide a shoulder to cry on. She obviously decides against, as her next text just says OK. Call me if you need to. Love you x.

I've got half an hour before I'm meeting Esther, and a large part of me wants to text her and say I can't make it, scurry back to the safety of my flat. But something about her voice when she said there was something she hadn't told me won't let me cancel, so I walk on, down street after street, heart pumping, until I find myself in the appointed pub.

Esther's not here, so I order a large glass of wine and find a seat in the corner, where I can feel the wall solid behind my back and have a clear view of the whole pub. There's a buzz of conversation, under which you can hear the sound of 'Fall at Your Feet' by Crowded House through the speakers. I used to love this song when I was at university, dreaming of a meaningful connection with some nameless, faceless, soul mate. As I look warily around the room, I think of all the other men in the world I could have ended up with, and how different my life could have been. But perhaps I never really had a choice.

I've just taken my first sip when I see her at the door, looking around for me. She's dressed in a bright red full-length coat, with her hair in a shining plump bun, cheeks flushed from the cold. She looks ten years younger than her age and has no idea that some middle-aged men are eyeing her admiringly. She spies me and waves, miming a drink. I shake my head, so she goes to the bar and two minutes later she's sitting opposite me, her G&T fizzing on the table between us.

'How was your day?' she asks, more as a conversational opener than because she wants to know, I imagine.

'Oh, you know . . .' I say, not meeting her eye. Where would I even begin? 'Yours?'

'Yes, good, thanks.' She's not interested in telling me about her day. She has her guard up around me; I felt it that day in her office. She doesn't want to let me in, and I can't blame her. I feel an urge to clear the air, to make the unspoken, spoken.

'Look, Esther, what we spoke about last time, when I came to see you. About how I treated Maria. I know you probably think I'm just saying it because I don't want you to think badly of me, but I am a different person now. I know what I did to her was awful, unforgivable. I know I made her life miserable, and I wish so much that I could go back and change that, but I can't. All I can do is acknowledge how wrong I was, and, well ... try to be a better person now.'

Esther fiddles with the straw in her gin and tonic, the ice cubes clinking against the side of the glass.

'OK,' she says finally, 'I can understand that, although I have to admit I can't always think rationally about our school days.'

Panic rushes through me again at the mention of school and I look around. A man waiting at the bar catches my eye and half-smiles. My chest tightens and I drag my gaze back to Esther.

'When I think about that time, I'm plunged back into it somehow,' she says. 'Everything I've achieved since pales into the background, and I'm back there, sitting on my own in the dinner hall, pretending to read a book. They stay with you, experiences like that. Change you. I know I'm successful now, and ...' she gestures to her appearance, unwilling to say the words, but I understand. 'But inside, there's a part of me still hovering there, on the outside looking in.'

I know what she means because despite our very different school experiences, I feel this too.

'Sometimes I'm talking to a woman I've met as an adult,' she goes on. 'Maybe a school mum, or someone at work, and they say something in passing about their school days, and it makes me realise that they were one of the popular ones. You know, they'll mention a party they went to, or their football captain boyfriend, and I just think, My God, you're one of them. And part of me—' she falters, reddening '—part of me feels *ashamed.* So I don't tell them who I was at school, I just laugh along and allow them to think that I'm the same, that my adolescence was filled with drunken escapades, giggly sleepovers, pregnancy scares. But it wasn't, was it? My experience of being a teenager would be like a foreign country to them.'

'I know this will seem hard to believe, but I understand a little bit of how you feel. My time at school was . . .' I trail off, unable to put it into words, especially to her.

She smiles, running a fingertip up and down her glass, making tracks in the condensation. 'Not the happiest days of your life? I've actually been thinking about that, since you came to see me.'

'What do you mean?' Time slows down a fraction. What does Esther know? What did she see?

'I knew you at primary school, remember.'

'Yes, I remember.' Wisps of cloud, floating across an azure blue Norfolk sky. Running through woods, breathless, to emerge on a huge expanse of sand, stretching on and on until it reaches the sea, and then beyond that the mysterious blue line where the sea meets the sky. Endless days spent on the beach, returning home at night with warm, salty skin, and sand in our shoes. Me and Esther, lying on our backs, side by side in her garden, not touching, unbroken blue sky above us, insects buzzing, the warmth of the rays on our sun-kissed limbs. Lying out as long as we could until the shadow of the house reached the last bit of grass, taking away the sun's warmth and turning the ground, and our bodies, cold. I remember all these things.

'I saw how you changed when we started at Sharne Bay High,' Esther says. 'You grew up faster than me. I was still a child at eleven, twelve, even thirteen. You went into yourself very early on, in the first year I think. And when you came out again, it was as if you'd made a conscious decision to be someone else. So anyone who'd known the old you . . . well, we had to go. It was all about Sophie, and the others. But you always seemed like you were on the fringes, never really part of the gang. Until the leavers' party. Something was different, wasn't it?'

I nod, hardly able to speak. Once I had moved on from Esther (and she was right, it had been a conscious decision), I had hardly given her a second thought, apart from making sure our past association was as little known as possible.

'*I* was different. I felt different. Like I was changing again, I suppose, or becoming the person I'd wanted to be all along.' I am feeling my way here, the truth stumbling clumsily out, unfamiliar on my tongue. My mind is whirring, unable to silence the nagging fear that I am still being watched.

'And did you?' she asks. 'Become that person, I mean?'

I stare into my wine. 'No, not really. But then, things were never the same. After that night, I mean.'

'No, they weren't.' It's Esther's turn to look down. She can't meet my eyes, I realise. What does she know?

I'm skirting too close to the truth here. I can feel it looming, like an iceberg in the ocean at night. I don't know exactly where it is, but I'm so frightened of hitting it unexpectedly, of feeling it crashing into me, tearing and splintering, sinking me entirely. Part of me wants to tell her everything, to let her in to this crushing fear that is consuming me. I want to shake her and make her hear me: *someone is watching me.*

My eyes slide back to the bar, but the man who smiled at me has gone. There's a woman there now with her back to us, her long brown hair in a loose ponytail. She begins to turn her head and my stomach rises up to my throat, but then I see her face and she's in her twenties, smooth-skinned and smiling at her friend who's just walked into the pub. I turn back to Esther.

'I saw Tim Weston.' I didn't even realise I was going to say it until the words were coming out of my mouth.

'What? Where?'

'After I came to see you in Norwich, I drove on to the coast. To Sharne Bay. I didn't even mean to, I just found myself driving that way. Did you know he lives in their old house? His mum sold it to him a few years ago, moved into a bungalow.'

'No, I didn't know that. Is that where you saw him then?'

'Yes. I went to look at my old house and then . . . I lost my way, and I found myself there.' As I say it, it feels unlikely, and I wonder how much of an accident it really was that I ended up outside Maria's teenage home.

'What was he like?' Esther asks in fascination. 'I always thought there was something a bit weird about him. He was so protective of her.'

'He was . . . OK, actually, under the circumstances. He was very kind to me about . . . you know. Said he didn't blame me.' I think back to our encounter. 'He seemed to know a lot about me though, which was weird . . . you too, actually.'

'What do you mean?'

'Oh, nothing much really, I suppose. He knew what we both did for a living, that's all. I sort of got the feeling he'd been keeping tabs on both of us.'

'I suppose maybe he feels like we're a link to Maria. It must be hard to let go. I can't imagine the pressure he must have been under, to be the only child left.'

'I know.' We are silent for a few seconds, each lost in our own thoughts. 'There was something else too,' I add hesitantly.

'What?'

'It's probably nothing, but ... just something else Tim said. When we were talking about what happened to Maria. He said, "She's tougher than she seems". Not, "She was tougher than she seemed". He spoke about her in the present tense.'

I expect Esther to laugh it off or suggest a slip of the tongue, but she does neither. She just stares at me, her face pale, the frames of her glasses harsh against the whiteness of her skin. We are suspended in uneasy silence for a few seconds, then she speaks.

'That was actually what I wanted to talk to you about.'

'What do you mean?' I can't look away although I am half-dreading whatever it is she's going to tell me.

'Every year since Maria disappeared, on my birthday, I get a present, delivered through the post.'

'OK.'

'It's a small thing, usually – candles, bath oil, a scarf. There's never a return address, or a card. Just a label: Dear Esther, Happy Birthday. Love from Maria.'

I put my wine glass down harder than I meant to, my hand jolting, the contents threatening to spill onto the table.

The chatter and buzz of the pub blurs around me, only Esther's face pinpoint-sharp.

'Every year since . . . ?'

'Yes.'

'Where are they posted from?'

'Different places – London, Brighton once, sometimes Norwich.'

'Norwich?'

'Yup, sometimes.'

'But who do you think . . . you don't think it's from *her*, do you?' My voice has dropped to a whisper. There's a pain in the palms of my hands and I realise that my nails are digging into the soft flesh.

'Believe me, I've considered all the options. I've stopped trying to figure it out to be honest. At least I had, until you showed up in my office. That was partly why I was so short with you. I was . . . freaked out, I suppose, at the idea that she's still alive, that the presents really are from her.'

'Did you ever tell anyone, go to the police?'

'I did take them to the police, after the first couple of years. They didn't take it seriously, though – I mean, there's no threat, is there? What could they do?'

I sit back in my chair, my mind skittering around. Is it really possible that Maria is still alive? And why am I only being persecuted now, if Esther's been receiving these presents for years? Am I being melodramatic to think that I'm in danger? I can't escape the fact that someone was watching me tonight. My eyes dart around, clocking everyone in the vicinity. Could that red-haired woman be her? Or one of that group of women by the bar?

Esther is watching me.

'I'm sorry, I didn't want to upset you. I just thought maybe you ought to know. Even though I'm expecting it, it still shocks me, seeing her name in black and white on the label, every year. I can't imagine what it must have been like for you to get that Facebook request.'

The desire to open up to Esther is very strong – the need to loosen this knot inside me that is being pulled tighter and tighter. The pressure in my head that has been building since the day I got the Facebook request threatens to reach bursting point.

'It's not just the friend request, Esther.'

'What do you mean?' She drains the last of her G&T and glances at her watch.

'I've had other messages, and the day I went to Sophie's, I'm sure someone was following me, and then . . .' I trail off, unwilling to admit how easily I was fooled into the internet date. 'Do you want a drink?' I say instead. Another glass of wine and I might just try to tell her the real story of what happened to Maria, start to let a little bit of light in.

'No, I'd better not,' she says, starting to gather up her things. 'I need to head over to Liverpool Street, my husband hates me being too late. What do you mean, though; you thought someone was following you?'

'Oh, nothing. It was probably just my imagination.'

She looks doubtful.

'Honestly, it's fine!' I say, attempting to sound breezy. I need to change the subject. 'I didn't know you were married.' Foolishly I'd imagined her to be as alone as I am.

'This didn't give you a clue?' She grins, waving her left hand in front of me, where I now see on the fourth finger a platinum band topped by a diamond solitaire.

'What does your husband do?' I'm panicking at the thought of being left alone, trying to keep her here longer.

'Lawyer, same as me.' She smiles. 'Boring!' I can tell she thinks it's anything but.

'Great.' I search my mind, but can think of no intelligent question to ask. She's a partner, I remember. 'Is he a partner too?'

There's an infinitesimal pause, and a cloud that I can't identify passes over her face. 'No, not yet.'

'Kids?' If I can just keep asking her questions, maybe she'll stay.

'Yes, two. One of each. You?' she asks, her eyes flicking to my ring-less finger so quickly that I almost don't notice.

'Yes. Just one.' The usual pang at that. At least now I'm divorced people have stopped asking when I'm going to have another. 'Henry. He's four.' I realise that Esther doesn't know that I married Sam. For some reason I am embarrassed about telling her. She's got her coat on now and there's no stopping her. In a few moments I will be alone again, facing my solitary journey home to an empty flat. What if someone is following me?

'Right, I'd better go and get my train, if you're sure you'll be OK. It was ... good to see you, Louise.' The words cost her, I can tell, and as she walks away, I'm overcome with an urge to run after her, ask her if we can't be friends. But I know it's hopeless. Esther seems willing to try and forgive me for how I treated Maria, and her. But she'd never forgive me if she knew the whole truth. Not in a million years.

Chapter 16

He's always been … protective. He knows what she's been through. Knows her childhood and teenage years weren't exactly a bed of roses. He just wants the rest of her life to be happy, that's all. Doesn't want anyone else to hurt her. The closer he keeps her, the safer she will be.

When she was pregnant, she thinks he secretly hoped she would give up work altogether, although that was never really going to be viable. She tries to push away the thought that he resents her professional success, that he'd prefer some slipper-shod hausfrau with dinner on the table. But it worries away at her, this feeling that he can't cope with her being more successful than him. He's not having a great time at work, and she feels almost reluctant to shout about her successes. She plays it down.

Pregnancy had another impact on their relationship too. Giving birth and breastfeeding not only ravaged her physically, they placed her in a new relation to her body. She didn't know what it was for any more. The things that had used to make her scream with pleasure left her totally unmoved.

She supposed she ought to have been pleased that he still wanted her. She had friends whose husbands didn't want to touch them after what they had seen in the delivery room: the blood and gore and screaming, ripping agony of it; they were repulsed by wives with loose-skinned bellies and leaking breasts.

She finds she has to reassure herself quite often. It's totally normal, what he wants to do. It falls within the range of normal. And what is normal, anyway? There's really no such thing, as long as nobody gets hurt. Although sometimes it does hurt, but then that's all part of the game, isn't it?

The main thing to remember is that he gets her. He knows her – he's the only one that does. She'll never find that with anyone else. And if she ever starts to forget that, well … he's there to remind her.

Chapter 17

1989

Sophie forgave me for bottling the tampon thing. In fact, she was really sweet about it, said she understood, I shouldn't have to do anything I wasn't happy with. She stuck close to me, walking with me in favour of Claire or Joanne, sitting with me at lunch every day. Maria stayed well away, thank God. I hardly saw her except in lessons. Everyone was talking about the leavers' party, which was happening in a few weeks' time, at the end of June, mostly about what they were going to take or how they were going to make sure the teachers didn't twig beforehand and ruin it. Sophie had this mad idea about doing some elaborate practical joke to send us out in style. Something spectacular, something that would make us go down in school history. I went over to hers and we watched this film called *Carrie*; I'd never been so scared. There wasn't going to be any pig's blood involved in Sophie's plan, but she said there would definitely be a big part in it for me. She didn't even tell Claire and Joanne about it. The only ones who knew were her and me, Sam and Matt. We needed the boys to get us the stuff, and, anyway, I think Sophie was trying to impress one of them. I didn't want to think about which of them it could be.

I knew I wouldn't bottle it again, wouldn't let Sophie down. I was sure then that I'd made the right decision, sticking with Sophie and the others. I saw Maria having lunch with Esther most days. She'd be fine. Esther was probably a better friend for her anyway.

The next big party was at Sam's house. I was properly invited this time, and not just because of Sophie. In fact Sophie said Sam had specifically asked her if she could bring me. I tried not to read too much into that. I got ready at Sophie's again, and we walked there from hers. I had no idea where his house was, so when we turned right by the fish and chip shop and started walking up Coombe Road, I was surprised. Not in a snobby way; I just never realised he lived up there. We walked past a gang of grubby little boys playing football on the street. One of them called out something rude to us but we ignored them.

When Sam opened the door his pupils were so large that his eyes looked nearly black. He enveloped both of us in a huge hug and then danced off back down the hall.

'God, he's having a good time already, isn't he?' I said to Sophie. I was hoping to convey my coolness, to let her know that I understood that he was on something, but she pursed her lips. The floor was carpeted in a sickly green and the wallpaper looked as though it had been there since the 1970s. Sophie pulled me down the corridor and into the kitchen at the back of the house. If the wallpaper was from the 1970s, the kitchen appeared to date from even earlier than that. Sophie sat me down at the Formica table, which had a sheen of dust and several burns on it. Her face was serious.

'Listen, we need to have a talk.'

I said nothing, picking with my fingernail at a chip on the surface of the table. Surely she wasn't going to pull away again, after I'd just got her back?

'We've noticed that you have a bit of an attitude about drugs.'

Who's 'we'? I thought, but didn't say.

'If you don't want to try anything, then, of course, that's up to you. But if you are going to be hanging around with us more, then that's what we do, you know? I wouldn't want you to feel left out.'

I thought fast.

'It's not that I have an attitude. More that I've never done anything except smoke a bit of weed, so I'm a bit unsure. What's E like then?'

'Oh my God, it's amazing. You'd *love* it. Everything's really beautiful and all the colours are really bright and you love everyone, and you just feel extraordinary. Light and happy. Like you could float away.'

'Sounds good,' I said lamely, embarrassed by my shameful naivety.

'It's more than good. Do you want to try one tonight?'

'Tonight? What, here? Oh, I don't know . . .' I was frightened of drugs, frightened of losing control, of embarrassing myself.

She shrugged, unsmiling. 'Like I said, it's up to you. I'm going to go and find Claire.'

She walked out of the room and left me sitting alone at the kitchen table. From the window I could see into the scrubby back garden. There were a couple of torn and rusty sunbeds, one of them lying on its side. I remembered how Maria and I had lain in the garden at Matt's house, and how relaxed I had felt in her company, alternating between desultory conversation and easy silence. I squeezed the inside of my mouth between my back teeth, chewing on the soft flesh, clawed by indecision. Was it too late to save what I had so nearly had with Maria? A proper friend – someone funny and interesting, who liked me for who I was. She'd forgiven me once – might she not do so again? I had tried to warn her, after all, about the tampon. All I had to do was walk out of this house, go home, and call her. It would be my final chance, I knew that, but still I felt she might give it to me.

The door flew open and I looked up, expecting to see Sophie back again, but my heart sank when I saw Tim Weston, closely followed by Matt Lewis's older brother. Tim ground to an abrupt halt when he saw me.

'Oh. I didn't know you were here.'

'Put these in the fridge, would you, mate?' Matt's brother said to Tim, shoving a couple of four-packs of lager into his hands and turning back to the party.

I pushed my chair as far into the table as it would go as Tim squeezed past me in silence. He removed one of the cans and put the rest in the fridge. He was halfway out of the door when he seemed to make up his mind about something and turned back to me.

'Look, stay away from my sister, OK?'

'Don't worry, I'm going to.' The harshness of my voice dismayed me, and I looked down, fiddling with the zip of my top. 'Is she here?' I asked more softly.

'No, of course she's not here,' he said, throwing himself

down in the chair opposite me and banging his can down on the table, causing lager to splash from the hole. 'Do you have any idea what you've done?'

'What d'you mean?' I said, not daring to meet his eye.

'She tells me stuff. I know what you've done to her. You may not know what she went through in London, but I do. This is the last thing she needs.'

'She's got Esther, hasn't she?' I muttered.

'Yes, and thank God she has, but you know as well as I do that being friends with Esther means she's cut herself off from ninety per cent of the rest of the year. And anyway, she wanted you. She liked you. And you let her down. And for what? That slapper in there?' He jerked his hand in the direction of the front room where the music was pounding. 'I hope you think it's worth it.' He stood up and pushed his chair back with a jerk, the legs screeching against the worn lino.

I sat at the table for a few minutes, not sure whether my legs would carry me if I stood up. Eventually I stepped towards the door, decision made, wondering only whether to tell Sophie I was leaving. However, just as I'd decided to try and sneak away without anyone noticing, the door opened again. I steeled myself for another conversation with Tim, but my stomach gave a foolish flip when I realised that it was Sam. His dirty blond hair was flopping into his eyes, the blue of which was almost entirely obscured by his dilated pupils.

'Lovely Louise! There you are!' he cried, causing a blush to spread up my neck, even though I knew that the affection he felt for me was purely chemical. He pulled me close and I hugged him back, feeling the heat of his body against my chest, my hands pressed into his back. I kept my eyes closed and inhaled, breathing in a mix of his worn leather jacket, a sweet and sharp citrusy smell and something else indefinable. An unfamiliar feeling rose in me, a desperate wanting that I could hardly name.

'Sit down with me?' Sam asked.

We sat down opposite each other and he smiled, reaching out for my hand. My heart was beating so fast I thought it was going to fly up out of my throat.

'Sorry about all this,' he said, looking around the kitchen.

'What do you mean?' I looked around at the rusty sink, the ancient yellow kitchen units, one door hanging off and a drawer completely missing, the chipped and stained worktop.

'You know what I mean. It's a shithole.'

'It's fine,' I said, squeezing his hand daringly. 'Who cares? At least you've got the place to yourself for the night. My parents never go anywhere. And even if they did, they'd kill me if I had a party.'

'My dad doesn't give a shit,' he said, his face darkening. 'I'm glad you're here though.' His smile reached down inside me, warming me from within.

I was about to reply when the door swung open once more, this time to admit Sophie. She smiled, looking pointedly at our linked hands on the table. Sam pulled his hand away and stood up, with a final smile at me.

'I'll see you in a bit, yeah?' he said. As he passed her, Sophie held her arms out.

'Where's my hug then, Sammy?'

Sam enveloped her in his arms, and she slid hers around his waist, watching me over his shoulder. When he headed back towards the living room, Sophie bounced down opposite me at the table.

'You two looked cosy,' she said with a wicked smile. 'So, what d'you think? Want to try it?'

I took a deep breath.

'Have you got anything I can take? Tonight, I mean?'

She smiled then, and I knew I'd passed the test. I also knew that whatever I'd had with Maria, it was well and truly over now. There would be no more chances.

Much later, I lay next to Sophie under a heavy goose-down duvet in her soft double bed as dawn broke. I felt as though I had passed through some invisible barrier into another world. I'd always felt at a slight remove from the group. My relationship with the others in it had always been filtered through Sophie, but taking the E had made me feel for the first time that I was really one of them. Images flashed through my mind from the night before: dancing, hugging, laughing; Sam's arms around me, lifting me up and spinning me around, everything a whirl of colour and light. Weak sunlight filtered through her Laura Ashley curtains and the birds began to squawk and chatter outside. I hadn't slept, running Sophie's idea over and over in my head. I had been a bit unsure at first but Sophie promised there wouldn't be any lasting effects – in fact Maria'd probably love it, might loosen her up a bit. Sam and Matt were up for it too; they thought it was a hilarious idea. We'd decided not to tell anyone else, not even Claire and Joanne. It was going to be our secret, just the four of us. I knew this would cement my place in the group – I was the only one that could do it. I just needed to hold my nerve.

Chapter 18

2016

I've had the lights on in here all morning but they haven't banished the October gloom, rain lashing from a gunmetal sky against the French windows. All week I've been putting off making a decision about the reunion, and even now the day has arrived, I still haven't clicked on Facebook to say I am attending. Polly is on standby for babysitting. I didn't want to tell her I was going, but I don't have anyone else who will have Henry overnight. She wanted to see the Facebook page so I haven't been able to hide it from her that Sam's going to be there. She was not impressed. I know she's only trying to protect me but she doesn't understand why I feel the need to go. She can't, because of the huge gaps in my story, the bits I haven't told her. She doesn't know how Sharne Bay pulls me, like a scar that itches, drawing your fingers to it, even though you know you should leave it alone to heal.

I'm completely happy for Henry to go to Polly's, but I do feel a pang when I see grandparents picking up Henry's classmates from the school gate. I can tell from the easy familiarity with which their grandchildren greet them that they are a proper part of their lives. For Henry, seeing my parents is an Occasion: he chooses his clothes with deliberate care, talks about it for days before, works himself into a state of anxiety, and is always ultimately disappointed when they fail to live up to his ideal. They've never shown an interest in looking after him, even when he was tiny and I was on my knees with exhaustion. They were sympathetic, but it simply didn't seem to occur to them that what I needed was for someone to take him away for a couple of hours. Maybe if we'd been closer before he was born I would have been able to ask for the help I so desperately needed, but the distance between us was too great to bridge by then. Twenty-three years of polite conversation had taken their toll and the time for honesty was long gone.

Sam's parents have never really been on the scene either. His dad died years ago, when Sam was at university, and although his mum flits in and out of his adult life, you wouldn't describe them as close. I used to try and get to the bottom of how and when she got back in touch, but he wouldn't talk about it. We were so close in some ways, but there were parts of him he never let me see. Henry's only met 'Other Grandma' a handful of times, so she's taken on something of a mythical status in his head.

I've chickened out of befriending anyone from school apart from Sophie on Facebook, so I'm reduced to poring over the little public information that is available on their pages – profile pictures mostly, although on some of them I can see photos and statuses that Sophie has liked or commented on. Matt Lewis seems to have picked up some small children, although they're not his; Sam met up with him occasionally when he and I were still together, although I never joined him, and he certainly didn't have kids then. He must have met someone who had children already. Claire Barnes has older children and is separated from her partner, judging from some of her and Sophie's exchanges.

I'm on my laptop at the kitchen table while Henry painstakingly eats a peanut butter sandwich, licking his forefinger and pressing it on the plate after every bite to catch any stray crumbs.

'My sister's not allowed peanut butter,' he announces. 'In case she swells up.'

It still hurts for me to hear him use the words 'my sister' about a child that isn't mine. He rarely mentions Daisy, or his stepmother. Of course he doesn't know that Sam left me for Catherine, but he obviously has an unconscious understanding that he is not supposed to talk to me about her or Daisy.

'Swells up,' he repeats. 'Like a balloon.'

'Right,' I say absentmindedly, absorbed in Facebook, wandering further and further off track, browsing through the holiday photos of someone Claire Barnes works with. My phone buzzes on the kitchen worktop as a Facebook notification pops up on the top right of my screen. I click on it, and everything in the room recedes until it's just me and the screen. It's another message from Maria.

> Going back to the scene of the crime? I'll be looking out for you, Louise.

Each message from her is like a blow to the head from an unknown assailant, leaving me reeling and confused. Henry is oblivious, totally focussed on his sandwich, protected by the egocentricity of small children.

This is never going to end until I confront it. I don't know what this person wants, but hiding here in my flat deleting messages is not going to solve anything. I stride into my bedroom and rifle through the wardrobe, discarding outfits: too work-y; too unflattering; too mumsy. I pack an overnight bag for Henry, and go online and book a room at the Travelodge on the outskirts of Sharne Bay. There's no way I'll get through this evening without drinking and the last train back to London from Norwich is way too early, something like ten o'clock.

There's still a part of me that wonders if I'm going to back out. But a few hours later, I'm in the car, dressed in the boring but flattering black dress I always wear when in doubt, make-up carefully done, high heels in the passenger footwell next to me. With Henry strapped in the back, I can't pretend any longer that I am not going to my school reunion. I can't ignore the messages either, and a tremor runs through me at the thought of what, or who, might be waiting for me at Sharne Bay High School. Layered on top of that fear is a tight knot of tension at the thought of seeing Sam, of being in the same room as him at an occasion that's not a necessary transaction, not a result of handing over our child. An occasion soaked in wine and nostalgia, emotions running high. I focus hard on the road, as if good driving will quieten the emotions that churn inside me.

At Polly's, Henry hardly gives me a second glance, struggling out of my embrace to go and find Phoebe, who he knows will happily read him the clutch of Thomas books he has brought in his backpack.

'Phoebe's got to go out soon,' Polly warns him. She turns to me. 'She's going to a sleepover. That little cow's going to be there.'

'What little – oh. Her.'

'Yes. Her. Listen, thank you so much for speaking to Phoebe about all that. It really seems to have helped. She went to the cinema with a couple of the others yesterday, they had a really good time. I think it really helped her to speak to someone who'd experienced the same thing.'

I smile weakly, wishing to God I'd never cast myself in this role of bullied schoolgirl.

'Now,' Polly goes on, looking at me sternly. 'Are you absolutely sure about this? Think of this as an intervention – an opportunity to change your mind. I'm not judging you or anything awful like that. I'm just worried about you. You've done so well to move on from Sam, you've been so strong. I don't want you to get sucked back into ... anything. You know what I mean. You could stay here. I have wine. You could watch *Strictly* with me and Maya.'

I am only tempted for a few seconds.

'No, I'm going. Honestly, Polly, I'll be fine. I'm not going because of Sam; I'll probably barely speak to him. I see him all the time, I don't need to go to a reunion to talk to him.'

'Yes, but you don't really speak, do you? You do all your communicating about Henry by text. Your only personal contact is passing Henry between you like a baton in a relay race. Which I think is a good thing, by the way. This is different: it's a social occasion, you'll be drunk, it's very emotive, being back at the place where you first met.'

'We didn't get together when we were at school. We were twenty-six when we started going out.'

'Yes, I know that, but you know what I mean. I was there when he left you, remember? I know what he's like, what you went through. I don't want you to end up back there.'

'I know. Thanks Polly. But I'll be fine, honestly.'

She reluctantly lets me go, extracting a meaningless promise from me that I'll leave if anything happens or I start to feel upset. The roads are unexpectedly clear and the drive goes by in a dream. It seems as if hardly any time has passed until I am pulling up on the road outside the school. I had thought about parking at the Travelodge and getting a cab to the reunion, but I've decided to leave the car here. This way, if I decide to leave after one drink I can get straight in the car and drive back to Polly's, and if I stay, I'll get a taxi back here to my car in the morning.

I am unsure about parking in the car park so I find a space on the road. I pull down the visor to check my face one last time in the mirror. I can hardly meet my own eyes. I could still turn back. It's not too late. I could go back to Polly's and watch *Strictly*, or just hole up in my room at the Travelodge. I sit for a few minutes, phone in hand, Polly's number up on the screen, thumb hovering. Two women I don't recognise walk past the car, chatting, laughing, clearly keyed up. They turn into the school gate and one of them howls, 'Oh my God!', her friend giggling and shushing her. Who are they? And if I don't even recognise them, what the hell am I doing here?

But then I see Sam, alone, walking easily and confidently into the grounds. My mouth feels dry and my tongue is taking up too much space in my mouth. For a minute I think I'm going to be sick, but it passes and the nausea is replaced by anger. Why should he get to waltz in there without a care, while I sit shivering and vacillating in a car that's getting colder with every passing moment? This is just as much my past as it is his. I turn off my phone, get out of the car and march firmly towards the entrance.

I am surprised to recognise the teacher manning the door as Mr Jenkins. He doesn't even look that old, and I suppose, although he seemed ancient at the time, he was probably only late twenties, making him early fifties now.

'Ah, hello there!' he says. 'And you are . . . ?'

'Louise Williams,' I say, my mouth dry with anticipation.

'Ah yes,' he says, clearly not remembering me in the slightest as he hands over my name badge. 'Looking forward to seeing all the old faces?' He smiles. 'Some of them have hardly changed a bit!'

I spend an unnecessarily long time fastening the badge to my dress, but when I can't spin it out any longer, I walk through the lobby into the hall, my fingers curled into my palms. It's the smell that hits me first. Like all schools, it smells of rubbers and disinfectant with a hint of old sweat, but the familiarity of this particular odour is like a smack in the face. It throws up memories I didn't know I had: queuing for chocolate in the tuck shop at break time, hot orange squash that scalded your fingers through the flimsy beige plastic cup from the vending machine, a game we used to play in the first year when we still called it playtime, called for some reason, now lost in the mists of time, 'That Game'. Of course there's also another memory, another night in this hall, this one not lost but branded onto my brain, leaving an ugly scar. I try to stem the images that flash through my mind, and the accompanying wash of shame: Maria, Esther, Sophie. Me.

With an anxiety bordering on panic, I realise I can't see anyone else on their own. Little groups form and merge, people flitting from one cluster to another with shrieks of recognition and overblown hugs and kisses. I am the only one who has come without the security blanket of a friend. Sam is over at the bar with his back to me, but I can't bear for him to be the first person I speak to. My eyes sweep the room, as they do everywhere I go now. There's a woman on the other side of the hall with her back to me, her mid-brown hair swept up into a complicated chignon, and as she begins to turn her head to speak to the man at her side, my heart slows and the room swims before my eyes; but then she looks behind her, laughing at something the man has said, and I can see it's not Maria at all. I recognise her, but like a lot of the people in the room, I struggle to put a name to her. Janine? No. Sarah? The two women who passed me in the car are whispering to each other and pointing in my direction, and for a horrible moment I think they are talking about me. But then I realise it's someone else they are interested in, someone chestnut-haired and beautiful. She is with a tall, dazzlingly handsome man, who has his arm wrapped tightly around her. I'm staring at the man, thinking how rare it is to come across someone in real life who is properly handsome in that movie star way, when I realise that the woman at his side is Esther. I'm absurdly, pathetically pleased to see her, and rush over.

'You said you weren't coming!' I want to hug her, but I know it will seem too much.

She looks embarrassed. 'Turns out I'm human after all,' she says, glancing at her husband. 'You know what finally decided me? You looking so surprised when I said I was married. This is Brett, by the way. Brett, Louise.'

Still clasping Esther with one hand, he shakes my hand with the other. 'Good to meet you, Louise. Can I get you a drink?'

'Yes, white wine, please.'

'Same for you, darling?' he asks Esther, who smiles her assent.

He releases his grip on her and goes off to the bar, and I turn to Esther.

'What do you mean, you're human after all?'

'I didn't think I cared what anyone here thought of me. Actually, I didn't want to care what anyone thought of me.' She's so scrupulous with herself, so honest about her own motives. 'But you know what? I've worked bloody hard to get where I am. I've got a great career, a gorgeous husband, two lovely children. I'm OK. I'm more than OK, in fact; I'm properly happy. And I'm afraid there's a little part of me – or maybe not so little – that wants to show them, people that might still be laughing about me, or even worse pitying me in a corner of their minds.'

'Well, I'm glad you're here. Do you even recognise anyone?'

We look around. There are vaguely familiar faces, but none of them belong to anyone who I knew well, or was even in our class. There were four classes of thirty kids in our year so there were a lot of them I barely knew.

'Ah. There's someone we know,' says Esther. There's a commotion over by the entrance, someone being embraced and exclaimed over. A man stands back from the group surrounding the new arrival, holding a large white fur coat and looking embarrassed and out of place. I know his face, but it takes me a couple of minutes to realise he's not an old school friend – it's Pete, Sophie's date from the night I went to her flat.

As I look over I catch Pete's eye and smile at him. After a couple of seconds he smiles in grateful recognition and gives a half-wave. Sophie is now engaged in animated conversation with three identikit, Boden-clad blonde women. When it becomes apparent that she's in no hurry to extricate herself, he comes over to Esther and me, and Brett, who is back from the bar with our drinks.

'Hi – Louise, isn't it?' says Pete.

'Yes, that's right. Well remembered.'

'Oh, I always remember names; it's one of my things. I remember everything anyone ever says to me too. It's a nightmare for my old friends, nothing gets forgotten.'

I turn to introduce Esther and Brett to Pete, but a woman I don't recognise has come up and started talking to them, so I leave them to it. I notice that Brett never releases his hold on Esther, his arm tightly glued to her back at all times.

'I didn't realise you and Sophie were serious. How long have you been together?' I ask Pete. I can't put my finger on why, but I'd got the impression that night in her flat that this was a new relationship, if it was even a relationship at all. Until he turned up, Sophie hadn't so much as mentioned his name.

'We're not really.' Pete looks embarrassed. 'This is our third date.'

'Your third date? And you're accompanying her to her school reunion? Jesus, that's a heavy old third date.'

'I know.' Pete shakes his head despairingly. 'I don't know what I was thinking. Well, I do actually. I've got this ... I suppose you'd call it a policy.'

'Policy?' This man is getting stranger by the minute. He seems a very unlikely match for Sophie from what I've seen of him so far.

'Yes. I got divorced a couple of years ago, which was fairly horrendous.'

'Oh, I know. Me too.' I wish the admission didn't make me feel such a failure still. Divorced by forty. I wouldn't normally admit it to a near-stranger, but the fact that he went first bolstered me. I'm not going to tell him that my ex-husband is here though.

'Really?' His face softens. 'You know then. So about a year ago I decided to get back out there. Put myself on a few online dating sites.'

'You met Sophie online?'

He looks defensive. 'Yes. Maybe it's been a while since you were on the whole dating circuit – everybody meets everybody online now. There's no stigma.'

'Yes, I know that.' Don't I just. 'It's more that ... it's Sophie. I can't imagine her doing it.' Sophie, who used to have all the boys hanging from her every word.

'Like I said, everybody does it. Anyway, when I first started, I was so quick to dismiss women – weird voice, nails too long, that sort of thing. My sister said I was deliberately picking holes in them to avoid getting involved. So I made up this rule for myself. If I go on a date with anyone, I have to go out with them at least three times – if they want to, obviously – and I have to say yes to whatever they suggest. As long as it's not illegal, or dangerous.'

'So you've ended up at someone else's school reunion? Someone you hardly know?'

'Yep. That's why I was so happy to see you. You count as an old friend in this scenario.'

I laugh and sip my drink, casting about for something to say, falling back inevitably on the obvious. 'What do you do?'

'I'm an architect – at Foster and Lyme.'

'Oh, I know them. They've put work my way in the past, when John Fuller was there?'

'He was before my time, but I've heard of him. So you're a . . . ?'

'Interior designer. Freelance now, although I used to work for Blue Door.'

Sophie pops up at Pete's elbow, looking annoyed.

'There you are,' she says to Pete. 'Louise, hi, you look great.' She kisses me automatically on both cheeks. 'Isn't this fab? Oh my God, look, there's Emma Frost, she's huge! And Graham Scott has got the most god-awful beard. And did you see Mr Jenkins on the door? I swear he tried to touch me up when he helped me put my badge on, didn't he, Pete?'

Pete shrugs.

'Do you remember all those stories about him, Louise? Natasha Griffiths, wasn't it? Ooh, I wonder if she's here. Pete, can you get us some drinks? More wine, Louise?'

As Pete ambles off to the bar, Sophie turns to me.

'Have you seen Sam yet?' she asks with ill-concealed curiosity.

'Not yet. I see him all the time though. We have a child together, remember?' Emboldened by the glass of wine I've already knocked back, I shoot back. 'Why have you brought someone you hardly know with you?'

Sophie's face falls. 'Did he tell you?'

'Yes, but only because I asked him how long you'd been together.'

Sophie looks embarrassed, and I can't believe I might have found the chink in her armour.

'I'd better tell him not to mention it to anyone else. You won't say anything, Louise, will you? I couldn't face coming here alone when I knew everyone else would be parading their husbands and pictures of their cherubic little children.' She could sound bitter, but in fact the overwhelming impression I get is sadness.

'Hey, I'm here on my own. I think lots of people are.' I put out a hand to touch her arm, pierced by an awareness of our shared history. It's painfully clear to me now that she used me at school to bolster her ego, but that's given me an unexpected insight into the insecurity that must have prompted her behaviour.

'Yes, but that's you, isn't it?' She shakes off my hand. 'It doesn't matter so much, no one's expecting anything from you.' Just like that the vulnerability is gone and she's back to slapping me in the face. 'God, where is Pete with that wine?' she huffs. 'Back in a sec.' She strides off towards the bar.

I'm pretty desperate for another drink myself, and I'm not the only one. You can tell that everyone in the hall is drinking fast in that nervous way you do when you know that the evening can't get started until everyone is at least mildly drunk. When I feel a tap on my shoulder, I assume it's Pete or Sophie with my drink, so I turn eagerly, but when I see who it is my heart sinks.

'Hi Louise,' Sam says with a wary smile. After our last encounter he's probably expecting trouble – weeping and wailing maybe, or at the very least sarcasm and barbed remarks.

I smile and plant a kiss on his cheek. 'Hi. How's things?'

'Good, I'm good,' he says, looking relieved. 'Where's Henry?' He looks around as if expecting to see him helping himself to the crisps laid out at the side of the hall.

'At Polly's. He's fine, he loves it there.' Already I'm bristling, on the defensive.

'I know, I know. No need to be . . . anyway.' He seems to remember where we are. 'You remember Matt, Matt Lewis?'

He gestures to the man next to him. I haven't seen him since our wedding thirteen years ago. He's put on weight and his hair is greying, but he's still recognisably Matt.

'Of course! Great to see you.'

I'm leaning in for a polite hello-kiss with Matt when there's a flurry behind me and Sophie descends on us, followed by Pete holding the drinks.

'Oh my God! You guys!'

She flings herself first into Matt's arms with a casual, 'Hey, gorgeous', and I remember that they are not virtual strangers like the rest of us. They still see each other. It was Matt who told Sophie about me and Sam. Next it's Sam's turn, and she throws her arms around his neck, giving him a lingering kiss on the cheek.

'Wow, you look great, Soph,' says Sam.

'Still got it!' She winks and nudges him with a flirtatious hip.

Pete hands me my wine and I take a gulp. It's sour and not even remotely chilled, but I plough on nonetheless. I'm clearly going to need it.

'So, what's the goss?' Sophie says. 'Who have you seen? My God, have you seen Graham Scott's beard?'

Matt exchanges a glance with me, raising his eyebrows very slightly and smiling, but I notice that his eyes are drawn straight back to her.

'No goss yet, Sophie. Give us time, we've only just got here.' Sam smiles. 'Anyway, you were always the one with all the inside info.'

'Oh yes, I know all and see all.' She laughs, wagging a finger. 'Don't try to keep anything from me!'

Pete is rummaging in his top pocket and pulls out a pack of Marlboro Lights. He sees me eyeing them and holds them out.

'Want one?'

'Oh, go on then,' I say with a smile.

'I thought you'd given up,' Sam says in surprise.

I want to tell him that there's a lot he doesn't know about me. That what he did to me has changed me, that I'm a different person now, but of course I don't. I simply shrug and follow Pete outside. As my eyes adjust to the dark, they are drawn to the corners, the shadows: the places where somebody could be hiding, watching. We perch on a low wall, shivering and wondering whether to go in and get our coats. The wind keeps blowing the matches out and it takes a few goes to get the cigarettes lit. I breathe out a plume of smoke and for the first time all evening I feel my body relax slightly, relishing the cold after the heat and barely suppressed hysteria inside the hall.

‘So,’ I say, ‘did you grow up somewhere like this? A small town in nowheresville?’

‘No,’ he says. ‘I’m London born and bred. Places like this give me the heebie-jeebies.’

‘Have you ever been to a school reunion? Your own, I mean, rather than some random woman’s you met on the internet.’

‘God, no. Can’t think of anything worse.’

‘Oh, OK,’ I say, stung.

‘Sorry, I didn’t mean that other people shouldn’t go to theirs, but it’s not for me, that’s all. I didn’t have the greatest time at school. Bit of a loner, I suppose.’

‘It’s OK,’ I say, thawing. ‘It is kind of a weird thing to do. I mean if it wasn’t for social media, nobody would know anything about the people they went to school with. We’d all just be getting on with our lives. I’ve actually heard of cases where people have got back in touch with their childhood sweethearts on Facebook and ended their marriages, gone back to their first loves.’

‘I stay right away from the whole thing,’ he says. ‘Apart from anything else, it just seems to me like a colossal waste of time.’

‘Yes, you’re probably right.’ There’s a silence, and I wonder whether if I wasn’t on Facebook, Maria would have found another way to reach out to me, to make me pay for what I have done. I’ve made it easier for her by putting myself out there, but it’s hard to hide nowadays, to stay completely off-grid. I take a long drag of my cigarette, and as the smoke burns fiercely down into my lungs, the fleeting sense of relaxation I’ve been feeling out here in the dark is replaced by a familiar unease, my shoulders hunching in response to it.

'So,' says Pete, with the air of a man deliberately changing the subject, 'you were about to tell me in there who you used to work for.'

We're obviously destined never to finish this conversation, however, because our attention is distracted by the sound of a man raising his voice at the top of the school drive. It's not a long drive, and there's a streetlamp right at the top of it. With a feeling of sick dread, I realise that standing under it and facing towards us is Tim Weston, gesturing and remonstrating with someone. The other person has their back to us and is wearing a black coat with the hood up. I can't tell from here whether it's a man or a woman, and although we can hear Tim's voice, the wind makes it impossible to make out what he is saying. Pete and I stand and peer up the drive, he presumably with prurient interest, me with rising fear, both of us straining but failing to hear. The freezing wind seems to be seeping into me, drilling right down to the bone. I squint my eyes, trying to make the shadowy figure into an adult Maria. Could it possibly be her, back here where it all began? Is that what this whole night has been about? I realise that I have no idea who organised the reunion, and haven't yet spoken to anyone who does. I take an unsteady step forward, narrowing my eyes, but as I do, Tim puts his arm around the other person and they leave, walking in the direction of the town centre. I sink back down onto the wall, all the breath punched out of my body.

'Wonder what all that was about,' says Pete. 'It's awful but I love seeing other people having arguments. Everyone's always so keen to show their best face to the world – you know, look at my perfect life, my wonderful family, this elaborate cake I've baked. I find it kind of reassuring to know I'm not the only one fucking things up.'

I force my mouth into a smile, but disquiet bubbles under my skin like a blister. I take a final, shuddering drag of my cigarette, stand up and grind the butt under my heel with unnecessary force.

'Once more unto the breach?' Pete says, standing up too.

We walk back towards the main doors together, and in spite of the cold, I can feel the warmth from him, our arms almost but not quite touching.

Chapter 19

1989

The evening started so well. Sophie brought round several dresses for me to try on, including the one that's now lying scrunched up on the floor beside me. It's a full-length emerald satin sheath ('I'll never wear it,' Sophie had said. 'It's so unflattering on me, it hangs off me in all the wrong places'), unlike anything I'd ever worn before: low cut, pulled in at the waist and off the shoulder, emphasising my curves and making me feel unexpectedly sexy and daring. I added some vertiginous black heels (again Sophie's cast-offs) and a diamond pendant necklace that my parents had given me for my sixteenth birthday, which glinted invitingly millimetres above my cleavage.

I sat doll-like on the edge of my bed whilst Sophie performed her magic. First she smoothed most of my hair back into a ponytail, which she twisted and secured with a diamante clip, expertly pulling a few tendrils free around my face.

Next she methodically layered foundation, powder,

bronzer and blusher before applying the glittery green eyeshadow I'd bought that week in Woolworths. She added black liquid eyeliner along my top lids with a cat-like flick at the outer corner of each eye, and finished with a slick of mascara to my upper and lower lashes. Ignoring *Just Seventeen*'s advice to do either dramatic eyes or lips, but not both, she added a deep plum lipstick that made my lips shine like fat, black cherries.

I couldn't see in the mirror from the bed, so when I stood up to view the finished effect, the stranger who looked back at me took my breath away. There was only the merest of hints, a barely perceptible uncertainty in my eyes, of the dumpy girl with the mousy brown hair who had started the process an hour before. I stood up straighter, pulling in my stomach and pushing my shoulders back. The mousy-haired girl shrank even further away as I took in my newly created hourglass figure, my glittering feline eyes, the diamond twinkling at my throat in the lamplight.

'He's going to love it,' said Sophie, and this time I didn't bother to pretend I didn't know who she was talking about.

Sophie went down the stairs ahead of me in a black Lycra dress so short you could practically see her knickers. I saw my dad's jaw drop in what I hoped was shock; although with disgusted fascination I detected a hint of something else on his face. As Sophie reached the bottom of the stairs to reveal me in all my glory, my mum's face was an uneasy mix of surprise, unwilling pride and something else, which could perhaps have been envy.

My dad recovered himself enough to play chauffeur ('*Your carriage awaits, ladies*'), but I caught the worried look he shot my mum. I loved the fact that I was worrying them.

I'd never felt any power over them before and it was intoxicating. They were frightened – of who I was becoming, of what I might do.

'Take care, love,' Dad said anxiously to me as he dropped us at the school gates.

'Thanks so much, Mr Williams,' purred Sophie as she ostentatiously unfolded her bare legs from the back seat, silver clutch bag in hand.

'You're welcome,' said Dad, looking studiously ahead of him.

As he drove away, Sophie and I looked at each other. I laughed breathlessly and she took my hand. 'Here we go!'

We tottered down the school drive towards the hall, where the music was already thumping. Mr Jenkins was standing behind a small table at the entrance welcoming people and wearing the most embarrassing shirt I've ever seen. He'd trimmed his beard and moustache and obviously thought he looked really cool.

'Good evening, girls. Bags please.' He looked Sophie up and down.

'What?' asked Sophie, her eyes swivelling towards me in panic.

'Bags, girls,' he repeated. 'Put them on the table here and open them please.'

My heart began to thump so loudly I couldn't believe Mr Jenkins wouldn't hear it. I tried not to look at Sophie as I fumbled with the clasp of my tiny black shoulder bag, opening it to reveal a small sequined purse, a mirror and the plum lipstick. He gave it back and then nodded at Sophie, who slowly laid her silver clutch on the table, pressing my foot with hers as she did so. Mr Jenkins lifted the flap and poked a finger inside, shifting the contents about. His finger paused for a second and he reddened, before handing the bag back to her.

'Have a good night, girls.'

We walked into the foyer and I turned to Sophie.

'Where is it? Why were you kicking me like that?' I hissed.

Sophie grinned and pulled down her dress at the front to reveal a small plastic bag of blue pills tucked inside her black lace bra.

'I was just messing with you! You should have seen your face! Good job Mr Jenkins didn't attempt a full body search, he was shocked enough at this!' She plucked a condom from her bag and waved it at me. 'Mind you, he'd love doing a full body search; he's such a perv.'

I gave her a half-hearted shove in the arm, and we walked in and peered around the hall. It was only 7.30 so not yet dark outside, but they'd closed all the curtains and put the disco lights on which had produced a strange twilight effect. Neneh Cherry's 'Manchild' was playing and nobody was dancing except Lorna Sixsmith and Katie Barr who are inexplicably obsessed with the song and know every word.

'There's Matt,' Sophie said, hustling me over to the 'bar', which obviously was only serving fruit juice, coke or lemonade. Matt was surveying the room, effortlessly cool in suit trousers, white T-shirt and Converse trainers.

'God, this is lame,' he said to Sophie. 'Are we really going to stay?'

'Of course!' said Sophie. 'Anyway, don't worry, I've got the supplies you and Sam sorted for me.'

She pulled down her dress again to show him the contents

of her bra, although this time she did it a little slower in an attempt to tease him. I could tell how much he wanted not to look, not to give her the satisfaction, but he couldn't tear his eyes away.

'Look, are you sure about this?' Matt turned to me, pulling his gaze from Sophie's cleavage. 'What if something goes wrong – really wrong, I mean?'

'Oh, for God's sake, don't be such an old woman!' Sophie said. 'It'll be fine – it's only an E. We do them all the time, don't we? Louise isn't worried, are you?' She turned to me impatiently.

'No,' I said untruthfully. In fact I was petrified, but I was keeping my fear, which was a small and solid thing, securely locked in the corner of my mind where I keep unpleasant truths.

'Louise is the one who's got to do it though,' Matt persisted. 'It's easy for you to say.' I was touched that he was willing to challenge Sophie on my behalf, despite his obvious attraction to her.

'No, it's OK,' I said. 'I want to do it.' I couldn't back out on Sophie again. She may have forgiven me for the tampon incident, but if I messed this up, she'd never speak to me again.

'Right, so that's settled. We'll see you later, grandma.' Sophie took my hand and hauled me off to talk to Claire and Joanne on the other side of the dance floor. As the conversation rose and fell, Sophie kept my hand in hers, squeezing it occasionally when one of them said something funny, or particularly dumb. She refused to let the other girls shut me out, deliberately including me in the conversation at every turn, and every time a doubt crept into my mind it was banished by the warm pressure of her fingers on mine. I fizzed inside with anticipation, with the pure joy of sharing a secret with Sophie that the other girls didn't know.

There was only one way into the hall, and I could see the door out of the corner of my eye. On one level I chatted and laughed and took the piss out of other girls' outfits, but all the time I was watching and waiting, hardly able to breathe for the weight of expectation that sat unmoving on my chest.

Around eight o'clock I was rewarded for my vigilance. Maria was wearing a midnight-blue knee-length dress that I'm sure we'd seen in Topshop that day we went to the fair. Her hair was loose and she was smiling at the girl next to her, with whom she was arm in arm. I had to look twice before I realised who it was. Maria must have done her own makeover on Esther as she looked pretty decent in a black skirt and dark red wrap-over top. She even had some make-up on. A couple of steps behind them, eyeballing the room like a bodyguard scanning for potential assassins, came Tim. The girls walked over to the bar, seemingly oblivious to everyone else and ordered two cokes, which came served with a straw, like at a children's party. Maria turned to Tim and asked him something. He shook his head. She looked annoyed and there was a short altercation, which ended with him stomping off to the other side of the hall and flinging himself down in a chair.

I felt Sophie's fingers tug on mine. 'Come on, let's go to the toilet.'

We crammed ourselves into a cubicle and Sophie reached inside her bra for the bag. She took out one of the tablets and put it into another small bag, which she laid on the closed loo seat. Taking a heavy Zippo lighter out of her bag, she started to hammer the pill in its bag. It soon began to break up into smaller pieces and after a few minutes had been reduced to a fine dust.

'OK, that should do it,' she said, holding out the bag, hand totally steady. 'Ready?'

Was I? I took the bag anyway.

'I'll go first, to avoid suspicion,' she said.

I waited for a few moments, eyes closed, fear and excitement sending tiny shockwaves around my body. As I walked back down the corridor to the hall alone, the bag of powder now wedged between my breasts, Matt and Sam were walking towards me. Sam's eyes widened momentarily at the sight of me, and as we drew near I could feel his attraction, tangible in the air between us. Again I felt the thrill of a power I'd never known before. This must be what it was like to be Sophie.

'There you are,' said Matt. 'You know you don't have to do this, right? If it's easier, you could just go home now, say you're not feeling well or something.'

I was moved by his concern, and by his understanding of the fact that I might need an excuse to give Sophie, rather than being able to say I'd simply changed my mind.

'Yeah,' added Sam. 'It's totally up to you. No one's going to think any worse of you or anything.'

Except Sophie. The words hung in the air and even though nobody spoke them, I knew they were in all our minds. I also knew that whatever they said, my decision was already made. I'd made it the night of the party at Sam's house, when I took the E, when I burned my bridges with Maria. If I failed tonight I'd lose Sophie too, and then what would I have?

'Well, as long as you're sure,' said Matt doubtfully. 'I'm going for a slash. Coming, Sam?'

'In a minute, mate,' said Sam, still looking at me.

All the doors to the classrooms along the corridor were closed. I had presumed they were locked, but when Sam tried the handle of the nearest one it turned easily.

'Come in here a minute,' he said.

I followed him inside. The blinds were drawn, and it was fairly dark although there was some light coming in from the corridor through the high panes of glass that ran along the room just below ceiling level.

'You look amazing tonight,' he said softly.

Little flutters rippled through me. I felt like someone else. This was a scenario I had played out so many times in my head, it didn't seem right that it could be happening in real life. I had my back to the wall and as he stepped towards me I rested my weight against it, not trusting my legs to support me. Sam put his hand to my face and traced a finger gently over my cheek and down the side of my neck. A shudder ran through my entire body. He leaned in and I could see his eyes coming nearer and nearer until everything became a blur. He kissed me softly, holding my top lip between both of his for a second before pulling back.

'Is this OK?' he asked.

I nodded, unable to speak.

He kissed me again, harder this time, his tongue exploring my mouth, pressing up against me so closely that I could barely breathe, hands running over the slippery satin of my dress, my insides turning hot and liquid in response. His fingers pressed hard into my flesh, a delicious pain that shot bolts of electricity through my body, and then I felt his hands slip behind me, searching for and finding the zip, beginning to slide it down.

'No!' I gasped instinctively, stiffening in his arms.

He jumped back as if I'd bitten him.

'Sorry! I thought you . . .'

'No, it's OK, I did, I mean . . . I do. It's just – I haven't . . . I'm not used to . . .'

He smiled.

'It's OK. I didn't mean to pressure you. You're just so sexy tonight.'

'Thanks,' I muttered, staring at the floor, hot with shame and fury at myself.

'It's OK, don't worry. Really, it doesn't matter. I shouldn't have pushed so hard. Let's leave it for tonight, yeah? Are you OK?'

'I'm fine,' I whispered.

'OK, I'll see you later, yeah?'

And with that he was gone, leaving me alone in the semi-darkness. I drew a long, shaky breath, only now feeling the coldness of the wall seeping into my back. How could I have been so stupid? Wasn't this what I wanted, what I'd been dreaming about for God knows how long? And what if he told Matt, who might tell Sophie?

I touched the package in my bra, small and unnoticeable to anyone but me. My resolve hardened. I wouldn't let this night be about what had just happened – or not happened – with Sam. This night would be about something else, something so big that no one would remember anything else about it.

Chapter 20

2016

The night wears on. The volume rises. There is laughter, lots of it. There are the promised eighties tunes and bad dancing. I find that there are people here that I know, or knew. Sophie, Maria, Sam, Matt – they've all loomed so large in my mind that I had forgotten that I did have some other friends, especially before that last year at school. Sam has disappeared, swallowed up by the crowd. I've done my bit, had a civil conversation with him. Hopefully I can avoid him for the rest of the night.

The mood in the hall is a potent cocktail of nerves and excitement; as the alcohol levels in our collective bloodstream rise, you can feel everyone slipping back into their teenage selves, as if their adult personas were only something they had been trying on for size.

Despite an ever-present watchfulness in my core, I'm actually having fun, and when Lorna Sixsmith goes off to the bar to get us more drinks so she can carry on telling me about her divorce, I am totally comfortable on my own. I look around the room, smiling in an alcoholic fug, wondering who else the evening will throw my way. A dark-haired woman in a blue linen dress smiles in friendly recognition across the hall and I wave back. I'm so glad I came now. Maybe this is exactly what I needed. Exorcise those demons.

Two women are heading my way, one tall with short blonde hair, expensively highlighted, one short and dark. I don't recognise them at first, but as they draw closer, smiling, the penny drops. It's Claire Barnes and Joanne Kirby.

'Oh my God, Louise!' says Claire, giving me a hug.

I hug her back and Joanne embraces me in turn.

'You look great,' says Joanne.

'Thanks, so do you both,' I say automatically.

'Isn't this weird?' says Claire. 'God, I was so nervous about coming.'

'Me too,' Joanne says fervently. 'Especially since . . . you know, being back here, where it happened. Maria, I mean.'

It's the first time I've heard her name mentioned tonight. I had thought that seeing as we were back here, gathered together in the place she was last seen, that she would be on people's minds, but it seems they have short memories. Not these two though.

'I've always felt so bad about her. I thought about not coming actually,' says Claire. 'It just didn't seem right, you know?'

For a minute I am confused. Claire and Joanne don't know what I did at the leavers' party, do they?

But then Joanne adds, 'I know. We were so mean to her. What shits we were.'

I realise she is talking about our daily campaign of isolation, rather than any particular incident.

'I've got teenage girls now myself,' says Claire. 'I'm always on the watch for anything like this. They get sick of me going on and on about it. If they ever say anything even slightly unkind about another girl, I jump down their throats.'

I tell them about Polly and Phoebe, and how upset Polly is, and they are sympathetic, suggesting more strategies that Phoebe could use to deflect this girl who is making her life a misery. They are kind, decent women, and I can imagine myself being friends with both of them if I'd met them as adults. We exchange promises to keep in touch, and I actually think we might.

I'm about to go and speak to the woman in the blue dress (Katie, it's Katie Barr, the Neneh Cherry fan) when Matt Lewis pops up beside me. I feel a wave of affection. Matt was always nice to me, wasn't he? He even tried to stop me following through with the plan at the leavers' party.

'Hey, you,' I say. Even in my drunken state it doesn't sound natural. I never say 'hey, you'. In fact no one says 'hey, you' apart from in American movies.

Matt doesn't smile; in fact he looks fairly grim.

'I've just been talking to Sophie. She told me about the Facebook thing. What the fuck, Louise?'

I look desperately round. Where is Lorna with those drinks? I spy her over by the bar; she's been waylaid by someone on her way back, laughing and chatting. She doesn't seem in any hurry. The bubble I've been floating around in is abruptly popped.

'What do you mean?'

'Who else knows? Who have you told, Louise?'

Despite the music, he's speaking quietly, so close that I can smell his slightly sour breath, see the pores in his skin.

'I don't know who knows ... I haven't told anyone, but maybe Sophie did, back then ...'

'We were all involved, Louise, and somebody knows. Think. Who have you told? Who else might know what we did?'

'I swear, I've never told anyone about what really happened. God, I don't want it to come out any more than you do. I was the one that ... you know ... you didn't do anything ...'

'Where do you think Sophie got the stuff from?' he hisses.

'Sam got it, didn't he?'

'From me! That's where he got all his stuff!' For a second I think he's going to hit me, but he takes a breath, unclenches his fists. 'Look, my life hasn't worked out the way I planned, OK? I messed up a lot of things, but I've got a new partner now, she has kids, they live with us. I've turned things around. I just don't want anything to fuck that up, OK? Not only did I get the stuff, I lied to the police. It doesn't look good, Louise.'

'I lied too. We all did.' I take a gulp of wine to try and wash away the bad taste in my mouth.

'Right. And we're going to continue lying, all of us. Whatever happens. Is that clear?'

'Yes,' I whisper, barely trusting myself to speak. I suppose I am as selfish as him – I don't want the truth to come out any more than he does, after all – but his ruthless disregard for the horror of what we did turns my stomach. How can he be back here and not feel some of the shame and distress that suffuse me?

'And if you get any more of these messages, I want to know. OK? Here's my number.' He scribbles it down on a piece of paper and shoves it into my hand. I put it carefully into my handbag, although I have no intention of ringing him, or of telling him about the other messages. I just want this encounter to be over.

'OK.' He seems satisfied, and with a surge of thankfulness I see Lorna finally making her way back to me, a brimming wine glass in each hand. Matt spies her too and makes his escape. I thought it was just me that couldn't leave the past behind but it appears I'm not the only one. Just before Lorna reaches me, Sophie bowls over, arms outstretched.

'Louise!' she coos, her fingers pressing into the soft flesh of my forearm. She's very drunk, I realise with a twinge of something that feels like fear. *In vino veritas.* Lorna hands me my wine and smiles at Sophie, who doesn't even acknowledge her. Lorna shrugs and says she'll see me later, rolling her eyes at me behind Sophie's back as she walks off, as if to say, she hasn't changed.

'Where's Pete?' I ask. Typical of Sophie to invite a near-stranger to an event where he knows nobody and then abandon him.

'Oh, I don't know, somewhere around.'

'So you told Matt about the friend request. You might have checked with me first.' I must be drunk myself, standing up to Sophie like this.

'Oh God, I'm sorry. Was Matt angry?'

I wasn't expecting contrition and it throws me. 'A bit, but don't worry about it. You haven't told anyone else, have you?'

She looks guilty. 'Only Sam.'

'Sam knows? When did you tell him? Tonight?'

'Yes,' she says quickly. 'Well, no actually. I phoned him the other day, after you came to see me.'

'You phoned him? Why? How did you even have his number?' The old jealousy rises in my throat, stifling me.

She sighs impatiently. 'Does it matter? I messaged him on Facebook to ask for his number.'

'But why did you want to talk to him about it?'

A strange look passes over her face.

'He was involved, wasn't he?' she says quickly. 'He got us the E. I thought he might have had the same message.'

'And had he?' I say, my head spinning. Why didn't Sam mention this when I dropped Henry off the other day? That must have been why he was weird, asking me if I was OK. And why didn't he say anything when I spoke to him earlier tonight?

'No, he hasn't had anything. Oh God, Louise, what are we going to do? Who's doing this?' I wasn't expecting this panic from her. *In vino veritas* indeed.

'I don't know. Have you had any messages from Maria? Since she friend-requested you?'

'Two.' Her eyes are huge, like a Disney princess.

'What did they say?'

'I had one not long after the friend request that just said "Still looking good, Sophie". And then another one this morning.'

'What did it say?'

'It just said "See you at the reunion, Sophie Hannigan". I mean, it's a message that anyone could have sent. Nothing scary about it, except that it's from her.' Her voice is a whisper and there is real fear in it. 'Oh God, Louise, what shall we do?'

'Why didn't you say all this when I came to your flat? Why did you act like it wasn't a problem?' My cheeks are flushed; she made me feel so foolish for being upset about the Facebook request from Maria.

'I've tried not to think about it. What we did ... I know it was wrong. And we all lied too, didn't we? We lied to the police. But maybe it wasn't all our fault?' She's pleading with me now. 'I mean, who knows what really happened? There was all sorts going on that night.'

'What do you mean?'

She just shakes her head and repeats, 'All sorts.'

I'm going to press her when Pete appears at her side.

'Oh, there you are,' she says vaguely, looking around, anywhere but at him.

'Yes, here I am,' he says, voice heavy with sarcasm. 'I can see you've been worried.'

'Oh, for God's sake, you don't need to follow me round like a ... like a fucking puppy. Just fucking grow a pair.'

She flounces off, stumbling on her heels, making a bee-line for Sam on the other side of the hall.

Pete's face is transformed, pale and angry. 'Nice friends you've got.'

'You're the one who's on a date with her,' I say crossly. There's a beat of silence and then we both start to laugh. It's as if all the tension bound up in the evening has been released in one steady stream of pure mirth, which goes on and on, longer than the joke requires, until gradually we stop, gasping, him pinching the bridge of his nose, me wiping mascara from under my eyes.

'So I guess there's not going to be a fourth date?' I say, when I can speak again.

'Oh yes, I thought I might take her to a wedding next. She can meet my parents, I can show her off to all my friends.'

'Sounds delightful. Or how about a work do, something to impress your colleagues?'

'Ooh great idea. I can tell them all about her job in "fashion".' He does ironic quote marks with his fingers.

'What do you mean? She does work in fashion, doesn't she?'

He snorts. 'Well, if you call working as a sales assistant in a clothes shop "fashion", then yes, I suppose she does. I mean, don't get me wrong, I don't care what anyone does for a living, it's just the pretence that gets to me. She wouldn't even have told me; it was just a slip of the tongue on her part when she was talking about meeting me after work.'

'But that flat in Kensington … how does she afford that if she works in a clothes shop? It must be worth millions.'

He looks at me strangely. 'You don't know her very well, do you?'

'Of course I don't,' I say, surprised. 'I hadn't seen her for over twenty-five years until the other week.'

'Aah,' he breathes. 'She didn't tell me that. She implied that you were old friends who were still in regular touch.'

'No, not at all.' Why would Sophie have wanted to give Pete that impression? 'So how does she afford it?'

'Simple. It's not hers,' Pete says. 'Belongs to some friend of hers who really does have a high-flying job, works away a lot in Hong Kong. Sophie house-sits for her when she's away.'

'Ohhh.' The note of glee in my own voice makes me uneasy. I take a glug of warm wine to try and keep the *schadenfreude* at bay, but it stings as it fizzes down my throat and sits burning in my stomach. So all is not as it seems in Sophie's world. No wonder she looked so shifty when I asked her if she lived there alone.

'I wonder why she told you,' I say.

'Well, once she'd made the slip-up about her job, she could hardly claim to be able to afford that place. And I think maybe . . .' he trails off, his cheeks reddening.

'Maybe what?'

'Well, if she thought there was a future for us, she wouldn't have been able to sustain the lie, would she? Her friend's due home from Hong Kong next week so she'll be back to her one-bed flat in Croydon.'

I half-laugh, not because there's anything particularly wrong with Croydon, but because of the contrast it presents with the elegant Georgian facades of South Kensington. I'm about to ask more when I feel a hand on my elbow, and turn to see Sam. The smile fades from my face. Up until now I've been feeling quite proud of how I coped with seeing him, but his fingers are a red-hot poker on my skin and I step back, folding my arms across my body.

Sam smiles at Pete. 'I'm so sorry, can I borrow her for a minute?'

Pete can offer no defence against the charm offensive that is Sam Parker.

'Oh, sure, OK.' He walks off stiffly, having no option but to head back to Sophie.

Sam turns back to me, and my confidence oozes away with every second that passes. I'm drunk now, my defences lower, and I'm struggling to maintain a calm exterior, desperate not to let him see the effect he can still have on me. I try to relax, deliberately allowing my arm to return to my side; take a slow sip of my drink. I can feel the heat and hustle of the crowd around me, but it's all at a slight remove. The room has shrunk to the two of us, held in our own private atmosphere where the air is cooler and the silences longer, and what we don't say has more power than our spoken words.

'So you know then.' I force myself to speak normally. 'About this Maria thing.'

'Yes.' He looks at me, puzzled. 'Why didn't you tell me? You knew, didn't you, when you dropped Henry off on Saturday?'

'Sophie said you knew then as well. She said she'd already phoned you,' I say, knowing I sound like a petulant child.

'Yes, I did, but I thought if you didn't want to talk to me about it I should respect that. It must have been horrible for you.'

He looks genuinely troubled and upset for me and with a stab of pain I remember the other side of him, how kind he can be. In many ways I am stronger and even happier without him, and I've coped better than I ever imagined I would on my own; but there are times when it would be wonderful not to be responsible for everything, when I would give up all I've gained just to have someone to take the burden of everyday life from me. Sometimes I'm not even sure if what I remember of our relationship is the truth, or whether time and distance has warped my perception. I don't even know if there is such a thing as the truth when it comes to relationships, or only versions of it, shaped by love and fear and the way we lie to ourselves and others.

'Have you heard anything more?' he says. 'From whoever set up the page, I mean?'

'No.' I don't want to let Sam in any more than I have to.

It's bad enough that he knows about this. I don't want it to be the way he seeps back into my life.

'And are there ... has she friend-requested anyone else?'

'Just one. Nathan Drinkwater.'

'Who is that, do you know?' he says.

'I've no idea. It's not someone from school, is it?'

'No, I don't think so. I've never heard of him. Look, Louise, you know I've always stood by you over this, don't you? I helped you, I was the only one who understood.'

He's right, and it's why I miss him so much still, despite everything. He is about to say more, but his attention is caught by Pete and Sophie across the hall, who appear to be arguing. She's laughing but he doesn't seem to be enjoying the joke; in fact he looks to be getting angrier and angrier. Sam eyes them with interest.

'Anyway, I just wanted to say I don't think you should mention anything to Tim about this Facebook thing if he turns up,' Sam says. 'It would be too upsetting for him.'

'I wasn't going to, Sam. What do you think I am, some complete emotional dunce?' I'm back on the defensive. I'd forgotten what conversation with him could be like. Like being pulled from a deep sleep straight up onto your toes, skipping around like a boxer, constantly alert for the next jab.

'No, of course not. Sorry, it was silly of me. I know you wouldn't do something like that.' There's a silence while he seems to be weighing something up.

'It's great to see you properly, Louise. How are you? Are you doing OK?'

He puts a hand on my arm again.

'I'm fine,' I say, taking a step back, wine slopping from

my glass and running down my wrist. I'm not so drunk that I've totally lost Polly's voice in my head, telling me to keep my guard up, not let him see any vulnerability. I swap my glass to the other hand and raise my wrist to my mouth to lick the wine, stop it running any further down my arm and onto my dress. Then I see Sam's eyes on my tongue and I stop, lowering my hand, the wine cold and sticky on my skin. He takes a step towards me and opens his mouth to speak, when there's a commotion on the other side of the room. Pete throws up a hand in what looks like disgust, Sophie flinching dramatically as if he were going to hit her, and strides off, out of the hall. Sophie glares after him, her face alive with rage and humiliation.

'I'd better go and see if Sophie's OK.' I need to get out of this conversation before things get out of control, before I start to lose myself.

Sam looks surprised and a little hurt. 'I thought we could have a catch-up. I know you don't want to hear about . . . you know . . . Daisy and all that, but there's other things – how do you think Henry's getting on at school? He never tells me anything.'

'Fine, he's fine. Make an appointment to see his teacher if you're that interested. I'll see you later.' I practically run away, not to Sophie, but to the relative privacy of the toilets. I lean against the cubicle door, feeling my heart beating all over my body. I put my hands on either side of me, pressing against the wall, as if that will stop me from falling. I can still feel the heat of his hand on my arm, his eyes on my tongue.

The rush of optimism I felt a short while ago has totally dissipated. When my breathing has slowed to something approaching normal, I go back into the hall and across the room I see Sophie and Sam deep in conversation, his hand on her arm. My stomach gives a little twinge. The jokey flirtation of their teenage friendship always upset me, and although I have kept it carefully filed away, my jealousy has never been far from the surface, threatening to burst out, ugly and full of accusation. There's also something else, something about the way his hand rests on her arm, that bothers me. I look around for someone to talk to. It's only ten o'clock, I can't admit defeat and leave yet.

Esther and Brett are sitting on the other side of the hall, holding hands and chatting animatedly to a couple of women I vaguely recognise. Brett has hardly left her side all evening, holding her hand, his arm around her. I guess she's more nervous than she seems. For the next hour I sit with them, nodding and smiling if anyone looks at me, laughing when they laugh, barely joining in the conversation. Being the first to leave seems like such an admission of defeat, but as soon as others start to do so, citing babysitters and early starts, I make my excuses too. I can't face saying goodbye to anyone else and I don't want to risk another encounter with Sam anyway, so I find my coat and slink out of the hall, dropping my name badge on the table as I go.

In the school car park I call the taxi number I carefully programmed in earlier and ask them to come as soon as possible, sitting on a low wall to wait. The sound of the music from the hall rises every time the doors open to expel small groups, coming out in twos and threes to smoke. All of them laugh about how rebellious it feels to be lighting up on school property, as if they're the first ones to think of the joke. My breath streams out as I sit unseen in the darkness and I pull my coat around me more closely. I've forgotten my gloves, so I fold my arms and tuck my hands under, hugging myself tightly.

'Hello again,' says a voice from the shadows.

'Oh my God, don't do that to me!' I jump up, clutching my chest.

'Sorry,' says Pete. 'I didn't mean to scare you. I was hoping you were still here though.'

'What on earth are you doing skulking around out here?'

'I couldn't stay in there. Sophie was being so vile to me, and I don't know anyone else. I didn't want to drag you away from your evening, so I thought I'd wait out here for you.'

'How long have you been out here?'

'Not sure. An hour?'

'But why are you waiting for me? What do you expect me to do about it?'

'Sophie booked us into a B&B, but I can't go back with her now.'

'A B&B? On your third date?'

'I know, I know.' Pete looks slightly shamefaced. 'Anyway, I thought maybe you could give me a lift back to London.'

'A lift? I can't drive, I've had loads to drink. I'm leaving my car here and staying at the Travelodge. Taxi'll be here soon.'

'Oh, shit.' He looks miserable. 'What the fuck am I going to do? The last train from Norwich back to London goes at ten. I've missed it by miles.'

I can't help smiling. 'It's your policy that's got you into this. Why don't you come back to the Travelodge? I only booked it today, I'm sure they'll have rooms. Where's your car, or did Sophie drive?'

'No, I did. She doesn't have a car. It's here too.' He gestures up the school drive. 'We drove over from the B&B, I was going to come and collect it in the morning.'

'OK, well, we can come over together tomorrow.'

We are silent in the taxi, both wrapped in our own thoughts. I check in first, then Pete enquires about a room.

'Sorry, we're full.' The young girl behind the desk is supremely uninterested in what this means for Pete.

'What, you've got nothing? Not even . . . I don't know . . . a room that's not made up? Or one you keep back for emergencies?'

'Emergencies?' the girl repeats, as if Pete has suggested he engage in some sort of deviant sexual practice with her. 'Like what?'

'Oh, I don't know.' He looks at me pleadingly. 'What am I going to do?'

We both know that there's only one solution that doesn't involve him calling another taxi to drive him around the cheap hotels in the area, one after another, in the vain hope that one will have a room. He knows that he can't suggest it though – it's too presumptuous – so he is tacitly leaving it up to me. I can't let him spend the night on a park bench. I turn to the girl.

'Does the bed in my room come apart? I mean, can you make it into two singles?'

'No.' She looks from me to him, her interest piqued.

'I'll sleep on the floor,' Pete says hastily. 'Oh my God, this is kind of you. Thank you so much.'

In the room, we are studiedly polite to each other, taking turns in the bathroom. I thank God I brought decent pyjamas and he declines to take anything off other than his overcoat.

'Look, you don't really have to sleep on the floor,' I say when he emerges from the bathroom. 'Just stay on your own side, OK?'

'Of course. That would be great. If you're sure.' Pete gets under the covers. If he was any closer to the edge he would be on the ground. I climb into my side and turn off the bedside light.

'Good night then,' I say stiffly.

'Good night. And thanks again.'

I pretend to fall asleep straight away, and soon his breathing evens and slows – either he's pretending too or he really is asleep. I stare at the hump of his back, barely visible in the darkness. At the time it felt like a basic human kindness to let Pete share my room. He seems totally decent, apart from his questionable taste in women. But here in the darkness I feel vulnerable. Who is this man? Eventually I fall into an uneasy doze, waking every half-hour or so until around four o'clock when, exhausted, I fall into a deeper sleep.

I slowly become aware of the noise of the TV news, and turn over. Light streams into the room between the gap in the curtains. The bed is empty, the door to the bathroom open.

'Pete?'

No reply. I look around blearily. His shoes and coat are gone.

Before I have time to wonder why the TV is on, the voice of the newsreader pierces my early-morning fug and her words begin to make their way into my brain.

'The dead body of a woman has been discovered by dog walkers in the woods behind a school in Sharne Bay, Norfolk, this morning. Police have not released the woman's name, but it is thought she was attending a reunion at the school last night. They are asking anyone with any information to contact them as soon as possible.'

Chapter 21

1989

Back in the hall, I scanned the room. It was getting darker outside now, so the strange twilight had been replaced by a more conventional disco atmosphere. The heat was rising and, as an overweight boy brushed past me on his way from the dance floor, I felt the dampness of his skin against my arm and smelled fresh sweat and cheap aftershave.

Sophie was talking to Matt; she flicked her hair over her shoulder, her eyes never leaving his face. She had to put her lips close to his ear to be heard over the music, and they gradually moved closer and closer together, the heat from him palpable even from where I stood across the hall. I saw Sophie put her hand softly on the side of his neck to draw him even closer to say something into his ear, and as she did so, Matt bent to kiss her. She pulled away giggling and gave him a playful push. I watched as she danced away from him towards Claire and Joanne, laughing coyly at him over her shoulder. When I looked back at Matt's face, he wasn't laughing at all.

Maria and Esther were sitting at the far side of the room talking animatedly, one of them leaning in every now and then to shout something misheard into the other's ear. There was no sign of Tim. As I watched I saw Maria look around quickly and take a miniature bottle of vodka out of her dress and top up the coke with it. Good. That would make her less likely to taste anything else in there.

I saw Esther gesturing to the door near them, Maria shaking her head, and then Esther leaving, presumably to go to the toilet. Maria sipped her drink, then put it down on the empty chair to her right, looking awkward in the way people do when they are unexpectedly left alone in a busy room. This was the best chance I was going to get.

I threaded my way through the room, watching Maria all the way. I probably didn't have that long, although Esther had gone to the smaller toilet block on the far side of the hall where there was more likely to be a queue. Maria was half-turned away from me, watching the dance floor as I came up on her left. I sat down in the empty chair next to her and she turned, smiling, assuming I was Esther back from the toilets. Her smile faded when she saw that it was me.

'What do you want?' Her hand went to the little gold heart around her neck, twisting it so that the tip of her finger bulged red either side where the chain was biting into it.

I thought fast. What was the best tack to take?

'I wanted to apologise – again.'

'Apologise? Seriously? Don't you think you're a bit late?' Maria gave a bitter laugh, her face hard with no trace of the forgiveness she had granted me at the party at Matt's house.

'I know. I'm sorry.'

'For God's sake, stop saying you're sorry! Where has

"sorry" been for the past two months around school? Where was sorry when you put that . . . that *thing* in my bag?'

'Well, that wasn't me, but I'm so sor—' I broke off, anticipating her anger.

'Just fuck off and leave me the fuck alone, Louise,' she said, standing up. 'I never want to see or speak to you again.'

She walked off across the hall, but as Esther wasn't back yet from the toilets she didn't really have anywhere to go, and I saw her hesitate at the edge of the dance floor, which had filled up since I sat down.

Adrenaline pumped through my veins, my skin tingling with a million pins and needles. I felt breathless with daring and alive with the fear of being caught. I slid my fingers inside my bra and hooked out the package. A group of boys jostled each other in front of me, one of them tripping over my foot. I knew him slightly, this boy. Johnny Majors. He wasn't cool, but he was funny, popular. He looked down with an apologetic gesture. I smiled, closing my hand around the plastic bag. *No problem*, I mouthed, the volume of the music making actually saying anything difficult. Johnny Majors smiled at me then, this boy that had never so much as glanced in my direction in five years at school together, his eyes taking in my curves, the flush on my cheeks. There was clearly something in me he had never seen before, something inviting and dangerous. There was a moment, just a heartbeat, where he almost sat down next to me. I had a vision of us talking, laughing, giddy on the newness of it. Imagined him kissing me as I slipped my hand behind me and dropped the little plastic bag and its explosive contents onto the floor behind the chairs, to be found and exclaimed over by the caretaker later.

Then my eyes slid from his laughing face to where Sophie stood on the other side of the hall, her eyebrows raised, gesturing furiously at me. I looked down at the floor, and saw Johnny's trainers retreating out of my view. I opened my hand and stared at the bag, at the innocent-looking blue powder. I remembered how the E had made me feel at Sam's party: light, unfettered, joyous. Would it be so bad to make Maria feel that way too? In a deep, secret part of me I knew the answer to that question, but I pressed it down so hard that it had no room to breathe. I buried the part of me that knew we weren't doing this to make Maria feel good; that we were doing it to humiliate her, hoping to provoke her into making a fool of herself. To go down in school history as the ones who dared to go that bit further. No silly pranks, no knickers on the flagpole. We would bring everyone together in horrified fascination as Maria came up, not knowing why she felt so uninhibited, so full of joy and love. We wanted to see what would happen, and that wanting was stronger than any worries about safety, or the morality of what we were doing.

I looked over at Sophie again, who was still staring at me, no words necessary to communicate what she was saying. I had a sense of being suspended, teetering on the edge of a cliff; and then I was falling, falling: opening the bag, tipping the contents into Maria's coke, stirring it frantically with the straw, willing the powder to dissolve quickly. My eyes darted around the room, but nobody was looking at me – and even if they did, all I was doing now was stirring my own drink. Unless you looked very closely, you wouldn't be able to see how much my hands were shaking. I looked down again into the glass – there was nothing to be seen now, it looked exactly as it had before. It occurred to me that actually, I hadn't quite fallen, not yet. I could take the drink to the toilets and pour it away. My hand hovered around the glass, but as I looked over to Sophie, I saw that she was beaming, her face alight with happiness, her hands aloft in a big thumbs up. Before I could change my mind, I forced myself onto my feet and went over to Maria, who was still standing uncertainly by the dance floor.

'It shouldn't be you who has to run away, or give up your seat,' I said, my heart thumping as much as the music. 'I'll go.'

She looked unsure.

'Go on – Esther will be expecting you to be there when she gets back. I'll go over there,' I gestured to the other side of the hall, where Sophie watched me with glee. 'I promise I won't bother you again.'

She glared at me suspiciously and then stalked back to her seat. As I walked over to Sophie, I looked back and saw Maria's hand go to her heart necklace again, twiddling it nervously. She picked up her glass, put the straw to her lips, and drank.

I think about this now, less than twelve hours later, sitting motionless on my bedroom floor. About the last time I saw her. After I'd mixed in the powder, I went to tell Sophie. She was elated, made a huge fuss of me. I didn't particularly want to do an E – I was high on the sheer daring of what I'd done – but she persuaded me. She'd taken one too, and when they started to kick in she led me onto the dance floor. For the second time in my life, I felt totally uninhibited, letting my body move to the music in any way it wanted. For the next two hours I thought of nothing else but the music and the physical, animal joy of giving myself over to it. The dance floor filled up (I don't think we were the only ones who'd managed to get something past Mr Jenkins) and after a while I lost track of everyone: Sam, Matt, even Sophie. Boys who had never looked twice at me were eyeing me in a new way. I felt as though I'd shed my skin and left the old me behind, lying discarded somewhere no one ever goes.

Eventually Sophie resurfaced, wanting to go to the bar and get water.

'Where have you been?' I asked her.

'Oh, around and about.' She gave a secret smile, more to herself than to me. I felt a tightening inside. Had she been with Sam, the two of them laughing about my frigidity, their heads close together, Sophie's perfect body radiating heat and invitation? Or with Matt, all thoughts of protecting me from Sophie's scorn driven from his head by his desire for her?

'Where is Maria anyway?' I asked. 'She must be coming up by now.' Lost in the moment, I had temporarily forgotten that this was what it had all been about. Of course it had never really been about Maria for me, only about myself and Sophie, and what this act could do for me, where it could take me.

Sophie smiled to herself again.

'What's so funny?' I asked. 'I thought you wanted to see her off her head. That was the whole point, wasn't it?'

She shrugged and looked around, but Maria was nowhere to be seen. I could see Esther crossing the room towards us, and with a lurch in my stomach I realised she was coming to speak to me.

She wasted no time on preliminaries. 'Louise, have you seen Maria?'

'No, not for a while. Why?'

I suppose at this stage I should have felt the shadow of what was coming, or at least a mild sense of foreboding, but I was still buoyed up by the euphoria that being someone else for the night had given me.

'She said you were talking to her earlier. What did you say?'

'I'm not sure that's any of your business.' I wondered uneasily how much Maria had told Esther.

'I think she's gone off somewhere. She said she wasn't feeling well ages ago, went to the toilet and now I can't find her.'

Perhaps it was then that the first tiny seed of doubt began to sprout.

'Maybe she's talking to someone outside, or in one of the classrooms?'

'Like who?' Esther said scornfully. 'You and your lovely friends have made sure that no one in their right mind wants to hang out with her. I thought you had better taste than that, Louise.'

Her words stung my cheeks with a shameful flush. I wasn't used to Esther confronting me like this. I preferred not to think about her, about how close we had once been.

'The only person I thought she might be with is her brother, but I can't find him either,' she went on.

Relief flooded me, mixed with disappointment that we weren't going to see Maria losing it on the dance floor like we'd hoped.

'She's obviously gone home with him then. You said she wasn't feeling well.'

'She would have told me if she was leaving. She wouldn't have left me here on my own.'

'Are you sure, Esther? How well do you actually know her?'

I could tell from her face that this had stung Esther exactly like I had wanted it to.

'You know what, Louise? Forget it. You obviously don't care or want to help. I hope for your sake nothing has happened to her. I'm going to call my mum to pick me up, so if you do see her can you tell her I've gone home?'

For a while everything was a blur of dancing and talking and laughing, and then before I knew it, it was midnight. Like Cinderella's coach turning into a pumpkin, the music stopped, the harsh lights were switched on, everyone was pale and sweaty and the room was just the school hall again.

After that, another blur. Maria's mum Bridget coming to pick her up: mildly concerned at first, becoming frantic with worry when Tim appeared and turned out to have been there the whole time and not to have seen Maria either. My dad arriving to collect me as Bridget was being led off to the school office to phone Esther's house. Hearing Mr Jenkins asking Bridget if there were any other friends they could try calling, and the heat that spread through me like a virus as she turned to me, rage and shame etched on her face, shaking her head – no, there was no one else. Hearing the words police and missing person and twenty-four hours.

The warm night had given way to a heavy summer downpour, raindrops thundering on the windscreen as Dad asked me what was going on. I tried to keep up a semblance of normal conversation, to pretend I was perfectly sober. Tried to pretend I was still his daughter, still the same girl who had left the house a few hours before.

And then there was just a space. I sat on my bedroom

floor all night and stared into it. A space where Maria should have been: dancing, going crazy, hugging people without knowing why. Being watched by me and Sophie, nudging each other and giggling. Waking up in the morning feeling like crap and not knowing what had happened.

But Maria has simply disappeared into this empty space, leaving only the shadow of a scornful laugh, a golden heart on a chain, a wisp of smoke in the night air.

Chapter 22

That night was the end of everything, and the beginning. The end of something is always the start of something else, even if you can't see it at the time.

What does she remember? The heat of the day that lingered on into the evening; the ceaseless rain that followed; the earth beneath her feet, solid and unyielding; the way she floated up above her body for a moment, wondering what was going to happen next, almost as if it had nothing to do with her at all.

Sometimes she doesn't know who she is any more. What she does know is that the girl she was died that night, and somebody else took her place. Ever since, this new person has been scrabbling for a foothold, clinging on to the rock face, dirt under her fingernails. Like trying to breathe underwater.

There are very few people in her new life that know about the old one. It's better that way. She avoids the awkward questions, changes the subject. Acts like she is a normal person, just like everyone else. When underneath her skin, guilt and lies crawl like cockroaches.

When you leave something behind you, you think that's it. It's gone. But you can't leave yourself behind. This is it; this is you, for life.

She's been ignoring the past for a long time, but she's beginning to wonder if she will be able to ignore it for ever. It lives in her, like a tumour or a parasite. Maybe now it's time to try and make sense of it, to wrench it out into the light, examine it. Face it.

Maybe it's only by going back that she will be able to move forward.

Chapter 23

2016

I sit in bed in the Travelodge, sipping metallic-tasting tea heavy with the unmistakeable tang of UHT milk, glued to the TV. The journalists obviously haven't been given any information, but they are spinning out the story nonetheless. The police clearly won't let them speak to the dog walker who found the body, so they've interviewed other dog walkers, who can only say versions of the same thing. No, they didn't see anything. No, nothing like this has happened here before. The empty space in the bed where Pete was gapes beside me, but I can't even begin to probe my feelings about that now.

My mind is twisting and turning, trying to make sense of it. I need to know who it is. Please let it be one of those nameless, anonymous women, the ones I didn't even recognise last night. The police will want to talk to everyone who was at the reunion, I am sure of that. I will call them, find out, and when I know it's a stranger, that will be it, it will be over. They've given a number to ring on the news, so I reach for my mobile, my thumb jabbing at the numbers.

They won't tell me on the phone, of course. They want to speak to everyone who was at the reunion and ask me if I can come in straight away to the makeshift incident room they've set up in the school hall. I call a cab, showering and dressing quickly, my need for the body in the woods to be a total stranger pressing within me like an overfull bladder.

In the cab I text Polly to check Henry's OK. She texts me back a terse, 'He's fine', with no kisses. It's not like her, but I guess she's in the middle of making breakfast or something. As we near the school I see police cars and a big, outside-broadcast van from the local TV station. A crowd of rubberneckers has already gathered, despite the fact that it's nine o'clock on a Sunday morning, and a freezing wind is buffeting in from the sea.

'Whereabouts you going, exactly?' asks the cab driver. 'Dunno if I can get all the way down here, looks like they might have closed the road off. You heard about what happened?'

He pulls over and I pay him, telling him I'll walk the rest of the way if I can. I climb out into the cold, my town-dweller's coat no protection against this vicious east-coast wind.

There's a police car blocking the road, with a young policeman in uniform standing beside it. As I cross the road, he comes over to me.

'Can I help you?'

I explain that I was at the reunion last night and have been asked to come in. His face changes and he asks me to wait for a few minutes while he speaks to someone. He moves away a little so that I can't hear what he's saying, muttering into his walkie-talkie. I stand awkwardly by the car, looking around. I am watching the reporter I saw earlier on TV trying to tame her flying hair into some kind of submission in preparation for another live broadcast, when the policeman comes back.

'OK, you can go down to the hall now. Ask for DI Reynolds.'

I retrace my steps from last night down the school drive, my neck buried in the collar of my coat, trying to control my breathing. It's a relief to get inside out of the wind. The hall looks different in the cold light of day. The disco, the debris, the banners from last night; it's all gone. At a nearby table Mr Jenkins is sitting alone, unshaven and pale. He takes the cup of tea proffered by a uniformed policewoman gratefully. I am reminded that I don't know who organised the reunion. I can't imagine it was the school itself; surely they've got better things to do. But somebody must have dealt with the school, set up the Facebook page, gone round with a bin bag last night and swept the floor, though I have no idea who. Nobody seems to be coming to talk to me, so I walk over to him.

'Mr Jenkins?'

'Yes?' He looks up, his face all dark shadows and worry.

'Hello. It's Louise Williams.'

'Oh, hello there. You were there, were you . . . last night?' He doesn't show any sign of recognising me, either from the reunion or from school. I suppose I was neither a brilliant student nor a particularly naughty one: completed my homework on time, didn't play up in class, achieved good if not outstanding grades. I slipped under the radar.

'Sorry to intrude, but I was wondering ... do you know who organised the reunion? Was it the school?'

'No,' he says. 'It was a former student who contacted us and asked if it would be OK to use school premises. She booked the bar and sorted the licence and all that, hired someone to decorate the hall, clean up afterwards, everything. Just asked that we provide a member of staff to man the door. She thought it would be nice to have that connection to the school. I didn't mind doing it.'

'Did you meet her? The woman who organised it?' I try to keep my voice neutral.

'No, it was all done by email.'

'And ... what was her name?' I struggle to form the words.

He looks around as if for permission from the police, but there's no one nearby. 'I suppose it doesn't matter,' he says doubtfully. 'Her name was Naomi Strawe.'

'Oh. Straw? As in dry grass?'

'No, with an e: S-t-r-a-w-e.'

I don't remember anyone of that name. My heartbeat slows a little.

'Was she in our year?'

'She said she was. I think there was a Naomi, wasn't there? Maybe Strawe was her married name. To be honest we didn't really check whether anybody was actually from the class of 1989.' He looks worried. 'I just assumed that anybody who wanted to come would be from your year – I mean, why else would you go to a reunion?'

'So did she show up, this Naomi?'

'No. That's the strange thing. There was a badge for her – she sent me all the badges of the people who'd said they were attending, and hers was one of the only ones left.'

Not the only one. There would have been a Tim Weston badge left on that table as well. I'm about to ask more, when I see a tall, bulky woman in a dark trouser suit making her way over to us.

'Louise Williams?'

I agree that I am, and she introduces herself as Detective Inspector Reynolds, asking me to come and sit down with her in the corner where there is a desk with a laptop and a few chairs.

'Thanks for coming in, Ms Williams.'

'Louise,' I say automatically.

'Louise. PC Wells tells me that you were here last night at the school reunion.'

'Yes, that's right.' I feel as if I am in a dream, floating above myself. What has happened to my carefully ordered life, where has it gone? How did I end up here?

'You've heard what has happened, obviously?'

'Yes, I saw it on the news.'

'So, as you know, we have found the body of a woman in the woods. The victim had her bag with her, so we've been able to make a provisional identification.'

'So . . . are you able to tell me?' Please God, let it be someone I don't know.

'Yes.' I can tell that she is watching me closely. 'The victim is Sophie Hannigan.'

My face somehow stays neutral but my body feels trembly and effervescent, as if my blood has been replaced with carbonated water.

'You didn't know her?' She sounds disappointed. She was expecting a gasp, tears, even a small scream. But as I stare at her unmoving, clearly struggling with the simple task of breathing in and out, the truth begins to dawn on her.

'You did know her?'

I nod without speaking and Reynolds sits in silence too, allowing me the time to process the information. She probably thinks I am in shock, but I am not shocked. All that happens is that the dull ache in my stomach that has been there since I first heard the news back in the Travelodge intensifies. It twists and grips. This is what I have been expecting all along.

'Yes, I knew her,' I manage eventually. Did I really? 'I mean she's not a close friend now, but she was once. I hadn't seen her since school, apart from once, a couple of weeks ago.'

'Why was that? Where did you see her?' She looks interested. I think fast. I can't tell her about the friend request from Maria; it brings up too many other questions, questions I don't want to answer.

'I contacted her when I found out about the reunion ... thought it would be nice to meet up beforehand. I hadn't really stayed in touch with anyone since school, and I thought it might be a bit much, turning up at the reunion cold, if you know what I mean. Meeting up with Sophie that night made the whole thing easier.'

'How did you get hold of her?'

'On Facebook.' I try to keep my voice level.

'And how was she, that night?'

'Fine. Looking forward to the reunion. She didn't seem to have changed much since our school days, not really.'

'And was there anyone she was looking forward or not looking forward to seeing at the reunion?'

'She was excited about it, but she didn't mention anyone in particular. I don't think she had any qualms or fears. She was one of those popular girls at school, you know?'

'Mm hmm.' She tries to maintain her blank facade but I can tell she wasn't one of those girls herself, and also that she knows I wasn't either. I can see DI Reynolds at sixteen, as tall and wide as she is now, her hair longer then, hanging greasily down her back, lumbering into the classroom, tripping over her chair, the pretty girls sniggering. Always at the front of the class, top marks for everything. Knowing, however, that popularity at school isn't everything, waiting it out, best results the school has ever seen, and then off. Off to university where she could reinvent herself, find her tribe.

'OK. Moving on to the reunion itself, do you remember when you last saw Sophie?'

'Around ten o'clock, I think.'

'Is that when you left?'

'No, I left around eleven, but I don't think I saw her later than ten.'

'Did you spend much time with her?'

'Not a great deal, no. We chatted, caught up, you know. There were a lot of people there.'

'And how did she seem?'

I think of Sophie clutching my arm, panicking. She was frightened.

'She seemed fine,' I say, unable to quell my own panic. I'm digging myself in deeper and deeper here, so scared of saying the wrong thing that I'm not telling Reynolds anything at all. 'Although, as I said, I hadn't seen her for years, so I don't know if she was her usual self or not.'

'Did she spend time talking to anyone in particular?'

'I saw her talking to Claire Barnes, Sam Parker, Matt Lewis . . .' I list a few more names, trying to recall each time I heard her laugh, saw her kissing people extravagantly, tossing her hair. Reynolds is taking it all in.

'And did she come to the reunion with anyone?' she asks.

I hesitate – just a tiny bit, but she's good, she notices straight away. For some absurd reason I feel guilty about dropping Pete in it, which is ridiculous as other people are bound to mention it.

'Sophie was at the reunion with a man. Pete.'

'A boyfriend?' Reynolds' ears prick up. I've got the stick and she can sense that I'm about to throw it for her. 'Do you know his surname?'

'No, sorry. I don't think he was exactly a boyfriend either; apparently they'd only been out a couple of times before. She met him online.'

'And she brought him to her school reunion?' She looks sceptical.

'I know. I asked her about that, but she said she didn't want to come on her own, not with everyone else married and talking about their children and stuff.' My voice falters and tears gather in my throat. Poor foolish, vain Sophie. I've been so busy berating myself for being wrapped up in what my teenage friends think of me, it never occurred to me until now that Sophie had cared even more than I did, with her pretend job in fashion . . . her borrowed flat . . . Pete. I think of Esther with her trophy husband glued to her side, passing round pictures of her children on her phone. None of us are immune, it seems.

'Take your time.' Reynolds' voice is kind, but she is watching me carefully.

'It looked like they were having an argument, towards the end of the evening. Not long before I last saw her.'

'And was that the last time you saw him? Did he leave without her? Or was he there looking for her at the end?'

It's like I've walked into a brick wall that I didn't even see coming. I've heard the expression about sweaty palms, but until now I didn't realise it was a real thing. I'm going to have to tell Reynolds that I spent the night with Pete. But how does that look? He was Sophie's boyfriend. Who would believe me if I say nothing happened between us in that hotel room? It will set Reynolds off on a chain of questioning that could lead to the friend request from Maria. They're bound to be looking at Sophie's social media accounts, but at the moment, all they will see from Maria is a couple of innocuous messages: *Still looking good, Sophie; See you at the reunion, Sophie Hannigan.* There's nothing to arouse suspicion there.

But if Reynolds suspects that I slept with Sophie's boyfriend on the night of her murder, she's going to want to look at me very closely. And if she looks at my social media, and finds the messages from Maria to me, she's going to have questions. Questions I don't want to answer. I can't bear for anyone to know what I did to Maria. And more than that, I can't risk the possibility of going to prison. Of course there's no body, but there are other people who know what happened at the leavers' party. Maybe not even just Matt and Sam – I wouldn't be surprised if Sophie let it slip to other people over the years. As Sam always used to say to me, it's just not worth the risk of letting anyone know what happened. And I have Henry now. If there's even the slightest chance that I could go to prison, I need to take what I did to Maria to my grave. I can't leave Henry without his mother.

I've spent so long hiding in the shadows, covering up the truth that I can't stop now.

'I don't know,' I say, my whole body itching with panic. 'I didn't see him.'

'Do you know where we might find him, this Pete?'

'Sorry, no. I only know his first name. And that he lives in London.'

'OK,' says Reynolds, leaning back in her chair. 'We'll want to speak to you again in due course, but if there's nothing else significant that you think we should know now?'

'No, nothing.'

'Just one more thing,' she says, pulling a brown envelope out of her inside pocket. 'We found something near the body.' She reaches into the envelope and pulls out a clear plastic bag. I can see what it is before she says any more, and it takes all my strength to keep my hands relaxed in my lap and my breathing steady.

'Have you ever seen this before?' she asks.

It sits there innocently on the table between us.

'No.' I try to answer naturally, evenly, speaking neither too quickly nor too slowly.

'Sophie wasn't wearing it?'

'No, definitely not. She was wearing a big, silver statement necklace.'

Reynolds doesn't say anything, just slips the clear plastic bag back into the envelope. A plastic bag containing a slender chain with a small golden heart hanging from it. Even though it's been more than twenty-five years since I last saw it, I would know that necklace anywhere. It haunts my dreams. Without a shadow of a doubt, that is Maria Weston's necklace. The one she was wearing the night she disappeared.

Chapter 24

2016

Polly takes a while to get to the door. She looks awful, like she's been crying. Her hair is unbrushed and there are dark circles under her eyes.

'Oh! What's the matter? Is everything OK?' I ask.

'Yes,' she says dully. 'Come in.'

I follow her down the hall, nonplussed. I texted her briefly before I left Norfolk to let her know what had happened, so I was expecting more of a reaction from her to the cataclysmic events of the last twenty-four hours. Of course, Polly has no idea of the implications for me, but it's shocking news nonetheless.

I pop my head into the sitting room. Henry and Maya are curled up together on the sofa, Henry sucking the soft edge of Manky.

'Hello, H. I'm back. Hi, Maya.'

They barely look up from the cartoon.

'Hi Mummy. Can I watch the rest of this?'

'Yes, of course.' Polly and I carry on into the kitchen and I swing myself up onto one of the high stools at the breakfast bar. I love the idea of a breakfast bar, but as usual the stool is uncomfortably small and I don't know what to do with my feet.

'Was he all right?' I say.

'Yes, good as gold. No trouble.'

'Where's everyone else?' The house is very quiet.

'Aaron and Phoebe are still in bed. Tea?' she asks perfunctorily, already filling the kettle.

'Yes, please.'

As the water boils, Polly comes to herself a little, as if she's making a deliberate effort to snap out of whatever state she is in.

'So, come on then, tell me. It was definitely this girl that you knew, the one you went to see the other week?'

'Yes, it was Sophie.'

'So had you talked to her much – at the reunion, I mean?'

'A bit. Not that much. There were so many people there.' I find myself playing it down again. It's easier since I'm lying to the police to tell everyone else the same lie. It frightens me how smoothly the untruths slip from my tongue, even to Polly. She's supposed to be my best friend yet she knows so little about me.

'It's so awful. The poor woman. Who do you think did it? Is she married?'

'No. Why?'

'Well, they say in ninety-nine per cent of cases it's the husband, don't they?'

'I'm not sure it's that high, but . . . she was there with a man though, a boyfriend.'

'Ooh, what was he like?'

I don't reply straight away, which Polly misinterprets.

'Do you think he did it?' She takes a biscuit and dunks it in her tea.

'No!' We are both a bit surprised by my vehemence.

Suddenly the effort of lying to Polly feels too much. I am so desperately tired of carrying this terrible weight around with me, and surely Polly would be the best person to help me to bear it. She loves me. She would understand.

'This is going to sound weird, but ... Pete – that's Sophie's boyfriend – spent the night in my hotel room.'

Polly's hand halts halfway to her mouth and half her dunked biscuit plops into her tea.

'What?'

'It wasn't like that. They had a row, and it was too late for him to get back to London on the train, so he came back to the Travelodge with me but they didn't have any rooms. So ... I said he could share with me. Nothing happened. We just went to sleep, and when I woke up this morning, he was gone.'

'Bloody hell, Louise.'

'I know.'

Polly stands up and crosses the kitchen, rummaging in the cutlery drawer for a spoon to fish the soggy biscuit out of her tea.

'How did it even come about?'

'Like I said, he and Sophie had a row, so he waited for me in the car park.'

'He waited for you? That's a bit creepy.'

'Not really ... I was the only other person he knew there – I told you I met him at Sophie's flat. He thought I'd be coming back to London.' Didn't he? A thought niggles at me – surely he knew how much I'd been drinking, can he honestly have believed I'd be driving?

'Still. You do realise you might have spent the night snuggled up to a murderer?'

Of course this has occurred to me, but I can't let that distract me right now. My mind is too full of other things.

'We weren't snuggled up. And he's not a murderer. He's a nice bloke.' Why am I defending him?

'Oh my God, do you fancy him? You do! You fancy the murderer!'

At any other time I would be delighting in Polly's ability to lighten any given situation, however grim. This one can't be lightened though. It's too dark.

'No, it's not that.' I don't really know how I feel about him. Maybe, if things were different, there would be something there. But they're not different. They are dark and ugly and Pete is entangled in it somehow.

'And seeing Sam? How was that?' she asks as she sits back down at the breakfast bar.

'Fine,' I say, thinking of wine running down my wrist, Sam's eyes on my tongue.

'Just fine?' says Polly, instantly suspicious.

'Yes, honestly. I hardly spoke to him.' More lies.

'Good,' says Polly. 'Probably just as well you ended up sleeping with that Pete bloke.'

'I didn't sleep with him! Not like that anyway.' It was probably the most peculiar night I've ever spent with anyone, and that's saying something.

'I know, you said. So what did the police say about the fact that you spent the night with him?'

I consider lying again but I can't bear for this to get any more complicated than it already is. 'I didn't tell them.'

'What? Why on earth not?'

Oh God, how to explain this to her?

'It was instinctive. I didn't really think about it. It just seemed better if they didn't know.'

'But why? Louise, don't be crazy, you can't lie to the police. Call them now – tell them you made a mistake. It's better if it comes out now, from you, rather than down the line.'

It's so hard to make her understand without telling her the truth about what I did to Maria.

'It's complicated. It's all to do with stuff that happened when we were teenagers. There's something I don't want the police to know. I . . . I can't explain.' My voice catches and Polly looks at me in concern.

'What on earth do you mean? Why can't you tell me?'

I shake my head, my face in my hands.

'Louise.' She pulls my hands away and looks me in the eye. 'There's nothing you can't tell me. Come on, we've been friends for what . . . thirteen years? You won't get rid of me that easily. What is it?'

I want so badly for her to understand. I can't bear feeling so alone with this. Before Sophie was killed, I could cope, I could manage it, but everything's spiralling out of my control. The thought of telling Polly everything, letting her in, feels like sinking into a feather bed.

'You know I told you that Sophie got the Facebook request too, from Maria, the girl who drowned? Well . . . I didn't tell you everything.' I breathe deeply, trying to get my voice under control.

'What d'you mean?'

'Sophie and I, we … we weren't always very nice to Maria.'

Polly frowns. 'Not very nice how?'

If I look up, I'll lose my nerve. 'We were … mean to her. When I told you that I'd experienced something similar to what Phoebe's going through … well, I did, but more from the other side.'

I daren't look at her. I swallow and continue.

'I was friends with Maria when she first joined the school, and then, later, well … I wasn't. Sophie didn't want me to be friends with her, you see, and Sophie was so … And then on the last night, at the leavers' party, the night she died, we did something terrible.'

'What did you do?'

I glance up quickly. Polly's face is pale, confusion written all over it.

Just say it. I close my eyes.

'We spiked her drink with Ecstasy. Nobody ever saw her again. She must have wandered off and fallen from the cliff.' I open my eyes and risk looking up. Straight away I know I've made a terrible mistake.

Polly is staring straight at me, white-faced and horrified.

'You spiked her drink? Were you not listening to me at all when I told you what's been happening with Phoebe? I can't believe you talked to my daughter about it, gave her advice when all the time you …' She pushes her stool back and stumbles off it, backing away from me until she hits the kitchen worktop, clutching it for support.

'Do you know why I look like shit this morning?' Her voice is harsh with accusation. 'It's because I've been up half the night with Phoebe. She was meant to be at a sleepover last night but I had to go and get her in the middle of the night after the mother became "concerned" because Phoebe was causing trouble and upsetting another girl. No prizes for guessing which particular girl came up with that little story. She cried for two hours when we got home. Two solid hours. Do you know what that's like, to watch your child like that?'

I shake my head.

'I'm sorry about what happened last night. It's awful. But it's not a good day for you to be telling me all this, Louise. Not after what I've just been through. I'm not in the mood to be understanding or forgiving, or whatever it is you want me to be. Not about this, not about teenage girls being fucking vile to girls who are supposed to be their friends.'

I had half-expected, and dreaded, ranting and raving but this hard, cold fury is worse. I thought Polly was in my corner, but of course she's not. She has children, and children trump everything, like a royal flush in poker.

'I think you'd better go actually. I need to focus on Phoebe today; I don't have any headspace for you . . . for this. I can't deal with it right now. I'll give you a call.'

I've known all my life that I couldn't tell anyone about what I did to Maria, but this thing with Sophie has thrown everything up in the air. I thought it made things different, but it doesn't, of course it doesn't.

As I drive away from Polly's house, I start to cry silently, and find that I can't stop. Henry is prattling away in the back about what he had for dinner and how Phoebe read to him before she went out. Thank God I didn't let him sit in the front as he had wanted to. I keep wiping the tears away with my hand, but more come. As I sit at the traffic lights, an old woman with a wheeled shopping trolley looks at me curiously.

I try to force my mind to concentrate on something else. I need to be not crying by the time we get home; I don't want Henry to see me like this. Naomi Strawe. I know there was no one of that name in my year at school. Strawe is an unusual name, one I'm sure I've never heard, although as Mr Jenkins said it could be her married name. I don't remember a Naomi though. I think of him spelling out the name, with his emphasis on the 'WE' at the end. The first two letter of Weston. With a churning sensation, fear beginning to shift within me, I whisper the letters out loud, jumbling them around in my head, the realisation gradually dawning. Naomi Strawe is an anagram of Maria Weston.

Someone followed me through the tunnel at South Kensington. Someone was watching me as I sat alone in that bar, waiting for a date who was never going to show. Was that someone there last night at the reunion, unseen, hovering at the edges, waiting for who knows what? I've been running on pure adrenaline since the initial, numbing shock of the discovery of Sophie's body, but that's wearing off now, and the implications are crowding in on me. I can't ignore the possibility any longer that Maria is still alive. Or if she's not, then whoever killed Sophie knows what happened to her; knows what I did. And Polly's reaction has hammered home another truth to me: I glance in the mirror at Henry's face, with its impossibly smooth skin, rounded, still babyish cheeks and long eyelashes fringing deep chocolate-brown eyes. Before today, even though I had let my other friendships slide, I wasn't alone, because I had Polly. But now, it's just Henry and me. We are completely alone, and we are in danger.

Chapter 25

2016

Once Henry is in bed, I pour myself a glass of wine. I wince at the taste, still suffering from the effects of overindulging at the reunion last night, but I need something to soften my sharp edges, to make sense of what is happening to me. In the sitting room I put the news on. Sophie is still the headline story. They've named her now, and Reynolds pops up, making a plea for information. They also give the cause of death, which hadn't been mentioned previously: strangulation. I feel sick, unable to stop imagining hands closing around her neck, the struggle for breath. Everything going black.

When my phone vibrates, I know with a dull certainty that it's going to be another message. I'm right.

> Oh dear, poor Sophie. We wouldn't want something like that to happen to you, would we?

I can't stay on the sofa, relaxing as though this is a normal evening, so I walk from room to room, jittery, jumping at every creak of the floorboards. Every now and then I sit down somewhere I never usually sit – the floor in the hallway, my back to the wall; on the side of the bath, the hard edges pressing into the backs of my legs. I keep imagining Sophie's broken body lying in the woods, still dressed in that ridiculous white fur coat, her beautiful caramel hair splayed on the ground; face white, lips blue, dark angry bruises on her neck. I think of the same fate befalling me: Henry in a small suit, solemn but not really understanding, clutching Sam's hand but looking around for me as if I might have just popped into another room.

I know the police will want to talk to me again and my body cramps with anxiety at the thought of what I have to keep from them: my night with Pete, the friend request and messages from Maria. I can't let DI Reynolds sense for a moment that there is more to this than meets the eye, that there is any hint of a connection between what happened to Sophie last night and that June evening in 1989. If they find out that Sophie's murder is linked to Maria's disappearance, it could start them down a path that leads to me, sixteen years old in an emerald green dress, a bag of crushed pills between my breasts. There are more ways than death for Henry to lose me, and I mustn't ever lose sight of that. I think of the conversations I had with Sam when we were together, about how we must never let our involvement in Maria's death become public knowledge; and of Matt so close to me last night: terrified, angry, his voice hot and urgent in my ear.

But now that my initial, instinctive response to lie to the police about our night in the Travelodge has died down, I realise what I have done. The police are going to be looking for Pete. They may even have found him already. Will he think, as I did, that the fact that we spent the night together is so open to misinterpretation that he needs to conceal it? He's got to be their prime suspect after all, and the fact that he left Sophie at the reunion and spent the night with another woman is bound to give the police pause. I can't rely on that, though. I need to speak to him before the police do.

There's a tiny part of me that wonders whether there would be a certain release in being found out, in being able to stop hiding and lying, to put down this heavy load that I've been carrying since I was sixteen years old. To be punished, yes, but maybe also forgiven. But then I remember Polly's reaction, and I know there won't be any forgiveness. And as I stand in Henry's room, draining the last of my wine, watching his flushed, sleeping face, I know I can never let this out. Quite apart from the shame of everyone knowing what I did, it's Henry who will keep me from speaking out. Even if it's only the remotest of possibilities, I can't risk going to prison and leaving my son without his mother. I'm going to have to carry this close to me for the rest of my life.

I sleep badly, my uneasy mind twisting and writhing. At two o'clock I wake with a start, drenched in sweat, certain I've heard a noise. The darkness is more than I can bear so I reach out a quivering hand to switch on the lamp. The house is in silence, but I can't shake the idea that something woke me. If Henry wasn't here I'd probably bury my head under the pillow and wait for morning, but I can't take that risk. In the absence of a weapon, I gulp down the stale water in the glass on my bedside table and slide out of bed with it in my hand. I steal around the flat, flinching at every creak of every floorboard, switching the overhead lights on as I go, leaving an eye-watering trail of blazing brightness in my wake. In the kitchen I swap the glass for a sharp knife with a gleaming blade, its handle smooth and cool beneath my fingers. I banish the darkness from each room in turn, all of them exactly as I left them, until the only place I haven't been is Henry's bedroom. I stand outside his door, dry-mouthed, my T-shirt clinging to me, cold and damp with sweat. I am paralysed by the fear that what lies behind it is all my worst nightmares come true. I have a strange sense that this is the last moment of my life as I know it, that I will look back and know that after this, things were never the same. I put my hand on the handle and push. My eyes are drawn straight to the bed. It's empty. The knife falls from my hand, landing with a soft thud on the blue carpet, and a second later I am on my knees, making a sound I've never heard from my own lips, a whimpering, like an animal in pain. Terror engulfs me, like a tidal wave. The breath has been knocked from me, coming only in short gasps between the low keening sound that I am making.

And then I see him. He's on the rug by his bed, fast asleep, still holding Manky to his face. He must have fallen out of bed without even waking, the thump as he hit the floor the noise that roused me. I fall to my knees next to him, burying my face in his hair, inhaling the sweet scent of him, weeping in sheer thankfulness.

In the morning I wake early, still shaky from the night's adventures. I've already looked up the address, so all I have to do is get us both dressed as quickly as possible and leave the house. I drop Henry at breakfast club at 7.30am; we're the first ones there. He soon gets over his confusion at my chivvying this morning, delighted to have the place to himself, running straight off to get the train set out.

It's dark as I walk towards the station, but I can see my breath in the stillness, a reminder that I'm still here, just. Some of the houses are still in darkness but there are squares of yellow light here and there and I glimpse the occasional domestic scene: a man in a suit on his sofa eating his breakfast, the flickering light of the TV casting shadows on his face; a smartly dressed woman checking her face in the mirror over the fireplace in her front room; a young mother at an upstairs window in a tired dressing gown, whey-faced and dead-eyed with exhaustion, holding her baby against her shoulder. I jump as a car revs into life as I pass, and when a tall man opens his front door and steps out into the street in front of me it's all I can do to stifle my yelp of fear. The man looks at me curiously before striding off ahead of me in the direction of the station. I stand for a minute, my hand on the streetlight, reminding myself to breathe in and out. When did I become this jumpy, terrified person? I give myself a mental shake and walk, more slowly this time, towards the station.

There's a café opposite the offices of Foster and Lyme so I order a coffee and settle myself in a seat by the window, eyes trained on the entrance. Suited figures are already going in and out. There's some kind of code that has to be tapped in, which should give me time to run out and catch Pete before he goes in.

I'm on my second cup when I feel a hand on my shoulder, making me jump and slop coffee onto the table.

'What are you doing here?' Pete's eyes stray furtively

across the road to where his oblivious colleagues greet each other, takeaway coffees in hand.

'I need to talk to you,' I say in a low voice. 'I'm sorry to ambush you at work but I couldn't think of any other way. I don't even know your surname. You know ... what's happened?'

'Yes, of course I know.' He sits down in the seat opposite me. 'It's so awful. I'm ... sorry. I know she was your friend. I spent the whole day yesterday walking around London, thinking about it, too scared to go home in case the police were waiting for me. I'm going to be their number one suspect.'

'So you haven't talked to them yet?' Hope flares in me.

'No. I know I'm going to have to. I just wanted to ... get my head together first. I'll call them today.'

'But aren't the police going to wonder why you haven't come forward before?'

'I don't know, I'll have to say I didn't see the news yesterday or something. Have you spoken to them?'

'Yes. I went into the school yesterday morning.'

'And did you tell them ... about us spending the night together?'

I look down, turning the salt pot around and around.

'No.'

I had anticipated anger but he looks more confused than anything else. There's something else, too. Relief?

'Why not?'

'I ... I'm not sure. I panicked.' I can't tell him that I am so used to lying about everything connected with that night in 1989 that the lie had tumbled out of my mouth before I'd had a chance to consider it. That my fear of anyone knowing what I did to Maria is so much a part of me that hiding anything that could possibly associate me with her disappearance is second nature to me. I need to tell him something though, give some idea of why I'm behaving like this. 'It's complicated.' I stare at my hands, my forefinger tracing patterns in the spilled sugar. 'When we were at school, Sophie and I, we … weren't very nice to another girl in our class. Maria.'

'What's a bit of schoolgirl bullying got to do with this? God knows we've all done stuff we're not proud of when we were younger.'

I so want to believe him, for this to be true, for what we did to have had no consequences. But there are no actions without consequences, are there? Even without the drink spiking, the way we treated Maria would have had an impact on her, possibly for the rest of her life. It would have affected her relationships, her friendships, her confidence. *Maybe it did. Maybe it's still affecting her now.* The thought skims across the surface of my mind, unbidden, and I see her in my mind's eye, not as smooth-skinned as she was and with a few lines on her face, but still recognisably Maria, with her hazel eyes and long brown hair, sitting in front of a computer, sending out her hatred over the ether to Sophie, to me.

'It's hard to explain. I just don't want it to come out more than it needs to. My – association with Sophie. The police already know that Sophie and I met up that night in her flat – the night you were there. If they find out I spent the night with her boyfriend, they're going to start digging around in the past, asking questions. This doesn't have anything to do with her being killed, I swear. It's just … past stuff that I don't want dragged into the present.' Any more than it has been already. 'Oh God, I don't know, maybe I should tell them. Call that detective, tell her I panicked, come clean?'

'Yes.' He doesn't look sure. 'You need to do what you think is best.'

'But you don't think I should?' I just want someone to tell me what to do, tell me everything's going to be OK.

He stares out of the window. It's starting to rain and people are walking faster, pulling their coats closer as if that will make a difference.

'I'm frightened of telling them,' he says, watching as raindrops ooze their way down the window.

'But why?'

His eyes flicker to me and then back outside again. I get the feeling that he's weighing something up.

'Well . . . just because, you know, I'm going to be their main person of interest, aren't I? Top of the list. Who do they always look to when someone's killed? The boyfriend. If they find out that I spent the night with another woman, a friend of Sophie's who I hardly knew – how does that look?'

'Not great,' I admit, although I sense he's not telling me the whole story. It's certainly true – who would ever believe that nothing had happened between us? There would be witnesses who could testify to seeing us talking and laughing together at the reunion. It wouldn't prove anything, but if the finger of suspicion is already hanging over Pete, this is going to make it worse. He must have been hovering around in the car park for an hour or so waiting for me, with no one to vouch for his whereabouts. I push down the vague feeling of unease that this thought gives me and turn back to Pete.

'So are you going to tell the police?' He holds my future in his hands.

'I don't know. Obviously I was going to, because I thought you would have told them already. But as you haven't ... well. I don't want to give them any more reason to suspect me than they already do.'

'What would you tell them, then? If you don't tell them we spent the night together?'

'I'll just say that Sophie and I argued and that I drove back to London and went home to bed.' His enthusiasm for the idea is growing.

'They'll know though, they'll be able to check traffic cameras, CCTV, that sort of thing. There's no way you could have got back to London without being picked up on some camera or other.'

'OK, well ...' He picks up a paper napkin from the table and folds it in half again and again, until it's too fat and tight to fold any more. 'I know. I'll just say I slept in my car. It was really near the school, I bet there's no CCTV there. All we need to do is hold our nerve and this will all blow over. We've done nothing wrong, and us spending the night in a hotel room has no bearing on anything to do with Sophie's death, so it doesn't matter if we don't mention it. We want the same thing here, don't we? For all this to be over.'

He must have read something in my face, because he blushed. 'Oh God, sorry. Look, I'm not a totally heartless bastard, you know. I do understand that someone's died here, and I know she was your friend.' Was she, though?

Certainly not now, and maybe not even when we were at school.

'The thing is,' he goes on, 'I barely knew her. I wasn't expecting to ever see or hear from her again after I walked out of that hall. To pretend I feel grief would be hypocritical. To be honest I'm struggling to feel anything apart from this . . . terrible fear. What if they can somehow pin it on me? I could be going to jail for the rest of my life.'

'Surely that couldn't happen, though? There wouldn't be any evidence.' It's not lost on me that you could say the same about my role in Maria's death. But the difference is that unlike Pete, I did do something wrong. And there are other people who know about it.

'Not physical evidence, no. But we did . . . you know . . . in the B&B before we went out.' He has the grace to look shamefaced. 'They'll be able to tell, won't they? That doesn't look great. And then we were seen arguing at the reunion. It all starts to stack up, and if they then find out that I spent the night with you . . .'

'Are you sure nobody saw us in the car park?' I say. 'No one saw us leaving together?'

'As sure as I can be. I didn't see anyone, did you?'

'No.' I trace my spoon around the bottom of my empty cup, circling the dregs of my coffee, my pulse racing from a mixture of caffeine and fear. 'Are you sure you're OK with this? I don't want to . . . pressure you into this, just because I've already lied.'

'No. This is what I want. We'll just keep it to ourselves, and everything will be OK. Why don't we swap contact details, in case we need to talk again?' He scribbles his mobile number on the back of a napkin and passes me another so I can do the same. 'Yes, I'm sure this is the best thing to do.' I'm not sure who he's trying to convince here, me or him, but I don't need any convincing. Since that first conversation with the police, my every instinct has been screaming not to tell, to keep my head down and my mouth shut. After all, I've already got someone after me. The last thing I want is to add DI Reynolds to the list.

Pete leaves the café and I watch as he crosses the road. He's standing by the entry doors, starting to tap in the code, when a car pulls up behind him, stopping on the double yellow lines. I watch, my heart in my throat, as DI Reynolds and a tall man in a dark suit get out of the car. Reynolds says something and I see Pete turn, his face inscrutable. They have a short conversation, and then Pete gets into the car and is driven away.

Chapter 26

2016

It's been a couple of days since my encounter with Pete, but I've heard nothing from him, or the police. I have to go and see Rosemary Wright-Collins this morning. I've been putting her off for a while but I've run out of excuses. It's going to be hard putting my professional hat on. Every time I try to get some work done, my mind grinds along in slow motion, imagination and creativity stifled by the constant whirring of my thoughts. My latest job for Rosemary is a flat in a Georgian townhouse in Islington (God only knows how much it cost) that needs redecorating throughout, having had the same owner for the last forty years.

I ring the bell. Rosemary takes a while to come to the door, and when she does, whilst she's impeccably dressed as ever, the epitome of sophisticated older womanhood, she's not her usual effusive self.

'Hello, Louise.' She stands there in the doorway for a moment with an odd, guarded expression on her face, before pulling the door back. 'Come in.' Inside, the flat is stunning, high-ceilinged and airy, but crumbling and in desperate need of care and attention.

'Wow, this is amazing, Rosemary. You must be so excited.'

'Yes, yes I am.' She doesn't seem excited as she leads me through the hall into the front reception room, her heels clacking on the original tiled floor. She's unwilling to meet my eye, standing by the enormous fireplace, rubbing at an imaginary speck of dirt on the mantelpiece with a manicured finger.

'So, where do you want to start?' I ask, trying to inject some enthusiasm into the proceedings.

'Before we do, Louise, there's something I need to talk to you about.'

Oh God. I've always thought she was loaded, but maybe there's a cash flow problem. I really need her. Without her, my business would be in serious jeopardy.

'OK,' I say. 'Is everything all right?'

'Yes, everything's fine. Sort of.' I've never seen her like this: hesitant, unsure. It's got to be a money problem. She turns to face me, clearly screwing up her courage.

'I had a rather strange email this morning.'

My stomach rises and flips, settling somewhere near the floor. Please God, no.

'From someone called Maria Weston.'

I open my mouth to speak but nothing comes out.

'I know it's not true,' she goes on quickly. 'I'm only telling you because I thought you ought to know.'

'What did it say?' I will myself to stay calm.

'She said you'd done a job for her, and that you'd messed up and left her in the lurch, that you were unprofessional and unreliable. She strongly recommended that I look elsewhere.'

'Right,' I whisper.

'I'm not going to, Louise. We've worked together for years, I know how good you are. I don't know what this is about and, frankly, I don't want to know. I don't want to get mixed up in anything messy though, you know? I want to keep our relationship strictly professional.'

'Of course, Rosemary. I think I know who's behind this,' I lie. 'I'm sure it won't happen again.'

We carry on with the consultation but things are very strained and I'm relieved when I get out of there. Maria is reaching out now; I can feel her icy presence slipping into every aspect of my life. I have a pressing need to talk to someone about all this, and the only person I can think of is Esther. Despite our chequered history, Esther has been kind to me and as I walk down the street away from Rosemary's flat I call her.

'Hello?' I can tell she's outside, the wind whistling at me remotely from wherever she is.

'Hi. How are you?'

'I don't know. Stunned. I can't believe it.' Why don't we believe it when something like this happens? We see it on the news all the time. Why should we be so surprised when it happens to us?

'I know, it's awful. Look, Esther, can we meet? I'd like to talk to you, about . . . you know, all this.'

'Really?' She sounds doubtful. 'Is there anything to say?'

'There is for me. I just need to talk to someone. Please?'

'Well, OK. I am in London today as it happens, I'm on my way to a meeting now, but I could meet you afterwards for a coffee – on the South Bank?'

I turn into Angel tube, wondering as I always do why

the escalator is moving a touch faster than the handrail. The platform is busy, and I stand with my back to the wall, breathing in the heat and the smell of dust and burnt rubber. I've always felt uneasy on tube platforms at what a small physical movement it would be to throw myself under the oncoming train. We think that the gulf between living and dying is huge, but on the tube platform I am always reminded that it's only one little step. Today as I press my spine into the oversized tube map on the wall, looking around me nervously, I can't stop thinking that on a busy day it's also just one little push. A hand in the back and a brief, hard shove that no one would even notice.

When I get to Embankment I push my way hurriedly through the crowds, desperate to escape the fumes and the crush, emerging into the cold, clear light. I scurry across the bridge, the Thames rolling beneath me, grey-green and dappled here and there by the shadows of fast-moving clouds. Platforms and trains, bridges and rivers – I'm so close, all the time, to death. To the possibility of death. Recent events have added a keenness to the blade but I've never been entirely free of it. It has been hovering for years, millimetres from my neck, on the verge of biting into my flesh.

Esther's already waiting for me outside the Festival Hall, her coat a scarlet stain against the monolithic building behind her. We hug tentatively.

'Do you want to get a coffee, or shall we walk a bit?' she says.

'Let's walk.' This conversation will be easier if I don't have to look her full in the face.

We talk about Sophie first, and although she is of course aghast at what has happened, I can tell Esther is struggling to say the right things. What do you say when someone who made your life a misery half a lifetime ago dies? We move on to the police, who have interviewed Esther briefly already, but who are going to talk to her again in more detail soon. It wasn't DI Reynolds she spoke to, but one of the underlings. Esther didn't cross paths at all with Sophie at the reunion so she's not high on Reynolds' list. I've got to go to Norwich tomorrow for another interview with her, and the thought of it lurks inside me like indigestion.

Esther and I walk in silence for a few moments, our tread punctuated by the trees that line the south side of the river, stark and leafless against the cold, grey-white sky.

'After you left the reunion, Lorna Sixsmith told me that you and Sam Parker had been married.' Esther turns to look at me, the wind whipping her hair around her face.

'Yes, we were.' I keep my eyes on the river, concentrating on the way the water is frothing around the edges, buffeting a discarded bottle onto the shingle. It still hurts, to think of us together. The pain is like a rope around my wrists: the more I try to wriggle free, the more it hurts.

'Why didn't you tell me?' she asks.

'I don't know ... I guess I thought you knew. I don't talk about it much,' I say, my voice clipped.

'How did that happen?' Esther, realising perhaps that her voice contains too much horrified fascination, qualifies her question. 'I mean, I wouldn't have predicted that. I know you liked him at school, but ...'

'You thought he was out of my league?' I don't mind. I always thought so myself.

'Not exactly that. But how did you even end up together?

Your parents moved away from Sharne Bay when you were at university, didn't they?'

'Yes. I didn't see Sam for a long time after that. We ran into each other in London years after I'd left university, when we were twenty-five, twenty-six.' I can still feel the breathless excitement of it, standing at the bar in a pub in Clapham, turning around to ask my friend Lucy what she wanted and being confronted with those blue eyes, almost as close to me as they had been the night of the leavers' party. I knew him straight away, of course, but it took him a second longer to catch on. When he did though he seemed genuinely happy to see me, pulling me into a hug and then setting me back from him, studying my face and laughing in surprise and delight.

We spent the whole evening together, one of those magical nights that you don't want to end. The warmth of the day still lingered in the air, and we sat knee to knee in the beer garden, drinking and swapping stories. Alone together in a crowd. Lucy and the others and his friends faded away until we found ourselves out on the street at closing time. When he bent to kiss me my insides turned to molten liquid, and I pulled him closer, my hands twisting and pulling his hair, his arms around me so tightly I could barely breathe. I grasped this second chance at happiness with him with both hands, and although it wasn't always easy, I held on to it for fifteen years. Until one day, two years ago, I found a text message on his phone that shouldn't have been there, and I felt it slipping through my fingers like grains of sand.

'And you ended up married?'

'Yes.' It seems wrong to parcel up those fifteen years of my life into such a brief conversation, but I don't have the words to explain it to Esther even if I wanted to: the breathless exhilaration of being with him; the thrill of the things he did to me; how he became everything to me, at least until Henry was born; the pain he put me through.

'And your little boy . . . Sam is his father?'

'Yes.' The sort of father who swings him up in the air until he's giddy with excitement, but doesn't want to clear up the mess when he's sick on the floor.

'So, do you think it was that bloke Sophie was with?' she asks, sensing that I don't want to say any more. 'That did it, I mean? You were talking to him, weren't you?'

'We chatted for a bit, that's all,' I say, careful not to sound too defensive. 'He seemed nice. I can't imagine him . . . doing that. But then I can't imagine anyone doing it, but somebody did, didn't they? It makes you realise, all these things you see on the news, in the papers – they've happened to ordinary people like us. They aren't special, they were just going about their everyday lives until something turned them upside down.'

'What about Matt Lewis?' she says. 'He always had a thing for Sophie, didn't he?'

For someone who wasn't part of our crowd, Esther is certainly very well informed. 'Well, yes, I think he did, but that hardly means he's going to murder her twenty-seven years later, does it?'

'I suppose. You don't think . . .' she hesitates. 'The Facebook request, the birthday presents?'

'I don't know, Esther. That's kind of what I wanted to talk to you about. I've had some more messages from her.'

'Saying what?'

I outline the content of the messages briefly. 'But Esther,

are we actually saying that she could still be alive? Where could she have been?'

Esther stops and leans against the railings, gazing over the river towards St Paul's, resplendent in the sunlight. 'I don't know. They never found her body, did they? But why come back now? How, even?'

'I don't know. But what Tim said, talking about her in the present tense . . . I saw him, you know. Outside the reunion. He told me when I saw him in Sharne Bay that he was going to go on her behalf, but then he didn't show up. Except . . . he did, sort of. I saw him outside, talking to someone.'

'Tim was there?' She looks at me questioningly.

'Yes. Well, not actually at the reunion. I saw him at the top of the drive, when I was outside smoking.'

'That's weird. I wonder why he didn't come in. I suppose maybe he changed his mind when it came to it? It's a pretty weird thing for anyone to do, when you think about it. Go to a school reunion, I mean. If you really cared about any of those people they would still be friends, and if you don't care about them, what on earth are you there for? Curiosity?'

'You went,' I say, stung by her words.

'Yes, and I wish I hadn't now. For starters I wouldn't be mixed up in all this. And it would have meant that I was able to leave the past in the past, but I couldn't. I can't. I had to show everyone – look at me now with my great career and my husband and my children. How bloody stupid. I should have just put it all on Facebook like everyone else.' Her hands tighten on the railings.

'It's not stupid, Esther. I didn't find out about the reunion until months after it was organised. Nobody had thought to let me know, and I felt crushed. If anything's bloody stupid, that is. Why should it even matter?'

'It shouldn't. But it does,' Esther says. 'It all matters. Part of me feels hurt that if she is still alive, she hasn't let me know. We were close, you know, before she died. She talked to me about a lot of stuff. Do you know about what happened to her at her old school? Did she ever talk to you about it?'

'She tried once, I think.' Slatted wooden sunbeds in the dark, breath rising in the night air. Two little fingers, linked.

'That boy that was obsessed with her – it was pretty bad. You'd call it stalking now, there'd be restraining orders and all sorts, but back then there wasn't much they could do unless he physically hurt her.'

She turns and we walk along the river in silence for a while.

'What is it you want, Louise? Why did you call?'

I want a night of untroubled sleep. I want to change the past. I want to stop looking over my shoulder on the tube platform, stop thinking about jumping or being pushed every time I cross a bridge.

'I'm frightened, Esther. I just want to know what happened to Maria; what happened to Sophie.' I want to know how much of it is my fault; if I'm next.

'Shouldn't you leave it to the police?'

She doesn't know I haven't told the police about the friend request from Maria. There's so much she doesn't know that it overwhelms me. I realise I have no idea what I'm doing here.

'Yes, you're probably right. Look, Esther, I've got to go, I need to get back to pick Henry up from school.'

'Oh. Right, OK. I'll see you sometime . . . maybe?'

'Yes, that'd be lovely.' I sound fake, as if I'm leaving a dinner party where I've had a really terrible time but am putting a brave face on it. 'Bye then.'

I turn back the way we've come and stride along, trying to look purposeful. The wind, which had been pushing us along from behind is now biting into my face, making my eyes water.

I am thinking about Tim, at the top of the school drive. Tim, whose adolescence was rocked and the fabric of his life changed for ever by the disappearance of his sister; Tim, who must have worked so hard just to attain an ordinary life: a home, a wife, a plump-cheeked baby. How has he carried on? How do you get over something like that? Or has he never had to get over it? Has he been pretending to grieve for a sister who is alive and well, and living under a false identity? And if that is the case, then what has she told him? How much does he know?

Chapter 27

He may have saved her, but that doesn't mean he has to keep on saving her. He tells her to stay quiet, not to rock the boat, live the life she's got. But she's not living, not really. She's just existing, getting through one day, and then another. But eventually those days will run out and what will she have to show for them?

Sometimes she wonders if maybe she could survive on her own. Throw off this dark, heavy cloak of secrecy that she has been wearing – just put it down and walk away, become the person she should have been all along.

Could she let someone else in? He knows the truth, and maybe that should be enough for her; not to be alone with it. She never could have got through it without him, she knows that much. Her faithful companion. Her partner in crime, forever complicit in the events of the night that changed everything.

She has lived her life in shadow, running and hiding. Yes, she can put a good face on it when she needs to, but inside she is still that girl. She's torn between the gut-twisting fear of anybody knowing who she really is, and the contrasting desire to be truly seen. Isn't that what we all want, really?

She wants to step out into the light and live the life she should have lived. She wants to be heard. She wants to be known.

Chapter 28

2016

The children who regularly get picked up by their stay-at-home parents at three o'clock are all lined up outside the classroom. Henry, of course, is not there and Mrs Hopkins looks at me in confusion.

'I finished work early today,' I lie. In fact I needed to see him, came straight from the South Bank to pick him up early. 'Can I pop my head in . . . ?' I point at the classroom. There's something about the way the after-school club children are sitting so neatly at their desks, coats on, bags on their tables in front of them, awaiting their next instruction, that pulls at my heartstrings. They're so small and already they've had to learn to conform. Henry is conversing quietly and earnestly with the girl next to him. It's the boy sitting on his other side that sees me first, Henry's friend Jasper. He starts tapping Henry frantically on the arm.

'Henry. Henry! Your mummy is here.'

Henry turns and his entire face lights up, fireworks going off behind his eyes.

'Mummy! What are you doing here?' He clearly wants to run to me, but looks anxiously at Miss Jones, the new teaching assistant, for permission.

'I finished work early today. Come on, shall we go to the park?' Again he looks to Miss Jones who smiles.

'Bye, Henry. See you tomorrow.'

As we cross the playground a large woman looms aggressively over the teacher in the neighbouring classroom. I've seen this mother before with her clutch of overweight, unruly children. This time it's the turn of the solitary boy amongst her brood, who stands beside her, belligerently kicking at his school bag on the ground next to him. She's obviously had the dreaded 'Can I have a word?' from the teacher at pickup time. Of course in her eyes her little angel can do no wrong, so she's not taking it too well, stabbing a finger towards the teacher's face.

At the park, Henry shouts with unabashed delight as I push him higher and higher on the swings. His joy is compounded by seeing his friend Dylan coming through the yellow gates with his mum, Olivia.

'Dylaaaan! I'm on the swings!'

Dylan comes running over. 'Come and play on the climbing frame,' he instructs.

'No, come on the swings!' Henry calls.

'No,' says Dylan sternly. 'Climbing frame.'

'OK. Stop me, Mummy,' Henry says, so I slow the swing and they run off together.

'Aw bless, they're lovely little friends, aren't they?' says Olivia, watching them fondly. I was getting more of a dictator vibe from Dylan but I don't burst her bubble.

'Shall we get a cuppa?' she continues.

We walk over to the little kiosk and order two coffees. I don't take my eyes off Henry as he runs around in the sand, every now and then falling to the ground. I realise Dylan is standing at the top of the climbing frame 'shooting' him.

'Did you hear what happened in the playground at pickup today? With Angela Dickson?'

'Who?' I say. Because I'm not often at the school gate when everyone else is, I'm hazy on who's who.

'You know, Angela Dickson, the—' she lowers her voice '—*fat* one. With all those kids.'

'Oh yes, I know.' I'm distracted by not being able to see Henry, but then he emerges from behind the toddler slide where he's been hiding from enemy fire and I relax, keeping my eyes on him. 'I saw her having a row with the teacher as we were leaving today.'

'Not just a row,' says Olivia. 'She punched Mrs Smithson!'

'Punched her?' I spin and face her. 'Oh my God! Did you actually see it?'

'Yes, I was still there talking to Mrs Hopkins.' Olivia is one of those parents who always has some pressing issue she needs to discuss with the teacher. I'm friends with her on Facebook, and every week she's airing some gripe with the school on there – sending home reading books that are not challenging enough for her genius child, that sort of thing. 'She actually punched her in the face.'

'Did they call the police?'

'I'm not sure,' she says. 'I saw Mr Knowles coming over.' Mr Knowles is one of the only male teachers at the school. 'Mind you, I wouldn't fancy his chances against Angela Dickson.'

My eyes flick back to the climbing frame, but Henry and

Dylan are not there. I look behind me, over towards the fort, but there's no sign of them. It's a big park with lots of equipment. They could be anywhere.

'Can you see the boys?' I ask Olivia.

'Oh, they'll be around somewhere. Let's go and sit on that bench, you can see pretty much the whole park from there.'

We walk over to the picnic bench and she sits down. I put my coffee on the table and scan the park anxiously. Olivia is still prattling on about the big school-gate news.

'I can't see them,' I interrupt her.

Olivia looks around casually, sipping her coffee.

'They're probably in the fort. Relax, Louise, they'll be here somewhere. Look, there they are.'

Dylan is running around and around a tree, making machine-gun noises, but I can't see Henry. My breath catches in my throat, but I try to stay calm. He's probably in the tree. That's where I've found him before, climbing so high I had to press my lips together hard to stop myself from shouting at him to come down. I walk over, trying not to run, forcing myself to breathe evenly. The closer I get the less it looks as if there is anyone in the tree. In the summer it's easy to hide in there, but at this time of year it's leafless and bare, and before I reach it I can see that the branches are not hiding him. Henry is nowhere to be seen.

'Dylan,' I say, too loudly. 'Where's Henry?'

'Don't know.'

'But you were with him just now, weren't you?'

'Yes. But then he started talking to that lady.'

Oh God. It's like a blow to the head. For a moment I think I'm going to pass out, but I gather myself, forcing my mouth into the right shapes to form words.

'What lady? Where?' I kneel down in front of him, taking hold of his arms.

'Don't know. Over there.' Dylan points in the direction of the fort, shakes my arms off and starts running round the tree again.

I start to run, my breath coming in gasps, calling his name. I get to the fort and bend down to peer in through the door. Two small girls with a doll in a pram regard me suspiciously. They are the only children in there. I turn and gaze frantically around the park.

'Henry!' I shout. I run the length of the park, looking behind every piece of play equipment, calling for him, louder and louder. Other mothers start to look around, wondering whether they ought to help me. There's always someone in here calling for their child, but there's a note of genuine desperation in my voice that is clearly worrying them. Olivia gets up and calls Dylan over, presumably to grill him further on where he saw Henry last.

I am on the verge of getting my phone out to call the police, all thoughts of my own safety, or reputation, entirely forgotten, when I see him. He's right at the far end of the park, standing with his back to me looking out over the gate that opens into the wider park. I come to a stop and emit something between a sob and a choke. Thank God. I carry on walking over to him, slowly now.

'Henry,' I call and he turns, smiling. 'Where were you?' I try to keep my voice light. 'I couldn't find you.'

'In the park,' he says.

'Dylan said you were talking to a lady.'

'Yes. She liked trains. She was asking me all about Thomas.'

My heart rate slows. Maybe she was just a mother, or a granny who'd brought her grandchildren to the park.

'Where is she?'

'She said she had to go. I was just waving to her.' I look across the park. In the distance I can see a figure in a dark coat walking towards the main exit.

'Did she not have any children with her?'

'No, she was by herself.'

'How old was she?' I ask, knowing as I do so what a pointless question this is to ask a four-year-old.

'Twenty?' he says, but that could mean anything from a teenager up to an OAP. Including a woman of my own age.

I am too shaken to stay any longer, and manage to persuade Henry to come home without a fuss by promising hot chocolate in front of the telly. As I strap him into the car, my phone vibrates in my pocket. I ignore it until I am in the driver's seat, Henry safely stowed in the back. Praying for it to be a work email, I tap the screen to wake it. It's Maria. As I read and re-read the Facebook message, the sound of Henry humming happily and tunelessly to himself in the back, full of pure joy at the thought of hot chocolate, feels like needles being driven into my ears.

> Henry seems like a nice little boy. I hope you watch him carefully. It's so easily done, isn't it? You turn your back for a second and they're gone.

Chapter 29

2016

I decide to drop Henry at school myself today, and after I watch him running across the playground and into the classroom, I walk round to the office, where gimlet-faced Mrs Harper sits as usual behind her glass screen. Her assistant Miss Wallis is nervously putting documents away in a huge filing cabinet at the other end of the office. I wait for the obligatory minute or two while Mrs Harper taps away furiously at her keyboard, attending to something infinitely more important than me. Eventually she swivels to face me.

'Can I help you?'

'I'm Louise, Henry Parker's mum.' I have to say this every time I come in here. I don't know whether she genuinely doesn't recognise me, or if she's punishing me for something: not being a regular at the school gates, or having a different surname to my child. 'I just wanted to double check the safety procedures around pickup.'

'Yes?' If she was wearing a lorgnette she would be lowering it. The temperature around us drops a few degrees;

I have done the unthinkable and questioned the school's competence.

'It's just, I have reason to be especially concerned at the moment, so I wanted to make sure that no one else apart from me can pick him up without my permission.'

'But you don't usually collect him yourself, do you?' she asks, her tone hinting at her disdain for me. It's all right for you, I think, with your nice little job in a school, working school hours only.

'No, he goes to after-school club,' I say, forcing my voice to remain neutral. 'But obviously that's a regular arrangement that the school knows about. I'm talking about other people picking him up.'

I catch a glint in her eye at the hint of a scandal. 'Do you mean his father?' She lowers her voice. 'Perhaps I should make an appointment for you to see the head . . .' She turns to her screen, clicking on the appointments diary.

'No! His father is fine.' She raises her eyebrows. 'I just mean anyone else.'

She sighs. 'Mrs Parker, I can assure you that we will not let—' she pauses for an infinitesimal amount of time, just long enough for me to register that she can't instantly call to mind which child belongs to me '—we will not let Henry go home with anyone other than a parent, childminder or usual carer without express permission from you.'

Williams, I think as I always do, my name is Williams; it's not the day for that particular battle though. I have no choice but to accept what she is saying, but I walk away with a heavy heart. I wish I could keep Henry with me all the time. When he's away from me the anxiety is a physical pain that runs me through like a sword.

However, there's no avoiding today's appointment in Norwich. I spent so long keeping away from this part of the world, building a new life for myself in London, and now it won't leave me alone, exerting a magnetic pull that I am powerless to resist.

Somewhere inside the glass-fronted building in front of me, DI Reynolds is waiting for me. What is she thinking? Is she wondering about me at all, or am I merely one of the many witnesses that she has to interview, the latest on a long list? Perhaps her training precludes her thinking like that. Maybe she has been drilled to always assume every witness knows something that could prove vital to the case. Or worse, maybe she has sensed something in me, a certain hesitation or guardedness. Is she going to grill me today, to come at me in some completely unexpected way? I have to be ready. I must be so utterly sure in my own mind of my story that she will not be able to trip me up.

I am shown to the interview room by a young woman in uniform who chats inanely to me as we walk through the corridors. We cover a lot of very British topics – the weather, traffic jams, the merits or otherwise of one-way systems. I can't work out if this is a calculated way of relaxing me before I get pounced on, or if she's just really boring.

Under the harsh lights, I perch on the edge of the moulded plastic chair, turning my cardboard cup around and around on the beige tabletop. I look around surreptitiously, trying to work out if there's a secret two-way mirror hidden somewhere like on TV, but I guess the CCTV camera on the wall is doing that job.

DI Reynolds is talking on her phone when she opens the

door, but she finishes the conversation quickly and smiles at me. She is bigger than I remember, although everything is amplified in this tiny room. I notice a raised mole on her cheek and red patches on her eyelids.

'Louise. How are you doing?'

'OK, thanks.' 'Very well' would be pushing it.

'This is DS Stebbings.' She gestures at the suited man who has followed her in, a tall man in his fifties who sits down next to her, opposite me. I recognise him as the man who was with Reynolds the day I saw them driving away with Pete outside the offices of Foster and Lyme.

Reynolds plunges straight in with her questions; there's no chitchat about the weather with her. We go over the ground we've already covered, but this time I'm prepared for the questions about Pete. Yes, I spoke to him earlier in the evening. He seemed perfectly fine, in a good mood. I saw them argue, but then I don't think I saw him again after that; he must have left. She's clearly pursuing this as a line of enquiry, but when she realises she's not getting anywhere, she gives up and moves on.

'OK. We have witnesses who mentioned that Sophie spent a lot of time talking to Sam Parker and Matt Lewis. Would you agree with that?'

'Yes. They were good friends of Sophie's at school.'

'More than friends, do you think? With either of them?'

'Matt had a crush on her back then but I don't know for sure if anything ever happened between them. They used to flirt, you know, but I think that was all it was, on her side anyway.'

'And Sam?'

'No,' I say instantly. 'Definitely not Sam.'

Too quick. Reynolds looks alert, interested. 'Why do you say that?'

'I don't know if you already know this, but Sam and I were married. We split up two years ago.'

'So you were . . . childhood sweethearts?'

'No.' What a repulsive phrase. She seems to think so too, the words foreign on her tongue. 'I didn't see him for years after we left school. We met again by chance in London ten years later, in ninety-nine.'

'So what makes you so sure that Sophie never had a relationship with him?'

'Well, I . . .' What is it that makes me so certain? Because she knew I liked him? Do I honestly believe that would have stopped her? Because Sam never mentioned it? Maybe he wouldn't have done; after all, it would have been ancient history by the time we got together.

My silence clearly speaks volumes to Reynolds and she moves on.

'And what about in the years since school – had Sophie kept in touch with Matt or Sam, or anyone else at the reunion?'

'I think she was in touch with some people – she told me when I saw her before the reunion that she still saw Claire Barnes, and Matt Lewis. Maybe some others too.'

'Was there any hint that she had had any sort of sexual relationship with Matt as an adult?'

'No, she didn't mention anything like that. Just that she saw him from time to time.'

'And Sam? Had she seen him since your school days?'

'He didn't see her while he and I were together, as far as I know. But I wouldn't know about the last two years. He . . .

he's married again, with a baby. We only speak because we have to now, about our son.' Bringing Henry into the conversation draws the knot in my chest a little tighter. Our son, who might be in danger because of me. Part of me wants to break down, to tell Reynolds everything, beg her to protect my son. But I try to rationalise it. How much danger can Henry be in? I won't be letting him out of my sight again after yesterday. He's safe at school. Sam's got him tonight, so I texted him this morning to ask if he had plans to take Henry out anywhere tonight, and he said he would be picking him up from after-school club and going straight home. He's four years old, so he's never alone. I can protect him.

Reynolds is still looking at me enquiringly.

'Things didn't end all that well,' I say. 'Between me and Sam.'

'How so?'

'He left me for someone else.' Even now I hate saying those words; hate the bald, hard fact of them. I wasn't enough for him, even though I gave him everything I had. 'Look, this hasn't got anything to do with what happened to Sophie.'

She makes a face that says she'll be the judge of that.

'OK. So how did Sophie seem, the night of the reunion? Is there anything that gives you pause, in the light of what happened subsequently?'

'She was fine. Happy, apart from the argument with Pete, although I have no idea what that was about. But to be honest, I wouldn't know whether she was her normal self or not. Like I said, I hadn't seen her for over twenty-five years, except for that one night a few weeks ago.'

'And you – you weren't in touch with anyone from school? Apart from Sam?'

'No. They weren't exactly the happiest days of my life.'

'What about Sam? You said he wasn't in contact with Sophie. What about other old school friends? Was he in touch with anyone?'

'He went out occasionally with Matt Lewis, but not often. I'm afraid I wasn't that interested. Happiest days and all that.'

I am prevaricating. It's less that I wasn't interested, more that I wanted nothing to do with Sharne Bay or our school days, and couldn't understand why Sam didn't want to cut the ties as well. On the nights he met up with Matt, I'd pretend to be asleep when he came in, mutter at him to tell me in the morning, and then when morning came find an excuse to be out of the house early.

'And what about the other people at the reunion? We're talking to the bar staff and the cleaners, of course, but there was a teacher there too, Mr Jenkins?'

'Yes, that's right.'

'I believe he was a teacher there when you were at school?'

'Yes, that's right.' Surely they don't suspect him?

'Did you speak to him at all, or see him at any point in the evening?'

'Mr Jenkins? Only when I arrived. He was on the door. Look, has someone said something?'

'What do you mean?' Her face is inscrutable.

'Well . . . when we were at school there were all these rumours about him. That he was . . . you know . . . a pervert. Liked sneaking around, watching the girls get changed, that kind of thing.'

'I see.' She's not giving anything anyway.

'But I've no idea if there was any truth to them. He certainly never did anything to me, and I never heard anything first-hand. It was always someone who knew someone. You know what teenagers can be like, how things get around. I wouldn't want to suggest that he . . . you know . . .'

'Of course.'

Reynolds looks intently at me, her hands face down on the table.

'I appreciate that you hadn't seen Sophie for many years, and that you didn't know much about her adult life, and of course we are pursuing various lines of enquiry,' she says. 'But we can't ignore the fact that she was killed at her school reunion, an occasion loaded with significance at the best of times. Was there anything that happened in your school days, anything at all, that you think may have a bearing here?'

I think of Maria's face, glaring defiantly at me from my computer; of Sophie silhouetted against coloured glass, gathering herself for what was to come; of Tim at the top of the school drive, gesticulating at a figure in a black coat; of a golden necklace, twisted around a sixteen-year-old girl's finger a lifetime ago.

'No,' I say. 'Nothing at all.'

Chapter 30

2016

Outside the police station, I walk steadily at a medium pace, in case Reynolds is watching me from an upstairs window. My car is parked in a nearby multi-storey, but I continue walking past the entrance, the rhythm of feet hitting pavement soothing me. Cars zoom past me with hypnotic regularity, a backdrop to my racing thoughts.

How have I ended up here, lying to the police again? I remember the other detective, a kind man. I never knew exactly how much Maria's mum Bridget had told him about me, but I don't think he ever suspected any foul play. Esther's testimony that Maria had been drinking was enough for him to conclude that a tragic accident was the most likely explanation. The rain that had begun to fall as we left the hall that night had continued all night, a relentless downpour that would have washed away any hope of physical evidence. Only Sophie, Sam, Matt and I knew exactly how tragic, and how far you would have to stretch the word accident, to make the official verdict anywhere close to accurate. At least, I think we were the only ones who knew.

Even though I have left the police station far behind, I still have the feeling that someone is watching me. I can feel the heat on my back, like the glare of the sun, ostensibly benign but with the potential to burn, to scald. I walk faster, hyper-alert, trying to look like someone in an ordinary hurry, perhaps with a train to catch, or late for an appointment. When I reach Norwich town centre, I duck behind a crowd of tourists and swerve into Marks & Spencer, its familiarity a soothing balm. How do they make all their shops smell the same? In the food hall, standing in front of the sandwich counter staring unseeingly at the tuna sweetcorn and chicken salad, I slowly become aware that someone is watching me. I try to keep my eyes on the sandwiches, but cannot stop the heat that rises to my cheeks. There's a harassed woman with two small children whinging for treats to my right, and next to her a greying man in a tired suit looking miserably at the low-fat section. My eyes slide beyond him and land on Tim Weston. He smiles and gives a half-wave, coming around behind the businessman and the woman with the children.

'Louise, hi. What are you doing here?'

'Buying a sandwich?' I give a breathless laugh, trying to conceal my discomfort. Has Tim been following me?

'Right. You came all the way to Norwich for a sandwich? They do have Marks & Spencers in London you know.' His tone is light but there's an accusation behind his words.

I give in. 'I've just been at the police station actually. Talking to them about Sophie Hannigan.' There's no point trying to avoid the subject.

'Oh God, yes of course, I heard.' His face falls. 'It's so awful. Do you ... know any more about what happened to her?'

'No, not really. They just wanted to talk to me, as someone that was there, you know. Someone that spoke to her at the reunion.' Why am I trying to justify myself to him?

'Right, right. It's just such a horrific thing to have happened.'

We stand there awkwardly for a moment.

'Which one are you getting?' he asks eventually.

I look down at the sandwich in either hand, shove one of them blindly back into the fridge, and we walk to the tills together. We pay for our sandwiches in silence, and walk out of the shop together and along the pedestrianised street.

'Which way are you going?' he says.

'Back to my car. It's parked near the police station.' I wave my hand in the general direction of Bethel Street.

'I'll walk with you, if that's OK?'

It's not OK, really. There's so much that's unspoken between us, not just on my side but on his too. I am uncomfortably conscious of how little I know him, and how I don't want him to know too much about me. We stand on the pavement waiting to cross a one-way street. Unfamiliar with the roads, I am looking the wrong way and as I step out, a car rockets towards me. My brain is moving slower than the car and as I hover in the road, I feel Tim's fingers close on the top of my arm and haul me back to safety.

'Sorry,' he says, seeing me rubbing my arm. 'Did I hurt you?'

'No, it's fine.' I give a shaky laugh. 'I think I'd be worse off if you hadn't grabbed me.'

'They're nutters, some of the drivers round here. Think they're at Brands Hatch.'

We cross carefully, and continue on our way in silence. I can't help thinking of the figure at the top of the school drive.

'So, you decided against going to the reunion then?' I ask eventually. I see Tim in my mind's eye, waving his arms and shouting, and then leaving with his arm around the small figure in black. Tim's face closes down.

'Yeah, I realised it would be a really bad idea. I've got my own life now. Best left well alone.'

Then what was he doing at the top of the drive? And who was he with?

'All that Facebook stuff,' he goes on. 'People from the past contacting you . . . it's so easy to get sucked in, but what does it all mean, really? You're better off focussing on your actual life, the one you're living. Our family was never the same, after what happened . . . to Maria.'

'Mmm.' I don't trust myself to speak, certain my voice will betray me.

'I felt like I'd be dragging it all up again for no reason, if I went. So you've . . . have you got no idea what happened to Sophie?'

'No, none at all.'

'I heard she brought some bloke to the reunion? Someone she hardly knew?'

'Yes, she was with a man. I'm not sure how well she knew him.' There's something about his interest in the details that makes me reluctant to share more than I have to with Tim.

'Sorry, I didn't mean to sound like I was gossiping, or making light of it,' he says as we walk, having clearly picked up my signals. 'I didn't realise you and Sophie were still close.'

'We're not. I mean, we weren't. I hadn't really seen her since school.'

'Oh, OK. It's ironic, I didn't go to the reunion because I didn't want to drag up the past, and then this happens and I feel like the past has given me a big old slap in the face anyway.'

'I know the feeling,' I say. However this situation is resolved, I cannot see how I am ever going to feel any differently to the way I do now. I've spent a lifetime with this weight on my shoulders. It has shifted and turned, been heavier at certain times than at others, but it has never lifted completely and I can't see how it ever will.

'I know what Mum thinks,' Tim says, 'but I've never believed that Maria killed herself. She was stronger than that, you know? Even when she had all that trouble at her old school in London, I never thought for a moment that she'd give up.'

For a heart-stopping moment I think he means that he suspects someone else had a hand in her death, but he continues speaking. 'I'm sure the police were right. She must have drunk more than she was used to, and got confused about where she was, or maybe she went to the cliffs to get away from everyone for some reason, to be alone. And then she must have stumbled or … I don't know. I thought I'd been able to stop turning it over and over in my mind, but this thing with Sophie, it's got it all churned up again.'

'What did happen, in London?' I've still never got to the bottom of this. Maybe it's time I did.

'Did she never tell you?'

'No, not really.' She had tried, but I hadn't let her. I knew if I let her get too close I'd never be able to pull back if I needed to.

'There was this boy in her year who she was friendly with. But then he started to want more, told her he was in love with her. She told him she wasn't interested, just wanted to be friends. But she felt a bit uncomfortable around him after that and pulled back, started spending less time with him. That's when it started.'

'When what started, exactly?'

'Notes in her bag at first, things like that: "Why won't you see me any more?"; "I know we're meant to be together". Then he started waiting outside our house in the mornings before school, wanting to walk with her, and then when she wouldn't he'd walk a few metres behind us all the way.'

'Did you tell anyone? Your parents?'

'Not at first. I mean, we used to laugh about it when it began. Also, I don't know, teenagers didn't tell their parents things in the eighties, did they? Not like they seem to now. The idea was that we got on with things ourselves. I hope my daughter's not like that when she's older.'

I know exactly what he means. Henry's still so little that he tells me everything that happens to him, his life an open book, but even Polly's daughters are much franker with her than I was with my parents. When I was a teenager, even before Maria disappeared, the life I had with my parents was completely separate from the rest of my existence – my real life, as I thought of it. When Polly asks her daughters how their day has been, she gets it all – the rivalries, the disagreements, the small kindnesses. She knows them. What my parents knew, and still know, is a highly edited version of me, a composite of who I was as a child and what I chose to show them of the person I was becoming.

'Then when he wasn't getting anywhere with that,' Tim goes on, 'he ramped it up. A couple of times she saw him outside our house late at night, looking up at her window. She didn't tell Mum and Dad about that, in case they thought she was encouraging it. And then the rumours started.'

This was what Maria had hinted at to me, but I hadn't wanted to hear it. I am overcome, as I have been so often recently, with an impotent sense of longing to go back and change the past. Change my behaviour, at least. I am a decent person now. I pay my taxes and go to the dentist. I recycle. I care about my friends, and about the world in general. But how do I reconcile that with the things I did when I was sixteen? I'm that person too, aren't I?

'What sort of rumours?'

Tim's face closes up a little. 'Horrible stuff. Sexual. But not only that she'd slept with such and such a boy, or whatever. He said she'd slept with girls too. I know that seems to be all the rage with teenage girls nowadays, but back then being called a lesbian was akin to being called a baby-murderer. Girls started to avoid her, even ones that had previously been her friends. Boys that had never even noticed her started sniffing around. And then a rumour went round that she'd slept with three boys at once. One—' he stops to control the tremor in his voice, biting his lower lip, and then spits out the rest of the sentence '—one in each hole.'

'But why did people believe him? If they knew her?'

'If you get enough people talking about something it

gathers its own momentum. And the idea that there's no smoke without fire is a powerful one. Think about famous men who've been accused of sexual assault. Even if they are completely exonerated, if the case is thrown out due to lack of evidence; even if the woman withdraws her statement. What's the first thing you think every time you see them on TV or hear them on the radio? "I wonder if he did it". That's what you think, every time.'

'So your parents decided to move? You told them in the end?' I remember that first day in the lunch hall; Maria explaining the cause for the move as 'a bit of trouble' at her old school; she was so determined not to carry it with her.

'Not exactly. He did that for her. He wrote them an anonymous letter signed by a "concerned well-wisher". Telling them about the rumours, these . . . things that were being said about her. Can you imagine hearing those things about your own daughter?'

I can't imagine it, can't imagine the pain and horror and sorrow of it. I think of Polly at her kitchen table, her voice dripping with barely concealed hatred for her daughter's persecutor. And of Bridget at the end of the leavers' party when she realised Maria was missing, her unflinching stare accusing me of an unknown crime.

'What was the boy's name? Do you remember?'

'Remember it? Of course. His name was Nathan Drinkwater.'

I stop dead on the pavement and a mother with a double buggy bangs into the back of my legs, tutting as she manoeuvres round me.

'Nathan Drinkwater? Are you sure?' Maria's only other Facebook friend, apart from me and Sophie.

'I'm hardly likely to forget it, am I? What's the matter?'

'Did anyone else know his name? Anyone from Sharne Bay?'

'Loads of people knew. Matt Lewis's cousin knew someone who went to our old school. I was fuming at the time when he told everyone. We came all that way to escape what had happened, but we couldn't. It followed us to Norfolk. I think it would have followed us anywhere.'

'What happened to Nathan? Did Maria ever hear from him after you moved?'

'No. I actually heard that he had died a few years ago, from a friend of a friend of someone who knew him. I don't know if it's true though.'

Is Nathan Drinkwater dead? If not, he doesn't sound like the type to give up due to mere lack of proximity. Could it really be him on Maria's friends list on Facebook? I wonder whether Maria continued to hear from Nathan after they moved, but told no one. And more than that, I wonder if he really is dead. And, if not, where is he now?

Chapter 31

2016

I had been hoping that my encounter with Pete in the café opposite Foster and Lyme would be my last; but as I emerge from the stunning Dulwich Village house belonging to one of my regular clients, Sue Plumpton, my phone rings and his name flashes up on the display. I am tempted to ignore it. There has been a comforting normality about today. I got absorbed in my consultation with Sue, and my head is brimming with ideas for one of her spare bedrooms, the latest in her house to get a makeover.

I envy Sue in her picture-postcard corner of London, divorced from a banker, her life filled only with tennis followed by lattes with 'the girls', walks in Dulwich Park with her Chihuahua Lola and dinner parties where she doesn't even have to cook the dinner. I smile, thinking of the M&S cottage pie for one I shared with Polly last time she came over – would that count as a dinner party, I wonder? I think about texting Polly to ask, and then remember with a piercing pain that we are not speaking.

Seeing Pete's name on my phone shunts my anxiety back into sharp focus. I am too frightened to ignore him; what if something's happened?

'Hello?' My voice sounds wary even to myself.

'Hi. How are you?' He sounds cautious too.

'OK. On my way back from seeing a client.'

'Where are you?'

'Walking past Dulwich College,' I say.

'Oh, that's not far from me. I can't get my head around the fact that it's just a normal school to the kids who go there.'

'I know! I always think that. When it's basically Hogwarts.'

'Right. I was wondering . . .' He pauses. 'Could we meet? I was going to suggest meeting in town but I'm working from home today, in Sydenham, so I could come and meet you in Dulwich – in the park maybe?'

I had been looking forward to getting home and making a start on my ideas for Sue's spare bedroom, but I know I won't be able to concentrate on that now, so I agree and we arrange to meet outside the café in half an hour.

I retrace my steps down College Road, turn right along the South Circular and five minutes later I'm in the park. Half of the well-heeled mothers of south-east London have congregated here today, and I'm in constant danger from kamikaze toddlers on scooters. Pete won't be here yet so I stroll past the tennis courts where some ladies (probably Sue's chums) are hitting genteelly back and forth.

Pete is five minutes early, but I'm already there waiting. I watch him dodging buggies and smilingly brushing off the apologies of the mother of an excitable toddler who rams into his legs on a tricycle.

'Hi.'

'Hello.' I find I can't meet his eye for too long and don't know what to do with my hands, pushing them into my pockets to keep them still.

'Do you want to get a coffee or . . . ?'

'No, I've had loads already today. Do you?'

'No, let's just walk,' he says, and we head off along the path.

'So, have you spoken to the police again?' he asks.

'Yes, yesterday.'

'And you didn't . . . ?'

'Mention our little rendezvous?' That sounded more bitter than I intended. 'No, of course not. We agreed, didn't we? You haven't told them, have you?'

'God, no. The last thing they need is another reason to suspect me.'

'So they do then? Suspect you, I mean?'

'Oh, I don't know. I think so, but of course they don't have any evidence so I'm hoping they're moving on, looking at someone else. All the time they're investigating me, they're wasting time when they could be looking for the real killer.'

'Maybe there's some forensic evidence that will put you in the clear? Surely there must have been something?'

'I hope so.' We walk on for a while, the sound of children's voices fading as we get further away from the play area. 'Can I ask you something?'

'OK.' I push my hands deeper into my coat pockets, balling my fists.

'Why are you so sure I didn't do it?'

'We spent the night together, remember?' Anxiety makes my words ugly with sarcasm.

'I know, but I could have done it before then. It was after eleven when we left, and from what the police said, nobody can remember seeing her after about ten o'clock. I had plenty of time to ... I don't know ... lure her down to the woods.'

I smile, despite the gravity of the situation we find ourselves in.

'That's partly why, to be honest,' I say.

'What is?'

'The way you said "lure her down to the woods". Nobody who'd really done it would describe it like that.'

'What would they say then?'

'I don't know, but luring someone to the woods is the sort of thing that would happen in a bad TV movie.'

'OK, but why didn't you suspect me before that?'

We're passing the lake and rather than answering straight away, I suggest sitting down on a nearby bench. One of the slats is broken at the end and I shift closer to Pete to avoid the jagged edge. He doesn't move away.

'Louise?' Our knees are almost touching, just a fragment of space between them. His hands are resting on his thighs, the skin around his fingernails chapped and raw as if he's been picking at it.

'I know it wasn't you, because I know who did do it.' The words tumble out in a rush, before I can stop them.

'What?' He jumps up and takes a few paces away from me, then turns back. 'What the fuck are you talking about? If you know who did it, why the hell haven't you told the police?'

'No, sorry, I'm explaining it wrong. I don't know who it is, but I do know that it's the same person who's been sending these messages to me, and to Sophie before she died. It's to do with what happened, when we were at school.'

'What, the bullying thing you told me about? And what do you mean, what messages?'

He sits back down, his anger subsiding. Tension flows out of me and the knot in my stomach loosens a little as I realise that I'm going to tell him everything. He's safe, he's got as much to lose as I have.

'You're not on Facebook, are you?'

'No, like I told you, I stay right away from social media,' he says. 'Full of nutters.'

'Well, I am,' I say, and begin my story. When I get to the leavers' party, I stumble over my words, watching him anxiously all the while for any sign of horror or disgust. He doesn't react though, or interrupt, but lets me tell him the whole thing, including the part about the Facebook messages from Maria, the internet date, the incident at the park. When I've finished, I shift away from him a little, allowing the broken slat to dig into the back of my thigh.

'So now you know. Whoever killed Sophie is the person who's been messaging me. Which means it's either someone who was around at the time, or . . . they never found Maria's body. Do you understand now why I don't want the police to make any more connections between me and Sophie than they have to? Why I don't want them to know I spent the night in a hotel room with her boyfriend?'

'I suppose so, but . . .'

'And do you hate me?' I ask, tears welling, ashamed at my childish need for reassurance.

'For what you did to Maria? No, I don't hate you. You were young. You made a bad decision, that's all. That's what people do when they're young. Yes, it had catastrophic, unforeseeable consequences, but it was just a bad decision. I think you've probably paid for it, haven't you?' He takes my hand, eyes pleading. 'But Louise, don't you realise? This could get me off the hook. If you tell the police . . .'

I snatch my hand back as if he's tried to bite it.

'No. I told you, I can't.'

'And I understand that, I do. But you could just tell them about the messages from Maria, you don't even need to say you bullied her, let alone go into the drink spiking.'

'They'll want to know why Maria has sought me out, what I did to her. They'll ask questions I don't want to answer.'

'But the Ecstasy, you said the messages don't mention that – the rest of it, it's just schoolgirl stuff. Nothing to interest the police.'

'But they'll want to know what Maria is talking about, they'll start digging it up. They'll find her, or whoever's sending the messages. Whoever it is knows what I did, and they'll tell the police . . . I can't bear it. You don't understand.'

Sam understood. He was the only one who ever did, and part of me longs to be back there with him in our bubble; the two of us against the world, with the promise of his silence to protect me.

Pete turns away from me and puts his head in his hands.

'You know that day in the café, when we agreed to keep quiet, not to tell the police?'

'Yes.'

'Well, I had another reason for wanting to steer clear of the police. When I was at university, there was this girl. We were friends, but she was . . . troubled, I suppose you'd say.

She used to stay over in my room in halls, but nothing ever happened between us, although I think she wanted it to. Then one day, there was a knock on my door. It was the police. They said there had been an accusation, a serious sexual assault. It was her. She said I'd tried to ... force her. You know. That I'd held her down, threatened to hurt her if she wouldn't ... But that she'd managed to get away before I could ... you know.' He has kept his gaze on the ground throughout this, but now he looks at me.

'I was exonerated back then; there was no evidence, because I hadn't done anything. But I know the police believed her and not me. They treated me like a piece of shit. And I heard the whispers in the corridors, felt the stares. And as for getting a girlfriend – well, no girl would come anywhere near me after that. And now I feel like it's all happening again. I know what everyone's thinking: Sophie and I argued, then I disappeared. There's no smoke without fire. Please, Louise. You have to tell the police about the messages from Maria. They'll be able to trace them. They can find out who's really behind this.'

'No,' I say quietly. 'They'll want to know why I've been lying to them, why I didn't tell them about the messages straight away. And anyway, I can't. There may not be any evidence, but I'm not the only person who knows what happened at the leavers' party. Whoever is sending those messages knows what I did. If I open the door to it, it's all going to get out. You won't be able to stop it. I could go to prison, lose my son.'

'You wouldn't go to prison, Louise. You're blowing this out of proportion. Think about it.'

Is he right? Have I built this up so much that my mind

is full of it, obscuring everything else? I've spent so many years hiding the truth that I don't know what's real any more. So many years with Sam, who knew what I had done and was as adamant as I was that we needed to keep it a secret. But maybe he was as blinkered as me, as unable as I was to think rationally about it.

Maybe; but for Henry's sake, I need to be around. Even if the chance of being prosecuted for Maria's death is miniscule, it's a risk I can't take.

'No,' I say. 'We need to carry on as we are, keep our heads down.'

He shakes his head, refusing to look at me. I take a deep breath. There is a part of me that thought there was something between us – just a spark maybe, but one that could be coaxed into a flame one day. But what I'm about to say will extinguish that little light entirely.

'Don't forget the Travelodge,' I say. 'I'm keeping a secret about you too, remember?'

As I watch him walk away, I wonder whether I will ever be able to have a normal relationship, or if my past is going to taint every aspect of my future. It's probably a good thing that he's gone – at least it's happened now, before I've had a chance to really get attached. It would have happened sooner or later.

I'm too mixed up, too dark; I'm just too alone to be with anyone else.

Chapter 32

2016

The last few days since my walk in the park with Pete have been very dark. I haven't had any client meetings, thank God, so apart from the school run where I hold Henry's hand tightly in mine all the way, I have stayed in the house, spending most of the time Henry is at school in bed. He should have been at Sam's this past weekend, but Sam asked if we could swap as he had something on, and I was only too happy to agree.

I know that I'm slipping behind with work, and that in a few weeks when it comes to light how little I've done for her I will be in danger of losing Rosemary altogether, but I can't rouse myself to action. I am jumpy, looking over my shoulder, the image of Sophie's body always in the back of my mind. I wonder if I will ever stop imagining myself on some other piece of ground, cold and lifeless. I save my energy for those hours between picking Henry up and his bedtime where I need to put on my best performance.

He's asleep now, shattered after the school day. He

wanted to go to the park again today, but after last time I can't face it. I am making a cup of tea when the doorbell rings. I jump and stare unseeing at the teaspoon in my hand. Who would turn up unannounced at this time?

I'm in my oldest tracksuit bottoms and sweatshirt, and I can't remember when I last had a shower. I run an exploratory tongue over my teeth and it catches on the roughness; I definitely haven't cleaned them today and possibly not yesterday either. If I stand very still perhaps whoever it is will go away.

The bell rings again, a double press this time, followed by a loud knock, official-sounding. What if it's Reynolds? If so then there's no point hiding; she'll track me down eventually. I put the teaspoon down, noticing as I do all the rings on the worktop from the spoons and cups of the preceding days. Have I actually eaten anything or have I just been drinking tea? I can't remember.

I edge into the hallway. A blurred shape waits on the other side of the frosted glass. I advance along the corridor, holding my breath, and then in a swift motion pull open the door.

'Oh. It's you.' I keep my hand on the Yale latch, unsure how long it's going to be before I close the door, and which side of it Sam is going to be on.

'Charming,' says Sam, his eyes flicking up and down, taking in my dishevelled appearance. 'No need to sound quite so excited.'

'Sorry, but . . . what are you doing here?'

'Again, charming. Traditionally in our country when a guest arrives at your home, you welcome them in, offer them a drink, that sort of thing.'

I step back, wrong-footed. 'Sorry. Come in.' He fills the hallway, as he always did. The flat was too small for him. He had filled every space in it. It's much more suitable for a spinster like me. Sam peers into the sitting room as we pass on our way to the kitchen.

'Wow, it looks really different.' He hasn't been into the flat since that time when I almost gave in to my loneliness and let him back in to my life. That was a good eighteen months ago, but I remember the way it felt: the longing, how much I wanted to let go. Since then, I've tried to make sure I only see him at handovers, which always happen at the door. On the odd occasion we have needed to meet to discuss something to do with Henry, it's been on neutral ground.

'Oh, I'm sorry, what did you expect?' My voice is harsher than I'd intended. 'That I'd keep it a shrine to you? Add a big photo of you over the fireplace?'

He looks stung. 'Sorry, I didn't mean . . . it looks nice. Just different.'

In the kitchen Sam looks around, clearly trying to keep his expression neutral in the face of the dirty cups, unswept floor and general air of neglect.

'It's not normally like this,' I mutter. 'Not had a very good few days.'

'It's fine, Louise, don't worry about it,' he says, looking worried nonetheless.

'Give me a minute, will you?' I say.

I dive into the bathroom and brush my teeth, splash cold water on my face and have a cursory wash, trying not to think about why I am doing so. In the bedroom I take off the stained sweatshirt and pull on something that at least falls into the daywear category, reappearing in the kitchen feeling slightly more human.

'Tea?' I ask, gathering up used bowls and stained cutlery and hastily wiping down the kitchen worktop.

'I'd rather have something stronger,' he says, pushing a crumb-strewn plate to one side as he sits down at the kitchen table. I snatch up the plate and shove it along with the rest of the dirty crockery haphazardly into the dishwasher.

'There's wine in the fridge. Can you get it while I . . .' I gesture to the dishwasher.

He stands up easily and gets the wine, reaching up to the top cupboard to get two glasses. He knows where everything is. I haven't changed a thing in here since he left. He pours us both a glass and pushes mine towards me.

'Sit down, Louise. Don't clean up on my behalf.'

I give up, promising myself that when he's gone I will throw off the lethargy that has settled on me since I saw Pete in Dulwich.

'So now you're in and you've got your drink, what are you doing here? Henry's asleep.' I sit down and take a gulp of wine. I'm not in the mood for games and it's liberating to realise that I don't care what he thinks of me, not in this moment.

'I came to see you, not Henry. I wanted someone to talk to, I suppose. About Sophie and everything. It's all so awful.'

He looks genuinely upset and I feel myself softening.

'I know. It's so hideous. Have you spoken to the police?'

'Yes, they were trying to make something of the fact that

Soph spent a lot of time talking to me and Matt. I mean, she was one of my best friends at school, of course I was speaking to her.'

'Was she really? One of your best friends?' When I think of my friends at school, I never consider any boys as part of that group. There were boys, of course, but in my sixteen-year-old head, boys couldn't be friends. There was always a difference, an edge, whether you fancied them or not.

'Not best friends maybe, but part of the gang. You know.' I suppose I do. My feelings about that time, about Sophie, Sam, Maria, they're so complicated. And now it's all got mixed up with the Facebook request, and what's happened to Sophie. I'm in a hall of mirrors, full of distorted reflections and false endings. I've lost track of which way I came in and I have no idea how to get out.

'Did you . . . mention the Facebook thing? Maria?'

He looks uneasy. 'No. I knew you didn't want the police to know and . . . well . . .'

'You got us the E,' I finish the sentence for him.

He twiddles the stem of his wine glass.

'It's made me think, you know?' he says.

'About what?'

'Oh, you know, the past. That kind of thing. You know what I mean?'

I raise my eyebrows, determined not to make this easy for him.

'You and I, we've got all this history together. It makes things easy between us, doesn't it?'

'Does it?' Things don't feel very easy right now. The air is thick with the unsaid.

'Oh, Lou. I know you're still angry with me, and you have

every right to be. I hurt you and I handled things badly. I am so sorry for that, I really am. But I hoped that maybe we could be friends. I thought ... that you might need a friend at the moment, one who understands. Who knows what really happened. I know I do.'

He's right, of course, that is what I desperately need. What I don't need is to get entangled with him again, to allow him to weave himself back into the fabric of my life. But he's the only one now who understands. He's standing below me with his arms outstretched and it's so tempting to let myself fall.

'Have you heard any more from ... whoever's behind this page?' he asks. I realise that he doesn't know there have been more messages. I daren't tell him about the one mentioning Henry. He'll be furious with me for not telling him at the time. Instead I answer him with a question of my own.

'Sam, do you think it's possible ... that Maria's still alive?' I am suddenly close to tears. 'What if the request really is from her? She must have worked out that she'd been given something. Or someone else has.'

He takes my hand and despite myself, my fingers curl around his.

'No, Louise. I don't think it's possible, honestly. Not after all this time. Whoever's doing this is just some sicko trying to scare you.'

'But Esther ... she's been getting presents from Maria on her birthday every year since she disappeared.'

'What?'

'She gets presents in the post, they say they're from Maria.'

Sam frowns, and I can almost see the wheels in his mind turning, trying to process this information.

'Sorry, who's getting these presents?'

'Esther Harcourt. From our year at school? I was talking to her quite a bit at the reunion?'

'I don't remember her.' He shrugs, and that one little gesture encapsulates the tragedy of the teenage years: the difference between the haves and the have-nots. Of course he doesn't remember Esther. She simply never crossed his radar, being neither attractive nor popular. I wouldn't have crossed it either if it hadn't been for my association with Sophie. I am overtaken by a desperate wish that I had never become friends with Sophie, that I had been brave and stuck with Esther. It's my own cowardice, my own craven desire for acceptance, for popularity that has led me here.

'It must be the same person who's put up the Facebook page,' he goes on. 'Like I said, some sicko. Do the police know?'

'I don't know. I haven't told them, but maybe Esther has. I know she went to the police when she first started getting them, but they weren't interested.'

He sits back in his chair, releasing my hand.

'Will you tell me what happens, next time you speak to the police?' he says.

'Yes, of course.'

'And you'll tell me if you get any messages on Facebook?'

I promise but I know it's a promise I won't keep. I am as alone as I've always been with all this. Polly still hasn't been in contact since I told her about Maria, and I can't let Sam in enough for him to help me. I don't want it to be the way he slips back in. I pour myself another glass of wine and he pushes his own towards me hopefully. I fill it. What difference does it make?

'So, how's everything else anyway?' he asks. 'Work?'

'Work's good. I've got another job on for Sue Plumpton – remember Sue?'

'How could I forget La Plumpton? Has she still got that awful little dog?'

'Lola? Oh yes, she's still going strong. If strong's the right word for what's basically a dog/rat hybrid. In fact I had to make sure I integrated her basket into the design for Sue's living room.'

'No!'

'Yep.' As soon as I start to relax into the conversation, it hits me that in spite of everything, I miss this. Before Henry was born, we would sit down together every evening at this table with a glass of wine and share titbits from our respective days. This tailed off in the early months of Henry's life, replaced by me walking up and down the flat in a haze of exhaustion, trying fruitlessly to soothe Henry as he screamed on my shoulder. Sam would retreat to the bedroom with his laptop and an attitude. We never got it back, that easy togetherness, even when Henry started sleeping through the night. Moving from a unit of two to one of three where one member was utterly dependent on the other two, shifted the balance of our relationship entirely.

I keep the conversation bubbling, asking him first about his work and then about some mutual friends that I've lost touch with since the divorce. Obviously there's an enormous elephant in the room that I am absolutely resolved not to mention, but unfortunately Sam strays onto the topic when

I ask about his mum. By the time he and I got together she was back in Sam's life, up to a point, but we never saw a lot of her, even after Henry was born.

'She's totally obsessed with Daisy, much more so than she was with Henry. I don't know, maybe it's because she's a girl. Spoils her rotten.'

I think with a pang of my little boy: his intense love for his cuddly toys, as if they were real; his dedicated application to any task he takes on; how seriously he takes the world. Can she really love this other grandchild more, just because she's a girl? Perhaps it's not that though. Perhaps it was me that was the problem. I had always sensed that Sam's mum was not a fan of mine, and I wonder, though I dare not ask, how Catherine is faring in that department. Now he's mentioned Daisy though, I can't skate past the subject completely. 'And how's that all going second time around? Fatherhood?'

'Oh great, great. She's wonderful, growing up fast, into everything.' He's saying all the right words but there's an edge to his voice that I recognise. I wait, refusing to fill the gap. 'Quite tiring though,' he says. 'Doesn't leave much time for . . . well, for anything else.'

I must have made a face of some kind, because he goes on.

'I know, I know, poor man, feeling left out, baby's taken his place. Quite the cliché, aren't I?'

He laughs, expecting me to do the same, but the story is so familiar to me that I can't even pretend.

'I'm sure it must be hard,' I manage, and then can't resist adding, 'Probably not as hard as being left on your own with a two-year-old.'

'Ouch. I guess I deserved that.' He runs a hand over his

head, all the way from his forehead to the nape of his neck. 'I'm sorry, Louise, I really am. And I know – well, it must have been hard for you last year, to hear that I'd had another child.'

Hard doesn't even begin to cover it. We went through so much to get Henry. All those bloody injections, the endless appointments. And my God, the waiting: total inability to concentrate on anything else; trying to hold off testing, because if it was negative I wouldn't know whether it was just too early or if it was a true negative. It was all so exhausting. And the pain of dealing with other people's pregnancies; at one point in my mid-thirties it had seemed like barely a day went by without a scan picture appearing on Facebook, or a group email coyly entitled 'News!'

'I'm happy for you,' I say, trying to mean it. I don't want to be this person, this caricature, the bitter ex-wife. 'It's given Henry a sister, and we always wanted that.'

'Hmm. Be careful what you wish for.'

'Oh Sam, don't say that.'

'No, no, I don't mean Daisy, of course I love her to bits, that goes without saying. But … it's not easy, that's all. Maintaining a relationship, or a life at all, when you've got a young child. I don't know, it didn't seem this hard with you.'

Of course it wasn't hard for him because I went out of my way to make things easy, to smooth his path. I went along with everything he wanted, I never said no, even if what he was asking was unreasonable. I made sure that his life carried on as normal, as far as was humanly possible. He was the only person in my life who really knew me, who knew what I had done and loved me anyway. I can suddenly see so clearly how much pressure that was for me, to be with someone to whom I always felt indebted. I had been grateful that he had chosen me, stayed with me.

'I'm sure it'll get easier as she gets older,' I say, knowing nothing of the sort.

'Oh yes, I'm sure it will.' He sounds equally unconvinced. 'Anyway, let's not talk about that. Do you remember Rob McCormack?' He launches into a story about a colleague, a man I met many times when Sam and I were together.

An hour later we're still at the table, halfway down our second bottle. It's as though I'm watching myself from a distance, unbalanced by a combination of wine and nostalgia, tinged with a longing that I don't want to think about. Part of me yearns to let go, to lose myself, to melt back into him as I've nearly done before, but at the same time I know I must hold back if I am to keep myself safe, to retain any trace of the equilibrium I've achieved over the last two years.

The conversation turns eventually and inevitably to Henry, reminding me of the other huge loss I suffered when Sam left me: I lost the only other person in the world who understands how wonderful, how perfect Henry is. The only other person who really gets him. We are laughing about the time he got a tiny plastic ball stuck up his nose when Sam glances at his watch and gives a start.

'God, look at the time. I really should go.'

I jump up immediately, putting the glasses and bottle on the side.

'Yes, of course, you'd better get back. I'll get your coat.' I hurry out into the hall to retrieve his jacket from the pegs by the door, and he follows.

'Can I pop in and see Henry?'

I recognise the yearning in his voice from all those lonely every-other-weekends, and push open Henry's door for him. The Thomas the Tank Engine nightlight casts an unearthly blue glow, and I stand in the doorway, watching as Sam kneels by the bed. As usual Henry has got too hot and taken off his pyjamas, his hair plastered to his forehead with sweat. Sam strokes the soft, silky skin on his back, and Henry shifts but doesn't wake, pulling Manky closer to his face.

Sam's face is closed as he comes back into the hallway, but I know how painfully aware he is of the price he has paid, not getting to do this every night. But then, it's a price I have had to pay too, because I don't get to do it either every other weekend plus the weeknight when he is with Sam. I hand Sam his coat and as I do so, my hand brushes his and I feel a jolt of electricity that tingles throughout my body. The moment hangs between us, hot and threatening. I can tell he's about to say something that he won't be able to take back, and although part of me wants to hear it, I know that if I do, all the work I've done in the past two years will be wasted. I snatch my hand back and the jacket falls to the floor. He stoops to pick it up and as he does, I slip past him and open the door, letting the cold air stream in.

'So, it was good to see you.' I lean forward and kiss him briskly on the cheek, leaving him with nowhere to go in terms of trying to kiss me. If he is bewildered at the sudden change of pace he hides it well.

'Take care, Louise. And let me know if . . . you know.'

'Yes, I will. Good night.'

I practically push him out of the door, closing it firmly behind him. Back in the kitchen, I lean against the worktop, hugging myself tightly because there is no one else to do it for me. I'm the only one who can take care of me, and I vow to do it better in the future. As the wind rattles the French windows, I stare out through the glass, but I can see nothing except my own reflection.

Chapter 33

2016

My flat doesn't feel the same any more. It used to be a safe haven, my refuge from the world. I don't feel safe here now though. I used to be thankful for Marnie, my upstairs neighbour, a woman in her fifties who seems to do nothing but go to her unspecified work, come home and go to bed. She's only a few metres above my head, but I hear practically nothing from her. When Henry was a baby and I paced the floor with him as he screamed, night after night, squirming in my arms, I thought she might come down and complain, but nothing. Now I would find it reassuring to hear footsteps creaking overhead, the sound of dinner being cooked, television being watched, friends coming over for a drink. But Marnie remains resolutely silent.

I can't stop turning last night's encounter with Sam over and over in my mind. I know I didn't imagine that moment between us at the door, and most of me is thankful that I didn't give in to it. But there is a tiny part of me that wishes I had allowed myself the relief of sinking back into him, of being held by him, soothed by the comforting familiarity of his touch. I give myself a shake, forcing myself to remember how things really were between us, especially at the end. I did the right thing. I can't put myself back two years.

Esther has called a couple of times today but I ignored it and she hasn't left a message. I've also had a call from DI Reynolds. I didn't answer that one either, but she left a voicemail asking me to ring her at my earliest convenience. If I don't call her back soon she's going to turn up here, armed with her questions and her indefatigable thoroughness. I know it's inevitable that I will have to speak to her again, but I'm trying to put it off as long as I can.

I'm scrolling unseeing through my emails at the kitchen table when the doorbell rings. I consider for a few seconds simply not answering it, but when it rings again, I walk slowly down the hallway, feeling almost resigned to whatever waits on the other side.

'Oh,' says Esther, looking down at my attire. Despite my best intentions, I'm back in the stained tracksuit bottoms and sweatshirt. 'Sorry.'

'It's fine,' I say, pulling the cord on the tracksuit bottoms tighter to stop them falling down. I'm relieved not to be facing Reynolds, but on the other hand I feel a vague unease. 'What are you doing here? How did you even know where I live?'

'Serena Cooke?'

Of course. My alter ego; the one who wanted to make a will.

'I figured you'd given your real address. It's too hard to think of a fake one on the spur of the moment.'

'Right.' We stand there for a moment, each unsure of the other's next move. 'Do you . . . want to come in?'

The kitchen is still a mess, but this time I can't be bothered to apologise, let alone tidy up.

'Tea?' I ask, moving some old newspapers off one of the chairs.

'Yes, please.' Esther hangs her coat and bag neatly from the back of the chair before sitting down. There's an awkward silence while we wait for the kettle to boil. Once we are both seated, mugs in hand, I wait for her to tell me why she's here.

'So I spoke to the police again,' she begins. 'Have you, too?'

'Yes.'

'So did they show you?'

'Show me what?' Oh God. I know what is coming.

'The necklace. Maria's necklace.'

My mind scrabbles around for the next lie, vacillating between telling her the police didn't show me, or saying they did but I hadn't realised it was Maria's, but somewhere in between the two the elastic band inside me snaps and my face crumples into hot tears.

Esther puts out a hand and touches my arm gently. 'Sorry, I didn't mean to upset you. Is it . . . the messages? Have you had any more?'

I get up from the table and take a piece of kitchen roll from the side to blow my nose.

'Don't be nice to me. Don't feel sorry for me. It's all my fault. Did you tell them . . . the police? That you thought it was Maria's necklace?'

'Yes,' she says, her face puzzled. 'Didn't you?'

'No. I didn't want them to connect me and Sophie to what happened to Maria.'

'But . . . surely they already knew you were all connected when you told them about the Facebook page?'

'I didn't tell them about that either.' My face flushes with hot shame, my blood running thick with all the things Esther doesn't know. 'Did . . . did you?'

'Yes, of course,' she says, bewildered.

So it's over. Reynolds knows. Tim will be getting a call soon, no doubt, and it won't be long before they come knocking on my door. With a heaving swell inside, I realise this is where it all starts to unravel.

'Well, I assumed you'd already told them,' she goes on. 'And didn't they find the messages from Maria anyway? On Sophie's computer?'

'Not as far as I know. If the police weren't looking for them, they would just seem like innocuous messages from a friend. As far as they're concerned, Maria's just another of Sophie's many Facebook friends. There was no reason for them to be suspicious, unless somebody told them about Maria.'

And now somebody has, and the police will be joining the dots, forming a chain that leads them back to a summer's night in 1989.

'I don't understand why you didn't tell the police about the friend request and the messages from Maria though?' Esther says.

'I didn't want them to connect me and Sophie to what happened to Maria in 1989,' I repeat.

'But why on earth not?' Esther looks utterly bemused.

It doesn't matter now. The police are going to find Maria,

or whoever is sending those messages, and they're going to find out what I did. It's all going to come out. There's no point pretending any more. There's even a kind of relief in it. Even so, I bury my face in my hands so I don't have to see her face when I tell her.

'What happened to Maria, whatever it was, it was my fault.' The words are muffled, but they are out there.

'Louise, it wasn't. I know you treated her badly at school, but we all do things we regret when we're younger. Things that maybe even horrify us when we look back as adults.' I can hear in her voice what it is costing her to say this, can hear the years of pain and isolation she suffered at school and the scars they have left.

'You don't understand. There's something you don't know.' I take my hands away and force myself to meet her eye. 'Do you remember at the leavers' party, you couldn't find Maria, and you came to ask me if I'd seen her? You said she'd said she wasn't feeling well?'

'Yes.'

'I know why she felt unwell. Me and Sophie had ... we did something ...' I clench my fists, take a shaky breath. Esther waits, says nothing. 'We spiked her drink with Ecstasy.'

Esther inhales sharply. I watch her face closely. She doesn't speak straight away, but puts a hand to her mouth and turns to look out of the French windows into the courtyard. She is miles and years away, turning events over in her mind, reconfiguring them to fit this horrifying new information.

'But what happened to her then?' she asks, turning back to me.

'I don't know. I never saw her again, I swear.'

Esther is silent again, and I hold my breath, awaiting my fate. I realise that, aside from the implications for me and Henry of the police finding out about what I did, I am dreading losing Esther when I was beginning to feel that I had found her again.

'So the Facebook thing . . . is that what it's about, do you think?' she says eventually. 'Does whoever's doing it know?'

'I don't know. They've never mentioned it.' Part of what is so frightening about the messages is that whoever it is never says anything specific. They offer only veiled threats, standing in the shadows.

'The Facebook page . . .' she stops. 'It couldn't be her, could it? Where would she have been all this time? Even on my birthday, when I get the presents, I've never really believed they could be from her. But the necklace . . .'

'I've considered every possibility, believe me. But Esther . . . what we did . . . can you . . .' Can you forgive me, is what I want to ask her, but I can't say it, I'm too frightened of the answer, and too ashamed of how selfish I am to need her forgiveness so desperately.

She looks down at her mug, picking at a small chip in the handle with her fingernail. 'You must have gone through hell when she disappeared. I can't imagine what that's done to you.'

'Honestly, Esther, when I look back I am utterly appalled at what I did, at who I was. Yes, I was insecure, yes, I was worried about losing my precarious place in the social pecking order, but everyone had to exist in that hierarchy, didn't they? But not everyone did what I did. Not everyone was so . . . weak. I look at my son, and if anyone ever treated him the way I treated Maria, I would want to rip them apart with my bare hands. I am a different person now. I really hope . . . well, I just hope you can see that.' I sit back down opposite her at the table, hardly daring to breathe.

'I think . . .' She stops and looks out of the window again. 'I think you've probably paid for what you did.' She looks back at me. 'I can see you're different now, Louise. I do see that.'

The tension that holds me in its thrall subsides a little and tears prick my eyes. I've told three people now, and two of them have considered me worthy at least of understanding, if not forgiveness.

'That's what—' I stop. That's what Pete said, I was going to say, but for reasons I can't articulate, I don't want her to know I've seen him. Something like shame fills me when I think about what I said to him, so I'm trying to keep it shut away. Then a strange thing happens, as if the thought of him has conjured Pete into the room.

'Oh, by the way, guess who I saw on the way here, at Victoria station?'

'Who?'

'That man Sophie brought to the reunion. Pete, is it? And here's the weird bit. He was with a woman, and not only that, they had a child with them, a baby. He was pushing the buggy. I wonder if Sophie knew he was married? I wouldn't be surprised.' Esther may have forgiven me, but Sophie still gets her scorn even in death.

'Oh my God. He told me was divorced at the reunion.' Has Pete been lying to me? If so, what else has he been lying about?

'I know! Do you think I ought to tell the police? Although

presumably they're already interviewing him so they must know he's married. I wonder how he's got that past his wife, being interviewed by the police and stuff.'

My mouth goes into autopilot and I express surprise and other appropriate responses to this news, keeping it light and gossipy. Inside I am reeling. Is Pete really married? He didn't seem like the cheating type. But then, what do I know?

At the door, I lean in to give Esther a goodbye hug, but something in her bearing – a barely noticeable hesitation, a momentary stiffening – makes me pull back. She wants to understand, but I don't know if she will ever get past this, if we can ever be friends.

When she has gone, I sweep through the house like a tornado, finding a place for everything that's lying around: dusting, hoovering, mopping the floors, changing the beds. When I've finished I get in the shower and stand under the jets for a long time, letting them rain down on me, warming me and washing away the grime that has accumulated since I left Pete in the park. I had thought we were getting closer but it strikes me now how little I really know about him. He could be anybody. Something he said to me at the reunion has been nagging at the edges of my mind, and now I remember what it is. He said he would never go to a reunion, described himself as a loner at school. I think about Maria in her childhood bedroom in London, peering out from behind a crack in the curtains. Nathan Drinkwater leans against a lamp post, staring up at her window, expressionless, just watching. I've imagined this scene before, but this time Nathan's face looks different. This time it looks familiar.

Chapter 34

She supposes there was always a darkness in him, a darkness she chose to ignore. Perhaps there was something in her that sought it out, deadly but unthinking, like a heat-seeking missile.

The first time, the things he did to her appalled her, scared her even, but even then there was a part of her that responded in kind: here he is. She kept the marks hidden under her clothes where no one else could see. He praised her, made her feel special, said that there had been a girl at university who thought he'd gone too far, who didn't enjoy the games like she did.

But then later, they didn't really feel like games any more. At first, she had enjoyed the thrill of letting him be in control, the delicious shudder of something that was close to fear. She was never really frightened though. But as time went on she could see something in his eyes, something different. It was like he wasn't there with her. He was somewhere else, with someone else. Someone he didn't care about hurting.

She had always sensed that there was something from the past that he wasn't telling her. Something darker even than the games he liked to play, when he gripped her wrists, put his hands over her mouth, around her neck even. Blurring the lines until she couldn't tell whether she was consenting or not: gasping for air, dizzy, bruised. Broken.

Perhaps it's simply not possible to truly know another person. When it comes down to it, we're all alone. Sometimes we don't even know ourselves.

Chapter 35

2016

I am determined to collect Henry on time today, but as so often recently, time slips away from me somehow, my mind full of the encounter with Esther earlier today. As I come panting round the corner, I can see I'm one of the last to turn up at the school gates for after-school club pickup. There are only a few children left standing by Mrs Hopkins and the new teaching assistant, Miss Jones. Most of them get collected at three o'clock by a parent (a mum mostly) or a grandparent (again, usually female). After-school club is for the unfortunates like Henry with two working parents and no helpful family members to take them home for cuddles and hot chocolate. The sky is clear with a sprinkling of stars already visible, and there's a smell of wood smoke in the air. I'm looking forward to scuffing through the russet leaves with Henry on the way home, and it's not until I'm fairly close that I realise that none of the children at the gate is Henry. Mrs Hopkins looks at me blankly. A tremor runs through me.

'Where's Henry?' My voice is spiky with fear.

'He was picked up at three . . .' She turns to Miss Jones. 'Wasn't he?'

Miss Jones looks concerned, but not overly so. She thinks it's a misunderstanding, something easy to sort out.

'Yes, his grandma picked him up.'

For a blissful half-second I think it's OK. My mum has come for an unexpected visit and decided to surprise him. She knows I hate the fact that he has to go to after-school club most days. But very quickly I realise it's not OK, not at all. Quite apart from the fact that she never voluntarily looks after him, Mum would never have done that without letting me know.

'His grandma?' My voice sounds unfamiliar, high and wobbly. Could Sam's mum possibly have decided it was time to get to know her grandson?

'Yes, an older lady, with long hair,' says Miss Jones, looking uncertainly from me to Mrs Hopkins. Sam's mum has an elegant crop.

'That's not his grandma! I don't know any older lady with long hair!' My knees buckle and I reach out, my hand finding the fence. A tiny splinter of wood skewers itself under the top layer of skin on my palm.

'He said it was his grandma,' Miss Jones says, more to Mrs Hopkins than to me. She's realised now the seriousness of what she's done.

'He's four!' I scream at her. 'Did you tell him she was his grandma? Is that what she said?'

'Well – yes . . .'

'He's four years old! He believes whatever you tell him! He thinks that when he loses his first tooth a fairy is going to come into his bedroom and replace it with money! I went into the office last week; I told Mrs Harper that I had concerns! You don't take the word of a four-year-old child, there are procedures, named contacts. Why did you just let him go?'

I'm up close to Miss Jones now, shouting in her face. Mrs Hopkins inserts herself between us.

'I absolutely appreciate the seriousness of this, Mrs Parker. Unfortunately I got called away to deal with a violent incident on the playground involving another parent. I left Miss Jones to manage pickup.'

'I bet I know who that was ... that horrible woman with the vile little boy.' Fear has loosened my tongue and Mrs Hopkins looks shocked.

'There was a message ... from the school office. Miss Wallis said you'd called at lunchtime.' Miss Jones has found her voice; her eyes are round with horror. 'You said that he wasn't going to after-school club, and that his grandma was picking him up. Henry seemed to know her ... I thought it was OK ... I'm sorry ...' She's starting to cry now but I don't have any emotion spare for her.

'That wasn't me on the phone! I never called the office! Mrs Harper should have told Miss Wallis that I had been in to check the safety procedures. And anyway, surely you don't let them go with anyone unless you know who they are. Don't you know anything?'

Mrs Hopkins intervenes again. 'You're absolutely right. This is a real failure on our part and I take full responsibility. We will be taking steps to make sure this doesn't happen again.' Her eyes flicker to Miss Jones. 'But for now, let's focus on where Henry is. Do you have any idea who this woman is?'

'No, I don't know. There isn't anyone.' I grip the fence harder and the splinter works its way further in.

The three of us stand there as if suspended in time, all looking to the others for the answer. In the depths of my bag my phone beeps. I scrabble frantically for it, hands shaking.

A new Facebook message from Maria Weston:

> I was right, Henry is a nice little boy. If you want him back, come to 29 Woodside St in Sharne Bay. Come alone. If you don't, there will be consequences for Henry. I'm waiting for you.

I drop my phone into my bag as if it's scalding my fingers.

'It's fine, I know where he is now,' I mutter. 'I . . . I've just realised who the lady is. It's OK, it's no problem. I forgot I'd asked her to pick Henry up.'

I don't think they believe me, Mrs Hopkins and Miss Jones, but what choice do they have? I run back towards the car, leaving Mrs Hopkins looking puzzled and extremely concerned. Miss Jones looks mostly relieved.

I tear out of the school gates, my phone already pressed to my ear. He answers on the third ring.

'Hi, Lou.'

'She's got Henry.'

'What?' says Sam distractedly. 'Who has?'

'Maria,' I say, panting. I'm already out of breath from running, but I can't slow down, mustn't waste a second.

'Hang on a minute.' I've got his attention now. 'What are you talking about?'

I tell him what has happened.

'What the fuck? Who's doing this? I'm calling the police.'

'No! She said come alone or there'll be consequences for Henry. She might hurt him if she realises we've called the police. I just need to get to him, to see he's all right. The police can come later.' If at all.

'Right, we'll go in my car. Thank God I'm working from home today. Where are you?'

Fifteen minutes later we're on our way. At every red light, I grind my teeth a little harder, my jaw wound tight.

'Oh God, oh God. What if Maria hurts him?'

'He'll be OK. It's just someone trying to scare you.' He doesn't sound convinced though and I can see the tremor in his hands as he changes gear. He's as frightened for Henry as I am, he's just trying to be strong for me. 'But Lou . . . you can't really think that Maria's still alive?'

I shrug, stare out of the window, dig my nails into my palm.

'I'll come in with you,' he says after a few minutes.

'No! You can't, I have to go alone.' If I don't, I know what will happen. Maria's already stepped over the line; done the unthinkable and taken my child. If she told me I had to cut my leg off to save him, I'd do it in a heartbeat. 'You'll have to wait outside.'

Sam looks at me with real concern.

'This could be dangerous. You've no idea who's in there.'

'I don't care. All I care about is getting Henry out of there. I don't care what happens to me. I never have. No one does.'

'Don't say that. I care what happens to you.'

I think of Sam's way of caring for me. I am better off without it.

'And I'm not the only one,' he goes on. 'Lots of people care about you.'

'But none of them really know me, do they? If they knew what I'd done, they wouldn't care quite so much, would they?'

'You've never given them the chance, Lou. Like you never gave me the chance. Even though I knew what you'd done, even though I was part of it, you still held me at a distance.'

'I wasn't holding you at a distance.' Tears are starting to flow unchecked down my face now. 'I had no choice, I was at a distance anyway. I've always been at a distance, from everything, ever since Maria disappeared. Being with you made it a bit better, I didn't feel so far away, because you knew, at least you knew who I was. So when you left me ...' I can't speak, great sobs wracking me. Sam reaches out a hand and takes mine, the contours as familiar to me as those of my own hand. I pull mine back and brush fiercely at my eyes, wiping away the tears.

'Don't,' I say. 'Don't touch me.'

He puts his hand back on the steering wheel and we drive in silence.

I wish that there was someone else to support me, that Sam wasn't the only person in my corner. I wonder whether he has ever been in my corner or if, and maybe this is true of most people, the only corner he is really in is his own.

We speed down the A11 in silence as the Norfolk landscape unfolds around us, the huge skies and endless fields pulling me back to them once more. The journey has never felt so long. There's an old train ticket in my bag and I tear it into pieces as we race along, each scrap tinier than the last. Neither of us knows Woodside Street, so as we enter the outskirts of Sharne Bay, I check the map on my phone again. We turn left off the main road onto an estate of boxy modern houses, all neatly tended gardens and sensible cars. Woodside Street is the third on the right and we drive slowly down between the bungalows.

'Don't get too close,' I say, panicking as we pass number 11. 'Stop here.'

Sam pulls over and already I'm opening the door, running down the street.

'Louise!' he calls after me.

'Stay there,' I shout, leaving him looking desperately after me. I am zinging with electricity; if anyone touches me they'll get thrown back like someone who's put a knife in the toaster. After these last few weeks of hiding, running, reacting, there's something almost freeing about doing something positive, taking back some of the control that has been wrested from me. I run down the street: 19, 21, 23, 25, 27. And then I'm there. Number 29 looks innocuously back at me. Whereas the other houses glow invitingly from behind closed curtains, the windows at number 29 are blank and unlit. I open the rusty gate and make my way up the path. The front garden is mostly paving stones with a few drooping weeds forcing their way up between the cracks. It's bordered by a narrow strip of flowerbed that looks as if it was once well cared for, but has been recently neglected.

The front door is blue, with two panes of frosted diamond-patterned glass in the top half. I am raising my hand to ring the bell, quickly before I can change my mind, when I realise that the door is ajar. Slowly, I push it open, reminding myself to breathe. The door gives a slow creak. I step inside, my boots squeaking on the dusty laminate floor, the sound echoing round the narrow hallway. There's a musty, unused smell of damp and long days with nothing to do.

The bungalow is double-fronted, and there is a doorway either side of me. I take a few steps further in, my ears straining for any sound in the silence. Cautiously I peer into the room on the left. It's the living room. By the light of the streetlamp outside I can see an old-fashioned green three-piece suite clustered around a glass-topped coffee table. A pine sideboard holds dusty trophies and china ornaments, and on the top shelf, sitting alone, I can just make out a photograph in a silver frame, elaborately curlicued. It's the face I've been looking at onscreen for the last few weeks: Maria's school photo. I step back and turn to look into the room on the opposite side of the hallway. It's also dark and empty, and looks like a spare bedroom, a double bed with a peach frilled eiderdown the only furniture.

Back in the hallway, my mind is screaming at me to run in, shouting Henry's name, but I need to take this carefully. I clutch the doorframe of the spare bedroom, trying to calm my breathing. The door straight ahead of me at the end of the corridor is closed. There are two doors identical to the ones I have just looked through a couple of metres further down the corridor. Both are tightly closed. I take a step, and another. Two more and I am standing next to the doors. I look from one to the other, and then reach out a cautious hand to the one on my left. Slowly, slowly I push down the brass handle. The door swings soundlessly open to reveal a bathroom, clean but old-fashioned with an avocado suite. Sick with fear, I take a step towards the bath and peer in. It's empty. I let out a stifled sob of relief mingled with terror. I pull the bathroom door to and turn to the door on my right, which I guess must be another bedroom. I put my hand on the handle, trying to stifle the panic that surges upwards in me, a silent scream, that I must not let out. As I push the door open, light spills through the gap, more and more of it until I can see the source, a standard lamp next to a desk.

A woman sits with her back to me at the desk, looking at a computer screen. Her long wispy grey-streaked hair hangs down over the back of her chair. She keeps her back to me, and I look frantically around the room, trying to take everything in before she turns round. There's a brand-new-looking wooden train set on the floor, the track set up in a complicated arrangement that with a lurch of fear I recognise as one of Henry's favourite layouts. On the wall in front of her, to the left of the computer, is a photo of me, the one from my Facebook page. Next to it is a photocopy of the article from the *Sharne Bay Journal* about me winning that design award, and a printout of Rosemary's testimonial from the homepage of my website. To the right there are photos of Sophie – lots of them. She poses and pouts from the wall, blowing me a kiss. There's even a cutting from the same paper featuring Sophie, immaculate even after a 10K run in pink fairy wings. On the screen in front of the woman, Maria's Facebook page is open.

'Maria?' I whisper. The woman pushes her chair back, stands up, turns around. I'm looking into Maria's hazel eyes, clear and cool. But the face is lined, her hands gnarled and loose-skinned. My brain struggles to make sense of what I am seeing. Of course Maria would be over forty now, I wasn't expecting a sixteen-year-old. But this woman is at least sixty-five. It's not Maria. It's her mother. It's Bridget.

Chapter 36

2016

I am frozen in the doorway. Bridget. Of course it's Bridget. Images flash through my mind: Bridget, hovering outside Maria's door with tea and biscuits, and hope in her eyes; Bridget in the rain and the dark, being helped to the school office, fear and rage etched into her features in equal measure; Bridget carefully choosing a birthday gift for Esther every year, the pretence that it is from Maria a sticking plaster over her shattered heart.

Why didn't I see this before? But then, how could I see it? I could never, if I lived for a million years, come anywhere close to the pain, the unendurable anguish that Bridget has suffered. I can see though how such a pain could grow over many years, fed only by dark thoughts and time, acres of unused time. Bridget has been tending her pain, sheltering it, protecting it, until the time came to use it. And now she is turning it outwards onto me.

'You look surprised, Louise. You were expecting someone else.' It's not a question.

'Where's Henry?'

'Did you really think Maria might still be alive? How on earth could that be?'

My mouth is completely dry and I am struggling to swallow.

'Where's Henry? Please . . .'

'No, she's not alive, Louise. She's not alive because you killed her.'

I try to force my mind to catch up with what I'm hearing, but it's dragging its heels, not wanting to acknowledge what is happening. How could Bridget possibly know? Who could have told her about the spiked drink?

'No . . .' I begin, my voice croaky.

'Yes, you did. Oh, you can say it was an accident, explain it any way you like. But a mother knows the truth. She didn't wander over the cliff by accident. She was smart. Even if she'd been drinking, there's no way she would have fallen by mistake. I'm the only one who knows what state of mind she was in at that time. I heard her, night after night, crying in her room when she thought I couldn't hear. One night it was very bad. I never got out of her exactly what had happened – all she would say was that it was happening again, like in London. And you were at the heart of it, Louise. Sophie Hannigan too – I could tell what sort of girl she was just by looking at her. But it was you that really hurt her. Do you remember the night she brought you home?'

Her eyes are bright and hard, boring into me like laser beams. I'm unable to speak, my mouth dry and claggy, but she goes on anyway.

'I saw the look in her eyes that night. I know she thought I was going over the top, with my tea and biscuits, but I could see that here was a proper friend for Maria, someone who could make the difference, change the course of her life. Well, you certainly did that, didn't you? She killed herself, and you and Sophie Hannigan are to blame as surely as if you'd pushed her over yourselves.'

My first, terrible, selfish instinct is relief. She's got it wrong. She doesn't know about the Ecstasy, doesn't know that we spiked Maria's drink. I've been so sure all along that whoever was sending the messages knew the truth that I've never considered any alternative. This relief though is swiftly tempered by doubt – she may not know about the Ecstasy but maybe Bridget hasn't got it completely wrong. How can I be sure Maria didn't kill herself? Esther doesn't think so, but who knew Maria better than her own mother?

'But ... the police,' I say, my voice thick and strange. 'They said it was accidental death, surely ...'

'The police! What do they know? What did they prove? There was nothing accidental about it. My daughter took her own life as a direct result of your treatment of her. I can't prove it, and the police will never be able to, but I know that it's true.' Her hands are trembling and her forehead is damp with sweat.

'And for years and years, you and Sophie have been walking about in this world, having jobs and boyfriends and husbands and homes and lives. And a child. You have a child. You took that away from my daughter, the chance to be a mother. The chance to know that terrible, overwhelming love, that fear, that sense that a part of your own body is walking around by itself in the world, totally vulnerable. And all this time my daughter has been alone in the cold sea.' Her voice is harsh, guttural. She holds tightly to the desk, as if she might fall.

'I wanted to be there, at the reunion. I wanted to see your faces, all of you, the ones that lived. Wanted to make a scene. And get some answers too.'

'You organised the reunion ... Naomi Strawe.'

'Yes. Seems stupid to you, I expect.' Bridget looks at me defiantly, daring me to agree. 'But I wanted Maria to be there too. She should have been there.'

'But you weren't there ... were you?'

'I was going. I wanted to go. But Tim stopped me. He saw me outside the school, on the road ... he wouldn't let me go in. He thought it wouldn't be good for me, and I couldn't make him see that I needed to. He doesn't understand. Nobody does.'

'That was you ... at the top of the drive, with Tim.'

'You saw me?' She's taken aback.

'Yes. Well, I saw Tim with somebody. I couldn't see who it was.'

'You thought ... ?' Her eyes glitter.

Had I ever really believed that Maria wasn't dead?

'You know that love, don't you, of a mother for her child?' Bridget says.

'Yes ... please, Henry, where is he? Is he here?'

She shakes her head, but I can't tell if she means he's not here, or that she won't tell me.

'My baby, my beautiful girl. When she was first born, she would only sleep on my chest, day or night. And even though I was demented with exhaustion, I didn't put her down. I held her, because that was what she needed me to do. I was amazed that I had grown her inside me, flesh of my flesh. And although of course she began to walk and talk, and eventually to have a life I knew little about, a part of her was still inside me. It still is. Is it any wonder I wanted to bring Maria back, to make you face what you have done?'

'No. I understand, I do. But I'm a mother too now, please—'

'How did it feel, when you realised I'd taken your son?' She interrupts me, won't give me a chance to allow any sympathy to creep in. 'Did you feel as if every drop of blood had drained out of your body? Did you feel you'd do anything – anything at all – if only he could be safe? That was what I wanted, Louise. I wanted you to feel a tiny fraction of what I have had to live with every day since 1989. People compare losing a person to losing a limb sometimes . . . "Oh, it was like losing my right arm", they say. It's nothing like that. You can learn to cope without an arm, without a leg. You never learn to cope with losing a child. You never get used to it. It never gets easier.' The words gush from her like waste from a sewage pipe.

'I hope my little messages have made you look over your shoulder everywhere you've been these past few weeks. I hope you've been coming to in the night with a start, jumping at every little noise; waking a little more scared each morning, a lumpen, heavy feeling inside; wondering if it's all worth it, if you can live the rest of your life like this.' Bridget is holding tightly on to the desk behind her, the skin on her hands stretched tight over the bones, her face flushed.

'I'm sorry. I'm so sorry.' It's all I can manage. 'Please, where is he?'

'Sorry's no good to me. I don't want you to be sorry. I want you to suffer, like I've suffered. I've been imagining it, every time I sent a message. Conjuring up the fear on your face, the dread in the pit of your stomach. Even following you wasn't enough, although I enjoyed the way you ran from me in that tunnel in South Kensington. I wanted you to feel what I feel, but I wanted to see it too, to see your pain with my own eyes.'

We stare at each other, eyes locked. She ought to be triumphant – this was what she wanted, after all. But all I can see is despair and terrible, endless pain.

'But why now?' I whisper.

'I didn't want to get in trouble with the police. Stalking, kidnapping, the police don't look too kindly on that. But it doesn't matter to me any more, not since the last time I saw the doctor. She looked so kind and concerned, was so terribly sorry to tell me, couldn't say for sure how long I had. But all I could think was: yes; now I can make Louise Williams and Sophie Hannigan pay for what they have done.'

Bridget is dying. My brain tries to process this, make sense of it, but the mention of Sophie's name has made the temperature in the room drop a few degrees. I take a step back, grasp the doorframe.

'You were so careless, Louise. Did no one ever tell you to be careful about what you put online? Photos of your little boy in his school uniform? Casual mentions of your local high street? Pictures of your house? You even moan on Facebook about having to put him in after-school club, so I knew you wouldn't be there at three o'clock today with all the proper mothers.' The knife twists, biting a little further into me.

'As for that internet dating site – God, you were easy to fool. All I did was paste in a photo from a catalogue. I didn't even take much trouble over the message. You must have been really desperate. And you waited so long! Half an hour! I had to order a second drink in that restaurant opposite the bar.' She laughs unpleasantly. 'I knew exactly where Henry would be and when. You should have taken better care of him. He didn't even have any idea that he shouldn't go off with someone he doesn't know. He was perfectly willing to accept that I was his grandma, chatting to me about his day, accepting sweets from me, telling me what he wanted on his toast.'

His toast. The kitchen. He must be in the kitchen. I tear myself away from the force field of pain and rage that surrounds Bridget, and run down the corridor. The door sticks for a second and then opens with a squeak.

'Oh thank God, thank God.' Henry is sitting on a high stool at the breakfast bar, a glass of apple juice in front of him, eating a slice of toast and jam.

'Hello, Mummy,' he says casually.

I run to him and pick him up, squeezing him to me, burying my face in his hair, his neck. Underneath the odour that school has added, of pencils and dusty floors and other children's sticky fingers, he still has his essential smell, the one I've been inhaling like a glue-sniffer since the day he was born.

'Hey,' he says crossly, wriggling out of my embrace. 'My toast.'

'Time to go,' I say breathlessly, trying to keep my voice light and casual. 'You can bring your toast.'

'I want to play with the trains again. My grandma said I could.'

'There's no time. Daddy's waiting in the car.' I tug on his hand. 'Come on, Henry.'

There's a noise in the hallway, the creak of the front door, footsteps on the laminate. Sam, I think with a rush of warmth, pulling Henry into the hallway.

'Mum?' calls a voice.

Oh God, it's Tim. Thoughts tumble through my brain. Is this how it ends? Is this the last thing Sophie saw? Tim bearing down on her, avenging the death of his beloved sister? I can't imagine that Bridget has the strength to have killed Sophie, so it must have been Tim. I want to tell Henry to go, to dodge Tim and run as fast as he can, but I know he won't understand what I'm asking him to do. It's clear he has not been frightened and has no understanding at all that we are in danger.

'Louise. What are you doing here?' There is panic in his voice. He stands in the corridor, filling the width of the hall, blocking our only escape route. I grasp Henry's hand a little tighter, my own slippery with sweat.

'I invited her,' says Bridget, stepping forward into the doorway of the bedroom. Tim doesn't move from the hall. I am caught between the two of them, like the king in a game of chess that is nearing checkmate, enemy pieces closing in from every side.

Tim takes a step closer. 'What has she told you, Louise?'

I pull Henry closer to me, feel his warm body pressing into my legs. He looks up at me, eyes round and trusting.

'Mum, what have you done?' says Tim, his voice urgent. 'What's Louise doing here?'

I try to will my legs to move, to run, to at least try and escape, but they won't obey my brain's command. It's like one of those nightmares where you're stuck in thick mud, being chased by a monster you have no hope of escaping.

'I told you,' Bridget says. 'I invited her.'

'I've just come from the police station. They told me about the Facebook page. It was you, wasn't it?' he says to Bridget. I look from one to the other in confusion. If Tim killed Sophie, how can he not have known about the Facebook page?

Bridget shrugs defiantly.

'They'll find out,' he says. 'They can trace these things. They'll know within hours that it was you.'

'Do you think I care about that?' she says, her voice cracking. 'I'm dying. Somebody had to bring them to account, those girls who drove Maria over that cliff.'

Tim's face crumbles and he moves a step closer.

'We don't know what happened, Mum. You have to let it go.'

'Let it go? How can I let it go? It won't let me go. There's something else too, something I need to know. He was going to tell me at the reunion.'

'What? Who was?' Tim runs a hand through his hair so that it stands up on end. Henry shifts even closer in to me and I put my arms tightly around him, stroke his hair. *It's OK*, I will silently, not daring to speak or move.

'Nathan Drinkwater.' Bridget spits the words.

'What are you talking about?' Tim says, confused.

'He sent me a friend request on Facebook. Well, he sent Maria a friend request. He said he knew I wasn't really Maria, but that he knew something about what really happened the night she disappeared. He said he had something of hers to show me that would prove it. He was going to meet me at the reunion, but then you were there and you wouldn't let me go in.'

'But, Mum, this is crazy. Nathan Drinkwater is dead. He died years ago.'

'What?' Her rage abates, and for the first time today, Bridget looks vulnerable, lost. 'He can't be.'

'He is. I looked him up, after Louise asked me about him when I saw her in Norwich. He died in a car crash in London. It was in the news, because he'd become famous in a very minor way, he wrote a couple of books, had a bit of success with them.'

'Then who . . .'

She looks at Tim, then at me, her face ashen.

'I don't know,' he says. 'But it wasn't Nathan.'

Tim seems to wilt slightly, resting his back against the wall and rubbing his eyes. It feels like a chance and with the lethargy of a few moments before lifting suddenly, I am galvanised into action. I pick Henry up in one smooth movement and run down the hall with him and out of the front door, leaving it swinging behind us. Along the path, out of the gate. When I reach the comparative safety of the pavement I put Henry down and look behind me, still moving, dragging Henry by the hand, to see if Tim is in pursuit. *Thump*. I run straight into Sam's chest. I clutch him, my whole body shaking uncontrollably.

'Daddy!' Henry says, all smiles, toast and trains forgotten.

Sam picks him up and holds him tight. Henry's legs and arms close around him like a vice.

'Thank God,' Sam says into his neck. 'I was just coming in, I couldn't stand it any longer,' he continues to me over Henry's shoulder.

'We need to go,' I say, half-running towards the car.

'What's going on? Who was in there? It wasn't . . .' he trails off.

'No. Bridget – Maria's mum. I'll explain in the car.'

'Bridget?' He's standing still on the pavement and I tug on his arm.

'Come on.'

With fumbling fingers I strap Henry into the back of Sam's car and climb into the passenger seat. I close my eyes for a second, adrenaline still coursing through me, but Sam's voice jolts me out of the moment.

'Louise! Is Henry all right? Did she hurt him?'

'No. He seems fine, he was perfectly happy when I got to him.'

'Thank God. He must be exhausted. Let's just get him home, and we can figure out what to do about Bridget in the morning.'

I rest my head back against the seat, my heart rate finally slowing. Now that Henry is safe, everything has lost its urgency. We head towards the main road out of Sharne Bay, Henry already fast asleep in the back. I stare out of the window into the darkness as it begins to rain, my thoughts broken only by the rhythmic sound of the windscreen wipers swishing gently back and forth.

As we swing onto the A11, the rain still beating a steady tattoo on the windscreen, I start to doze off, my head at an awkward angle against the window. I'm just slipping into that delicious state of total relaxation where you know you're going to fall asleep but you're still conscious, when Sam's voice jolts me awake.

'I can't believe it was Bridget. What did she say?' He sounds anxious.

'She blames me for Maria's death. Sophie too, but mostly me. The messages were about frightening us, punishing us for how we treated Maria.'

'But how does she know—'

'About the Ecstasy? She doesn't. She thinks Maria killed herself. That's why she blames me. Because of how I treated her. It was never about the Ecstasy.'

'So she's got no idea what really happened? She put you through all this, frightening you nearly to death, taking our child, just to get you back for a bit of schoolgirl bullying?' I can sense his anger rising, his knuckles white on the steering wheel.

'She lost her child, Sam,' I snap. 'Neither of us can begin to understand what she's been through.' I try to think of Bridget as she was the first time I saw her – smiling, so hopeful with her tea and biscuits, but I can only see her as she was today: hollow cheekbones, suffering etched into her face as if someone had carved lines into it with a Stanley knife.

'I know, I know. Sorry. It's just the worry of this afternoon, Henry going missing like that. I thought we'd lost him, Louise.' I reach out and put my hand on his knee and he covers it with his own. In the back, Henry stirs and whimpers. I turn round, removing my hand from beneath Sam's, and reach back to stroke Henry's leg.

'It's OK, Henry, go back to sleep.'

I look out into the darkness, thinking aloud.

'The thing is, Bridget can't have killed Sophie. She wasn't even there for a start, and she wouldn't have had the strength anyway. Sophie was strangled.'

'It must have been Tim, then,' says Sam.

'No,' I say. 'He was there in the bungalow just now. He'd only just found out about the Facebook page himself. He'd been at the police station, they'd told him. He didn't know, Sam. He didn't know anything about it. And why would he have had Maria's necklace anyway?'

'Well, I don't know about the necklace, but as for not knowing about the Facebook page, that's what he would have said, isn't it?'

'I don't think he was lying.'

'Well, then . . . maybe it had something to do with Nathan Drinkwater,' Sam says, swerving out to overtake a lorry.

'What?'

'Nathan Drinkwater. You told me at the reunion that Maria was Facebook friends with him too, remember? He was that boy who was totally obsessed with Maria, wasn't he? Before she moved to Sharne Bay? I remember Matt Lewis's cousin telling us about it at the time. Maybe it's got something to do with him.'

'But he's . . .' I trail off, unwilling to finish that sentence, my mind racing. When I told Sam at the reunion about Nathan Drinkwater being on Maria's friend list, Sam said he'd never heard of him. How can he be bringing Nathan up now if he doesn't know who Nathan is? I repeat it in my head again, trying to convince myself. Sam doesn't know who Nathan Drinkwater is. Does he?

I close my eyes again but the relaxed feeling has gone. My mind claws around, trying to fit the pieces together, but they don't seem to belong in the same jigsaw. Bridget's reason for sending the Facebook messages is clear: she wanted me to feel at least a fraction of her unendurable pain. She's been nurturing that pain for all these years, allowing it to grow, to curl its tendrils around all the other thoughts in her brain, choking them so that they withered and died, leaving only itself.

But Bridget didn't kill Sophie, and I don't think Tim did either. They weren't there that night, I saw them leaving, despite the lure that was drawing Bridget: the promise of information about her dead daughter, and something else – a tangible piece of evidence. A necklace?

I think of Sophie at the reunion, laughing with the boys, telling them she knows all and sees all. And then later, in her panic about the Facebook messages, she told me there had been 'all sorts' going on at the leavers' party. What did she know? What did she see?

I had assumed that the Nathan on the Facebook page was the real Nathan, that Bridget had tracked him down as she had done Sophie and me. But Bridget said Nathan had contacted her, not the other way around. And Nathan Drinkwater is dead. Anyone can be anyone on Facebook. It's easy to hide behind a faceless page on the internet. A broken, dying mother can pose as her dead daughter to wreak revenge on the girls she blames for ruining her daughter's life. But somebody was playing Bridget at her own game. Somebody else was posing as the boy who forced the Westons from their home, made them abandon their whole life to start again in a small town in Norfolk. Someone who knew that Nathan Drinkwater was the one person that whoever was posing as Maria wouldn't be able to resist replying to.

We drive on in silence, broken only by occasional shifting and muttering from Henry on the back seat. I daren't look at Sam lest my face betrays what I am thinking, so I turn to look out of the window. I try to look beyond my reflection, out into the darkness, but I can't ignore my face, looking back at me in shadow, eyes wide. I can't believe Sam can't hear my heart pounding.

I should know better than anyone that things aren't always what they seem. It's like when someone tells a story about something that happened when you were there, and it's not at all how you remember it. It might be they're telling it a certain way for effect, to make people laugh, or to impress someone. But sometimes that's simply how they remember it. For them, it's the truth. That's when it becomes hard for you to know whether what you remember is the truth, or whether it's just your version of it.

I realise I've been trying to hold on to the idea of Sam as a decent person because he's Henry's father, but Sam has lied to me before, and lied well. Even after I found that text from Catherine on his phone he continued to lie, until it just wasn't possible any more and he left me to be with her. All the lies, the betrayals, the many ways in which he hurt me crowd in on me, stifling me. The times he held me down and it became more than a game, the times he put his hands to my throat playing out a fantasy that wasn't mine.

I wrap my arms around myself, although it's warm in the car. I've spent so long sitting in darkness, lying not only to others but to myself too. But the door is open now. Just a crack, but it's open. And the light is streaming in.

Chapter 37

2016

As Sam parks outside my flat, reversing into the tiniest of spaces, all I can think of is getting away from him. My mind is veering from one thing to another and I can't think about what to do next, what I'm going to do about this strange new reality that I find myself facing. I concentrate on getting Henry into bed, on how that is going to feel, that moment when I lock the door behind me and we're safe, and I can think.

As soon as the handbrake is on, I'm unbuckling my seat-belt and opening the door.

'Thanks very much. I'll just grab Henry and get him into bed, and we'll speak soon, OK?' My voice sounds high and tinny, completely unlike my normal voice.

'It's OK, I'll bring him in. He's so heavy when he's asleep.'

'No, it's fine,' I squeak. I clear my throat. 'It's fine,' I repeat, lower and calmer. 'I can manage.'

'I know you can, but I'd like to help you.'

Before I can reply, Sam is out of the car and unstrapping

Henry. He lifts him swiftly out of the seat. Henry's eyes half-open and then close again, his head heavy on Sam's shoulder. Sam shifts him onto one hip and heads up the garden path without speaking. I have no choice but to follow, rummaging in my bag for the key.

I open the door and stand aside to let Sam and Henry in. For a few wild seconds, I think about running, shouting for help – surely Sam wouldn't hurt Henry – but it seems ridiculous and anyway, where would I go? I don't know any of the neighbours. And as I look at Henry's sleeping face over Sam's back, I know that it was never really an option. Everything I thought I knew has shifted, like coming into your bedroom to find that someone has moved everything very slightly out of its normal place. I can't leave Henry alone with Sam; I don't know what he is capable of. I follow them in and close the front door behind me.

Sam goes straight into Henry's room and puts him on the bed. Carefully he takes off his shoes and school uniform and eases him under the duvet dressed just in his Thomas the Tank Engine pants. Something about the way he does it makes me wonder if I've got this all wrong. Surely the person who knows that there's no point putting pyjamas on our son because he'll only wake in the night and take them off, can't be the person who has done . . . I'm not even sure what it is he's done. I can't articulate it to myself, even inside my own head.

Sam comes out, leaving the door open a crack as we always do.

'I think we need a drink after all that, don't you?'

Before I've had a chance to answer, he heads straight down the hall to the kitchen and opens the fridge, taking a half-drunk bottle of white wine out of the door. I follow him into the room.

'Look, Sam, I'm tired. Can we maybe do this another time?' *Just leave, please leave.*

He takes two glasses from the top cupboard. I vow to completely reorganise the kitchen tomorrow if . . . if . . . my mind tries to finish that sentence but I close it down.

'I don't want a drink. Please, Sam, I just want to go to sleep. Let's do this another time.'

I step forward boldly and take the glasses out of his hand and put them on the kitchen worktop.

'It's late. I'm exhausted. Please?'

He shrugs.

'OK, if that's what you want.'

I follow him back down the hall, hardly daring to hope that it's nearly over, that he hasn't realised he's slipped up mentioning Nathan. A minute more and I'll be locking the door behind him, and then I will be able to think.

He puts his hand on the Yale handle, poised to push it down.

Come on, I will him silently. *Open the door.*

His hand stops. He turns to look at me. *Just open the door.*

'I can't, Louise.' His voice breaks, and on the door handle I can see his fingers shaking.

'What do you mean? Can't what?' *Breathe, just breathe.*

'I can't leave. Not yet. I'm sorry.'

'You can.' I try to control the rise in my voice, to disguise the fear, the panic.

'No, it's no good.' With a dart of pain that surprises me, I see there are tears in his eyes. In fifteen years together I never once saw him cry. He looks down. 'You know, don't you? Because of what I said in the car, about Nathan Drinkwater?'

I look down too, at the whorls and knots in the oak floorboards that we chose together, the dust gathering in the corners by the door mat.

'I don't know anything.' My voice is a rasp, constricted by the muscles in my throat, which are seizing up, barely leaving room for the air to flow in and out.

'You do, I can see it in your eyes. I told you at the reunion that I'd never heard of Nathan Drinkwater, and now you know I was lying. You're frightened of me. You know.' He's not angry. In fact I've never seen him look so desperately sad, and the love and despair on his face screw the knot inside me even tighter. I sway slightly, my head spinning.

He reaches out to touch me but I jerk my arm away. His face falls.

'Come and sit down,' he says. 'Let me explain.'

He doesn't wait for an answer, but walks back to the kitchen, his tread heavy and slow, reluctant. I hesitate outside Henry's room, his nightlight glowing through the crack where Sam left the door ajar. I gently pull it closed and follow Sam down the hall on legs that will barely carry me.

Sam has taken the wine bottle from where he left it on the worktop and is sitting at the table pouring two glasses. He gestures for me to sit down next to him, so I do, my body heavy, filled with lead.

'Remember when we first got together, Louise?' he says, twisting the stem of his wine glass. 'We were so happy, weren't we?'

I would agree with him no matter what he said, but this

one is easy. Yes, we were happy. For the first time in my life, I was with someone who knew what I had done and still loved me. It lessened the burden of guilt somehow. When he kissed me outside that pub in Clapham, I felt lighter than I had done in years.

'It was such a relief to be with you. You loved me so completely, so . . . innocently.' It seems a strange choice of word considering the things we had done together. He must have seen something of this on my face, because he insists, 'It was innocent, Louise. Or maybe pure is a better word. The things we did together, we did out of love. You wanted it as much as I did, didn't you? I never forced you, did I?'

He is almost pleading. I shake my head. No, he never forced me. Or perhaps more accurately, I never said no. A shiver runs through me, revulsion laced queasily with the remnants of desire. At first it had been liberating to be released from the confines of the vanilla sex I'd had with previous boyfriends. There was something about the letting go, the relinquishing of control, that excited me, freed me. But there were times, especially after Henry was born, where things went further than I was comfortable with. I thought it was because I'd become a mother, that I'd changed. But I didn't say. I never said because I could feel him slipping away from me by then and I didn't want to give him a reason to leave.

'I didn't want to hurt Sophie, I swear.' Sam turns the wine glass around and around in his hand, the liquid slopping about dangerously.

'No, of course not,' I say, tasting bile. Oh God, what did he do?

'I just wanted her to be quiet, to stop saying those things,

things that someone else might have overheard. But she wouldn't shut up, she just kept on saying it, saying she'd seen me with Maria at the leavers' party, asking me what happened, if Maria had said anything, if I said anything to her. I kept telling Sophie it was nothing, nothing happened, that I left Maria in the woods, that she was fine the last time I saw her.'

'What are you talking about? What do you mean you left Maria in the woods? When?'

He doesn't answer, just twists the wine glass even more furiously.

'Sam?' My need to know is overriding the fear I feel. Am I on the brink of finding out the answer to the question that has been clawing at me since I was sixteen years old? 'Is this something to do with Matt?' I think of Matt's eyes boring into mine at the reunion, his insistence that we should all keep quiet. A wild hope surges in me that what Sam is about to tell me is that he has been covering up for Matt all these years.

'Matt? No, it's nothing to do with him. He's just worried that it'll come out that he supplied the E.' My heart sinks. 'It was hard,' he goes on, placing his glass carefully on the table. 'Seeing you still so torn up about it, all those years later. Knowing that with just a few words I could put an end to your guilt, your shame. But also knowing that it would mean the end of you and me. The end of us.'

I stare at him, wanting yet not wanting him to continue. He takes my hands in his, enfolding them, his thumbs circling my palms over and over. He puts his face in my hands, so that I can't see his eyes as he speaks, the words rushing out, unstoppable, his hot breath on my hands.

'You didn't kill Maria, Louise. I did.'

Chapter 38

Louise doesn't talk to anyone about the details of her and Sam's sex life. She is too ashamed of her response to being dominated, pinned down, helpless. She did tell Polly a bit when things got bad after Henry was born, but even she doesn't know the full story.

When Louise was a teenager, and into her early twenties too, it was all the rage to talk to your girlfriends about the intimate details of your sex life – the mechanics, the quirks, the sounds, the things that went wrong. Nothing was off limits. But then something happened. Around the time she and Sam got together, her friends started to think about getting married, and actually to do so, and she found that those conversations tailed off. Was it because they had made their choice, and couldn't admit to anything that was less than perfect? Not so easy to laugh at the sexual foibles of someone you're going to have to spend the rest of your life with. Not so funny any more.

The conversations where she might have been able to bring up her own sex life dwindled away, and she didn't want to be the one to introduce the topic. She would have liked to have had someone to confide in, to check how far from the norm their sex life was, especially in the last couple of years when things got really out of hand. She reads obsessively on the subject, googling BDSM and rape fantasies, reassured when she sees studies that say this falls within the 'normal range' of fantasies, horrified when she reads articles linking it to real sexual violence.

Things got worse the second time Sam was passed over for promotion, and then again after Henry was born. He thought that motherhood would level things out, that he would become the important one. But Louise's business went from strength to strength and he was left behind. But of course she could never leave him behind. Not him, the only one who knew her. If only Louise had known what he had done, how very different things might have been. Who might she have become without a lifetime spent building a wall around her to make sure no one could get in? Of standing on cliffs or bridges wondering what it would be like to just give in, to step forward and not have to be any more?

Sam always felt the need to prove himself, to prove that he was still the dominant force in her life. He should have known that he didn't have to prove anything to her because she loved him so completely, had always loved him since the days when she watched him flirting with Sophie Hannigan in the school cafeteria. Louise had always thought there was nothing he could do that would make her stop loving him. Nothing at all.

Chapter 39

2016

I am totally rigid, my stomach drawn in so tight that it's holding the rest of my body together. I could be made of glass, hard and smooth and cold to the touch. One move could shatter me. I keep perfectly still on my chair, hyper-aware that Henry is asleep only metres away.

'What happened?' I don't sound like me, my voice thin, barely denting the silence that fills the kitchen, this room where we spent so many nights talking, eating, laughing. Carefully, I pull my hands from his and place them, trembling, in my lap.

'Do you remember that night, Louise?'

Of course I remember. He knows I do.

'I was good, wasn't I?' He sounds like Henry, seeking my approval. 'To start with? I had you alone in that classroom and I could have pushed you much further, but I knew you were scared so I stopped. I was good. You remember, don't you?'

'Yes.' Urgent hands on green satin, his fingers digging

into my flesh harder and harder, his tongue in my mouth, everything hot and blurred. And then me, alone in a classroom, my back against the cold wall, cursing myself for my inexperience, my frigidity.

'You wanted me, but you were scared. You didn't deserve to be forced, Louise. Later on you enjoyed our games as much as I did, didn't you?' The pleading tone is back and I nod, the reflex to make him feel better still strong in me. 'But you weren't ready, not then.'

I remember how humiliated I felt when he left me in the classroom, and I am surprised to feel a pang of sympathy for my teenage self. I've never felt sympathy for her before, only guilt and disgust and shame.

'But Maria, she was different. I'd heard the stories about her, we all had. The things she had done. I didn't need to feel bad about doing anything to her, because there was nothing she hadn't done before.'

I want to tell him they were all lies, those stories, made up by someone else who had thought he could take what he wanted from Maria Weston, but I am frightened of him now, so I say nothing. If I let him talk, help him to believe that whatever he did wasn't his fault, maybe he will go.

'I saw her leaving the hall, stumbling and clutching at the doorframe for support, putting a hand to her mouth. I followed her down the back path towards the woods. She was panicking, didn't know what was happening to her, needed to get away. I wanted to make sure she was OK. After all, I knew what she had taken and she didn't. I was looking out for her.' He turns his anxious face to me.

I try to look reassuring. I nod; yes, you were looking out for her.

'Just before she got to the woods, I saw her trip and fall so I called out. She turned, and I ran to catch up, asked her if she was OK. That was what Sophie saw. She'd been watching Maria too, following her, to see if she was coming up on the E.'

'Sophie saw her that night? She never said.' I think of Sophie when I went to see her at her flat, laughing about the friend request. *What, the girl who drowned?* Her studied unconcern must have masked a fear and guilt that matched mine.

'I didn't know either, not until she called me after you'd been to see her at her flat.'

'Why didn't she tell the police, at the time?'

'She was like you, wasn't she?' says Sam. 'So scared of what you had done, of what would happen if anyone found out. She just thought it was better to say nothing at all. That was all Sophie had seen, after all. Me and Maria, walking down to the woods. When we spoke on the phone before the reunion, I thought I'd persuaded her that it was nothing, that she should forget it. But then at the reunion, she kept going on and on about it. She was frightened, rattled by the Facebook messages; she wouldn't leave it alone. I think she really thought there was a chance Maria was still alive, and that I knew something about it. She was drunk, and her voice was getting louder and louder. People were starting to look round, to wonder what we were talking about. She was going to cause a scene. I had to get her out of there.'

'Where . . .' The words stick in my throat. I breathe deeply and try again. 'Where did you go?'

'I told her I'd remembered something from the leavers' party, something that might help her, suggested we go for a walk outside to talk about it properly. She was desperate for answers, couldn't agree fast enough. I said ...' His voice falters. 'Louise, you have to understand, I only did what I did because I needed to protect my family. I didn't want my children to have a father who was in prison. I didn't want this one bad decision I made when I was sixteen to ruin their lives. I couldn't let that happen.'

I nod vigorously, desperate to appear supportive.

'I said we should walk down to the woods where we couldn't be overheard,' he goes on, his voice quieter now. 'It was really quite cold by then, so we got our coats, and I put my hands in my pockets, and I could feel that there were gloves in there, so I put them on, just to keep my hands warm, you know?'

Oh God. Poor Sophie.

'We walked down the path to the woods, and I was still hoping that she would leave it alone, still trying to think of something I could tell her that would satisfy her curiosity. But then she started saying we should tell the police, and ... that was when I panicked, Louise. Why did she have to drag the police into it? I couldn't have her telling the police about seeing me with Maria that night, could I? I couldn't let this one mistake ruin the rest of my life, my children's lives.'

'So you ...' I whisper, not able to finish the sentence.

He puts his face in his hands.

'I didn't mean to. Didn't want to. You have to believe that, Louise.' His voice is muffled, the sound only just escaping between his fingers.

'But all those years ... you let me believe that I was responsible for Maria's death ... you encouraged me to keep it a secret too.'

I can see now with frightening clarity how much it suited Sam, encouraging me to feel guilty, not to tell, all the time subtly reinforcing the idea that what I had done meant that no one else could ever understand me, or love me. He didn't want anyone poking around in the circumstances of Maria's disappearance any more than I did. He needed to keep me close, and to keep me quiet.

I look now at this man who I loved for so long, who I still love, the father of my child. It's as if someone has twitched away the veil I have kept so carefully suspended between me and the reality of what he was becoming after Henry was born. I worked so hard to pretend to myself that things were OK, but now I force myself to face the truth. Motherhood didn't turn me into a prude. It was Sam who changed, not me. He resented the time and love that Henry took from me, and the energy that I poured into making my business a success, and so he pushed harder, needed more. He pulled me ever further down the road that led away from the fantasies we had played out together, games that I can't pretend I hadn't enjoyed, towards something darker, more sinister. Something real. Is that what happened with Maria? Did she do what I never did? Did she say no? I have to know, I owe it to her. I can feel the chain that binds me to Maria stretched taut between us. She deserves to have somebody know the truth about what happened to her.

'What happened, Sam? At the leavers' party?' I try to sound matter of fact, concentrating on steadying my breathing, keeping my voice low.

'I wanted to tell you so many times, Louise. You have to believe that. But I couldn't risk losing you and Henry.'

But you threw us away, I want to say to him. If you were so scared of losing us, why did you leave us?

'I saw her fall, so I ran down the path and took her hand to help her up. Told her we'd walk a bit to clear her head. She was panicking, clutching onto me, didn't know what was happening to her. We took the path through the woods. It was darker in there, the moonlight couldn't reach us and she held me even closer in the darkness.' The words are rushing out of him now, as if they've been waiting inside his mouth for years, locked up, squirming to get out.

'I talked to her about other things,' Sam goes on. 'Tried to take her mind off how she was feeling. We came out of the trees and walked down to the cliff edge, the sound of the sea crashing against the bottom of the cliffs. We sat down. I started to stroke her hair, just gently. She was enjoying it, all her senses were heightened anyway because of what you had given her. She tipped her head back, and I stroked the side of her neck, like I had done to yours earlier.'

I can see Maria, her throat white and exposed in the starlight. Moonlight dancing on the water, the taste of salt in the air.

'She turned to me then, her pupils huge, asking me why she felt like this, saying she hadn't had all that much to drink. I knew why, of course, but I couldn't tell her.'

Oh, Maria, I'm sorry. I'm so sorry.

'And then I leaned in and kissed her. She kissed me back at first, she really did, Louise. She wanted it. You have to believe that.'

I want to believe it, to believe him.

'And then ... we were lying on the ground, me on top of her, and she ... she was wriggling, trying to get out from under me, but I thought . . . I thought she was enjoying it. I thought it was a game. Like with you, later, you know? Just pretending.' Yes, like me. But I had lost track of where the pretending began and ended.

'So I carried on.' Sam's words bring me back to the room, back to myself. 'She wanted it, I'm sure she did. The things she'd done – you heard about it, didn't you? We all did. She was trying to push my hands away, but it was a game, it must have been because in the end she stopped and let me do it.'

I think of Maria, so small and slight, surely no more than eight stone in weight, pinned beneath Sam who was nearly six foot by the time he was sixteen. No wonder she stopped fighting, all alone on the cliff, the roar of the waves drowning out her screams.

'And then afterwards, I thought she would lie there for a minute like I needed to, to compose myself. But as soon as I rolled off her she scrambled to her feet, pulling her dress down and staggered off in the direction of the school. She was all over the place. I ran after her, asked her where she was going. She said she was going to tell everyone what I'd done to her.'

Even though I know with a creeping sense of dread how this story must end, a small part of me rejoices at this tiny act of defiance.

'What I'd done, Louise? What about what she'd done? She went down there with me. She wanted it as much as I did. But then she started going on about her wrists and her mouth, she said there were marks and blood. I hadn't meant to hurt her, of course, but sometimes there would be marks, wouldn't there? On you? It didn't mean you hadn't wanted it.'

I remember a girl I used to work with noticing a weal on my wrist once and asking me about it. Unprepared, I stammered something about burning myself on the oven. She looked at me strangely and avoided me ever after.

'I told her no one would believe her, not with her reputation, but she just walked off, and then she started shouting 'Rape!' at the top of her voice. She was walking into the woods, shouting it over and over again. I ran after her again and this time I stood in front of her and took hold of her arms. I said it wasn't rape, she had to stop saying that word, but then she spat in my face and called me a rapist, asked me if I knew what they do to rapists in prison.'

I want to weep and rage and cheer at her strength.

'And that was when I knew she meant it. She was going to tell, no matter how bad it made her look, no matter whether anyone believed her,' Sam says. 'And even if they couldn't prove it, there would be people who would never look at me the same way again. That would have been it for me, Louise.' His voice breaks, tears threatening. 'It would have been the defining event of my life, always and forever the boy who was accused of rape. I couldn't let her do that to me, Louise, couldn't let her ruin the rest of my life. You see that, don't you?'

I am so used to believing him, so used to seeing him through his eyes rather than mine, that I am almost sucked in, lulled by his version of himself: the innocent victim, falsely accused, terribly wronged. But he's telling me this at the wrong time. If he'd told me years ago, before he cheated on me and left me and our son, when I was still under his spell, I might have believed him, felt sorry for him. I might even have understood. But I have seen unbearable pain in a mother's eyes, and a golden heart on a slender chain. I have taken off my blindfold.

'I had no choice; you have to believe me. I couldn't have her going around saying these things about me. I had to . . . had to make her . . . be quiet.'

Oh, Maria, forgive me. I think of Bridget, the pain of what she thinks happened to Maria etched on her face. Finding out the truth will finish her. But, of course, I realise as I look at Sam next to me, she'll probably never find out. I think of Sophie's broken body. I know what happens to people who know too much about Sam.

'It took a long time, longer than I thought.' His voice is small, and again I am reminded of Henry confessing to a childish crime – stealing sweets from the cupboard or breaking an ornament he wasn't supposed to touch. 'But in the end she was quiet. I couldn't leave her there, so I decided to try and get her over to the edge of the cliff. It had started to rain by then and she kept sliding out of my arms – I was shaking so much, and she was so heavy. But I managed to get her there in the end, and lay her down on the grass. I was crying by now, Louise, really sobbing, so I nearly didn't see.'

He stops and takes a swig of wine, the glass slipping between his fingers, his face covered with a light sheen of sweat.

'As I knelt beside her, I saw something that nearly changed the whole thing: her eyelids flickered. She was still alive.'

Ice floods my veins. He had been given a second chance, and even then he had not taken it.

'I looked out to sea and thought about the rest of my life,

and what it would be like if I stopped now, ran back up to the hall, called an ambulance. It would be OK at first, I could say I'd found her like that – I'd be the hero. For a while. But then I thought of her face as she spat at me; when she woke up, I knew that the first thing she would say would be that lie again: rapist.'

I clutch the sides of my chair. All the years we spent together, our wedding day, the heartache of IVF, the joy of having a child, it's all been swept away. I had thought that him leaving was the worst thing he could do to me: ruining everything, wiping away all our previous happiness, sullying my memories of our time together. How wrong I was.

'I could see her necklace glittering in the moonlight, winking up at me. I had this idea that it could identify her, if they found her body much later, that it would still be there, around the . . . the bones of her neck . . .' His voice peters out and he covers his eyes with his fingers, rubbing them as if trying to erase the memory.

'So I took it off and put it in my pocket,' he continues, his eyes still hidden.

My God, Sam has had Maria's necklace ever since. Where did he keep it? I shiver at the thought of it, that I could have come across it by accident at any time, clearing out a drawer or rummaging at the back of the wardrobe.

'And then I . . . pushed her over. She . . . I couldn't see very well, but I heard the splash as she hit the water. Then she was gone.'

The tides must have been his friend that night. Maria's still out there somewhere, just bones now, or what's left of bones when they've been in the sea for all that time. My God, I let her down so badly.

He looks up, eyes pleading.

'I couldn't have people thinking those things about me, could I, Louise? I don't know if anyone would have believed her, but mud sticks, doesn't it? I couldn't go through the rest of my life as the one who was accused of rape. Nobody would ever have looked at me in the same way again.'

I think back to that night: I remember speaking to Sophie, to Esther; I remember Bridget arriving, the revelation that Maria was missing. But what I realise now is that Sam wasn't there. He wasn't there when I was dancing, oblivious to everything except the beat of the music and the chemicals surging through my bloodstream; he wasn't there when the lights came up; he wasn't outside as Mr Jenkins took Bridget to the office to call the police. No, he was weaving his way through the woods, through the rain, sodden and mud-soaked; running through Sharne Bay, keeping to the back streets, until he reached the safety of that little house on Coombe Road; he was taking off his clothes and shoving them into a bin bag; he was showering until the brown water streaming off him ran clear.

Sam reaches out and strokes my hair, entwining the strands around his fingers, a chilling reminder of our previous intimacy. I sit motionless in my chair, desperately trying to order my thoughts.

'But . . . Nathan Drinkwater . . . why . . . ?'

'I had to find out who was sending those Facebook messages. Sophie called me after you went to her flat, told me about the friend request from Maria, and your visit to her flat. Why didn't you come to me, confide in me?'

I shrug as if I'm not sure, but I know why. I was trying to make sure his strong fingers couldn't reach into my life any more. I didn't want him to assume the role of confidante, take charge of my life again. I wanted to deal with it on my own.

I think of that day with Pete in Dulwich Park, and of my dark suspicions when Esther told me she'd seen him with a woman and a baby. I had just assumed that if Pete was lying to me about his domestic situation, he could be lying to me about something else too. If only I had known that I was looking for Nathan Drinkwater in entirely the wrong place.

'I thought that whoever had set up the Facebook page must have known the truth about what I had done,' Sam goes on, the words coming thick and fast now, as if he's been waiting for a chance to confess. 'I needed to find out who it was. I figured that if they cared enough about Maria to set up this whole Facebook charade, then the name Nathan Drinkwater would make them sit up and take notice. Matt Lewis's cousin had told us all about Nathan and I'd never forgotten his name. And I was right, of course; she couldn't resist a message from Nathan. I just didn't know until tonight that it was Bridget. When "Nathan" told her that he knew something about the night of the leavers' party, and that he had something to show her, she couldn't agree fast enough to meet him. I didn't tell her what it was, this proof. I wanted to wait and see who I was up against before I showed anyone the necklace. It was her suggestion to meet at the reunion, around the side of the school. So I waited, but no one showed up. When I realised no one was coming, I went back inside. Dropping the necklace in the woods was a mistake. I still don't know how it happened. It must have fallen out of my pocket in the . . . scuffle. It was only later that I realised it was gone, and it was too risky to go back and look for it.'

I know why Bridget didn't show. She bumped into her son, who assumed she was there to make trouble or to torture herself even further by looking at the class of 1989 who made it to adulthood, and he persuaded her to leave. Thank God he did. I wonder with a shiver what Sam was planning to do to whoever showed up, if they had. In his version, what he did to Sophie and Maria were desperate acts, a pair of terrible mistakes borne out of sheer panic in the heat of the moment. This is who he is, the man I married, the father of my child. Up until now it has been that which has horrified me, that the man I loved could do the things he has done. But he arranged to meet Bridget in cold blood. That was no mistake, no temporary moment of madness. I can see him now, standing in the full glare of the truth, outlined against it in stark relief. And I am afraid, not just of who he is and what he has done. I am afraid of what he is going to do next.

Chapter 40

2016

My whole body is tensed, like a bow drawn, ready to fire. Every fibre of my being is on alert, not only trying to work out my next move but also listening for Henry, terrified that he's going to wake and come into a scene he'll never be able to leave behind him. I daren't even think about the other possibility, the one where he never gets a chance to remember. With Henry asleep in his room, Sam has me trapped here as effectively as if he had tied me to the chair with iron chains.

Sam untangles his fingers from my hair and I struggle not to flinch as he runs his hand briefly down the side of my face.

'I remember when we first got together,' he says. 'I used to wake in the night sometimes to find you staring at me like you were trying to imprint my face permanently in your brain. It was so easy, being with you, especially after the years before. I'd never been looked after the way you looked after me, cared for me. I was the centre of your world. And we were happy, weren't we? But when Henry came along, I can't pretend it didn't change things. I got shifted out from the centre, replaced. I was left hovering somewhere around the edges, peering in. I loved Henry, of course I did, but I didn't love what he did to you, to us.'

Tears start in my eyes for the first time tonight. I knew things had changed after Henry was born. Once the obligatory six weeks were up, Sam had expected things in the bedroom to return to normal. Except what he wanted to do wasn't normal, even for us. It was as if someone had flicked a switch in his brain, and the games we had played before were no longer enough for him. It was as if the illusion of hurting me no longer satisfied him. He wanted to see real fear in my eyes.

'Don't blame Henry,' I whisper.

'I don't,' he says simply. 'I blame you.'

I can't stop shaking. I sit on my hands, unable to predict what they will do otherwise. I can't scream because I might wake Henry, and even if I did, what would happen? Would anyone hear? What about silent Marnie upstairs? Would she call the police? Or simply pick up the remote control and turn up the TV?

Sam pushes back his chair and the chair leg screeches against the floor. I wince, listening desperately for any sound from Henry's room. But there is nothing, only silence, as Sam gazes out of the French windows into the darkness.

'Oh God, oh God.' He beats his forehead gently against the glass. 'Why did I have to mention Nathan?'

I am struck by a memory of another time: a time when Sam went too far. He had really hurt me and he knew it. He was standing just where he is now; penitent, begging me to forgive him. Of course I did. I didn't know then who I would be without him; if I would even be anyone at all.

'Just pretend you didn't,' I blurt. 'I won't say anything. Just go, please. I'll never tell anyone, I swear. Please Sam. What about Henry?'

He turns to me with tears in his eyes.

'I'll look after Henry. I love him as much as you do. You don't think I'd hurt him, do you?' I don't want to think so, but I don't know; I don't know anything now.

'Henry needs me, Sam.' I slide my shaking hands out from under me and grip the edge of the table. 'Children need their mothers.'

'He'll be OK, like I was,' he says, but there's no feeling in his voice now. His eyes look out into the darkness where he can see nothing, and I know he is miles and years away, in that grotty little house with cigarette burns on the Formica kitchen table.

I think of how Henry wakes me up every morning by putting his face so close to mine that when I come to, all I can see are his eyes, blurred and out of focus, his eyelashes tickling mine and his hot breath on my face. Of how he gets into bed with me, pressing his small, warm body into mine, curling into me as if he would like to get back where he came from, inside my body. Me and Henry, we used to be one, I want to say to Sam. We may look like two, but really, we are one.

Sam walks slowly back around the table and sits down next to me, turning his chair so that we are knee to knee. He closes his eyes and reaches out to stroke my hair with first one hand and then the other. I begin to shake violently and saliva rushes to my mouth.

'I'm sorry, I'm sorry,' he says under his breath, eyes still closed. He puts his mouth to my hair and kisses it, breathing me in. I sit very still, my breath coming fast, feeling the blood flowing around my body, right down to my fingertips. His hands are running over my hair, smoothing it down, just as he used to as we lay in bed at night, me falling asleep to the soothing rhythm of his stroking. I should run, fight, do something, but I am practically catatonic with fear. The hideous shock of what is happening combined with the familiar feeling of his hands on me, gentle yet filled with terrifying intent, has paralysed me.

'You have to be quiet, Louise, please, please be quiet,' he murmurs into my hair, and I can feel him glancing anxiously towards the room where our son is sleeping peacefully.

His hands are moving lower now, his lips still pressed to my hair, his fingers curling gently around my neck. The strange torpor begins to lift, but it's too late. I am already struggling to breathe, his fingers squeezing harder and harder. My shallow gasping breaths are the only things that break the silence that we are locked into by our love for Henry, our desire to protect him from this scene. I scrabble uselessly at his hands, trying to get between them and my neck but there's no space, they're closing in.

'Shhh,' he whispers into my hair. 'Don't wake Henry.'

I pull desperately at his fingers but he's too strong, and I can feel myself fading, surrounded by the shadows of the other times I felt his hands around my neck, in our games. They were never this tight, though. I was never this close to darkness.

I can feel the chair solid beneath me, just as it was this morning when I ate my breakfast here in this room. The things are still there on the side, unwashed: two plates coated in toast crumbs; one cup, half an inch of cold tea in the bottom; a glass filmy with sticky fingerprints, just a dribble of apple juice remaining. Are they going to be the last things I see?

I can't pull his hands from my neck so I stop trying, instead flailing wildly around trying to find something, anything that I can use to get him away from me. It's getting harder and harder to get any air into my lungs, worse each time I try. I'm going, I can feel it; it won't be long now. My vision starts to blur around the edges and the kitchen where I sit with Henry each night as he tells me about his day swims in front of my eyes, melting into a haze of pain and fear. Oh Henry. My hand hits the kitchen worktop beside me and I grope around, unseeing, hoping to find something I can use to hit him, or at least shock him into releasing me, but there's nothing there, my hand is grasping thin air.

'Shhh,' whispers Sam again, his lips on my ear now, caressing it gently. I try to mouth 'please' but nothing comes out and he's not looking at me anyway; he's lost in a world where what he's doing is OK, just one of our games, his way of showing his love for me.

'It's OK, Louise, just be quiet, shhh. Everything's going to be OK.'

But I have spent too long being quiet. Too long pretending everything is OK, repainting the last few years of our marriage in bright colours. As the edges of the kitchen cupboards bleed into the ceiling and blackness closes in, it no longer matters if Henry wakes up. What matters is staying alive. With everything in me I kick out, but there's nothing there. I'm kicking uselessly into space. I try again and this time my foot catches a chair leg. I hook my foot under the seat and thrust my leg up as hard as I can. There is an almighty clatter as the chair crashes to the floor.

Sam's hold around my neck loosens and as his face looms back into focus I can see panic in his eyes. For a few seconds we are both suspended in time, and then a small voice calls from the bedroom.

'Mummy?'

Summoning every ounce of strength I can muster, I jump up from my chair, pushing Sam's hands away. I have a sense of his arms falling slackly to his sides as I run into Henry's room, slamming the door shut behind me and sinking to the floor with my back against it, knees to my chest.

'It's OK, H, go back to sleep,' I whisper across the room, but his eyes are already closed, the noise of the chair having woken him only briefly.

I can hear Sam's footsteps padding down the hall and I close my eyes, feeling only the hard contours of the door against my back and the soft weave of the blue carpet beneath my fingers. I breathe in the smell of Henry's room: washing powder, Play-Doh and the faint but unmistakeable scent of Henry himself. I've been here in this room so many times in the dark like this, inching away from the cot or the bed, desperate not to make even the tiniest noise that would wake Henry and mean I had to start the whole settling him to sleep process again. I think of the hours I spent sitting beside him with my hand on his back, getting colder and colder, terrified that removing my hand was going to cause him to shift and start crying. That seems like another life now, a life where a woman I don't recognise soothed her child to sleep and then climbed back into bed into the warm embrace of her loving husband. I want more than anything now to go to Henry, to hold him, but I daren't leave the door, straining against it, ready to push with all my strength.

The footsteps stop and I feel a pressure against my back as Sam pushes gently at the door. I brace myself, feet flat to the floor and lean back, eyes closed, the taste of saltwater in my mouth from the tears rolling unchecked down my cheeks. Sam's feet cast a shadow under the crack of the door against the glow of Henry's nightlight.

'Please Sam,' I say, my voice croaky and unfamiliar. The pressure lessens, but the shadow remains.

'Please don't do this. You love Henry, I know you do.' I keep my voice low, my eyes on the small, sleeping figure on the bed across the room, alert for any sign that he is waking.

'I know how much it kills you to be away from him, even for a week. And he loves you. He loves the good in you, like I did. Like I do. Think of what it was like for you, growing up without your mum.' Desperation has made me daring. Sam never talks about the missing years where he didn't see or hear from his mother. 'Don't make that Henry's life too. Don't let him grow up without me. He trusts you, Sam. Think of the way he looks at you, the way he slips his hand into yours when you're walking down the street together. The way he doesn't just wrap his arms around you when you pick him up, but his legs too.'

I need to throw everything I can at this.

'And what about Daisy, and Catherine? I know you love them too. Don't do this to them. Don't let Daisy's father be this person. Please, Sam, please . . .' My voice gives way, no more than a rasp now, my throat burning.

I sit there in silence as the seconds pass. After a minute, maybe two, the shadow under the door disappears and again

I hear footsteps, but I can't work out which way they are going. Has Sam gone back to the kitchen or towards the front door? I daren't open the door to see, daren't move from my position on the floor, petrified that at any moment I will feel the slow press of the door against my back, and there will be nothing I can do. So instead I sit there motionless and shivering as hour after hour passes, leaning against the door, my back throbbing with pain, occasionally uncurling a leg to stretch away the stiffness. I once fell asleep on the floor in this room when Henry was a baby. At the time he'd never slept longer than two hours at a stretch, but that night he slept from midnight until 5am, at which time I jerked awake in a panic, frozen and stiff, to find that he had rolled onto his front for the first time ever. With his face turned away from me, all I could see was a bundle of blankets in the gloom and I was utterly convinced for a few seconds that he had stopped breathing, smothered to death while I lay beside him.

Tonight though, there will be no sleep. I keep my silent vigil until the grey morning light begins to seep under Henry's train-patterned curtains and I see him stirring. We can't hide in here for ever, so I stand up and go over to the bed, lie down next to him, feeling the warm, solid mass of him in my arms.

'Is it breakfast time?' he says sleepily, curling his arm around my neck.

'Yes. Yes, it is. Jam toast?' I ask, in as normal a voice as I can muster, every word like swallowing broken glass. 'Shall we have it in your bed, as a special treat?'

He smiles widely and releases me, starting to arrange his cuddly toys in preparation for breakfast. I stand up and walk towards the door. I pause with my hand on the handle, wondering what awaits me on the other side, whether this is the moment where Henry's life is changed for ever, irrevocably ruined. Very slowly I push the door open into the silence and peer to my left down the hall in the half-light. The kitchen door is slightly ajar. I look right, towards the front door, which is closed. The flat looks the same, yet it feels entirely different. It's no longer safe, no longer my home. I don't know what's lurking around the corners, hiding in the shadows.

I walk down the corridor, hesitating just before I reach the sitting-room door. Taking a deep breath, I swing around through the doorway. It's empty, exactly as I left it. I do the same with my bedroom, the pristine still-made bed irrefutable evidence that last night really happened. Next is the bathroom: also empty. From the doorway I can see my face in the bathroom cabinet mirror. My skin is sallow and there are dark shadows under my eyes, which are spidered with red. Something moves behind me and I spin round, my heart hammering, but there's nothing there: just the flickering of the sunlight through the bathroom blind reflected on the wall behind me.

I tiptoe down the hall towards the kitchen. My breathing is laboured and I wonder what damage has been done as I try to inhale and exhale as quietly as I can. As I reach out to open the kitchen door a sudden noise makes me gasp and jump back, but seconds later I recognise it as the sound of the wisteria rattling against the French windows in a gust of wind. With a surge of bravery I thrust the door open. The wine bottle and two glasses sit abandoned on the table, and the chair I kicked still lies on its side on the floor. In the dawn light, the room is full of shadows, but Sam has gone.

I pick up the chair with shaking hands and pour the wine from the glasses down the sink. As I do so, I hear a noise coming from the hallway. Oh God, no. I dart out, every inch of me in fight mode, but it's just Henry coming out of his room and heading for the bathroom. I breathe deeply, gathering myself; then while he's in there, hurry to the front door and double lock it, putting the chain on for good measure.

Back in the kitchen, I fill the kettle, take bread from the breadbin and put it in the toaster; assemble butter and jam, plate and knife, all the while staring at my hands as if they belong to someone else.

When Henry's toast is ready, I take it along with my phone and a cup of tea into his room. I climb into bed beside him, careful not to disturb the breakfasting bears.

'Thank you, Mummy,' Henry says with his customary graveness.

'You're welcome,' I say, sipping my tea and pulling him close. I am thankful beyond measure that he has no idea what happened here last night, but his innocence, his blind faith in the happiness of his own life, and mine, breaks my heart this morning.

I tap away at my phone, stumbling over the keys, as he painstakingly tears his toast into small pieces, giving one to each bear. A few minutes later my phone buzzes, and even though I know Bridget won't be messaging me any more, my stomach lurches in response.

Twenty minutes later, as I stand at the sink rinsing toast crumbs from tiny plastic plates, the doorbell rings. I advance slowly up the hall, wiping my hands on a tea towel.

'Who is it?' I say with difficulty, my voice hoarse.

'It's me,' she calls.

I stumble to the door, fumbling with the chain, my fingers slipping on the locks. Finally I get it open and there is Polly, her hair wild and unbrushed, still in her pyjamas with her oversized Puffa coat over the top. She takes in the pallor of my skin, my bloodshot eyes, the faint marks on the sides of my neck.

'Oh my God,' she says, and takes me in her arms. My legs give way beneath me and I crumple into her, sobbing with relief, finally able to let go.

Chapter 41

2016

The frosted grass crunches under our feet as we walk through Dulwich Park in the winter sunshine. Henry holds tightly to my hand, as he has done ever since we heard the news. I've only told him that Daddy has had to go away for a bit, the words sticking in my throat, but he seems to sense there is more to it, and hasn't asked me for any details. He's been asking about his sister though, so I am trying to screw up the courage to arrange a meeting with Catherine. I suspect we've got a lot in common.

It's two weeks now since I emerged from Henry's room to find Sam gone. I sat at the kitchen table with Polly as we waited for the police to arrive, drinking tea, my muscles slowly relaxing, warmth inching back into me. Henry hummed tunelessly in the sitting room over the reassuring click and clack of his trains as Polly and I talked. I told her things I had never spoken about to anyone; about Maria, about me and Sam, what he had done to me, what I had let him do, and how it had made me feel. I sensed something different between Polly and me: a barrier maybe, one that hadn't been there before? But as we talked, I realised it was the opposite: a barrier had been taken away, the one I had been putting up every time I saw her since we met. She can see me now, all of me.

We had fallen into a comfortable silence when the doorbell rang, a shrill reminder that I couldn't stay cocooned in the flat with Polly for ever. DI Reynolds was her usual professional self, but there was a certain solicitousness that hadn't been there before. Unlike on the previous occasions that we'd met, the words came pouring out of me like a river. I told her everything. She said that given the passage of time, and Sam's subsequent actions, it was unlikely that any action would be taken against me, either in relation to Maria's death or my obfuscation over the Facebook messages. I didn't ask whether Reynolds would be telling Bridget and Tim about my part in the events of that night in 1989. The Facebook page has disappeared and I've heard nothing from either of them since the day I ran from Bridget's bungalow, towards what I thought was safety.

Reynolds had news for me too: a hiker walking the coastal path had called in Sam's car just an hour before, abandoned near the cliffs at Sharne Bay. It was at the bottom of a rough, almost impassable track that led from the main road down past the school woods to the cliffs. The driver had crashed into a tree and simply left the car where it was, its front left bumper crumpled into a pine tree, shards of glass from the headlight sprinkled all around.

I can't help but think of him now, bumping down that track in the darkness, past the woods. Did he think of Sophie then, or Maria? Or was he thinking of Henry and

Daisy? Perhaps of Catherine and me as well. Ever since I got Maria's friend request, the question of what really happened to her has consumed me. I no longer have to speculate, but I have paid a terrible price for that knowledge. Perhaps it's no more than I deserve.

Henry tugs my hand, pulling me towards the play park. I am reminded of the last time I was here, and try to keep my thoughts from straying towards Pete, and our conversation last week. It had taken every drop of courage I possessed to pick up the phone, but I knew I had to apologise to him, needed the slate to be clean so I could start again. I got the apology out of the way first, but he was puzzled when I then asked after his wife and child. I didn't do it pointedly; I just wanted him to know that I knew, and that it was OK. That nothing he could do would come close to what I had done, and that I understood I was in no position to judge anybody. I don't think he was sure whether to be angry or amused that I had made such a quick and easy assumption, when in fact the woman and child that Esther saw him with were his sister and her baby.

In the play park, Henry jumps onto the roundabout and I push it round and round, his solemn face flashing past me again and again. He's so like his father, a constant reminder of what I've lost. In my mind's eye I see Sam, so beautiful at sixteen with his dirty blond hair flopping into his eyes, struggling down that path, Maria a dead weight in his arms. So assured, so popular. What was it in him that made him able to cross that line, and cross it more than once? All those years that we were together, shouldn't I have been able to see it? I don't think I was ever able to see him clearly though; my eyes were clouded by history, by shame; by love.

I think of Maria's last moments, of how frightened she must have been, and of Bridget, her whole life irrevocably ruined. Sam's revelation doesn't absolve me. I still did what I did to Maria, I still played my part, and I'll never be able to atone for that. But I can't live the rest of my life in shadow. I have a reason to move on, to move forward into the light, and he's here, spinning before me, his cheeks glowing in the biting December wind.

Henry holds out his hands, wanting me to stop the roundabout. As we walk over to the swings, his mittened hand slips inevitably into mine again.

'Mummy.'

'Yes?'

'Where *is* Daddy?'

'I told you, didn't I? He's had to go away for a bit, to do some work.'

'But where has he gone?'

The dark day looms at me from the future, the day I will have to tell him who his father was. Sam has been in the papers, and all over the internet. I will never be able to hide it from Henry. But for now, I will let him hold on to his pink-cheeked, bobble-hatted, unbearable innocence.

'Not far. He's got to work away for a bit, that's all. Shall we get a hot chocolate?'

He gives a little skip of delight. He's so easy to distract now, but that won't always be the case. I won't always be able to keep him with me either. The day will come when I have to let him walk to school by himself, or go to the swimming pool with his friends. He'll accuse me of being overprotective then, and he'll be right, but I will have my reasons.

My head says that Sam is gone, but I can still feel his hands around my neck; still feel him somewhere deep inside me, like a parasitic worm, buried in the darkest, worst part of me. He could be at the bottom of the ocean, or he could be here in the park, watching us as we walk across the grass. I may never know, and perhaps that will be my real punishment for what I did to Maria. Not the messages from Bridget, not even that night in the flat with Sam, but a lifetime of looking over my shoulder, never quite knowing. Always wondering.

My phone buzzes in my pocket and I feel the usual, instinctive lurch of alarm, even though I have deleted my Facebook account – not just from my phone, but altogether. It's a text from Polly, telling me she's running late but will be here with the girls soon. These days I try to keep in touch with people in person, rather than from behind a screen. I'm no longer holding on to the edges of my life; I'm reaching out, rebuilding it from the fragments that were left.

My parents came to stay for a few days after it happened, and although we didn't exactly have a Hollywood-style emotional breakthrough, I could feel their quiet support, and it meant something. Dad sat on the floor with Henry and played trains. Mum made me endless cups of tea and cleaned the bathroom. I felt closer to them than I have in years.

My clients have been really understanding too. Rosemary apologised for how she treated me that day in Islington, and promised me she wouldn't consider using anyone else.

Henry and I reach the café and I automatically scan the room, wondering if I'll ever be able to go to a public place without looking for Sam. It's steamy and noisy, full of families: kids clamouring for cake, parents wiping mouths and moving cups of coffee to stop toddlers knocking them over. I walk to the counter, Henry's hand still glued to mine, and order two hot chocolates. There are no free tables so we take them outside, wondering if it's warm enough to sit out there.

Henry looks up at me anxiously. 'What do you think, Mummy?'

A small cloud begins to pass over the sun and a shadow crosses the grass towards us, turning it darker green as it moves across. I have a choice. I can stay in this limbo for ever, sitting frightened in the dark, or I can take control and move on. I can let what I did, and what Sam did to me, define me, or I can try to learn from it and live a better life as a result.

The cloud passes and the sun re-emerges. I sit down at an outside table, placing Henry's hot chocolate carefully opposite me. He sits down too, and if anyone is watching us, they will see us together, smiling at each other here in the sunlight.

A note from Laura Marshall

Thank you so much for reading *Friend Request*. If you enjoyed it, I'd love to hear what you think.

As a debut author, it's still astonishing to me to think that real people are reading this story that for so long existed only in my head. Although none of the characters are based on real people, I did use a lot of my own experiences at school to inform the 1989 chapters, so it would be great to hear if they resonated with your own teenage years. Did that pressure to fit in with the cool crowd feel familiar to you? Did you know a Sophie? (Who didn't?!).

If you have any thoughts on the book that you'd like to share with me, you can find me on Twitter @laurajm8, on my Facebook page LauraMarshallAuthor or on Goodreads. You can also sign up for my newsletter on my website www.lauramarshall.co.uk, for news, giveaways and updates on my next book, which I'm working on now. If you have a moment, it would be wonderful if you could leave a brief review online, to help other readers discover the book.

I'd love to hear from you and thanks again for reading.

If you enjoyed *Friend Request*, read on for an exclusive extract from Laura Marshall's next bestseller,

Three Little Lies

Coming summer 2018

Chapter 1

July 2006

Olivia

My little boy. He looks so alone up there. It's the first time he's worn a suit since he left school, which God knows feels like five minutes ago, although it's over two years. It seems only yesterday that I was sending him off to school for the very first time, his hands lost in the sleeves of a jumper I'd bought with growing room. I can see that boy in his face, which is the same to me as it's always been. Yes, of course he's changed, but the new faces have just been layered on top of his original face, the one that only I can see now – smooth-skinned and perfect, a sprinkling of freckles across his nose, his expression completely open.

It's closed now though, seemingly emotionless, although I'm not fooled. I'm the only one that can feel the tremors running through him, because they run through me too. Flesh of my flesh. Until a baby is around six or seven months old, it has no idea that it's a separate person to its mother.

Up until then, it thinks they are one person, which is why separation anxiety kicks in around this time. Eventually, the baby gets it, but for the mother it never goes away. You and your child are, always and for ever, one. You feel every cut, every mean remark, every heartbreak.

'Court rise.' There's a bang on the door signalling the judge's imminent arrival, startling Daniel who looks instinctively up at me for guidance. I try to smile but my lips won't press themselves into the right shape. His eyes sweep the public gallery hopefully, even though he knows Tony won't be here; can't face it. I can't face it either, but I'm here anyway. It's merely the latest in a lifetime of things I couldn't face but still did – getting up five times a night to feed him or soothe his crying, spending endless Sunday mornings watching him playing rugby in the freezing rain, driving him all over the country to play piano concerts, sitting beside him all night the first time he got drunk, too petrified to sleep in case he choked on his own vomit. Everything I've done has been to protect him, to make things better. This is what we do, we mothers. I need to keep reminding myself of that, whatever happens, whatever I've done. It was never about me. It was for Daniel.

The judge sweeps in, a caricature from a bad film, all frayed wig and florid cheeks, the jury watching him expectantly. They are nervous, over-awed; it's probably the first time most of them have been in a courtroom, let alone been a crucial part of the process. Some of them let their eyes flicker to Daniel, but they don't linger on him long. What is it that makes them look away? Disgust? Fear? How much do they already know about him, about what he is accused of?

I lean forward, resting my arms on the rail. I will be

here every day until this is over. I can only let myself see a positive outcome, where he is exonerated – the witnesses discredited, the ... *victim* admitting she lied. We will take a taxi home and I will put him to bed and he will sleep, and his body and mind can begin to restore themselves.

I can't countenance the alternative. I shudder at the idea. For me, as for most people, prison has always been an abstract concept; at most, I have driven past them, imagined the prisoners inside, but as a race apart. They are criminals, not ordinary people. Completely alien to me and my way of life, something I will never come across or have to think about. Well, not any more. When you have other mothers as friends, the conversations move on over the years. First it was all sleepless nights and nappies, first words and potty training; then schools, friendships dramas, puberty, GCSE choices. Most recently, it was drugs, sex and alcohol. I thought they would be the last problems we would have to deal with before I forged a new relationship with my sons, an adult one. I imagined them taking me out for lunch, consulting me for advice on home improvements; hugging me again, like they did when they were little, but this time it would be them making me feel safe instead of the other way around. I never in a million years imagined I would be here, in an unknown landscape where none of my friends can, or would want to, follow me. I would swap places with any of them in a heartbeat.

The judge sits down, and so does everybody else apart from the prosecution barrister who turns to the jury to make his opening statement. And so it begins: my little boy's rape trial.

Chapter 2

Friday 15th September 2017

Ellen

Sasha's not in when I get home from the studio, so I put on a CD of Olivia's recording of Purcell's *Dido's Lament* full blast. Of course I've got everything she's ever recorded downloaded, but this is my absolute favourite, softer and more intimate than her famous version of Mozart's Queen of the Night aria. It was the first thing I ever heard her sing live, and there's something about slotting the CD into my old hi-fi that feels right. I played it on the show today, shoving down any misgivings I had about whether Sasha might be listening. She would have been at work; there's no chance they were playing Simply Classical in her office. I doubt any of her colleagues have even heard of such a tiny digital radio station unless she's mentioned it, which I doubt. She hardly even talks to me about it, a silent signal that she disapproves of my choice of work, redolent of the Monktons as it is. Classical music was their world and she rejected it utterly, as she has done everything connected with them since the day she moved out.

It was different for me, though. I loved it as she never did. My parents weren't ones for listening to music. My mum listened to Radio 2 in the kitchen sometimes, and they had a few CDs in a dusty stand in the front room, one of which might be put on if they had friends round, but they didn't care about it. It didn't stir any emotion in them. I went through the motions of fandom when it came to the bands other girls liked, blu-tacking posters to my wall and even going to a couple of gigs with Karina, but my heart was never in it. It wasn't until that first concert where I sat in the darkness next to Daniel, heart pounding, tears in my eyes, Olivia's voice pouring over me, into me, like warm water, that I understood what music could be.

I lie down on the sofa, wanting to relax into the music but keeping one hand on the remote control, alert for Sasha's key in the door. I hadn't been expecting her last Friday – I thought she was going out straight after work – but she'd come home around 7 o'clock in a foul mood and found me listening to Olivia. She hadn't said anything about the music, but I could feel her displeasure, radiating out like soundwaves, invisible but powerful. I'd switched if off and tried to talk to her, but she'd stomped off to her room, saying she was tired. There was definitely something up with her but I never got to the bottom of it. Tonight it's not Sasha's key but the door buzzer that interrupts me, jerking me upright like a marionette. I hastily turn off the music and take the few steps into the hall.

'It's Jackson,' says a terse voice on the intercom. No hello, how are you. Not for Jackson the fripperies of the normal greetings that oil the social wheels. I sigh and buzz him up, waiting until I hear his footsteps in the hallway before I open the door.

'Is she here?' he demands, sweeping past me into the front room.

'No, she's not back from work yet. Was she expecting you?' I am chilly, matching his brusqueness note for note.

'Clearly not,' he says, flinging himself down on the sofa, legs apart. 'I went to meet her from work ... as a surprise.' He has the grace to look shame-faced about this last bit. We both know he was checking up on her. 'She hadn't been there all afternoon. The receptionist told me she left at lunchtime, and her phone's going straight to voicemail. If she's not here, where is she?'

'How the hell should I know? I'm not her keeper.' I try to maintain a cold note of indignation, but a thread of worry tugs at a far corner my brain. Where is she?

'You're not far off,' he says. 'Best friends, aren't you? So close? Tells you everything?'

A small voice in my head wonders if this is true, but I want it to be, so I agree.

'Yes, she does, and whatever you're thinking, it's not true. She's not seeing someone else, Jackson. She's really not. She loves you.' This last part sounds weak even to me. I'm not sure that she does. The rest of it doesn't ring entirely true either. Twelve years of friendship should give you a certain understanding, a shorthand. We shouldn't have to tell each other what's going on, how we're feeling. We should just know. Usually I do, but in the last week or so, since she came home in such a strange mood, Sasha's been distant, evasive, brushing off any attempt on my part to get her to open up. Jackson deflates a little with the realisation that I genuinely don't know where she is, and I lower myself onto the edge of the armchair.

'What's going on with her, Ellen?' His bluster has evaporated, and with a jolt of surprise, I realise how much he likes her. 'I mean, she's always blown hot and cold, but this is something else. It's not the first time I've caught her out in a lie recently.'

'What do you mean?' I say, torn between my discomfort at discussing her like this, and my need to know. What has she been lying to him about?

'Oh, I don't know … not being where she said she was going to be, or being … evasive. Cagey.'

'She's always been a bit like that, though.' This is true. She liked to retain an air of mystery, even when we were teenagers and had little to be mysterious about. 'That's just how she is. It doesn't mean … '

'That she's shagging someone else? Oh, grow up, Ellen. She's not this perfect super-human being, you know. She's as flawed as the rest of us. If not more so.'

'I know,' I say, stung. 'I never said she was.'

'No, you never said it,' he says scathingly. 'But we can all see it, what you think of her, how much you love her.'

'She's my best friend!' My cheeks are hot. 'And what do you mean "we can all see it". Who's "we"?'

'Forget it.' Jackson picks moodily at a loose thread on his jeans.

'Look, she's not here, and I have no idea when she's going to be back,' I say as firmly as I can, standing up and moving towards the door. I don't want him here, cluttering up our flat with his accusations and insinuations. 'When she gets back, I'll tell her to call you, OK?'

'I think I'll wait,' he says, taking out a pack of cigarettes and a lighter. 'She'll have to come back sooner or later.'

My instinct is to acquiesce, but I force myself to speak. 'I'd really rather you didn't. And you can't smoke in here.'

He sighs theatrically and puts the cigarettes back in his pocket.

'Fine, I'll go. But make sure she rings me as soon as she gets back.'

'I'll tell her you were here, Jackson. It's up to her if she wants to ring you or not.'

After he's gone, I go straight to the kitchen where my phone is charging and call Sasha. Her voicemail clicks in straight away. I listen to her message as if there's going to be some clue contained in it. *Hi, this is Sasha's phone. I'm not available right now so please leave a message.* She's smiling as she speaks, you can hear it.

'Hey, it's me. Jackson's been here kicking off about you not being at work. Where are you? Call me when you get this.'

I replace the phone on the side, and lean back against the worktop, staring out of the window. There's not much to see from this side of the flat. The next block of flats is about five metres from ours, a strip of potholed concrete in between. A couple of old-style punks with Mohicans live in the flat opposite. Sometimes they smile and wave when they're in their kitchen cooking, but there's no sign of them today. You can just see a section of pavement on the route that leads to and from the station, and there's a steady stream of commuters making their way home from work. None of them is Sasha. That thread tugs at me again; memories push against the door I closed on them years ago.

I sit down at the tiny kitchen table by the window, taking a biro that has found its way into the fruit bowl and twiddling it round and round, ink staining my fingers where it's leaking. She would normally be back from work by now, entertaining me with tales of her day, pouring us both a large glass of wine, rooting around in the fridge for something to cook. It's one of my favourite times of day when I'm in, although I'm not a traditional nine to fiver, what with irregular shifts at the station and other freelance work.

I'm hungry, but there doesn't seem much point cooking just for me. I toast a slice of bread, and eat it without a plate, gazing out into the evening. As the sky darkens, the frequency of the passers-by decreases, but there's still no sign of Sasha. I call her again, but it's still going straight to voicemail. The nagging voice in my head that I've been trying so hard to ignore is louder now. I put Olivia's CD back on to try and drown it out, but it's a mistake because it brings those days back, and what had started as a whisper – a question, a suggestion – becomes a voice that I cannot quiet.

What if he's back? It says. *What if he's had enough of his new life in Scotland? What if he's been waiting, biding his time, lulling you into a false sense of security? Waiting for one of you to let your guard down, to slip up? What if he was waiting for her outside work? What if he followed her down the street, cornered her in a dark alley, bundled her into a car?*

No. She's gone out somewhere, her phone's out of battery, that's all. She'll be back soon, smelling of wine and cigarettes; she'll take me in her arms, hug me, affectionate and blurry, slurring her words, full of gossip, indiscreet as ever. We'll sit and talk late into the night as we often do; in the morning I'll take her in a cup of tea and we'll half-watch

Saturday Kitchen on the telly in her room while we look at clothes online, planning an afternoon shopping trip.

It's almost completely dark now, but still I sit here. I haven't turned the kitchen light on, so I am able see outside rather than staring at my own reflection. The pavement is more or less empty, just the occasional latecomer from work, head down, speeding along, or groups of friends on their way to the pub, chatting and laughing. Meanwhile I sit here, watching, waiting; trying to stop the voice that forces its way into my brain, seeping around the walls and locks I have constructed to keep it out, reverberating through me. The voice that reminds me that ten years ago, Daniel Monkton was sentenced to ten years, five of which he spent in prison, and five on probation, his every move scrutinised. That tells me Daniel Monkton is free to go where he pleases now, and contact who he likes. The voice that says Daniel Monkton is back, and he wants to make us pay for what we did.

Send Laura Marshall a friend request . . .

On Twitter @laurajm8

On Facebook laurashallauthor

www.lauramarshall.co.uk

Be among the first to hear her news, views and win copies of her next book.

#FriendRequestBook